Greek
Heroes

Other books by Geraldine McCaughrean

Greek Heroes

GERALDINE McCAUGHREAN

OXFORD
UNIVERSITY PRESS

OXFORD
UNIVERSITY PRESS

Great Clarendon Street, Oxford OX2 6DP

Oxford University Press is a department of the University of Oxford.
It furthers the University's objective of excellence in research, scholarship,
and education by publishing worldwide in

Oxford New York

Auckland Cape Town Dar es Salaam Hong Kong Karachi
Kuala Lumpur Madrid Melbourne Mexico City Nairobi
New Delhi Shanghai Taipei Toronto

With offices in

Argentina Austria Brazil Chile Czech Republic France Greece
Guatemala Hungary Italy Japan Poland Portugal Singapore
South Korea Switzerland Thailand Turkey Ukraine Vietnam

Oxford is a registered trade mark of Oxford University Press
in the UK and in certain other countries

British Library Cataloguing in Publication Data

Date available

ISBN 978-0-19-274202-5

3 5 7 9 10 8 6 4 2

Typeset by AFS Image Setters Ltd, Glasgow

Printed in Great Britain by
Cox & Wyman Ltd, Reading, Berkshire

Contents

Perseus

1

For Fear of Things to Come

They have no feelings, you see. Oracles. How could they?

Suppose you could look into the future and read there every downfall, every disaster, every desire unfulfilled, every death and all decay, every dark damnation in store. Could you go on caring?

If oracles had feelings, they would hold back. They would bite their tongues. They would turn away their heads into the shadows and keep silent their secrets.

'There will be good times; there will be bad times,' they could say. That much would be true. There is always good and bad to come.

But no. Their mouths let fall the future like water from a bubbling fountain, and never a thought for how it will poison those who eagerly drink it in. Still, poison is to be expected of snakes. And the oracle at Epidaurus was, after all, a serpent.

King Acrisius of Argos went to visit the Epidauran oracle to enquire whether he would ever have a son.

'You have a daughter. Your des-s-scendants will people a great nation. Be content,' hissed the oracle.

King Acrisius hesitated. So many more questions crowded into his mind: so many things he wished to know about the future.

'Will my country's enemies attack? Will the rains come? Will the harvest ripen? Will my people thrive?' He might have asked any of those. But no. He asked the one question that every foolish man wants to know:

'How will I die . . . die . . . die?' The question echoed around the walls of the gloomy comfortless temple.

'They all as-s-sk that-t,' said the oracle, with a contemptuous flick of its green-scaled head. 'How dull you are. How tedious-s-s.' The yellow, lidless eyes rested on Acrisius as if he were already dead and forgotten. 'Pers-s-seus-s-s,' hissed the oracle.

'What's that? An illness? Is it painful? How? When?'

'Pers-s-seus-s-s,' said the oracle again irritably. 'Your grandson, Pers-s-seus-s-s, will kill you . . . in good time.'

'But I haven't got a grandson!'

The oracle yawned. 'You have a daughter, haven't-t you?'

'But she's not even . . . ' Acrisius interrupted himself with a heartfelt cry that echoed round the temple. 'When? When? When?'

'*When your time is done,*' breathed the oracle coiling itself, like a rope on a ship's deck, into a flat, tidy circle. 'You have as-s-sked your fill. Come no more, Acris-s-sius-s.'

The king stumbled on shaking legs out of the clammy temple, and was stunned to his knees by the sunlight outside. Behind him, the oracle whispered to itself scornfully, '*Why do they always-s as-s-sk it? They none of them think they will die. S-s-so why do they go on as-s-sking?*'

* * *

4

'Danaë! My darling Danaë!' Acrisius said it a thousand times on his journey home. 'My own daughter's son will kill me? Never! Such a gentle, loving girl! She would never allow it! Ah, she could never give birth to such an unnatural son!'

After another mile he thought, But suppose the child took after his father? What father? Danaë's not even married. And what monster could she marry who would breed such a son? No, no, the oracle is mistaken. Not possible. Not possible.

After another ten miles he thought, But suppose the child's a lunatic—moon-touched—or cursed with a dreadful temper—or clumsy—or given to accidents . . . Poor Danaë. Better not to give life to such a brat . . . Better not to marry than to give life to such a brat . . . Better never to meet a man than to marry and give birth to such a brat . . . Better she were . . . Then Acrisius turned up his collar and looked around him, guilty at the thoughts in his own head.

On his return from Epidaurus, he set about building.

His architect said, 'Yes, yes, I understand you. A high, round tower. But what is it *for*, your majesty?'

His clerk of works said, 'Yes, yes, I will follow the plans—thick walls, no staircases, only one floor near the top. But what is it *for*, your majesty?'

His daughter Danaë said, 'Yes, yes, father. It's a remarkable piece of building. Very . . . er . . . tall. Very . . . er . . . interesting. People will come from far and wide to see it. But what exactly is it *for*?'

'Is it a watchtower?'

'Is it a lighthouse?'

'Is it a mill?'

'Is it a silo?'

'Is it a chimney?'

'And why does it have no door?'

Acrisius said not one word. When his tower was built, while the winches and hoists were still in place, he invited his daughter—his lovely, unmarried daughter, Danaë—to enjoy the view from the tower's summit. While he stood at the bottom, she rode in a brick-basket up the funnel of stone to the wooden platform at the top.

'Oh, father! I think the stonemason must sleep up here! There's a little bed. And a table. And a basket on a rope and . . .'

'And how is the view, Danaë, my dearest?' called the king, and the echo made it sound like a sob in his throat.

Danaë crossed to the little barred window. As she did so, there was a deafening clatter of scaffolding, and a squealing from the tackle-block, and a snaking of falling rope. 'Father! Father! The winch has gone! The hoist has collapsed! Help! How am I to get down? Oh, be quick, father. It's a fearful height. I'm dizzy to look down! Father! Father?'

But though her calls tumbled down the tower like pebbles down a well—'Why, father? *Why?*'—no one stood at the base to hear her.

'I'm sorry! I'm sorry! I'm so sorry!' murmured Acrisius, tripping through the folds of his robes as he ran towards the palace. His daughter's cries clamoured out of the small, barred window like the peals of a bell at the head of a belltower. But he covered his head with his arms, his ears with his hands, and he howled down the noise: 'She *shan't* have a son! She *shan't* marry and have a son! There'll be no grandson! There'll be no killing of grandfathers. Let her live there and die there. *Well, and what's wrong with that?*'

The eyes of his servants and ministers rested on him, empty of comment.

'Well? She can have anything she wants—food, games, dresses . . . Well? She's only a woman, isn't she? She's mine to do with as I choose. And she'll never miss what she's never had!'

The eyes of his servants and ministers rested on him, but their mouths spoke not a word.

'Well? I could have killed her, couldn't I? I could have, couldn't I?'

The eyes of his ministers and servants rested on him with not so much as a raising of eyebrows.

'But someone tell her to be quiet!' he shrieked, driving his fingers into his ears until he coughed himself into a silence.

After a while, Danaë was silent, too. She stood long hours at the barred window of the tower and watched the sun rise, the moon set, the spring ripen, and the autumn leaves fall. She saw the dark shadow of the tower fall towards the palace like an accusing finger, and she saw her father cringing in the window of his chamber.

At first she called. And then she wept. And then she thought. And then she sang, for the sake of hearing a voice ring back off the curving walls.

The citizens of Argos looked up now and then and said, 'She's singing again.'

'I couldn't sing, could you?'

'She's a sweet girl.'

'He's a cruel father.'

'A stupid man . . .'

'A wicked king . . .' Then they shivered and went on their way.

But someone else heard Danaë singing, and stopped to listen—stopped and listened and looked and liked what he heard and saw. High in heaven, Zeus, king of the gods, swung a leg lazily over the side of his hammock of cloud and peered down on the tower's round roof. Danaë stood warming herself in the beams of sun that slotted through the barred window and painted a bright, striped square on the floor.

As the sea has an endless appetite for the rivers of the world, so Almighty Zeus had an appetite for beautiful women. 'Poor *soul*,' he said mournfully. 'So all *alone*,' he said earnestly. 'So badly treated,' he said indignantly. 'And so very *pretty*.'

Standing in her pool of light, Danaë stretched herself and turned her face to the warmth of the sun. 'Oh, for someone to talk to! Oh, for someone to share this loneliness! Did I ask so much of life that the Fates have abandoned me here? What would I ever ask for again if I only had my freedom? A little home somewhere—a husband to care for, maybe—a little baby . . . ' Her arms cradled the air tenderly, and high above the tower a rumble of thunder sounded like a groan of longing.

Doesn't the largest river thread itself out of a tiny spring? Doesn't the largest bird hatch out of an egg? Can't all the words in the world be spoken by a single small mouth? It was no great feat, then, for Zeus, father of the gods, to thread his great form through the small barred window of a prison tower. He simply transformed himself into a shower of gold, and poured himself down a shaft of sunlight into Danaë's lonely cell.

Coins and ingots and gold dust pelted her like hail so that she reeled and fell on her back and drew up her knees and cried out in fright. But it was not unpleasant— just a little startling.

When she got over her astonishment, Danaë gathered up the gold into her lap and sat turning it over in her fingers. It was warm to the touch—but then that is the nature of gold—warm and soft and pliable. It was not the first time Danaë had counted gold or fingered precious metals.

Though it was perhaps the first time the king of the gods had experienced anything so *very* agreeable.

After a time, when it was dark, she got up and went to the window. 'You! Hey, you!' she called down softly to a passing soldier of the guard. 'A skirtful of gold if you'll help me to escape from this terrible prison!'

The guard slouched against the wall of the tower and snorted with laughter. 'And where would you lay your hands on gold, princess?'

Danaë lifted her lapful of treasure and tipped it out through the bars. Looking up, the astonished soldier saw a shimmering, glinting chute of spinning light cascading down on him. He threw up one arm across his face, to protect himself—and reached out the other hand, greedy for the gold.

But it was only a trick of the moonlight, for no coins or ingots of gold bombarded him. The spinning light seemed to dissolve away in mid-air, and the guard was sent sprawling by a sudden gust of wind.

So Danaë remained in her tower, alone. She might even have thought the shower of gold nothing but a dream but for an occasional flurry of gold dust around the floor when the winter wind blew in.

Nine months later, Danaë gave birth to a boy.

'A baby? She's had a baby? It's not possible!' cried King Acrisius when they told him. 'She's been locked in that tower for two years! She hasn't so much as sneezed on a man! Don't bring me these lies!'

'A boy, your majesty,' was all the messenger said. 'She has called him Perseus.'

'Kill it! Kill them both!' screamed the king, his voice

breaking in the dryness of his throat. 'Well? Why does nobody move? Why does nobody obey me?'

Ministers of government shuffled their feet. 'It wouldn't be wise, your highness. The country would rise up against you. You . . . You've been less than popular since . . . since the . . . er . . . tower, sire. We think there would be riots—open rebellion—protests—ballots—voting—*republicanism*.'

Acrisius suppressed a cry of alarm. 'Very well. Fetch a trunk.'

'A trunk, your highness?'

'A trunk. A trunk. Are you deaf? A coffer—with a lid and a latch. Take it down to the beach . . . And break open the tower.'

Then his ministers ran. They picked up the hems of their robes and they ran—with crowbars and sledge-hammers and ropes and winches, and they broke open the walls of Danaë's tower. While they were doing so, the crying of her newborn baby rained down on them like the ringing from a belfry. So delighted were they at the king's change of heart that they hurried to fetch him just what he had asked for—a solid oak chest with a lid and a latch—and to set it by the shoreline.

Only later in the day, as they watched it wallow out to sea did they curse themselves for fetching it, and spit on their own hands because they had helped Acrisius in his wickedness.

2

An Unwelcome Suitor

For Acrisius had his soldiers force Danaë and her baby son into the wooden chest, and closed the lid on them, and locked it with a key.

'Father! Father! What did I ever do that you should hate me so much?' cried the muffled voice of his daughter. 'What crime did I commit that you should imprison me in the tower and now in this . . . this . . . *coffin*?'

But the only reply was the shriek of a seagull and the slap of its big orange feet as it strutted up and down the ridged lid of the floating trunk.

Back on the shore, hissed by the scornful sea, Acrisius hugged himself in both arms but would never again feel loved. His ministers looked at him with faces as hard as rocks, with eyes as blank as the seashore pebbles.

'Well? I didn't execute her, did I? I didn't kill the baby! Nobody can ever say I murdered them! I just . . . I just . . . sent them away.' And the ministers' eyes turned away from the king and rested on the troughing ocean. Already the maze of waves hid the bobbing trunk from sight. Everyone there thought it had leaked already,

already filled, already sunk with a silent thud to the crab-infested sea-bed and the shifting, corpse-cold dark.

A fresh wind was blowing. Skittering over the wave-tops, sharp as stones, a rattle of icy spray spattered Acrisius's face.

Watching from somewhere beyond the horizon, Zeus, king of the gods, was not well pleased to see his own son posted, like a message in a bottle, out to sea. He cut a notch in his lightning staff to remind him of a debt unpaid, a wrong unpunished, then swept home to the holy mountain of Olympus. The hem of his cloak sprinkled the ocean with hail behind him. The hail rattled on the lid of the wooden chest (very like gold coins). And the slipstream swirling behind the great god dragged that portion of the sea, scarf-like, into a different ocean where dolphins tugged it further still in their beaks. Finally, the wooden chest grounded— bang—on a shoal of whelky, submerged rocks. The brass bindings broke, the nails were jarred loose, the seams opened, and the sea rushed in.

If Dictys's nets had not at that very moment scooped up the remains of the wooden trunk into his little fishing boat, the Princess Danaë would have surely become no more than a hank of hair and a rag of cloth washing to and fro in the water.

Dictys forced open the metal latch and lifted the lid. To his astonishment, a pair of white arms reached out at once and placed into his slippery hands a baby boy. 'Warm him! Warm him, for the love of heaven!' cried Danaë, and rose up out of the chest like the goddess of love first rose up from the waves.

Love herself could not have seemed more beautiful in Dictys's eyes. As he pushed the small, cold baby inside his shirt, against the warmth of his chest, he found his heart beating fit to leap out through his gaping jacket. 'Your servant, lady. Your eternal servant,' was all he could say, all he could think. Danaë put her cold, wet hand into his, and stepped into the shelter of his boat.

And there, you might say, she stayed for eighteen years. And had they remained, the three of them, on that little fishing boat, the oracle's prophecies could never have come true.

But as soon as Danaë had told her story, Dictys was all impatience to present her to the king of his country. A princess—a great beauty—a mother and her son cast adrift on the sea and brought to the shores of his kingdom! It was surely news fitting for a king's ears. 'And the palace is surely a far more fitting place for you to stay than my poor little fisherman's hut,' said Dictys breathlessly.

'I'm perfectly comfortable here,' said Danaë, curled up in front of his hearth.

But nothing would prevent Dictys from rushing to the palace of King Polydectes with news of his wonderful discovery.

King Polydectes of Seriphus was a man of distinction. Not for him the scurrying, round-shouldered, guilty gait of Danaë's royal father. Polydectes walked with his chest thrown out and his cloak trailing, flicking his hands to right and left to draw attention to his many, many possessions. For Polydectes collected beautiful things— china, glassware, silver ornaments, gold plate, pictures, statues, chariots, trees, tapestries, lamps, clothes, furniture, armour, horses, and dancing girls.

Oh, and wives.

'You didn't *gasp*,' said Polydectes, pursing his lips peevishly when Dictys was admitted to his presence. 'Everyone always gasps at the amazing beauty of my palace.'

13

Dictys bowed low and apologized. 'I was so very breathless with running, your majesty. I've run all the way from the harbour!' And he told the king about Danaë and her baby cast out to sea in the wooden chest. But perhaps if Dictys had not been so quick to mention Danaë's beauty, then Polydectes might have simply yawned and gone back to watching his dancing girls.

'Did you say "beautiful"?' asked the king, sliding languidly off his couch like a lizard. 'How beautiful?'

'Oh, the angel fish with their streaming rainbow fins are not more beautiful, your majesty,' said Dictys. He really did not mean to recommend Danaë like a carpet salesman selling a rug, and afterwards he cursed himself for speaking so feelingly.

'I don't greatly care for fish,' said Polydectes thoughtfully. 'Except the stuffed variety. But you can tell this sea-going princess that once she's washed the seaweed out of her hair she may come here to the palace. If she's as good as you say, I might condescend to marry her.'

Then Dictys gasped, though not at the beauties of the king's royal palace. 'What have I done?' he asked himself in horror.

Danaë had no wish to marry King Polydectes. She sent word to say so—politely, respectfully, and with due gratitude.

The king summoned her to the palace and, having once seen her, issued a Royal Proclamation that he would marry Princess Danaë the very next day.

'You do me a great honour, your majesty,' said Danaë, 'but I don't wish to marry you tomorrow.'

'Next week, then. Not a day later,' snapped the king.

'You misunderstand me, my lord. I mean that I don't wish to marry anyone at all.'

When Danaë refused him a fourth and fifth time, the king became surly and cross. When she refused him for a

14

year and then for ten years it became an obsession with Polydectes. 'I *will* have her. No woman refuses me!'

But Danaë chose to stay with Dictys the fisherman, and though they were poor, and had nothing to eat but the fish Dictys caught, the three of them were happy: Danaë, Dictys, and Perseus.

Perseus grew like a pollarded willow—all the more beautiful for standing by the waterside and suffering the cuts of Fate. His hair leapt towards heaven in a thousand curled question marks, and his eyebrows seemed always raised in wonder. His eyes were so pale a brown that they were almost gold—round like two golden coins. He learned a leaping confidence from the sea and a stillness from the rocks. He learned cunning from the wrasse who feels its way silently over the sea-bed, and fierceness from the shark; he learned wisdom from the dolphin and recklessness from the bass who feeds under the pounding surf. But not even the whale calf who swims in the great shadow of its mother through ice and storm could teach Perseus anything about loyalty.

'I shall protect you, mother!' he said, every time King Polydectes sent his messenger to rattle at the door. 'Though you have no husband to look after you, I shall take care of you and keep you from harm!'

He went fishing with Dictys, and as the tides counted in and counted out eighteen years, Perseus grew to be a man.

'I've done asking! I've done requesting! I've done inviting!' raged King Polydectes. 'Send troops to the fisherman's hut. Send them when the fisherman's away at sea! Tell them to fetch the woman Danaë here. I *will* have her! I *must* have her for my wife!' The idea of Danaë was by now a madness in his blood. All his other fine possessions held no delight for him. All his other wives seemed ugly. He only wanted what he could not have. The wanting nagged and chewed and clawed at him. 'I will marry the wretched Princess Danaë, and I'll marry her today!'

So the soldiers beat at the door of the fisherman's hut. 'Open up! Open up, in the name of the king!'

The door opened, and there stood a young man— hardly more than a boy—with a startling shock of golden hair, and pale, round, almost golden eyes. 'Good-day, gentlemen,' he said brightly.

'We've come for the woman, Danaë.' The captain of the guard stepped forward, but Perseus put up one hand.

'You are welcome, I say, to stand on our doorstep. But come one step inside, and I'll be obliged to throw you out again.'

Meanwhile, at the palace, King Polydectes put on his finest robe and turned down the covers of his great marriage bed. 'I should have done this long before now!' he shouted at the parrot dozing on the perch by the window. 'I'll teach this woman how very unwise it is to slight a king—very unwise!'

'King very unwise,' repeated the parrot.

Eagerly, Polydectes watched from the chamber window for the patrol to bring his bride. At last they straggled into view—a scuffle here, a flurry of dust there, a raising of voices, a few smudged words. Polydectes was excited to think of Danaë struggling like a pretty moth in a web. But strain his eyes as he might, he could not see her among his soldiers: he could only see them squabbling and brawling among themselves:

' . . . head hurts . . . '

' . . . took us by surprise . . . '

16

'. . . got the better of you, you mean . . . '

'. . . who's going to tell the king . . . '

'Tell me what?' bawled Polydectes from the window. 'Where's my bride? Where's Danaë?'

'It was that son of hers, your majesty! He took us by surprise! He's a little demon, your majesty . . . strong beyond his years . . . used magic, I'd say.' They poured out their excuses at the king's feet, then delivered the message Perseus had sent them away with: *Say my mother shall marry whom and when she pleases!*'

Polydectes wiped the flecks of foam from his lips and slammed the shutter shut. 'Perseus! I'll wager it's that lad who's poisoned his mother against me! Well, if he's the only obstacle . . . Wisht! Tread carefully, Polydectes. You can't kill the brat and hope his mother will love you after . . . ' A sneering smile broke over Polydectes's face. 'No. This calls for subtlety—a plan, a plot. If Perseus is the problem, Perseus must be *put out of the way.*'

So the king looked around among the little tribal kingdoms, and found himself a princess—any sorry little princess—and announced that he would marry her. Silver trumpets swore to it: proclamations spoke it from every pillar and tree: *'Rejoice and pay tribute! King Polydectes will marry the Princess Nemo! Presents will be graciously received.*' And he let it be known that his heart had sickened of the obstinate Princess Danaë.

It was a great relief. Danaë unclenched her anxious little fists, and the fisherman Dictys laid aside his rusty old sword (for he had thought to fight to the death rather than see Danaë forced into marriage). 'I shall catch fish enough to feed the wedding guests,' he said. 'That will be my tribute to the king.'

'My gratitude and blessing will be my tribute,' said Danaë (who had not a penny to call her own).

17

'And I shall pay tribute, too!' Perseus declared recklessly.

Standing close by (according to the king's instructions) was a palace courtier. He immediately burst out laughing—a loud, forced, humourless laugh which drew every eye. 'Did you hear that? *Perseus* is going to pay tribute! Little *Perseus* is going to give the king a wedding present! Barefoot Perseus! One-shirt Perseus! Fish-stinking Perseus is going to offer tribute to the king! What will it be, then? A few seashells? Or a piece of driftwood?'

The colour rose into Perseus's cheeks as it rises into the sky at sunset. His eyes flashed brighter than freshly minted gold. And he ran all the way to the palace and knelt on one knee in front of King Polydectes. Strangely enough, the king seemed to be expecting him.

'I hear you mean to bring tribute to me and my new bride, lad. How very kind. The duke here has promised ten horses. The count over there is giving a summer house? And what had you in mind to give me?'

'Name it, your majesty! Name it and I shall bring it! You shall have whatever you ask, sire!'

So Perseus fell into the king's trap, and the king hinnied and snorted into his cup of wine and spattered his clothes blood-red. '*Anything*, Perseus? Well, let's make it . . . no, no. Let me see . . . I wouldn't like to insult you with a paltry challenge . . . ' He strolled up and down the room, pretending to rack his brains. 'Let's make it the . . . no, no, that would be too difficult, surely . . . Although you did say *anything*, didn't you?'

'Anything, your majesty!'

'Then let's make it *the head of Medusa*!' The king turned quickly so as to catch the tremor of fear and horror that must surely shake Perseus to the core. But he was disappointed. Perseus did not so much as flinch.

'Very good, your majesty. The head of Medusa. It will be my honour to lay Medusa's head at your feet, sire, before the next moon has waned!'

Braggarty little fool, thought the king, smirking as best he knew how. That's the last boast *he'll* make.

At the door, Perseus turned and seemed about to ask something. Mercy? Pity, perhaps? The king's eyebrows lifted superciliously. 'Yes? Was there something, boy?' Perseus blushed, shook his head, and left.

But in the courtyard outside he stopped a palace servant and asked in a little whisper, 'Excuse me troubling you. But do you happen to know what or who Medusa is?'

3

Taking up Arms

Medusa was a thing of sea shanties and travellers' tales and nightmares. Medusa was Fear itself clumsily parcelled up so that she spilled out into rumour and legend; she was a hissing at the corner of the world; a horror just out of sight of the corner of the eye. Medusa was vile.

She had been beautiful once—beautiful such that the eye that saw her could not bear to look away. Her eyes had been so beautiful that the Sea-Shaker, the Earthquake-Maker, the sea god himself, Poseidon, loved her and wanted to possess her. But she was a flirt and a tease, and put Poseidon to the indignity of chasing her all over the city of Athens. The waves of the ocean-god sluiced through the streets—a tidal wave of desperate passion.

Medusa ran at last into the purified and holy temple of the goddess Athene, and there she allowed her chaser to catch her. The building was overarched by surging water which swept into the temple and tumbled the beautiful Medusa in a glittering embrace.

But oh, when he withdrew, Poseidon's wave left the sacred holy altar stained white and the walls caked with salt and the offerings of the worshippers scattered about and ruined. So angry was the goddess Athene when she saw this vandalism, when she saw how Poseidon and Medusa had defiled her holy place on the earth, that she cursed Medusa and made her as ugly as her two immortal sisters, Euryale and Stheno. Poseidon looked at her once and banished her and her sisters to the driest desert in the world—to Libya—so that he might never lay eyes on her again. And Medusa swore, there and then, that whosoever she laid eyes upon . . .

'But *how* is she vile?' Perseus asked the fisherman Dictys.

'No one has lived to say.'

'Then if you can't tell me what she is or why she's hideous, won't you tell me where I can find her?'

'No. I don't know. And if I did, boy, I would tear out my tongue rather than tell you. You're the light of your mother's eye, and if you go on this foolish quest you will leave her all in darkness.' And he pulled his cloak over his face and would not speak another word about Medusa. But Perseus was as determined as ever to carry out his promise to the king.

From the terraces of Olympus, Medusa was just a small, distant, green, squirming thing. A whole forest of cedar trees had been planted to block the view a little, so that the gods and goddesses should not be put off their breakfasts.

'I have a thing or two to do down there,' said Zeus, greatest of the gods, waving a hand towards the distant landscape.

His wife Hera lifted her brown eyes, lash-fringed like the deep carpets of the silent underworld. 'What kind of a thing, husband?'

'Oh—dreams to deliver to young heroes,' said Zeus generally. 'That sort of thing.'

'Which particular young hero?' asked Hera, trying to follow the line of his eye when, every few moments, he darted a glance towards the shores of Seriphus.

Zeus tugged at his beard irritably. His wife was disagreeably shrewd, and took it to heart whenever she found out about his little love affairs. Most unreasonable. What were a few paltry kisses? And couldn't he spend his kisses where he chose? His mouth fell into a pout. What were a few extra *sons* scattered about the earth, strong as bulls, with the valour of lions, or with eyes like golden coins. And Zeus could not help being interested in them, could he? His human sons?

After a day or so, the king of the gods got up and tiptoed away, hoping nobody would notice. Weather fronts closed behind him, the blue stratosphere buckled and the holy mountain shook, so that berries fell from the bushes and streams changed course. But the gods, sprawled idly along the terraces, pretended not to notice the ruler of heaven picking his way down towards the plain. Only Hera breathed fast and furious through her regal nose and said, *'Bastards!'* Her nymphs-in-waiting pretended not to hear.

Perseus, lying on his face in bed, had thought he was fully awake, puzzling over how to find Medusa. But a sudden milkiness clouded his thoughts. He lay spread-eagled between waking and sleeping, dimly conscious of being unable to turn over.

Zeus leaned low over his son and whispered in his ear: *'Go to the ghastly, grey-eyed Graeae. Ask what they would rather not tell you. Ask where you may find the Nymphs of the West. You hear? But take care, boy. Take care.'*

22

All the doors and windows in the house banged, and Perseus rolled over on to his back, suddenly wide awake. 'I had the strangest dream . . . ' he started to say. But Dictys had already risen and gone out fishing, and his mother, troubled by dreams of her own, was scurrying about fastening the shutters and bolting the doors.

By the time Zeus returned to Olympus, he trailed behind him a dismal train of anxiety that bent trees at the shoulder and creased the clouds into a scowl. He gnawed his lip, and threw himself down on his throne with his fists knotted in his beard. The lesser gods pulled their robes closer round them against the chilling of the air.

'A fine young man, that,' said Hermes loudly to Athene, casually preening the feathers on his heels.

'A fine warrior lad, yes,' said Athene, examining the point of her spear.

'Who is? What?' Zeus looked up.

'Oh, we were just discussing that boy Perseus, son of Danaë. An excellent little hero in the making. Remarkable background. Nobody quite knows who his *father* was— someone quite exceptional, that's plain.'

Zeus sat back on his throne and stroked the knots out of his beard. 'Now you speak of him, I think I do recall the boy. Good family, you think?'

'Oh undoubtedly—And so handsome, too.'

A glint of pleasure crept into Zeus's eye like a single fish into a lake. 'Now you mention him, I do believe I've seen him once or twice. Didn't I hear somewhere that he's made some wild, foolish promise to find Medusa and cut off her head? Yes, I'm sure I did.'

'How very brave!' 'How enterprising!' said Hermes and Athene simultaneously.

Zeus looked pleased and only a little suspicious.

'In that case, I shall lend him my sickle-sword!' declared Hermes.

'And I shall lend him my shield!' cried Athene.

Zeus beamed with delight. 'How nice! How very generous! It pleases me greatly to see you taking such an interest in the little people of the Earth. Encouraging enterprise. Helping the courageous. Yes, indeed. Excellent!' He jumped up from his throne and went to deal with affairs of the Divine State, a new spring in his ten-league stride.

Hermes and Athene looked at each other and the goddess of war shrugged. 'Well, I can't bear it when he sulks. Besides . . . I'd be glad to see Medusa's head in a bag.'

'Why?' asked Hermes, startled by her ferocity.

'I hate her. Never mind why,' said Athene, who did not like to speak of that white salt caking the walls and altar of her holy temple. 'I hate her, that's all. So let's help that bastard Perseus as much as we're able.'

They spat on their palms and shook hands in a pact: no word of helping Zeus's son must ever reach Hera, his jealous wife.

At each temple in turn, Perseus prayed for the help of the gods on his quest to find and kill Medusa. As he turned away from the altar of the goddess of war, a dazzle of light struck him in the face like a blow. An oval metal shield lay on the steps. Perseus thought it must have been left lying in the hot sun and had grown incandescent, for it was so bright that it left scorch marks on his vision. But when he picked it up, it weighed no more than a mirage—a shiny, eye-deceiving pool of light. He half expected it to disappear off his arm.

Realizing that here was a gift from the gods, he shut his eyes tight in thankful prayer. Behind him, there was the sound of a scythe striking down a stook of corn, then a metallic twanging. He spun round and saw a sword—a curved sickle of a sword—wedged deep in the solid stone of the temple step, its hilt pointing the way he should go.

Perseus turned his golden eyes to the sky and thanked whatever power had sent him these strange, fantastical presents. He took up the sword and set off to run, thinking not to stop till he found the Graeae (whatever they were) and Medusa (whatever she was) and sliced off her head. *'How can I fail with the gods helping me!'* he crowed.

His steps led him directly to the sea-shore, where the sand made him sink and stagger, and the sea barred his way. His fingers accidentally brushed the sharp blade of the sickle-sword, and drops of blood spotted the stainless face of the silver shield.

Then the breaking waves seemed to say, 'You are still mortal, Perseus—a thing of flesh and blood—a weak, vain thing that will one day die.' And his heart quailed inside him as he stood beside the vast ocean, on the shore of an unfriendly world.

Far away, in a kingdom Perseus knew nothing about, blood also spattered the sea-shore. And bones littered the sand. And deep footprints filled up with water on the rising tide. They were not human footprints, but hooked, lizardly tracks scuffed through by the great following scar of a dragging tail. And the bones and blood were not human bones or blood but all that was left of goats and sheep and pigs tethered among the dunes. So far, the people of Ammon had fed the sea-monster on livestock. So far they had kept it away from the bolted city gates, with tethered sacrifices.

It was not enough. Each time the monster erupted from the sea, like a tongue from a mouth, it devoured their offerings quicker than the time before. Then snuffling on towards the city wall, it dangled its dew-lapped head over the palisades and let its saliva drip. They could hear its panting, they could hear it grind its teeth, they could hear the hooked feet scratch at the wall. One day soon it would shoulder its way through the crumbling masonry and take the meal it craved—human flesh.

4

The Grey-eyed Graeae

Like a wire pulled tight, the western horizon thrums and trembles for one fraction of a blue second as the sun sets. The sound of it echoes through the whole hollow ocean. And in this region of shadow, where the floating islands of the world have drifted and collided and grown together like cartilage, live the Graeae.

Death never sails this far. So they never die. Only their bodies die, little by little, around them. A hand withers. A shoulder droops. A spine closes, vertebra by vertebra, into a brittle, rigid stick. So long have they stayed there, decayed there, that only one eye remains between the three, and only one has a tooth in her jaw.

But such an eye! It can see a voyager coming a hundred miles away. And such a tooth! It can eat him at a sitting and leave nothing for the gulls.

'Give me the eye, sister! It is my turn for the eye!' The seeing Graea claws the eye from its socket with a big-jointed finger and fumbles it into the outstretched palm of her sister. For they share the eye, all three.

'Give me the tooth, sister. I have a sailor here ripe for the eating!' The chewing Graea claws the tooth out of her black gums and fumbles it into the outstretched palm of her sister. For they share the tooth, all three.

Only while the eye was out did Perseus dare to move or blink or breathe. Only in that moment of blindness did he dare to crawl closer across the Graeae's midden of litter.

'What's that, sister One? I thought I heard a rattle of bones. Is someone near? Give me the eye quickly!'

'I look and I see nothing, sister Two. It is not your turn yet for the eye.'

'My mouth is watering, sister. I could swear someone eatable was near. Give me the eye!'

'I look and I see *no one*, sister Three. Wait your turn, can't you? Wait your turn.'

Only as the eye changed hands did Perseus creep closer and closer to the foul sisters squatting on their haunches around a cauldron of boiling jellyfish and seaslugs.

'Give me the eye, sister. It *is* my turn for the eye!'

So like an oyster gouged from its shell, the single, soft, wet, grey eye is scooped out of its socket. 'Here, then. Don't snatch, sister! You might damage it!'

'Who snatched? Who snatched? It was my turn and you've given the eye to sister Three! Sister Three! Give it to me and wait your turn, you selfish hag!'

'Who, me? *I* don't have it. I didn't take it! Have you dropped it, you clumsy crone? Have you dropped our eye in the dirt? You fool!'

'I didn't drop it! I haven't touched it!'

'Well, a hand took it from my hand! One of you took it! Admit! Admit!'

'I admit,' said Perseus. 'I have the eye.'

The voice was so close to their ears that they swatted and snatched at it as they would a mosquito. Their purse-gathered lips opened in gasps of surprise and howls of rage. He lifted one plait of brittle grey Graea hair and rested it in the palm of another Graea.

'Sister! I have it by the hair! Give me the tooth so I can bite the thief to mammocks!'

'Sister! Sisters! It has me by the hair! Give me the tooth so I can bite off its head!'

But out of the tangle of knotty hands, Perseus plucked the tooth as well, then sprang away to a safer distance. Six old hands patted and scraped the dirty ground, searching, hunting, desperate.

'Peace, sisters, and let me help you. Have you lost something? Let me help you find it, with my two good eyes.'

The Graeae crawled towards him across the ground, reaching and snatching towards the sound of his voice. He skipped out of reach. *'It has our tooth! It has our eye! Oh, sisters! What shall we do!'*

Perseus said, 'What can you mean? Can it be this you're looking for? This sharp yellow tooth like the head of an axe, and this one soft, wet, grey slippery eye? Surely not. Such ugly things. I think I'll throw them into the sea.'

'No, no!' The Graeae froze, heads up, hands outstretched.

'Or shall I tread them underfoot?'

'No, no!' The Graeae scurried closer, their tears only in their voices, for they had no eyes for crying.

'So shall I sell them to you for a word or two of wisdom?'

'Give us back our eye! Give us back our tooth!'

'Or shall you starve in everlasting darkness?'

'WHAT DO YOU WANT?' they howled.

'Tell me where I may find the Nymphs of the West,' said Perseus. 'I need their help to find and kill the Gorgon called Medusa.'

The Graeae, supported on knuckles and knees, sagged pitifully. 'The Nymphs of the West? That secret is all we have left of value!' said sister One. 'While we keep the sight of them hidden from all human eyes, no one can compare our old age with their youth! We shall keep the secret of them until they are grown old like us. Then you may know.'

'Then I shall toss this eye and this tooth into the cauldron with the jellyfish and the seaslugs,' said Perseus briskly, and indeed he almost dropped the slippery eye, because his hand was wet with sweat.

'*NO!* Give us back our precious parts, and we'll tell you!'

'Tell me, and I'll give you back your parts. Speak!'

The Graeae sank down, like torn sacks emptying. They slumped along the ground. 'Follow the weed line. Follow it to their cave on the other side of the kingdom,' said sister Two.

'You fool, sister! Now he'll never give us back our parts!'

Perseus was indignant. 'What do you take me for, ladies? Here! Here's your precious eye, and here's your tooth. I, Perseus, honour my bargains!' (But even so, he threw their stolen parts on to the ground between the three. And when he last looked back, they were in danger of kneeling, or leaning, or slapping a hand down on the cold, wet, slippery, round, grey eye.

'Wait till I have it!' shrieked one. 'Listen how I'll tear him like bread in the breaking!'

'Calmly, sister! Calmly!' said another, squatting back on her haunches as she pushed home the single, dirty tooth. 'If that thief out there thinks he's going to kill Medusa, he'll be turned to rock like the rest soon enough. Rock heart and brain. Rock lights and liver. Rock. Rock. Rock!' And she rolled on the balls of her ancient feet and laughed, for want of an eye to weep.

* * *

30

He followed the line of seaweed that circled the shore of that blue-black land. Whether the weed floated on the third wave or drew a fly-blown line along the high-water mark, he followed it. And it led him to the mouth of a cave. He had leaned one hand against the portal, to untangle the bladderwrack from round his feet, when a single vowel echoed down the cave.

'O-o-oh!'

He looked up and saw a girl as young as the Graeae were old, as beautiful as they were ugly, as naked as they were ragged, and as happy as they were sad.

'Oh, sisters!' she exclaimed softly after a moment spent staring at Perseus. 'This is nice. Do come and see this.'

Her two sisters came printless over the wet sandy floor of their cave. 'Is it a stork?' they said. 'It's standing on one leg.'

'Did it come out of the sea or out of the air? It is nice, yes, sister. Such pretty eyes.'

'I'm looking for the Nymphs of the West,' said Perseus, and the girls scattered, as angelfish scatter at the blundering in of a shark. Curiosity soon brought them back.

'Did it speak?' said one.

'It looks rather like us, in a two-legged sort of way.' She dropped her voice to a whisper. 'Do you suppose it's *one of the gods*?'

'I'm not one of the gods,' said Perseus. 'I'm just a person . . . ' He was about to say 'the same as you'. But looking them up and down there, this was blatantly untrue. 'I'm just a man.'

'What's a man?' said the Nymphs, who had lived unseen, unknown, unvisited all their lonely, lovely lives. 'Is that like a sailor? We've heard tell of sailors.'

So Perseus tried to explain. And when he had told them about men, he told them about cities and ships, clothes and chariots, horses and sheep, maize and apples, money and markets, kings and beggars, wars and festivals. It was all new and strange to them; they had heard none of it before. He tried to tell them about Love, too, but found he knew nothing about it and fell silent.

The Nymphs sprang and skipped about him while he talked, stroking his hair and plucking at things. 'You're wonderful! You're making it all up! You're amazing! Take us with you and show us these things!'

Perseus apologized and said he regretted that he could not, at least until his work was done. 'But you can teach me now, and tell me what I don't know. Where can I find Medusa and how can I kill her?'

The Nymphs looked suddenly sad. They would not answer at first. One of them, twirling her fingers in Perseus's hair remarked, 'It must be awful to be a rock.' Frankly, Perseus thought it rather an irrelevant comment.

Then they drew him by the hand into their cave, and showed him a painting on the wall. The oldest Nymph pointed in turn to three ghastly, winged women, saying: 'Stheno . . . Euryale . . . Medusa.'

A coldness gripped at Perseus's skeleton, and he found it difficult to move; the portraits were so vile that his gorge heaved. The three faces staring out from the wall were round, with flat, splayed noses and tongues dangling from between tusk-like teeth. They were crudely drawn, he told himself, for the hair was a daub of fat green strands, not hanging down but standing out in all directions. He looked more closely, and his flesh sweated drops as cold as those that ran down the cave walls. They were not locks of hair sprouting from the heads at all.

They were snakes.

* * *

'Medusa turns things into rocks,' said the oldest of the Nymphs. 'Anything that looks at her.'

'How do you know?' asked Perseus. 'You've never left this beach, this cave. You've never met anybody but each other!'

The Nymphs shrugged and sucked their thumbs and scuffed the sand with their toes. 'We just know. We've always known. I suppose we were born knowing. We were put here to know, I suppose—by the gods. We have the Things-to-Keep-Safe, after all.'

'What are they?'

The Nymphs sniggered at his ignorance. 'The *Things*, of course. For the One-Who-Will-Come. The Helmet and the Wallet and the Shoes.' (They had gone back to examining him, unfastening and refastening his belt and unpicking the seams of his tunic and licking the intriguing drops of sweat off his neck.)

'Do you suppose that could be me?' asked Perseus modestly.

The idea quite overwhelmed them. They rushed about the beach bumping into each other and tugging at their hair. They shrieked and laughed and wept and yelped, 'Him! It's him! He's the One-Who-Will-Come! He is! He is! We knew it all along!'

They fetched from the cave a black, bulging shoulder-bag and laid it at his feet with all the pride of cats presenting a dead bird or a half-eaten mouse. The bag was so black that it seemed to absorb all the light: he could not see what weave of cloth it was, but it smelt slightly dank and mouldy. 'The Wallet of Pluto,' said the Nymphs.

'Pluto, the God of the Underworld?'

But they only shrugged. That was the name they had always known, always used.

Perseus pushed his hand into the bag and snatched it

33

out again. He had touched something warm and fluttering like a bird. He tipped the bag upside down on to the beach, and a helmet and a pair of sandals fell out. The sandals had feathers decorating their heels—rather unmanly and tasteless, thought Perseus, who preferred plain clothes himself. But as they lay on the beach, the feathery shoes began to tremble. They rolled on to their soles and pattered shyly around Perseus and roosted again alongside his feet. The Nymphs were enchanted. Perseus felt a little foolish, but he put on the sandals anyway . . .

And the next thing he knew, he was walking off the ground. He found footholes in the air, and sprinted up among the seagulls. *'I can fly!'*

It was hard, at first, to keep his head from tumbling between his feet and not to turn upside down like the clapper in a bell. But before long he stood in the air like a swimmer treading water in an ocean of sunlight.

He shouted out his thanks to the gods, and settled gently on to the beach. The Nymphs were nowhere to be seen. Wedging his shining shield into the sand to serve as a mirror, he picked up the helmet which had also been in the bag, put it on and stood back to admire himself.

Nothing.

The shield's perfect mirror showed him each blade of grass, each dune, each sandpiper, each dying wave. But no Perseus. The Nymphs, who had fled from the wonder of his flying crept back out of their cave: 'Ah. He's gone. The-One-Who-Comes has flown away and left us with nothing but his shield . . . '

'Oh, you gods!' cried Perseus in horror. 'Is this a punishment for my boasting? Have you taken my body away from me? Have you turned me into sand? Am I a spirit? *Am I dead?* Is that all my sandals were for—to fly me to the Underworld?' His voice echoed deep inside the cave, but there was no reply. He kicked at the sand, and

it hissed against the bright shield. He ripped off the helmet and threw it down in disgust.

And there he stood, his fear and fury reflected in the shield's mirror, and there lay Pluto's Helmet of Invisibility spinning on its bright, miraculous crest, jaw-straps flying.

'Nymphs! Nymphs! Where are you? Come out and speak to me! Come back and tell me where to find the Medusa! I can fly! I can make myself invisible! What monster is safe from me? I could kill the whole world and never stop for breath!' And he swung his curved sword and laughed out loud. 'What can Medusa do to *me*, the darling of the gods?!'

'Kill you, what else?' said the oldest Nymph from where she stood in the mouth of the cave. 'She has only to sit where she sits, and you have only to look at her to be turned into stone. How will you kill her without looking at her?'

She was so certain he would die that Perseus faltered, and the showy flourish of his borrowed sword went astray and caught the rock of the cavern entrance. The impact jarred his arm in its socket and bruised his hand. He dropped the sword and put out his fingers to touch the damp stone. The words of the Nymphs rang around his head: 'It must be awful to be a rock.'

Far away in that kingdom which so far troubled Perseus not at all, the boastful King Cepheus bragged that his city walls could keep out any sea-monster. But the people did not believe him. Neither did they believe that the sea-monster would be fobbed off for ever with goats, sheep, and cattle. Besides, their livestock was gone. They were living on bread. In fact, they were starving for lack of bread.

And every night the sea-monster came and hung its head over the city walls and drooled its saliva on to the streets.

5

The Gorgons

It was like watching a shrimp stray into the fronds of an anemone, or a fly bumble into a spider's web. For the gods, watching from the height of Olympus, it was sport to see unwary travellers meet the Gorgons.

How did the travellers come there? Sometimes sandstorms sent them astray in the heart of the desert. Or sometimes it was the misreading of a map. For some a reckless dare. Or a stampeding camel, carrying its rider off the desert trail. Or the rumour of a magic place. For a dozen reasons, travellers regularly came to that barren everlastingness of yellow sand where the horizon vibrates like hot wire. But they never came away.

At the centre of the desert stood the three Gorgons. The great desert winds had long since torn away their shadows and carried them around the world to drop as nightmares on the pillows of a thousand beds.

But even the worst nightmares could not compare with the sight of the Gorgons: those bony, stumpy wings, those snouting noses, those tusks bulging through rubbery lips, those dangling tongues, those eyes oozing red rheum, those serpents writhing out of skulls to knot and flicker in scaly green tresses. The Gorgons' eyelids drooped idly, for their snaky hair had a thousand eyes to scan the desert for passers-by. Stheno, Euryale, and Medusa crouched in a seeming forest of stalagmites—rocky pillars rounded and shaped by the wind, caked in desert salt and stained by the droppings of vultures.

Look close. Those are not stalagmites. Those stumps are all that remain of travellers who died where they stood, in the single split-second of seeing Medusa.

Imagine feeling your flesh creep with horror, the tiny hairs stand up rigid on your forearms and, looking down in time to see those hairs turn brittle, that hand turn grey and lose its pattern of blue veins. Imagine your sleeve suddenly weighing like stone, your flesh like bone, your feet becoming sealed to the rocky ground; your joints freeze, your muscles stiffen, the blood stops still, the heart falls like a boulder through the hollow of your body, the brain drops into the jawbone, the eyeballs dry and harden into blind, round pebbles. Then stillness, darkness, nothing . . . for evermore.

That was how death came to the travellers who strayed into the lair of the Gorgons. That was what the gods regularly watched—unmoved—from the heights of Olympus, like watching a shrimp sucked into an anemone or a fly bumbling into a spider's web.

Only when Perseus, son of almighty Zeus, was flying in his winged sandals towards the Gorgons' desert did the gods stir themselves uneasily and muster along the parapets of heaven and whisper to one another, peep and peer earthwards, and twist their gauzy robes between anxious fingers. The rumour had quickly spread—that Perseus's fate was of *particular* interest to Zeus.

'Such a pleasant boy,' said Athene. 'Those golden eyes. Most appealing.'

'So very reckless.'

'So very daring.'

'So very pious.'

'So very promising.'

'Oh yes. I'll find a good place for him in the Halls of the Dead.' They all turned and stared at Pluto. 'Well? You don't fool yourselves, do you, that he can succeed? How is he to kill Medusa without looking at her? *Feel* his way? Blunder into her with his eyes shut? Grope up her backbone and take hold of a handful of hair and one-two off-with-her-head? Suppose he picks the wrong one? Stheno and Euryale are immortal. He may be invisible with my old helmet on, but then what? So he'll be an invisible rock instead of a visible one. So the vultures will fly into him and break their beaks, and the Gorgons will stub their toes against him. No, I'm telling you, by sunset I'll have to go down there and chisel his soul out of his body and take it inside my helmet down to the Underworld. That's the only compliment I'll pay to your Perseus there. He can't hope for better.'

The gloomy god of the Underworld was startled by a sudden tightening in his black robe, as Zeus took hold of him from behind by collar and sash and shook him furiously. 'Silence! Unless you want me to pitch you down to your everlasting halls and bolt the doors to keep you there. Where is Hermes? He must carry a message for me to the Gorgons and forbid them, in my name, to harm any more mortals!'

But the Gorgons were creatures of the Earth and loathed the gods for their beauty and had sworn never to obey the commands of Zeus the Almighty.

'Where's Athene? She must go to the boy and tell him it's impossible! It can't be done. Perseus must give up his attempt. Let him put some other head into his wallet. I'll give him some monster's muzzle to take to Polydectes instead!'

The gods and goddesses turned away their heads, embarrassed to see their king howl and rage with fear. Zeus raised his fist and in it was a thunderbolt large enough to break the horizon's trembling wire and shatter the Gorgons and their forest of rocks.

Then his wife, Hera, came and stood on the parapet of heaven between Zeus and his target. 'Husband! You disturb all Olympus with your noise! What great disaster is about to happen that can make the king of heaven lose his dignity? Is a god in danger? Is one of the Immortals in peril? No? Then why such a shameful display? For a little mortal? A speck of flesh? A comma in history? Anyone would think this boy meant something special to you. One foolish little worshipper? Since when did we reach down and dabble in Fate? Even the noble hero Odysseus never stirred you to this kind of passion. Tell me, *husband*. Why should you concern yourself with this *Perseus*?'

Then Zeus might have said, 'Perseus is my son. What's that to you? I am king of the gods. I'll father what children I like. I'll do as I please.'

But then there would have been a rift in heaven—civil war like sheet lightning in the skies, and Chaos. All these thoughts passed through Zeus's mind as he stared into the liquid brown eyes of his wife. And he did not say, 'Perseus is my son.' He said:

'You are right, my dear. What is the fate of one young mortal? It's just that this boy—what's his name again?—Perseus, showed uncommon promise. And you know how sentimental I am. Pah! Let him go! What's it to me?' Then he pulled the hood of his robe forwards over his head and walked away across the sky, stepping from cloud to cloud.

The gathering of gods broke up, with awkward gestures and muttered comments, and left none but Hera looking down from the parapets of heaven. An unpleasant sneer buckled her top lip. 'Now, Perseus—look on the Gorgons and be turned to stone, and let the sands blast you and the vultures perch on you and the winds grind you down to dust!'

Sunlight flared up off the shield Perseus was carrying across his back as he flew; it reflected so brightly that the stab of it hurt Hera's eyes and she had to look away.

Perseus knew better than anyone how difficult it would be to cut off Medusa's head without looking at her. He considered waiting until the moon had set and following the sound of the hissing snakes. But how then could he be certain of beheading the right Gorgon? Besides, the night is rarely so black as to hide a thousand pairs of watching eyes or the black bulk of a body against the paler sand. How much of a glimpse must he catch of the Medusa to be turned to stone? He had no way of knowing. Like a child peeping out between its fingers, he had a great yearning to see what could be so very terrible that it turned a man to stone.

Perseus knew when he was approaching the lair of the Gorgons. Even the birds were not immune to the dreadful magic of Medusa's eyes. Those which looked down as they flew over the ugly sisters plunged out of the sky—clay pigeons felled by their own curiosity. Perseus took his direction from the distant thud and crack of breaking vultures, and by the sight of them plummeting out of the sky a league away.

He flew over an oasis, and there below him an Arab woman was combing her hair, using a pool of water for her mirror. All of a sudden, the Arab woman dropped her comb with a splash and stared up: she had caught sight in the pool of the reflection of a young man flying overhead.

'By Zeus! By Athene! By all the gods!' cried Perseus, somersaulting through the air. 'Would it work? Could it work?'

He thought of turning back and asking the Nymphs, but would they know? He considered retracing his steps and asking the grey-eyed Graeae, but he knew they would only lie to him. He called out to the gods, *Will it work? Will it work?* But there was no answering sound except the shriek and crack of vultures thudding to earth half a league away. There was only one way of finding out if his idea would work: he would have to try.

He practised over the desert sands. Flying on his back like a swimmer saving the life of a drowning friend, he held the shield over his head and stared into the reflection on its inside. The hollow curve made everything reflected in it look smaller, further off. But he could see the waves of sand speckled by stones, the lizards running to and fro, the spiny fruit of the cactus as red as a man's heart. He put on the Helmet of Invisibility and became no more than a flash of light, a streak of whiteness, a brightness too bright to see.

'Before I was born it was decided,' said Perseus aloud to himself. 'Whether I shall kill Medusa or Medusa will kill me. My fate is already written in the brain of the oracles of the world and no wishing will change it. So let's find out what the Fates have in store for me!' He rolled on to his back and held the shield over him; it shielded him from the great heat of the noonday, and it reflected every spiky shrub, every scorpion, every beetle and butterfly below him.

The Gorgons lolled, flaccid and fleshy, among the rocky remains of their victims. Their soft rolls of fatness were piled up around their feet, and their stumpy wings drooped from fleshy shoulderblades. Their horrible claws crammed pebbles and guano into their tusked mouths, and between mouthfuls their tongues hung out over their double chins, drooling repulsively. Like the thrums of a rug, green snakes coiled densely out of their bony skulls and tasted the air, first one way then another, with forked, flickering tongues. Some short, some long, they knotted and writhed and hissed, and now and then the Gorgons scratched in among them with a piece of stick.

'You're looking older today, sister,' said Euryale with a sneer.

'So? So what if I am?' retorted Medusa. 'I'll have to grow a lot older before I'm as ugly as either of you!' But the anger rising through her veins made the snakes on her head break out in a deafening hiss. She hated her sisters when they reminded her that they were immortal whereas she must grow older and older and one day die. 'You're only jealous!' she taunted them. 'Just because I was loved once. Just because Poseidon gave me his . . . ' But she broke off, because a crawling of her infested scalp told her that something warm-blooded and alive was close at hand. 'Who is it? Who's there?' The snakes tossed and groped upwards from her head, but neither they nor she could see anything—only sense a closeness, a dangerous closeness.

Medusa shielded her eyes with her small fat claws and looked up at the empty sky. But it was noon and she was dazzled; the sun left marks on her eyes like little swordcuts. Her flat grey nose smelt human flesh, even so. 'Sisters! Sisters! Is someone coming? Is someone close at hand? Why doesn't it turn to stone? And why can't I see it? Oh, Poseidon, is it you come back to me? Are you playing a trick on me, my lover?'

Reflected on the inside of his shield, Perseus saw below him the cairns of rock which had once been men and women. He saw the rags of clothing still blowing around them, the looks of fear fixed for ever in stone. Then he saw a green-clawed foot and the feathers of a stubby wing and a roll of flesh and a green strand of seeming hair . . . and then at last three faces looking up to search the sky.

He felt his blood run cold. He felt the hairs on his arms and neck lift and prickle. He saw the reflection of his own face go grey—a ghastly grey as all the blood fled out of his lips and cheeks. Had his ruse not worked, then? 'Is that my fate?' he asked himself. 'Is this how it feels to be turned to stone?'

But his heart kept pounding, and his hand kept hold of the shield and his eyes went on seeing—though it was a sight almost too loathsome to bear—the three crouched shapes of the Gorgons. He drew his curved sickle-sword. He feathered his flight. He sank low over the hideous sisters—straight out of the dazzle of the noonday sun.

But which was Medusa? He had only one chance to guess right, for if he hacked at the neck of the immortal Stheno or Euryale, they would drag him out of the air. The snakes could sense him: they groped towards him, they strained in their bony sockets to reach up and pierce him with poisonous fangs. He lay in the air above them as close as a swimmer to the thick green weed of a river bed; his back was almost brushing them. *But which was Medusa?*

'MEDUSA!' he shouted at the top of his voice, and it seemed to him that one face turned before the rest. He dropped the dark cloth bag over that one (like the hangman's blindfold) and that was where he let his curved sword fall.

It is difficult, in a mirror, to tell left from right, to judge distances, to aim a blow. Medusa spread her wings and threw up her arms to tear free the bag covering her head. One hand struck Perseus and knocked off the

Helmet of Invisibility. But the sword of Hermes fell as true as a beam of sun. And when Perseus pulled tight the cords of the black bag and clambered up through the scream-filled air, the bag weighed heavy and jerked in his grasp.

To Euryale and Stheno, Perseus seemed to materialize out of the very air over their heads: one moment there was no one; the next there was this bird-man shouting a name, loosing a sword stroke. They lunged and they clawed, but all they found in their grip was a tuft from the crest of a helmet and a scrap of cloth from a tunic.

When they saw the swaying stump of their sister—like a tree struck by lightning—they let out such a screech of grief and rage that several of the stony figures shivered into sand then and there. The immortal Gorgons spread their dirty wings and beat the air so hard that it must have bruised. Ponderously they lifted their great weights into the air and took off in pursuit of Medusa's murderer.

6

Winged Pegasus

All that was left of Medusa rocked on its claw-like feet—like a volcano after the Earth's core has blasted off its peak and left only a gaping crater red, red, red with welling magma.

Just as the blood flowing from a cut will flow until it has cleansed the wound, so Medusa bled until out of her body was washed something . . . Something white, something huge, something shapeless and lumpen slumped on to the ground. It was as brilliant a white as ocean spray. Little wonder, for it was the child conceived by Medusa in her days of beauty—the child of the Earth-Shaker, the Earthquake-Maker Poseidon, god of the sea. It was a horse.

And yet it was not a horse, for lying along its back, gradually breaking, unfolding, spreading, flapping, two immense wings rose up until their topmost feathers met. Unstained by his mother's blood, Pegasus the Winged Horse was born, as wild as temper.

His shadow fell huge on the Libyan sands, then only as large as an eagle, then only as small as a hawk, as Pegasus leapt higher and higher into the sky, snaking his white neck, flaring his dark nostrils, and trampling the air with his white hooves. Foam spumed from his lips and flecked all his sweating neck and flanks, and his eyes rolled in a vengeful frenzy.

The two Gorgons, for all their stumpy wings, were so enraged by the murder of their sister that they kept pace with Perseus who dared not look back over his shoulder. He was unaccustomed to flying, and his limbs were tired with struggling to keep his balance in the air. Once, twice he stumbled into a somersault, pitching end over end. Behind him he could hear the Gorgon sisters shriek with triumphant, joyless laughter and gain on him a little. The wallet with Medusa's head in it weighed heavy as a boulder; he feared the black cloth must split and let fall his trophy; but it only banged, banged against his thigh. He had thought the writhing of the snakes inside was a simple reflex—like chickens who go on running about after their heads are cut off. He expected that one by one they would wilt and die. But the snakes did not die at all; their hissing went on as loud as ever.

And that was not all that escaped the bag. Seeping through the black cloth, Medusa's blood dripped, dripped on to the desert below. And as each gout of blood touched the ground, it bored a deep, small hole in the sand. A moment later, out of each hole wriggled a green serpent, its fangs charged with a deadly venom. The blood of Medusa seeded the world's deserts with snakes.

The rhythmic beat of the white horse's wings seemed to be counting away Perseus's life in seconds—five, four, three, two—as with each stride it gained on him.

'Kill, horse! *Kill!*' shrieked the Gorgons. 'Bite him! Trample him! Kick him! Ride him down! *Ride him down!*'

A shadow fell on Perseus as the horse leapt over him and cut off the sunlight. The boy saw the hooves falling on him. He pulled in his head and heels and tumbled through the air so that Pegasus completely overshot him. But now he was trapped between horse and Gorgons. He flew back the way he had come, holding his shield in front of him so as not to see the hideous sisters. What if their gaze, too, could turn a man to rock? Then Perseus would fall like a meteorite to the ground and become just one more boulder in a desert of boulders.

So intent was he on not seeing the Gorgons that he collided with Euryale in mid-air. There was a squeal and a grunt, and two hooked hands came round the edge of the shield and pulled it downwards. And there he was, face to face with that snout, those tusks, that great lolling tongue. His despair gave Perseus a superhuman strength and he wrenched free his shield. But though his blood ran as cold as meltwater and his flesh crawled, he did not turn to stone at the sight of Euryale or the smell of her foul breath. She struck out at him with the thing she happened to be holding in her claw—his own magic Helmet. In fending off the blow, he raised the sickle-sword, and its wire-sharp blade cut through the chin-strap of the Helmet and brought it crashing into his face. Somehow, with the back of a hand, with the rim of the shield, he crammed it on to his head—just as Stheno flew up beneath him and snatched at his winged feet.

He felt their touch—it was scaly and dry, like a crocodile, and grazed his skin. But a moment later— when they might have torn him in two between them— they were bawling and brawling with each other. 'Where did he go?' 'What have you done with him?' 'Did he melt? Did we dream him?' 'No! I can smell him still!'

The invisible Perseus half swam, half flew out of their reach. A whooping triumph swelled in his throat and he wanted to laugh at their squabbling, and to taunt them. But as he went to put away his sickle-sword, a blow in his back knocked all the breath out of him in a pained, panicked cry. Pegasus, startled by his invisible foe and maddened by the scent of him, flailed at the air with his front hooves and snapped with his long, white teeth.

The only safe place in all the wide skies seemed to be astride the beast's back. And that was where Perseus found himself. He flung Athene's shield across his back, he crammed the Helmet of Invisibility down so hard on to his skull that he could barely see out, and he pushed the sickle-sword through his belt. Then he clung on grimly with both hands and both knees. The bag containing Medusa's head thumped into the animal's white ribs, and winged Pegasus felt for the first time in his short life what it was to be ridden by a man.

He took off at a gallop that set Perseus and his baggage clattering. The Gorgon sisters, by the time they realized what was happening, could only pant and grunt after the shrinking speck of white, until it disappeared over the horizon. All that remained of their sister was a trail of wriggling serpents on the desert below.

Pegasus bucked and reared, stretched round and bit, but nothing would dislodge the rider from his back. He was so intent on the struggle that he failed to notice the vast barrier of a mountain rising up into the sky ahead of him.

The gods lining the parapets of heaven to watch had a marvellous view. For Pegasus was flying directly towards Mount Olympus, his great wings cutting elegant sweeps through the air, his head turned away to snap at his invisible rider. (To the gods, of course, nothing is invisible.) 'Here they come!'

'What a horse!'

'Isn't that your shield, Athene?'

'Isn't that your sword, Hermes?'

'Aren't they your sandals . . . ?'

'Look out!'

'I say, have a care!'

Suddenly the sleepy, languid gods were scattering to left and right; some dived to the floor, some were bowled on to their backs as Pegasus, mindless of the mountain in his way, flew straight into it, pulling up his head only at the last moment. His hooves clipped the escarpment.

And where they did so, a redness spurted out. Perseus saw it and exclaimed, 'What? Now even the world is bleeding! *Can* cliffs bleed?'

It was not blood at all. Pegasus, having sweated himself to a parching thirst, flew in a circle and paused to drink at the red, welling stream now cascading down Olympus's cliffside. He drank and snickered and staggered and rose up again on lopsided wings.

When he had gone, the gods hurried down as fast as dignity would allow, and dabbed at the stream with their fingers. They scooped up the red liquor in their palms. They stained their robes reaching for more.

'Look! It's all running down to Earth,' said one. 'We should dam it up. This is too good for the little mortals down there—too strong for their silly little brains.' But somehow the dam was never built, and the wine continued to flow from the highest slopes of Olympus, down through the vineyards of Greece. Hippocrene they called it: 'wine-of-the-horse'—and gods and men delighted in it equally, though it made them all as drunk as ticks.

Having drunk a gallon of hippocrene, Pegasus mellowed. The animal sagged at the shoulders and lowered his lids against the brightness of the sinking sun. Horse and rider sank down into the long shadows of Africa.

In Africa there stood, in those days, a man more bent at the shoulder, more heavy at heart than even King Acrisius of Argos. His lot in life was dreadful: to hold up the sky for ever and to keep it from crashing on to the Earth beneath. The icy clouds buffeted his face and the birds perched in the corner of his eye and eagles nested in his cavernous ears. But when the sun glared in his face, or the flinty stars drove their sharp points into his bent neck, he could not fend off the pain, for his hands were everlastingly spread to support the level sky. Just once he had known a moment's relief when Hercules the Strong had taken his place in return for a favour. But Hercules had tricked Atlas back into his never-ending ordeal.

Heavy as the heavens were, there was something heavier still which Atlas had to bear. It was the fear of his fate. For an oracle had prophecied Atlas would lose his life one day at the hands of a son of Zeus.

'How can I die when I'm immortal?' Atlas had demanded, half scoffing, half angry. But no answer came to his question, and at length fear took the place of scorn and anger. Fear gnawed away at Atlas's heart as it gnawed at the heart of King Acrisius. Only one emotion was stronger than the fear. Standing in that one remote spot, unable to move and surrounded by dark, trackless Africa, Atlas was as lonely as One.

Perseus and Pegasus landed late in the gloomy evening. Both were as exhausted as each other. Perseus took off his Helmet and wiped his face.

'By Zeus! That was clever! Where did you spring from?'

Pegasus pranced and bucked and rolled his white lips back off his white teeth at the sound of the booming voice. Perseus snatched out his sickle-sword: 'Who's there? Show yourself!'

'Look up, young man. You are camped in the lee of my left leg. No call to disturb yourself. I never sit down. But if you would care to move round to the front, it might be easier to talk. I'd be heartily glad of your news, young fellow. You are most welcome to my humble realm. My name is Atlas.'

'I've heard of you!' exclaimed Perseus, suddenly wide awake. 'Your hospitality is famous throughout the world!'

'Is it? Is it indeed? How pleasant. How very nice to know. Do feel free to light a campfire. I can provide a bird or two from my humble larder.' And he swatted a brace of songbirds which had been singing overloud in his ear. The sky tilted momentarily, and a sprinkling of stars fell.

While Pegasus slept, Perseus built a fire and cooked himself some supper, and entertained Atlas with the story of his quest for the head of Medusa.

'And you mean to say that you—a small mortal from Seriphus—have cut off Medusa's head?'

Perseus smiled rather smugly. 'I do believe I had a little help from the gods,' and he showed the shield and the sickle-sword and the bag. Atlas looked doubtful.

'Why should they help you? No offence, boy—but why exactly should the gods take it into their heads to help some penniless boy with the smell of fish on his hands? Show me the head. Go on. Show me. I daresay you've been killing lizards or lopping willow trees.'

Perseus was not offended. A cocksure arrogance was stirring in him—the one that had made him promise Medusa's head to King Polydectes in the first place. He felt about him in the darkness for the wallet. (If it was hard to see in the daylight, it was impossible to find in the dark.) 'My mother has often told me the story of how I came to be born. And it seems to me—though I can't quite work out the way of it—that my father must be one of the gods themselves.' He laughed at a sudden extravagant idea: 'Maybe even Zeus himself!' His hands still mislaid the nasty, writhing bag in among the long grass.

'Liar! *Liar!*' bawled Atlas, kicking out at Perseus and scattering the campfire in a flurry of sparks. The sky quaked like the skin of a drum, and the echo ricocheted between ground and cloud, plain and planets. *'Liar-iar-iar!'*

Bowled head-over-heels by the kick, his arm over his head to protect him from the ear-splitting noise, Perseus was too startled to cry out.

'YOU? You worm! You squirt! You braggart! You, the son of Zeus? Ha! I laugh at the idea, see? Ha ha!!' Atlas was leaning down so low that the whole pallet of the sky on his back sloped at a dangerous angle and planets slid into unlucky alignments and the stars jostled. 'Get off my land! Get out of my realm, you boasting whelp, or I'll kick you all the way from here to the Hesperides! You're a boasting storyteller! Your father's some sailor who took your mother's fancy—some beggar, some wretch, some dwarf . . . ' Perseus could see Atlas's eyes, large as moons, bulging with rage. They reflected a few red sparks from the scattered fire.

'Is this the famous hospitality you show your guests?' cried Perseus, but his voice was choked with amazement and drowned out by Atlas howling, 'Liar! *Liar!* LIAR!'

'And I say I *am* the son of Zeus. Or how else would I have killed the Gorgon?' The clouds were shaken clear of the moon, and Perseus could at last fumble his way to the lost black bag. It wriggled under his touch. He pulled open the cords, and holding the bag from underneath, so that the cloth fell back over his hand and arm, held up Medusa's head. 'See it for yourself, if you don't believe me!'

Atlas stared.

*   *   *

He is staring now. Although his staring eyes you might mistake for white scars on a hillside and his gaping mouth for a cave. You would take his hair for a plantation of trees and his bent back for the bare upper slopes of a mountain range. For Atlas was turned to rock by the son of Zeus.

His bones are buried deep now—like strata of rock. Loose earth blown in on the wind buried him, and grass took root in the earth and blurred every sharpness—his elbow, his knees, his heel, his jaw . . .

Clouds covered the moon again. In the darkness, Perseus could not tell what had happened. One moment Atlas had been towering over him, raging, shouting, deafening him with insults. Now the African night was quiet. The smell of sweaty giant was gone. After a few seconds the chirruping roar of insects filled up the silence. Somewhere, a wild animal howled. The horse Pegasus, so white that he glowed in the dark, woke up and pawed the ground in an ecstasy of nervousness.

Perseus thrust Medusa's head back into its wallet without looking at it. He was disappointed that Atlas had (apparently) stormed off without bothering to see the convincing proof of Perseus's heroism. But it was also a relief not to have to fight the giant. After all, the man was as big as a mountain!

He picked up all his bits and pieces of baggage and leapt astride the winged horse once more, before Pegasus could bolt for freedom or remember his hatred towards Perseus. Up among the stars, riding out the tantrum which followed, Perseus came to the conclusion that this steed of his might be a little on the stupid side. Tantrums are often the last resort of the stupid.

7

Two More Visitors for the Oracle

The ruins of the old tower were falling! His legs would not carry him out of the way! First single bricks then whole sections of wall, wooden beams, iron window bars, winches, a little bed, and table all hurtled down on him, burying him alive. He tried to cry out, but his mouth filled up with dusty mortar. Then the whole tower, with infinite slowness, keeled over and fell on him so that no amount of digging would ever rescue him from under the rubble.

King Acrisius woke up screaming and threw off his bedclothes as though they were crushing the life out of him. Wiping the sweat from his face with a pillow, he went to the window and looked out. The tower had long since been pulled down, of course—immediately after the first nightmare he had given the order for it to be razed to the ground. But the bad dreams went on, night after night.

Could that be what the oracle had meant? That little Perseus—little drowned Perseus, little dead drowned Perseus—would leave behind him such nightmares as to stop up Acrisius's thumping heart?

Or was he not really dead at all? Had Acrisius's daughter and grandson really sunk and drowned in that leaky chest? He imagined them still down there after eighteen years, holding their breath.

For eighteen years? No! It was impossible! Danaë and Perseus had not lived so much as an hour . . . well, not so much as a day . . .

Perhaps a week, if the chest had floated . . .

And if it had floated, might not some ship's captain have seen it and taken it aboard and smashed the lock and found . . . ? Acrisius shuddered with a sudden cold.

'Boy! *Boy, where are you?*' His footpage tottered into the room dizzy with sleep. 'Tell the stables to make ready a chariot, I must go to Epidaurus.'

'Now, sire? In the middle of the—'

'*Now!*' And Acrisius threw the pillow he was clutching, though it missed the boy and only toppled a valuable, carved bust of the king. The sculpture fell on to the marble floor, and the hollow head shattered.

Acrisius thought he could see loathing in the eyes of the oracle at Epidaurus. He was wrong. Oracles have no feelings. But Acrisius tended to see loathing in every pair of eyes that looked at him. It was only the reflection of his own guilt.

'What-t is-s it this-s-s time, Acris-s-ius-s-s?' hissed the oracle.

The king's voice was shrill and loud with hysteria. 'I just came to tell you you were wrong! You were, weren't you? Admit it. You were wrong!'

'I am never wrong,' said the oracle turning away its hooded head, 'and fate is unchangeable.'

'So-ho! Tell me now that Perseus is going to kill me! You can't, eh, can you? You can't, see!'

'Pers-seus-s-s is going to kill you, Acris-sius-s-s,' said the oracle implacably. 'You may go now.'

'But I . . .'

'You what-t, Acris-sius-s-s?' said the oracle, without the smallest note of curiosity. 'I s-s-see blood on your hands-s, s-ssir. Bes-st go home and wash-sh-sh it off.'

Acrisius snatched his hands back inside the sleeves of his robe and rushed outside, his diaphragm quaking with horror. In the daylight he was mightily relieved to see that the redness in his palms was only where he had clenched his fists so tight that his nails had cut the skin and made it bleed. Dreadful if the oracle had meant something else . . .

'But I didn't murder anyone!' he blurted out loud. 'I just put them in a chest.'

So perhaps they were not dead.

'But they must be dead. I killed them!' Try as he might, Acrisius could not make up his mind which was true, which he wanted to be true. He went home and commissioned spies to keep watch the world over for news of his dead daughter and his dead grandson.

After he had gone, the oracle had a second visitor.

'Two kings-s in one day,' observed the serpent, and a slight sneer creased the hard rim of its mouth. 'What do you want, Cepheus-s-s?'

King Cepheus, who had come in disguise with his hood pulled far forward over his face, sat down sharply on the floor; his legs trembled too much to hold him. He had a horror of snakes.

'A friend of mine has a problem,' he began.

'Come come, Cepheus-s-s. Don't ins-sult my intelligence-ce. Friend, indeed. You wish-sh to know how

56

to be rid of your s-s-sea-mons-s-ster.' In the oracle's mouth, the beast's name seemed as long as its body.

'Yes-s-s . . . I mean "yes",' said Cepheus, trying not to catch sight of the weaving, waving head or the flickering fangs.

'Why did Pos-seidon s-send it agains-s-t-t you?' asked the creature, although the question sounded like a statement.

Cepheus answered in a guilty rush. 'Because my foolish wife bragged that our daughter was more beautiful than the mermaids. And those vicious women—fish— what is a mermaid exactly?'

'A mammal,' said the oracle yawning.

'Well then, those vicious mammals went whining to Poseidon, and he took a piece of this and a bit of that and moulded it all together into . . . into . . . well, you've seen it, haven't you? There, inside your head? It's hideous!'

The oracle ducked down and poked its round green head round Cepheus's hand to stare him in the eye. 'Because it is s-so very s-s-serpent-like?' hissed the serpent menacingly.

Cepheus gave a scream and cowered backwards. 'Not at all! No! But it keeps eating things, doesn't it? Goats and pigs and sheep and cows and horses. And last night it pushed down a wall and walked through the streets of Ammon. *For the love of the gods! What must I do to save my kingdom?'*

There was a long, terrible silence before the serpent said, 'Why did you was-ste t-time t-travelling here, Cepheus-s-s? You know full well what s-s-sacrifice you mus-s-t-t make.'

'*No! NO!* Not Andromeda! Not my daughter! Not my lovely, innocent daughter! Not her! Have pity, won't you? Say my wife! Say my prime minister—I wouldn't mind that! But not Andromeda! Her marriage is all arranged! There must be some other way!'

The oracle stared at the ceiling until King Cepheus had shouted himself silent. 'I promis-se you this-s-s, Cepheus-s-s, Andromeda will never marry Agenor. That is not-t her fate. Deck her with jewels-s, then chain her to the flat-t black rock by the s-sea. You know the one. Andromeda is the only apology Pos-seidon will accept-t for the ins-sult to his mermaids-s-s. It is her fate.'

A week later, the Princess Andromeda sat at the family dinner table, along with her betrothed, the handsome Prince Agenor, and wondered at her parents' strange behaviour. First her father had presented her with a necklace and a belt of the most exquisite lapis lazuli set in gold. Now her mother was sobbing silently into her sleeve-ends. They both sat stabbing the food on their plates as though it had done them an injury. And neither spoke, though Agenor leapt up from time to time to look out of the windows. He swore he could hear the sea-monster scratching at the city wall.

'What are you going to do about it, father-in-law-to-be?' he asked in his sharp, nasal voice. 'I have to tell you, it's very difficult indeed to organize the wedding— everyone is so nervous of the wretched beast. And I do hate to see darling Andromeda so anxious. And there's so little *food*! I thought I'd wear my purple. What do you think, dearest? It suits me well, don't it?'

'Yes, Agenor. It suits you very well,' whispered Andromeda, her thoughts taken up with her parents' odd behaviour. 'You still haven't said, father. Did the oracle know a way to be rid of the sea-monster?'

King Cepheus choked on a mouthful of bread, and his daughter had to bang him on the back. He caught hold of her hands for a moment, then let go as if her fingers were too hot to touch. 'Yes, Andromeda. The oracle knew what must be done.'

'Excellent!' declared Agenor, draping the curtain-hanging over one shoulder to see if the colour suited him. 'We'll have the wedding the day after it's done. I thought we'd have sports afterwards, to entertain the guests. Have you ever seen me throw a discus, dearest darling Andromeda?' He picked up a plate and seemed about to demonstrate, but Andromeda gently took it away from him and put it back on the table.

'Tell us, father. Will it be very difficult?'

Cepheus covered his face with his hands. 'Yes, daughter, it will be the most difficult thing I've ever done.' And pulling his robe over his face he rapped three times on the table.

Suddenly armed soldiers leapt into the room at every door and window—big, ungentle men with necks as broad as their shaven heads, and arms covered in battle scars. One seized Andromeda from behind, pinning her arms to her sides in a fierce embrace.

'I say!' protested Agenor. 'Let go of my dear darling betrothed!'

The king and queen fled the room, colliding at the doorway and struggling with each other to be out of the sight of their betrayed daughter. 'I'm sorry! I'm sorry! I'm sorry! It's all your mother's fault!' wailed Cepheus over his shoulder, and Queen Cassiopeia shouted and slapped at him in bitter denial. 'She has to die, Agenor!' cried Cepheus. 'The oracle says so! It's her fate! She has to be chained to a rock to feed the sea-monster! The mermaids demand it! Forgive us, boy. Forgive us, Andromeda! Forgive us!' His footsteps pattered away along the echoing corridor pursued by the queen's sobbing.

In the soldier's arms Andromeda stopped struggling and stared after them, breathing fast and shallow. Then she turned her eyes to Agenor whose sword was half out of its sheath. 'Will you let them do this to me?' she pleaded.

The sword slid home again with a thud. 'Poor dear darling Andromeda,' he said flatly.

The soldier lifted Andromeda as though she were a piece of army baggage. 'Help me, Agenor! You won't let them feed me to the monster! I know you won't! Not you! Not if you love me!'

'Ah.' Agenor studied the sleeve of his robe and, with extreme concentration, began to pick at a blob of candle-wax which had stained it. 'Well, if it really is the only way to satisfy the horrible thing . . . '

'Agenor! *Help me!*' Her hands reached out towards him as the soldier carried her out into the gardens. A host of butterflies flew up off the bushes and flowers. '*AGENOR!*'

Her young man hurried down the seaward path after his betrothed and the squad of brutal soldiers. He raised his voice and called, 'It's a terrific honour for you, of course, dearest! I only wish it were my fate to save Ammon from the sea-monster! People will always be grateful to you after this! And if the oracle says it's your fate, who am I to argue?'

'Agenor, I hate you!'

'Now, now. You don't mean that. Think about it. It's an immense honour, if you'll just think about it . . . and I'm sure the unpleasant part will be over very quickly . . . '

'*Mother! Father! Agenor!*'

The chains hung waiting from the smooth black rock by the sea-shore—high up to fasten her wrists and low down for her ankles. As Agenor's high-pitched voice droned on at a distance—'an honour really . . . a very great public service . . . '—the bull-necked soldier

60

manacled her with the iron rings. Then he pinned her to the rock with his shoulder while he put the tip of his sword to her delicate robe and slit it from throat to hem. The two pieces fell away into the eager, gaping sea and left her in only the necklace and belt of lapis lazuli and gold.

At the sight of this, Agenor's voice died in his throat and he covered his face with his hands and stumbled away up the cliff path whimpering, ' . . . soon be over . . . soon be over.'

'Sorry about him,' said the soldier gruffly. 'No loss as a husband, that one.' His stubbly, scarred cheeks were red with blushes. Both he and Andromeda watched her torn white robe wash to and fro in the water before it sank slowly out of sight. 'Orders, see. Orders . . . Well. I'd . . . er . . . I must be going, lady. Good luck.'

A wave broke against the rocky platform and they were both deluged in bitter spray. 'I'm afraid you must be awful cold, lady. I hope the sea-monster won't be long in coming.'

'If I were your daughter . . . if I were your wife . . . would you leave me here to die such a death?' pleaded Andromeda.

'Fate's fate, lady. There's no changing that.' His nervous glances said that he expected the sea-monster at any moment to lurch up out of the water at their feet. He sheathed his sword, saluted her once, and hurried back up the cliff path in awkward leaping strides. Andromeda's head sank on to her chest, and her yellow hair, spilling down her body, clung to her spray-wet skin.

As far away as a migrating bird, Perseus rode Pegasus across a cloudless sky. The winged horse had not given in to its rider, but it was stupid, easily fooled, and Perseus had only to put on his Helmet of Invisibility to catch and mount the beast whenever he wanted.

Below him the sea was an amazement of different colours. Shoals of krill, rafts of seaweed, underwater reefs and eddies of surface wind made patches of green, white, and turquoise. Dolphins left dotted trails, and flying fishes burst like fireworks into the air. Diving gulls pelted the water, and the dark shapes of sunken ships lay whirled round with bright shoals of fish.

He thought the sea-monster, too, was a ship's hulk until, with a flick of its tail, it moved off in lazy undulations through the water below him. The glare off the waves smudged its shape and colour. He did not see clearly its barnacle-encrusted back, its hooked fins, its banks of jagged teeth, the fronded, raggy barbules that waved around its massive, dew-lapped mouth, nor the six legs that dangled from its scaly underbelly. He wondered that there could be such strange beasts in the world. But moving far faster than any water-borne creature could swim, Perseus overtook the cruising monster and flew on in hope of sighting land. He was unsure where he was and which way he ought to be flying.

'I trust in the gods to direct me,' he said out loud, his face cocked towards the sky. But there were few gods available to see or hear him at that particular moment.

Most of those on Olympus had gone down to Africa to see if the rumours were true—that the immortal Atlas had been turned into a mountain by a teenage boy with a clutter of magic baggage.

8

Love at First Sight

At first she was nothing more than a patch of white and gold and flashing lapis lazuli, seen out of the corner of his eye. Even when he came closer, he did not quite believe what his eyes were telling him—that someone had chained this beautiful young woman to a rock to be splashed by the angry sea. It was Pegasus who decided the matter, settling down on to the slippery platform to drink from a rock pool.

At the sound of the horse's clattering hooves and fanning wings, Andromeda, who had her eyes tight shut and her hair over her face, began to scream and scream and scream.

With an angry flick of his sensitive ears, Pegasus wandered off along the foreshore and left Perseus standing dumbfounded on the sacrificial platform of black granite. Remembering his manners at last, he quickly removed the Helmet of Invisibility and put it under his arm. It left him no hands free to cover his ears; he did wish she would stop screaming. 'Please don't alarm yourself, madam. My horse is unpleasant but remarkably stupid.' Andromeda's eyes opened, wide and round as whirlpools—and Perseus was sucked in and lost everlastingly in fathoms of love.

'Your horse?' she said. 'Who are you?'

'Were you expecting someone else? I'm sorry. I'll go.'

'Don't go,' said Andromeda hastily.

It was difficult for Perseus to know what to say. He had never seen a naked woman chained to a rock before. He looked at his feet for lack of knowing where else to look. 'Aren't you rather cold?'

'Perished,' said Andromeda.

'You're extraordinarily beautiful, if you don't mind me saying so.'

'Come back tomorrow. You won't think so then,' said Andromeda.

'I could stand here and look at you for ever.' Having dared to glance at her face, he could not now unfix his eyes.

'Then you would be eaten, too, and I'm sure I don't wish that on anyone,' said Andromeda.

'Eaten?'

'Why do you suppose I'm standing here, young man?' she asked irritably. 'In other circumstances I might enjoy talking to you, but I have a great deal on my mind just at the moment. Must you stare so at my jewels?'

'What jewels?' said Perseus. 'What do you mean, "eaten"?'

So Andromeda explained how her mother had bragged, how the mermaids had taken offence, how Poseidon had assembled the monster, how the oracle had spoken her fate. The waves broke tediously up against the rock, and they were both wet through before she had done.

'I think that's the saddest story I ever heard,' said Perseus, wiping saltwater off his cheek with the heel of his hand.

'I'm so glad you enjoyed it.'

'And this sea-monster is due here shortly?'

'Any moment.'

'Then I'd best hurry. Which way is your parent's palace?'

'Why? Do you want *supper*?' she hissed, straining forwards from the rock though it twisted her arms in their sockets.

'No. No time. I just want to be sure they'll let me marry you if I kill this sea-monster . . . You wouldn't mind, would you? Marrying me, I mean? Only I've been in love with you ever since I laid eyes on you, and my mother said that if I ever loved a woman I ought to marry her before anything else. Unlike my father, you know. Whoever he was. You see . . . '

'Sir!' said Andromeda. 'I would marry your horse if it saved me from being eaten! You don't have to ask my mother and father! I'll marry you! I'll marry you!'

While Perseus pondered this, a large wave slopped over his feet and made the wings on his sandals sodden. 'No, no. I think I really must ask your mother and father for permission. Mother told me if I met a woman I loved I must ask the blessing of her mother and father. Unlike my father. You see . . . '

'*SIR!*'

He was loath to stop looking at her, but at last tore himself away and set off up the path to the royal palace. 'Oh, I forgot! I should lend you my cloak!' he called back.

'*LATER!*'

'Oh, and I'm very honoured that you're willing to marry me.'

Andromeda did not answer. Winged Pegasus had wandered back along the beach and was licking her thoughtfully with his long, rasping tongue, savouring the salty taste of her skin.

When he finally found King Cepheus and Queen Cassiopeia, they seemed very pleased with the idea of Perseus marrying their daughter. They were scornful at first, until he told them he had just beheaded Medusa. Then they could not promise their blessing quickly enough. Perseus was quite flushed with pleasure. 'At home they call me One-Shirt Perseus,' he said.

King Cepheus stood holding the door open. 'You're welcome. You're welcome. Now go and fight the sea-monster! Please!'

'Of course it's most selfish of me to want to marry a princess when I have no money to buy her clothes or feed her on anything but bread and sardines . . . '

'He wants money,' said the queen, grabbing her husband's sleeve. 'Promise him money, Cepheus. Promise him anything.'

'Oh, I didn't mean—'

'Half my kingdom!' cried King Cepheus falling on his knees in front of Perseus. 'Half my kingdom is yours if you kill the sea-monster and save Andromeda!'

'Oh, I—'

'—But do HURRY! The monster comes at sunset, and the sun is already dipping in the sea! Go! Go! Go!'

Perseus rearranged all his baggage—his shield and wallet and sword and helmet—and hovered away across the garden, disturbing the butterflies for a second time that day. In the distant sea, a dark shape was cutting its way inshore through the smooth, gleaming swell, along the scarlet path of the setting sun. For a moment it looked as though Poseidon's monster was swimming in blood.

At the sight of the monster, stilly watching her from among the waves, Andromeda fainted. The beast was transfixed; the answer to its longings was suddenly there. It had been

66

formed and made to hunger after Andromeda. As Poseidon took a piece of alligator, a shred of shark, a morsel of whale, a section of moray eel, and moulded his ravenous, vengeful monster, he poured into its sea-cold blood all the heat he had felt for Medusa, all the hunger he still felt for beauty, all the violence he normally reserved for causing tidal waves and earthquakes. So the monster thought and dreamed and pictured and bayed for Andromeda. And when it found her staked out as a gift, its ecstasy was horrible to see. It leapt and pranced in the sea, and its tongue lolled out through its thousands of teeth. Its nostrils were full of her sweet smell. It scraped its clawed fins on the shallowing sea-bed and stretched out its neck . . .

A dart of light glimpsed out of the corner of its eye was all that the monster saw of Perseus. But at the first clash of the sickle-sword across its steely neck, the monster threw up its head and sent its attacker tumbling through the air. The Helmet of Invisibility fell into the sea; the wallet holding Medusa's head dropped too, into a bed of seaweed, and the shallow water closed over it. Perseus steadied himself, his winged feet trailing in the surf, then pitched himself at the monster, striking with sword and shining shield.

The beast was enraged at being kept from its sweet, delicious prey. But Perseus, having lost Medusa's head, was every bit as angry. He rained blows on the monstrous snout, and teeth rattled into the sea. But the scales of its skin were tougher than leather, and the lash of its tail quick to find its mark. It coiled around Perseus and held him under water until he thought his lungs had turned to stone inside him.

At last the creature brought its captive close to its mouth, to rend him in its teeth. Then Perseus was able not only to snatch a breath of air but to jab the tip of his sickle-sword into the lolling pink tongue. The beast loosed an ear-splitting whistle through its gills and, throwing Perseus aside in disgust, turned back towards its chief prey—Andromeda.

Its two stumpy alligator legs mounted the platform of black rock and began to pull the rest of its long body up out of the water. Perseus—his shield gone now and floating like a bright reflection on top of the waves—swam with his sword in his fist, and pulled himself astride the broad, finny back. The beast lost its hold and they both slid off the rock and under water where they rolled over and over and over in a deadly embrace. Perseus cut himself on his own sword and on the sharp scales of the monster; pain and the smell of human blood drove the creature to a greater madness. The nasty fronded feelers around its mouth sucked and groped at Perseus's head, and the gills opened and closed in panting, evil-smelling breaths. Through the gill-flaps Perseus drove in his sword, and with one more massive shudder which threatened to pin the boy against the black rocky cliff, Poseidon's sea-monster went suddenly limp.

As flaccid and buoyant as a dead whale, it lolled in the water, feet uppermost, only its heavy skull resting on the sea-bed. Perseus pulled himself on to the sharp-edged platform of rock and lay like a man dead, at Andromeda's feet.

'My hero!' she said, reviving. 'I love you. But who are you?'

'Perseus,' he replied, squeezing the sea water out of his golden hair. 'And I love you, too.'

When he went to gather up his belongings, the shield had beached itself like a little round boat. The wallet containing Medusa's head he never expected to find, for it had fallen in among the waving, rust-red fronds of a thousand sea anemones and a forest of seaweed. But when he swam to where he had seen it fall, he barked his knees on a sharpness, and cut razory slashes in the soles of his sandals as he stood up on the shallow, solid stuff. It was red still—as blood-red as the anemones had been—but was as brittle now as shale or flint. It was weirdly beautiful, but dead, and the bag rested on top of this delicate reef, within ready reach of Perseus's dipping hand.

A singularly unpleasant thought crept into his mind, as he slung the wallet across his shoulder, and the head banged against the small of his back. He began to realize that Medusa's magic was still seeping out of this nasty trophy of his: a magic which could turn living things to stone.

They called it coral, afterwards—that brilliant, blood-red, brittle, shining, stony stuff. Its beauty made it precious, and it was prized by mermaids and princesses alike.

As for Pegasus, he was nowhere to be found. He had seized the chance of freedom, catching the warm noon breezes under his wings and losing his whiteness among canyons of creamy clouds. It would take a better man than Perseus to tame the son of Medusa.

9

In-laws

'Splendid! Splendid!' cried King Cepheus over and over again, while Queen Cassiopeia simply wept with joy.

Andromeda sat silent in the circle of Perseus's right arm. She spoke no word of reproach against the parents who had fed her to a sea-monster.

Cepheus could not help remembering how he had knelt on the floor and pleaded with Perseus: the boy looked so very young and ragged sitting there, in a borrowed tunic, bloody and bruised and beaming with delight.

'I never thought, when I woke up this morning, that this would be my wedding day,' said Perseus. 'As for the matter of half your kingdom—'

The door burst open then, and Agenor minced into the room on tiptoe, wearing his finest robes and a great many jewels. He ran to Andromeda and would have kissed both her hands if she had not snatched them away. 'Dearest darling Andromeda! I am overjoyed at our great good fortune! My prayers have been answered! The gods have spared you!' and he took Andromeda in his arms and kissed her.

Perseus's heart sank a thousand fathoms.

But Andromeda broke away and rapped Agenor sharply across the muzzle as she might a dog that had bitten her. 'How dare you! How dare you even speak to me, you coward!'

A dreadful silence fell over the room. Agenor turned very pale, but chose to ignore the trickle of blood leaking from his nose. Turning to the king he said, 'When will you make my joy complete, sire? When shall the wedding be?'

'Ah well, Count Agenor . . . ' began Cepheus haltingly.

He seemed to be in difficulties, so Perseus came to his aid. 'Andromeda is going to marry me, sir.'

Agenor peered down his nose at Perseus for a moment, then looked around the room with exaggerated astonishment. 'Did somebody speak?' he asked.

Andromeda crossed the room and took hold of Perseus's hand. 'Perseus of Argos says he is to marry me. It is his reward for saving me and killing the sea-monster when there was *not a man in Ammon who dared* even to speak out for me. I would ask you to stay for the wedding at sunrise, Agenor, but I don't believe *dogs* are allowed inside the Temple of Aphrodite.'

Nervously the king whispered something in the queen's ear.

Agenor could not ignore the second insult. He turned on his heel and swept towards the door, head thrown back and the breath whistling in his nostrils. In going, he declared theatrically, to everyone present, 'Married at sunrise, you say? We shall see about that. *We shall see!*'

He was no sooner gone from the room than he was forgotten: Agenor had that quality about him. The king might wring his hands and gnaw his lip, but Andromeda and Perseus could think only of their wedding.

The night gardens of Ammon were stripped of flowers to deck the Temple of Aphrodite. The statues in the streets were draped with scarves and streamers, so that each time the wind blew, it lent them a kind of dancing life. Andromeda, dressed in a white robe, laid her jewels of gold and lapis lazuli on the altar of the goddess, in token of her gratitude for such a husband. And Perseus, in his borrowed tunic and still cluttered with bags and sandals and shield and sword and helmet, clanked his way to the temple on foot rather than alarm people by flying there. He laid aside the weapons at the door of the temple, of course.

Small bells were being rung to welcome bride and groom, as the sun hatched out of the land and rose up over the peaceful city of Ammon. And if, off-shore, the embittered mermaids hissed and whispered among themselves, their spite could no longer reach the beautiful Princess Andromeda.

Only the spite of Agenor could do that.

As the ceremony began, there came a violent drumming of spear-ends against the marble floor, and into the temple, as brash and bullying as drunken schoolboys, came Agenor and twenty, thirty, fifty of his friends and followers.

'Stand aside, *boy*! A real man has come to fill your place. This is my bride and my wedding. You've kept my place warm for me, but now you can step aside. Agenor is here to arrive a lord and leave a prince.'

Perseus looked to the king. It was neither the time nor the place for brawling, and surely the king would send Agenor away with a single word of command? But the king said nothing, and the queen only wept.

Agenor snorted with contempt. 'What? Did you think the king would favour you before a *count*, you thick-necked peacock?'

Andromeda threw back her head in proud disdain. 'But *I* favour him, Agenor. I favour him before you. Who would prize a soldier who hid while the battle was on and claimed the booty when it was over?'

'What does *your* opinion signify, woman?' piped Agenor. 'We are talking kingdoms here, and thrones aren't thrown away on coarse-handed fishermen. Of *course* he could gut your sea-monster! Gutting fish is his trade!' His followers all laughed, loud and long. And suddenly the king had changed sides.

'It's true, Andromeda. Where he comes from they call him One-Shirt Perseus. How can you give yourself to a boy they call One-Shirt Perseus? How can I share my kingdom with a boy they call—'

The queen joined in, and though Andromeda put her fingers in her ears, she could still hear the soft, insinuating, pleading voice:

'Think of it, dear. One-Shirt Perseus. It would be a disgrace. We'll give Perseus here money—a lot of money. Then he can go back to catching his fish, and you can marry your childhood sweetheart—your dear Agenor.'

Andromeda cried out with revulsion, and clung to Perseus who whispered something into her ear, something not touching on Love.

Meanwhile, the spears had begun to strike the marble floor again. Agenor's followers began to chant over and over again, 'One-Shirt Perseus! One-Shirt Perseus!'

'Stand aside, boy, or we'll cut you down where you stand,' said Agenor. Perseus indicated that he had no sword, but Agenor's friends drew out their blades all the same. There were even archers there who laid arrows to their bowstrings and took aim on Perseus's unprotected body. The chanting went on: 'One-Shirt Perseus! One-Shirt Perseus!'

73

'You didn't stand aside as I told you, boy,' said Agenor, wagging his finger. 'Now I think it's time for a blood sacrifice on the altar of Aphrodite—to ensure a happy and fruitful marriage between Andromeda and I.'

'NO!' Andromeda screamed and covered her eyes. The archers drew back their bowstrings. The swordsmen were impatient to finish off the work the arrows began.

Impatient. Impatient they stood, and impatient they stand—their weapons up, their teeth bared, their cheeks folded like dogs' masks. They saw Perseus reach inside the wallet that lay by his feet. They heard him shout a word or two at Andromeda. They saw the hand draw out something green, repulsive and writhing. A nasty smell struck their nostrils, and curiosity plucked at their brains. But then their nostrils smelt nothing more, their brains struggled no more after understanding, and their eyes— their eyes which had focused on something so hideous that no eyes should ever have seen it—froze over. Their eyes froze over like winter ice sealing a hundred ponds, and they were stone, stone, stone dead.

The treacherous king and his silly queen sit, even now, like their own statues. The people of Ammon have long since shuffled them away out of sight, ashamed that any king of theirs should break his sworn word. And the Temple of Love is sealed up, like a tomb: not a tomb for the frail, loved corpses of the dead, but an everlasting prison for the stony remains of Agenor and his hard-hearted friends.

Perseus returned the head of Medusa to its wallet and hoped to lead Andromeda gently out of the temple before she could see what had happened to her mother, father, and one-time suitor. But she opened her eyes and stared around her. She reached out curious fingers to touch the stony arrowheads, the stony eyes, the stony bristles of the fur-trimmed robes.

People say that she was unnatural not to shed a tear, not to rage and run mad, not to shun the man who had turned her mother and father to stone. But after being chained to a rock for a day waiting for a sea-monster to lurch up out of the sea at your feet, who can say how you or I would behave? At any rate, Andromeda turned her back on her mother and father and one-time suitor (whose heart had always been stone anyway). She tied her fate to that of the man they called One-Shirt Perseus but who in truth was the son of Zeus.

10

The Reluctant Bride

There was another wedding planned for that selfsame day, another royal marriage, another marriage to which the guests came armed with swords.

No sooner had Perseus left on his quest for Medusa's head than King Polydectes made plans for his wedding. All well and good, you might say, since Perseus had gone in search of a wedding present. But Polydectes sent word spurning the little tribal princess named as his future bride. Now that Perseus had gone to certain death, the way was clear for the wedding Polydectes had always intended: to the boy's lovely mother, to Danaë.

Danaë woke to find the fisherman Dictys leaning over her.

'Get up, lady. Quickly. The king's men are coming along the waterfront. I fear the king means to have you, as he always said he would. Get dressed quickly. We must go—leave the country. Polydectes is never going to accept your "no" for an answer.' While Danaë dressed, Dictys grabbed up some flasks of water, some loaves of bread and a cheese.

'But I can't leave the country, Dictys. Or how will Perseus ever find us when he comes home?'

The words were in Dictys's mouth to say, 'Perseus won't be coming home. By now Perseus is a lump of stone standing in the gritty desert winds, wearing away to a memory.' But he could not break Danaë's heart. 'Then we shall go to the Temple of Athene, madam, and plead sanctuary. Polydectes won't dare send his troops into a temple: it would bring down the wrath of the gods on his head.'

Danaë was pleased by the idea. 'And then in a day or two Perseus will be back, and he'll shame the king into abandoning this madness.'

Dictys wanted to say, 'Perseus won't be home in a day, nor a week, nor a year, nor a lifetime, unless rocks can walk or dead men travel. And the king is too mad with desire to give over his wooing.' But what was the purpose in frightening Danaë? So Dictys said nothing, only dragged down a fishing net off the roof rafters and stepped quietly out of doors.

The troops of King Polydectes fell on the little hut as though it was the strongest of fortresses. They attacked with shouts and brandished swords, meaning to cut down the peaceful fisherman and carry away his friend in chains. To their astonishment, Dictys merely looked up from mending a large net spread on a bench before him, and did not run for shelter or dash to seize a weapon. Their running faltered, their sword-tips dropped.

Then he had them. For he rose up and flung the net. It fell lightly over their heads and entangled every latch of their armour, every thong of their sandals, every finger that tried to throw it off. While the troops lay cursing in the netting, Dictys called Danaë from the hut and ran with her towards the arches, spires, and pillars of the nearby city—to the temple of Athene and to sanctuary among the cold, stony-eyed statues inside it.

Within minutes the temple was surrounded by seven platoons of guard, all brandishing swords, all bellowing for Dictys and Danaë to surrender. The king himself came to stand on the temple steps and shriek his outrage:

'I shall have you, Danaë of Argos! I shall have you! How long do you suppose you can hold out against me without food? Without drink? Soon you'll come out of there begging me to marry you. And I shall take you—oh yes, I shall take you, *Princess* Danaë. But not for a wife. I shall have you for my handmaiden, my slave, my *ornament*. And do you know the first task you shall do for me? Fasten that fisherman's grinning head on a pole as a warning to anyone else who might be tempted to thwart me. Think on, Danaë. I, Polydectes, I, King of Seriphus, always have my way in everything. Come out now and beg my forgiveness. On your knees, beg my forgiveness!'

'Wait till Perseus comes! Wait till my son Perseus comes home!' cried Danaë's defiant voice from the shadows. 'He'll teach you the manners your mother should have taught you!'

'Perseus? One-Shirt Perseus? That *boy*? That braying donkey? He's dead and gone, lady, dead and gone.' And the words splashed through the temple of Athene like icy water, to break upon the altar in a thousand shivering echoes.

After their marriage at a wayside temple, Andromeda and Perseus did not hurry back to Seriphus. They walked and rode and sailed, and now and then Perseus laid aside his luggage and took Andromeda in his arms and flew with her, wearing his winged sandals. But they always had to settle to earth again by the shining shield, golden sickle-sword, the black wallet and battered helmet. Perseus could not bring himself to leave them strewn about on foreign soil like so much litter. As well as helping him complete his task, they made him feel special, fortunate, blessed, smiled on by the gods. 'Did I ever tell you how I came to be born?' he said to Andromeda.

'I think you did mention it,' she answered patiently. But she did not mind when he told her all over again. She found it very easy to believe that Perseus was the son of Zeus. But then she was in love with him, after all.

The days came and the days went, and the bread and cheese were eaten and the water was gone. Hunger and thirst entered the temple of Athene like stealthy spies in the pay of Polydectes, to drive Danaë and Dictys out into the open.

'Since you saved my life, you have done me kindnesses without number, Dictys,' said Princess Danaë after many hours of silence. 'Will you do me one last act of friendship?'

'Name it,' said the fisherman.

'I would rather die than be a slave to Polydectes. Please. Friend. Kill me with that knife of yours and spare me the shame of surrendering.'

Dictys, who had been sitting on the steps of the altar carving a piece of wood, dropped his knife in astonishment. 'What kind of talk's that? What about Perseus? What about your valiant son? Have you forgotten that he'll be here soon to—'

But Danaë interrupted him. 'If I have fooled myself, I'm sure I never fooled you. My reckless, silly Perseus is dead and turned to stone by Medusa. If death could come as quickly to me, I'd welcome it—especially from the hands of a good friend. Will you do this for me, Dictys? Will you kill me before Polydectes loses patience and bursts in here with his soldiers?'

Dictys picked up the knife and studied it for a long time. Then he said, 'I'm sorry, Danaë. I can't find it in me to do you that service. The truth is, I've been in love with you for some twenty years now, and it's not in my power to kill someone who's so much a part of me.'

Danaë might have wept or she might have laughed, but she only gave one long sigh. 'Oh, Dictys, I *wish* you had said so before now. The truth is, I've loved you myself for quite ten or fifteen years. How very pleasant life could have been.' Her voice trailed away as the early morning sounds of the siege army waking and stirring outside ended the silence of the night.

'My patience is gone, Danaë! My siege is over!' King Polydectes's silhouette seemed to fill the bright doorway of the shadowy temple. 'Lend me your spear, lieutenant; there's a smell of fish in here. I must harpoon that gaping guppy of a man before I lay hands on my new slave.' He came on into the temple, and at his back came a line of soldiers whirling swords so briskly that the air cried out in pain.

From the palisades of heaven, the goddess Athene uttered a scream of outrage—her blood-chilling war-cry heard on a thousand battlefields by the dying heroes of the Middle World. *'Enter my temple armed, would you, you infidel! Break my sanctuary, would you? Make war on the innocent and soil the white walls of my holiest places with blood?'* She drew back her hand, wielding the great spear of war which had not flown since the Siege of Troy. And she took aim on the heart of King Polydectes.

But another hand seized hold of the tail of the spear and wrenched it out of her hand. There stood Hera, queen of heaven. The jealousy burning in her eye cast strange, green shadows into the hollows of her lovely face and made her curiously grotesque. Athene protested: 'He's defiling my temple! He's breaking my sanctuary!'

'Then you may kill him tomorrow. Today he shall live.' Hera's voice was like the keel of a great ship grating on gravel.

'But why, madam? Why?'

A sneer rifted the features of Zeus's wife and narrowed her large brown eyes. She spoke in a voice heavy with sarcasm. 'Don't tell me that you are the last in heaven to know? That Princess Danaë won the love of my all-glorious husband and bore him a son? Why, the story is all over Olympus! I am the laughing stock of heaven! Listen? Can't you hear them sniggering at me behind their hands? So. This little mortal held Zeus in her arms, did she? Then I have a hankering to see her in the arms of a man less to her liking. Let Polydectes take her. Let him kill the fisherman in front of her very eyes. Then you may throw your spear if you want. But not before. I forbid it.'

So Athene laid aside her spear and turned her back on the little creatures of Earth far beneath her. Better not to see: better not to look.

Hera looked. The jealous queen of heaven threw herself down on her stomach, her chin on her hands, and watched the temple in distant Seriphus. The sneer on her face was transformed to a malicious grin. It may have taken her twenty years to find out about Zeus and Danaë and the tall tower and the shower of gold and the baby boy called Perseus. But now she knew, somebody must pay. 'Bastard,' she said under her breath. 'Revenge on you, bastard Perseus.'

Polydectes put his spear-point to Dictys's throat and grinned. 'You're a traitor, Dictys, a traitor. You've thwarted the will of your king. You've done your best to stop me taking what's rightfully mine. I'll sink your boat and I'll burn down your home and I'll bury you at a crossroads where a million feet will trample over your grave!'

Dictys might have replied (though not to plead for his life). But he had the strangest impression that someone was holding him by the scruff of the neck and whispering in his ear: *'Close your eyes, Dictys, and whatever happens don't open them again until I tell you!'*

Polydectes reached out a hand and grasped Danaë's arm. 'Get up, slave. Get up and kiss me. Then maybe things will go easier for you. Kiss me and tell me you love me.'

Danaë might have replied to the king (though not to say that she loved him). But she had the strangest impression that someone was holding her other arm and whispering in her ear, *'Close your eyes and whatever happens don't open them again until I tell you!'*

In as long as it takes to lift off a helmet, Perseus appeared on the steps of the altar of Athene. He was carrying no sword, no shield, and wearing no armour, but he carried, across one shoulder, a dark-woven satchel. Polydectes thought he must have crept out of the shadows. After the initial surprise, he laughed out loud. 'Well! If it isn't One-Shirt Perseus come back to defend his mother! Well? Where's my wedding present, you braggart? Where's the head of Medusa you promised me?'

'Here,' said Perseus.

'Here.' It was the last word Polydectes ever heard spoken. It was the last word ever to lodge in the tiny trembling hairs of his soldiers' ears and tumble into their understanding. 'Here.'

Then their ears were turned to stone. The temple's burning incense was scentless in their nostrils. The sight of the lovely Danaë and her golden-eyed son blurred and was shut out of their eyes. For they had seen the thing in Perseus's fist—the green, writhing head with its lolling tongue and tusky teeth and staring, staring, glaring, Gorgon's eyes.

After he had put away Medusa's head, Perseus had to break the stony fingers of the king to free his mother from the cold, cold grip. He told her and Dictys that they could open their eyes. But Danaë could only look around her for a moment before closing them again in horror.

'What have you done, boy?' said Dictys under his breath. 'What have you done to all these young men?'

Andromeda came threading her way between the statue-figures of the soldiers and comforted Danaë who was trembling violently. 'It's the looks on their faces!' explained the older woman in a ghastly whisper, and Andromeda said, 'I know. I know.'

11

The Games

'For the love of Nature! Take that head away from him before he does any more harm!' Hera, queen of heaven, jabbed her finger into Zeus's giant face. 'First Atlas! Then Cepheus and Cassiopeia and now Polydectes and half his royal army! Who next?'

Zeus too was furiously angry. He had been found out by his wife, and he hated to be found out.

Hera nagged on and on. 'What does he think he's doing? Two royal courts turned to stone! A hundred and fifty people standing about for ever and a day, in plain view, in the middle of towns! While Medusa had her den in the middle of a desert, she was only a legend. She didn't kill as many people in a year as Perseus has killed in a ten-days! He's toting her head about the Central Sea like a travelling magician!'

The laments of a hundred households rose up on the hot midday air and clamoured at the gates of heaven, mourning their stony sons and husbands dead at the hands of Perseus. Zeus had been embarrassed by his own son, and he hated above all things to be embarrassed.

Still his wife went on nagging, nagging, nagging him

incessantly, carping about the past, harping back to the subject of Danaë. 'You don't love me any more. It's not enough for you that I bring you ambrosia every morning and hippocrene every night. No! You must go changing yourself into bulls and swans and showers of gold and so forth to win these miserable little mortal women, peopling the world with children too godlike to sit still and too human to handle their magic. Is this all the king of the gods is good for—making mischief among his worshippers? Is it? Well, is it?'

Zeus sprang up suddenly from his throne and in the shockwaves that shook the blue sky round about a thousand cumulus clouds foundered like galleons. 'Silence, woman! Don't you understand anything?' Hera stared defiance at him until she realized, too late, that he would seize on her and shake her out of heaven's window by her thick brown hair. 'Don't you understand? Fate must take its course! Fate decides everything! We gods have to obey it just as surely as every pig or dog or scorpion down there on earth! What? Do you suppose *I* wrote the future in the brains of the oracles? Do you suppose *I* can change fate to please one jealous, ignorant goddess? At the corner of the world the Three Fates are spinning the future even now, and nothing I can say—I, the king of the gods!—can change what's destined to happen today or tomorrow or next year or a thousand years from now! It was *time* for Perseus to be born—that's all. It was *time* for Medusa to die! The strands of fate had simply come to an end for Cepheus and Cassiopeia and Polydectes! Who will it be today? Do you think *you* can decide? Do you think you'll be the undoing of my son Perseus, you silly, jealous woman, unless you are the chosen instrument of his fate?' By the time he had finished shaking his wife, a thousand nesting birds had risen up and fled Olympus. (But then that, too, was their fate.) 'Now tell Athene to go and get back that death's-head,' mumbled Zeus. 'Before Perseus can do any more damage. For pity's sake.'

But there was no need to wrest the tools of the gods away from Perseus. One glance at his mother's face after the killing of Polydectes, and he went straight away and laid the bulging black bag on top of the shield, on the altar of the goddess of war. To one side he laid the feathered sandals, on the other the golden sickle-sword and Helmet of Invisibility. The stone figures of Polydectes and his troops glared at him as he did so, and by the time he had threaded his way between them to the door and out into the sunlight he felt like a small boy who has played with fire and accidentally burned down a city. In his bare feet he could no longer fly. He passed a hand through his golden hair and knew he would never again be invisible till his soul drifted free of his body at death. His hip missed the weight of the sickle-sword and he knew he would kill no more sea-monsters.

For a moment he was so overwhelmed by the terrible thought of being ordinary that he dashed back into the temple—pushing through the petrified forest of frozen figures. But when he reached the altar, the sword and sandals were gone, the black bag and helmet had dissolved away, and he was in time only to see the shield reclaimed. It stood on its end, the head of a Gorgon painted in its centre—a painting so realistic that Perseus feared for a second that he would be turned to stone by it.

But it was, after all, only a painting, and his flesh remained flesh, and his blood went on running. It ran cold as the goddess herself, Athene, stepped out of the shadows and lifted the shield on her forearm. He would have continued to stare into her grey eyes, for there was something beautiful past bearing in them. But she lifted her shield until its topmost rim covered her face and only the feathered crest of a warrior's helmet showed above the shimmering metal. He was forced to close his eyes against the blinding brightness.

And when he opened them again, Athene had gone. She left her temple astride the winged horse Pegasus which she rode back to the slopes of Olympus. Those who glimpsed her flight through the sky said they had seen a new goddess in the heavens bearing a shield too fearful to describe, and mounted on a winged horse.

Nothing remained for Perseus. Nothing? The beauty and love of Andromeda? The kingdom of Seriphus? The treasures of Ammon? Perhaps, after all, he was a little better off than before he left on his quest, when his only possession was the nickname One-Shirt Perseus.

'You must choose your throne, Perseus,' said Dictys. 'You can't go about casting down kingdoms and leaving whole nations without a leader. The time for adventuring is over. Maybe you won't prove a better king than Polydectes or Cepheus, but you must at least try. Andromeda will help you. Well? Where will you make your kingdom?'

Perseus was horrified. He was not yet twenty years old. Except for a few overcrowded weeks, he had done nothing, been nowhere, met no one, learned nothing except about catching fish and killing monsters. It was no apprenticeship for wearing a crown.

At last he said to Dictys and Danaë, 'This is my wish. You two shall rule over Seriphus on my behalf—on the condition that you marry and move to the palace. It doesn't seem right for a king and queen to live in a fisherman's hut. Then, if you'll give me your fishing boat, Andromeda and I will sail to Argos, the land where I was born. I shall make my peace with my grandfather and tell him everything that's happened to us. I tell you, mother, I can't rest easy until I know just why he locked you in that tower or why he set us both on the sea to drown.'

'I don't bear him any grudge,' said Danaë taking Dictys's big, gnarled hands in her own. 'Everything has turned out for the best. I hope you don't harbour any thoughts of revenge.'

Perseus's face was a picture of innocence. 'Why would I bear a grudge, mother? Look what fate has brought *me*.' And he took hold of Andromeda's small, soft, white hand. 'But I don't want to be a king just yet, so let me make this one last journey. Please.'

There was no more hope of dissuading him than of dissuading a river from giving itself to the sea. He set sail before the week was out, with Andromeda to help him raise the sail and to cook the sardines he caught on a line dangled into the wake of the little boat.

'He is coming, Acrisius! He is coming!'

The tower in the courtyard came striding on tree-root legs and bent its shoulders and pushed a human face up against the window of King Acrisius's chamber. The cell bars took the shape of a toothy mouth which writhed and grinned as it whispered, *'Here comes your fate, as the oracle promised! Here comes your grandson to smash in your head!'*

Acrisius gave a scream and awoke standing by the window with his arms pushed out into the night to fend off his nightmare. One step more and he might have plunged to his death in the courtyard below.

He mopped his brow on the curtain and called feebly for his page-boy to help him back to bed. 'Tell the admiral to make ready the fastest ship in the fleet. I've got to . . . I've got to . . . leave Argos for a while. Never mind why. If my ministers of state ask you where I've gone, tell them I've . . . no, no. Better nobody knows. Don't tell anybody. But alert all the ports along the coast and tell them to keep a sharp look-out for any ship carrying a traitor called Perseus. An assassin called Perseus. You hear? A thousand pieces of gold to anyone who kills Perseus before he can set foot in Argos. He's coming. I'm sure of it. The same dream every night for a week. He's coming! And I won't stay here to be murdered in my own bed! Put the army on full alert!'

The sleepy page-boy only half-listened to the old king's ranting. The army of Argos had been on full alert for a year, and the ports kept watch night and day for the 'traitor' Perseus who had driven the king half mad merely by staying alive.

Rumours had travelled as far as Argos of superhuman deeds of courage performed by a youth with golden eyes, called Perseus—a boy loved by the gods, armed with magic and terrible in the destruction of his enemies. So eager was King Acrisius for news that he paid sea-captains whole chests of gold to hear stories of Perseus's exploits. Then when he heard their news, he had them thrown headfirst into the harbour for daring to say that Perseus was still alive.

When he fled Argos in terror, for two days he would not tell the captain of the ship which way to steer. He would not name a destination because he could not think himself where to go. All he wanted was to run to some corner of the Earth where Perseus would not find him. Let the boy seize his throne. Let the boy claim Argos for his own. Just as long as Acrisius did not have to die. Just as long as the oracle's prediction was wrong. Just as long as Acrisius could go on living, could go on living . . .

You might ask yourself what kind of a life it was to cling to—racked with nightmares and haunted by guilty fear. But to some men death is so infinitely terrifying that they spend their whole lives running away from it, as though it were a dog on their heels. They never have breath or time enough to enjoy living.

'Truly, sire, I cannot help but ask you again—*which way must I steer?*' said the ship's captain as patiently as he knew how. 'I must put in for ship's stores if nothing else.' The king looked at him—suspicious, terrified. 'If I might suggest it, your majesty, why not call in at Larissa in Thessaly? See the Games. Watch the athletes. They say there's no finer entertainment on all the shores of the Central Sea—javelin, discus, high jump, foot races, wrestling . . . '

'Yes, yes. All right,' snapped the king. 'But listen here! When we dock on Thessaly, no word of where you're from or who I am. Right? I am incognito. Anonymous. Nobody. I don't have a name. Understood?'

'Nobody,' repeated the captain obediently. And it seemed to him, looking at the little hunched creature muffled up in its cloak, darting fearful glances over his shoulder at every squeal of the gulls, that King Acrisius was right. He was nobody: nobody at all.

The Games at Larissa were a riot of fanfares and flags, processions and presentations. Young men in white tunics, wearing their muscles like snake-wrestlers, stood about the arena, dusty to the knees and bleached gold by the sun. The tiered seats of the amphitheatre banked up towards the bright blue sky in multi-coloured rings, and acrobats were performing sideshows for the queues of people still hopeful of buying seats.

Perseus and Andromeda, who had interrupted their voyage to Argos to watch the Games, stood near the entrance, drinking cooled wine, when the prince of

Thessaly himself stopped for refreshment. He eyed the Princess Andromeda from head to foot, and decided he was in the company of nobility.

'And whom have I the pleasure of addressing?' he enquired, flourishing the hem of his short cloak as he bowed.

'Perseus of Ammon, Seriphus, and Argos,' said Perseus, recollecting how he had once been called One-Shirt Perseus.

The prince was quite put off his stride. He broke off his elaborate bow and popped upright. 'Zeus! Really? What, the hero who cut off Medusa's head and killed Poseidon's sea-monster? Zeus! Really? Why wasn't I told?' Perseus blushed. A little crowd began to gather. 'But why aren't you competing? The whole idea of the Games is that the best from all nations should compete with each other! What's your sport? Running? Jumping? No! Javelin, of course!'

'Well actually I . . . ' Perseus, who had grown up working, without ever a moment for sport, racked his brains to think what sport he might have been good at if he had had the time. As Dictys's apprentice, it had been his task to throw out the marker buoy at the tail of each fishing net. He said, 'Discus. That's my sport. Throwing the discus.' And before he knew it, the prince of Thessaly had hurried him away to the competition tents to chalk his hands and choose a discus from the rack of shining pottery discuses. They looked for all the world like a row of kitchen plates.

Perseus was flattered. He was confident. He watched the other discus throwers whirling themselves round on one foot before hurling the discus off the palm of one hand and out across the arena, and he was certain he could throw his just as far. Had he not the strength of a god in his shoulderblades, the power of an immortal in his blood?

'Good luck,' said Andromeda and kissed him before hurrying away to find a seat among the crowd.

'And now! As a guest of the prince of Thessaly himself, a late entrant in the discus-throwing!' bellowed the crier, his words whirling up the great dished sides of the arena. 'Perseus of Ammon, Seriphus, and Argos!'

Perseus rubbed more chalk into his palms because they were sweating.

Acrisius, sitting behind the throwing circle, in the third tier of seats, felt sweat pour down his brow and back and hands. He shuddered violently, so that the girl newly sat down beside him asked if he was ill. 'No!' he said. 'No,' and peered through spread fingers towards the throwing circle and the young man standing there.

His hair was an upward rush of gold, like a volcanic eruption; his arms and legs were scarred and bruised from some recent fight; his eyes were golden slits closed down against the sunshine, like the coins posted into the mouth of a dead man . . . He was beautiful. He reminded Acrisius very much indeed of his daughter Danaë, the daughter he had loved so much.

Perseus spun himself round, shoulders down, arms outstretched. The crowd laughed at his appalling style—but they had to cheer the great long throw he made—a man's length further than any other discus on the field. The stadium fell silent as Perseus made ready for his second throw.

Watching, anonymous, just one man hidden among the thousands of other spectators, knowing he would not be recognized even if the boy saw him, Acrisius was struck by a sudden torrent of happy thoughts. This is my grandson. This is my heir. This perfect, beautiful young man bears my family name. This is what that helpless little baby grew into—a man who can throw a discus further than any man else; a man who can slay sea-monsters and cut off a Gorgon's head; a man famed throughout the Middle World; a man with the blood of gods flowing through his veins; a man already a legend; already a myth; a man, if ever there was one, to strike pride into his grandfather's heart.

He could not help it. He could not stop himself. Acrisius reached out his old, veined hand and plucked the robe alongside him: 'That's my grandson out there,' he whispered, and his eyes were full of tears, so that he did not clearly see what happened next.

Perseus mistimed his second throw. He let go of the discus a half-turn too soon, and instead of it flying out across the arena, across the measuring marks on the ground, it curled out of the back of the throwing circle and into the crowd.

There was silence, then a rising clamour of curiosity. 'Where did it fall? Was anybody hit? Is anybody hurt?'

Andromeda looked down at the old man lying in her lap. The discus had struck him in the head, but it was a clean blow and there was no blood. He looked simply as if he were asleep, and a single tear had crept out of one eye and down his cheek.

'He said he was your grandfather,' was all she could tell Perseus when he came climbing up the tiers of seats like a madman, tearing at his golden hair and rending at his clothing with chalky hands. Choking with remorse, he lifted up the old man's body and carried it out of the stadium, weeping aloud.

12

Blind Fate

'It was fate, not you, that killed Acrisius.' That's what they all said. 'It was foretold by the oracle. It was written in the stars before you were born. It was Acrisius's fate to die like that!'

But Perseus would not be comforted. He crouched over the body of his grandfather and wept for three days and nights. Then he placed it on the foredeck of his boat and continued on his journey to Argos—a coming home for the dead king and a coming home, too, for Perseus after nearly twenty years of exile.

News travelled ahead of the little boat, and by the time it put into port, the streets of Argos were lined by crowds. The statues were draped with scarves and the ground strewn with flowers. Flags beckoned him into port and a mob waited to greet him.

'Hail to Perseus, slayer of Medusa, slayer of Poseidon's sea-monster, and heir to the throne of Argos! Hail to him who killed the mad tyrant Acrisius and closed his mouth for ever! Hail to Perseus, king of Argos!'

Perseus leapt over the prow of the boat and scattered the mob with his fists and with curses. 'Silence! Hold your tongues! Death to the next man who calls me king of Argos! *There's* the king of Argos—on my foredeck! Give him the funeral of a king and drape the houses in black—not like this with flowers and ribbons! What kind of men are you to rejoice at an old man's death?'

'But he was a tyrant!' said the women of Argos open-mouthed. 'Just like Cepheus and Polydectes, and you turned them into stone! You're a hero, so you are. Everybody says so.' And they stared after him as he climbed the harbour path, and wondered.

For three days more Perseus locked himself away in the palace and sat at the window of Acrisius's bedchamber and stared out at the spot where the long-demolished tower had once stood: his birthplace. At last Andromeda came to him and said, 'Think what Dictys told you. It's time to be a king. Don't think badly of yourself. You're a hero, after all. Everybody says so.'

Then he covered his face with his hands and rocked to and fro on the window seat. 'No, Andromeda. Don't you see? If it was fate for me to kill Acrisius—and the gods know I didn't mean to!—then it was fate for me to kill the sea-monster, fate for you to love me, fate for Medusa to fall to my sword. I didn't *do* anything! It doesn't matter what I *do*, everything will turn out just the same. The fates are weaving the future now. They have been since the start of Time, and they'll go on until there is no more thread and Time itself comes to an end. I'm nothing. I'm no one. I'm a puppet dangling on that cord the fates are weaving. There's no such thing as a hero—only a man with a destiny. Not the great traveller Odysseus, not Theseus the Minotaur-Slayer, not even the giant Hercules. And not me, for all my bragging. Everything we ever did—good or bad—was no more than our role in an everlasting play. Tomorrow I'll go to see the oracle at Epidaurus and ask what lies in store for me.

Then I'll know everything that's planned. What else is there to know?'

The ministers of state had shyly gathered outside the door. They pleaded with him, stretching out before them the crown of Argos on a golden tray: 'Lord Perseus, be our king! Give us a king! We must have a king!' But he slammed the doors on them.

'Never! Never! I'll never wear that crown! There's blood on it. Blood!' The ministers went sadly away, thinking that Acrisius's grandson was proving just as mad as Acrisius had been.

They did not argue when he exchanged realms with King Megapenthes who ruled over an insignificant little kingdom along the coast from Argos—a land of shepherds and fishermen and vineyards and olive trees.

On his way to the temple at Epidaurus, Perseus was surprised not to pass any travellers coming away from the shrine. And when he arrived, the place seemed deserted. The door of the dank, dark sanctuary was strung with cobwebs, and no tributes lay on the steps, only a plate holding a little dirty rainwater.

He ducked inside and could see . . . nothing. The torches along the walls were burned down to extinguished stumps, and the dish of holy oil had long since burned away on the marble altar. In the thick, touchable darkness Perseus stumbled up against the tarnished rods of the tripod itself—the throne of the serpent oracle. Something hissed close by his ear. For a moment his blood ran cold as he recalled the snake-haired Medusa.

'What-t do you want-t? Who are you? Get-t out-t and leave me in peace-ce-ce.'

'Is that the oracle? Are you here? I can't see you.

'I'm Perseus of . . . I'm Perseus, son of Danaë, come to learn what the future holds for me.'

Something smooth-scaled touched his body and reared up; the pale diamond of a snake's head lunged towards his face. 'Don't-t you know? Haven't-t you heard? Why must you t-torment me like this-s-s? I'm *blind*. I'm us-seless-s to you, Perseus-s-s. I'm blind, blind, blind!' The snake interrupted itself. 'Pers-seus-s? I remember that-t name. You were to kill your grandfather, Acris-sius-s-s of Argos. Is-s he dead yet?'

Perseus said nothing, choking on tears.

'Nobody comes-s to tell me, you know? No one comes-s to tell me how the world runs-s. For centuries-s I told them the future. Now I'm not us-seful to them, and they leave me in ignorance. And no one pays-s tribute!'

'You're blind?' said Perseus slow-wittedly. 'How? Blind?'

'S-someone has cut the threads-s of fate. With shears, so they say. Sh-shears! Ah! They might as well have sh-sheared through the stalks of my very eyes-s. My inward s-sight is gone. I who looked into the future can s-see *nothing*. Nothing! As blind as the Cyclops after Odysseus-s drove in his sharpened stick. Blind! Now nothing is certain. Nothing is s-s-sure. The s-strands of fate are cut-t! The future is cut loose like a sh-ship that cuts anchor!'

Perseus felt about for the snake's weaving head and held its scaly hood between his two hands. 'The gods of Olympus bless you with everlasting darkness! You've told me the best news a man could ever hear!'

The serpent pulled away from him, unaccustomed to the touch of human hands. 'But now I sh-shall starve for want of tributes-s-s—s-starve for want of worshippers-s!'

'You shall never starve,' promised Perseus. 'I, King Perseus of Little Tiryns, swear it. I will shower you with tributes! I swear it! Don't you understand? At last every man and god is free of those spinners in the corner of the world. They had us trapped like flies in a spider's web: the Three Fates. But now we're free to be cowards or heroes or madmen or kings or fishermen or fathers or fools! Our futures are our own to make!' And he ran with the serpent in his arms, outside the cave where, for the first time in centuries it blinked its lidless eyes at the sights of the present world. It trembled in his arms, afraid of the light.

The oracle could no longer see into the future. For the future lay unwoven, invisible . . .

. . . like a child in the womb waiting to be born . . .

. . . like a bottomless well of untasted water . . .

. . . like a page of white paper still to be written upon by Perseus and the heroes who came after him.

Hercules

1

The Son of Zeus

The first time Zeus created Humankind, he used gold. Of course he did. Zeus had every precious substance at his fingertips, and an eye for beauty. Unfortunately the Race of Gold had an eye for beauty, too, for no sooner were they moulded and cast and buffed up to a shine than they began to prance and preen, and pride themselves on their looks.

'How beautiful we are! How fine! How precious! Who will treasure us? Who will admire us? Who will worship us and do our bidding?'

Zeus melted them down and ground their golden bones into dust which he sprinkled into the rivers.

The second time, he used silver. It had a ghostly loveliness and was agreeably soft within his clever hands.

The Race of Silver was elegant and effete. They did not prance about or flaunt their sinuous silvery beauty. In fact they scarcely moved at all. When they were not thinking beautiful thoughts, they were gazing at spiders' webs sprinkled with dew or stroking the silky strands of each other's hair or watching their breath cloud their own shining kneecaps. When they lay down and slept, they rarely woke up again.

Zeus piled hills on their sleeping forms and turned instead to bronze. The Race of Bronze was bursting with energy and needed little sleep. It was tireless and hard-working and brutally strong. It tore down spiders' webs in gathering wood for its forges, and on these forges it made spades and mattocks and hoes, armour and knives and spears. Once the Race of Bronze discovered war, they were happy indeed. The fields lay fallow and the beds unslept in . . . for the Men of Bronze were busily slaughtering one another with mace and arrow and sword.

Zeus had no need to destroy them. They killed each other, leaving their brazen bones scattered about among the ruins of their fallen forts.

There was nothing left but iron. Iron and earth and clay. Rather than dirty his hands, Zeus gave the work over to Prometheus the Titan. Once, before their conquest by the Olympians, the Titans had ruled Heaven and Earth. Now Zeus could snap his fingers and the few surviving Titans were obliged to do his dirty work.

But it was a good choice. Prometheus was a master craftsman. Despite being given such poor quality materials, his big hands twisted the iron into a delicate filigree of bone, and clad it in coarse clay with a topknot of grass. He lavished the tenderest care on his little manikins and grew fond of them, for all their imperfections.

When they asked *Who? When? Where?* and *What?* Prometheus taught them the Sciences. When they gazed up at him, in their innocence, and asked *Why?* he taught them the Arts—Music, Painting, Poetry, and Dance. When they shivered in their furless, goosy skin, he even climbed to the mountaintops and plucked a glimmer of Fire from the wheel of the Sun Chariot to warm Mankind.

Zeus was enraged. 'Steal fire from the gods? Give fire into the hands of those . . . those . . . *termites*? I'll make you pay, Titan! I'll make you wish you were never born. I'll make you wish you had become extinct like the rest of your kind!' And he took Prometheus and chained him, spread-eagled, against the Caucasus Mountains, a prisoner for all time. Eagles tore at his unprotected stomach, from dawn to dusk, feeding on his liver, rending at his liver, shredding it with their beaks. But because Prometheus was immortal and because the liver can heal and renew itself, there was no end to his Titanic pain. There was no end to Zeus's revenge. There was no end to the guilty knowledge in every Human heart: *'We* did that to Prometheus. He stole fire for *us*. He is suffering for *us*.'

Why do I tell you this? I don't know. It all happened thousands of years before Hercules was born.

And yet the picture would not be complete without that background skyline, without those distant crags specked red by Prometheus's torment. It tells you something about the gods. It tells you something about strength and weakness, about tyranny and freedom.

'Strangle him. Bite on him. *Crush him in your coils!*' raged the queen of the gods, thrusting her face so low that her cheeks flushed with blood.

The two serpents coiled around the base of her throne were as thick as jungle creepers and sleeved in overlapping scales as large and green as leaves. They blinked their hooded eyes, and their forked tongues flickered lovingly around her cheeks and ears. 'We hear, O Hera. Yes-s-s, Hercules-s-s sh-shall die.'

'Another woman's child,' she seethed.

'We hear, O Hera.'

'Fathered by my husband!'

'He dies-s-s, O Queen.'

' . . . made me the laughing stock of all heaven!'

'S-s-surely not, O Queen.'

'Imagine! The king of heaven preferring a common mortal woman to me, his sloe-eyed queen!'

'S-s-sloe-eyed, but not slow to see,' whispered the grovelling serpents in her ear. 'We go, O Queen, to s-s-strangle the puny child in his cradle, to s-s-smother him as he s-s-sleeps-s-s.' And they slithered across the marble floor of heaven like two streams of fetid green water, trickling over the brink of the clouds.

The baby's cradle stood in the shade of the eaves, and his hands reached for the lazy flies that circled overhead. His mother Alcmene was indoors sleeping through the heat of the day. So too was the king she had married after Hercules was born. Not a grand king, nor one who lived in a grand palace, but one who had come to love his little stepson. His gardens were greenly watered, and the air was filled with the scent of azaleas, and with silence.

So at the sound of a scurrying rattle, the baby smiled and looked around. Two heaving heaps of green, quivering and shivering, fumed like compost heaps on either side of the cradle. Out of the thorny heaps, horny heads rose up, wavering; gaping wide red mouths with flickering tongues and bared, pronging fangs. Venom dripped on the bedclothes and scorched large, sizzling holes.

'*Strangle him. Bite on him. Crush him in your coils,*' murmured the leaves on the trees. The baby boy laughed out loud at the ducking dance of the serpents' swaying heads. He reached out and took each by its thick green throat.

Their hinged jaws gaped. Their tails slumped, coil upon coil, into the crib on top of the baby's legs. Their thrashing rocked the wooden bed so that its feet thumped on the wooden verandah. The noise woke Queen Alcmene in her room overhead, and looking out of her window, she clutched at her hair: 'My child! My Hercules! Save my Hercules! O Zeus in heaven, our baby!'

The young child looked up at her and smiled at the sight of his mother's face. And he held up the snakes— one in each hand—as if to say, 'Look what I've got!' He jabbed his nose into their red mouths, saying, 'Aboo! Aboo!' Venom trickled down their scaly trunks.

First he knotted their necks. Then he knotted their tails. He plucked off their scales like petals off a daisy, and he bit into their soft, sheeny bellies to see what was inside.

'*Dead! Dead! My darlings!*' murmured the wind in the hollow trees of the garden.

At last Hercules dropped the serpents out of the crib and watched rather sadly as their lifeless coils slumped one by one out on to the floor. Then his mother came running along the verandah outstretched like a bird, her clothes billowing. He turned on her a pair of doleful eyes, then looked over the side of his cot at one of the snakes and said, with a trembling chin, 'Broke it.'

For all Hercules was not his own son, King Amphitryon took a burning pride in the boy as he grew. No expense or trouble was too great when it came to his education. One tutor was not enough: the king's stepson must have three—one to teach him wisdom, one to teach him sport, and one to teach him music. Eminent men they were, all three. But neither Rhadamanthus (with his wise sayings) nor Linus (with his lutes) could fire Hercules with a desire to learn. Only his sports-master, Chiron, could do that. Perhaps the fact that Chiron was a centaur—half man and half horse—made the difference. From discus-throwing to steeplechasing, there was no sport at which Chiron did not excel, and Hercules longed to be like him. Because Chiron told him to, he found it no hardship to get up early, go to bed early, and run and exercise for long hours every day.

One day the centaur said, 'Never touch strong drink, lad.'

'When do I ever get offered strong drink,' said the eleven-year-old Hercules laughing.

But Chiron stamped his hind hooves and said with uncharacteristic fierceness, 'Promise me!' Hercules promised without a second thought.

Not that Hercules was slow at his other subjects. In fact he played a lute rather well, though his fingers had a tendency to snap the strings. And he soon knew every one of Rhadamanthus's wise and pompous sayings, and would teeter and stoop along the corridors wagging his finger and, in a piping voice, doing his Rhadamanthus impersonation: 'The heart is bigger than the fist.' 'A bad man may be punished by the gods but only a good one is envied by them.' 'Folly is the fool's choice.' 'Hardship is the hero's pride.' Whether he understood them, that was a different matter. He learned the words . . . and he did do a splendid impression of Rhadamanthus. It was a pity there were so few people to appreciate it. When his mother saw it, she only told him not to be disrespectful.

In those days, Thebes was a small place, keeping itself to itself. It was uncommon to see strangers in the area unless they were passing by on the road. So Hercules looked once and looked again when he saw two women in a tree one day.

He had been stalking a deer through the woods, and his eyes ached from searching out its blotched hide among the dapple of the trees. He lost sight of it for a moment, and when he once more discerned a moving shape among the blobby sunlight, it was not the deer at all but a woman dressed in austere grey. She went and stood in the hollow of a tree—as if it were a doorway—and Hercules's eye was drawn up the trunk to where another blousy-looking woman in dark red and black slouched along a branch, like a kill draped there by a lion. 'Greetings, Hercules,' said the second woman in a liquid, mellifluous voice. 'Come nearer. There's so much I could give you . . .'

Hercules was rather embarrassed: the other woman, upright in the alcove of the tree, made him feel uncomfortable, watching him with her uneven, grey eyes. Even the birds were not singing: they had been thrown off-key by a skirl of unearthly music blowing through the wood. 'Yes, come nearer, Hercules. Show us what manner of man you are.'

Man! Ha! He was only thirteen! So to overcome his awkwardness and a feeling that someone was about to make a terrible mistake, he moved towards the tree doing his funny 'Rhadamanthus' walk, tottering and hinnying and wagging one finger in the air.

As he reached a spot beneath the branches, the woman in red rolled startlingly off her perch and dropped down behind him. Her feet made hardly a sound. Her arm circled his shoulders and her mouth pressed against his ear: 'I know what *you'll* choose.'

In some panic, Hercules looked to the other woman but she had folded her arms across her chest and remained inside the hollow tree. Her face was quite blank: she simply said, 'Well? Which *do* you choose? Hardship or happiness? Danger or daydreams? To struggle and to suffer, or to sleep?'

Hercules giggled maniacally. 'I think you've got the wrong . . .'

'You are Hercules the Strong, aren't you? Son of Alcmene?' snapped the grey woman.

The other, in red and black, ran her fingers over the muscles of Hercules's arm. 'Oooh, yes. He's strong all right.'

'And slow-witted seemingly. Well? Choose, boy. You're privileged, you know. Most don't get the choice. Hardship or ease? We haven't got all day: other people have fates to be decided.'

Afterwards, people asked him, 'What possessed you? What came over you? Who in their right mind . . . ?' But at the time it wasn't like that. Hercules simply felt awkward, and the words they were using brought to mind all Rhadamanthus's pompous, ponderous sayings. So he put on his Rhadamanthus stoop, and did his comical Rhadamanthus walk, and recited two or three epigrams in the scholar's thin, piping voice. Anything to break the tension.

' "Hardship is the hero's pride." "Fame was never found in bed." ' (He wagged his finger: it was a very good impersonation.) ' "Failure is easy, success is hard!" '

The grey woman's eyes, at first dismayed by the faces he was pulling, suddenly flashed. 'True! That's perfectly true!'

The red woman's hand slipped off his stooping shoulders. 'You mean you choose hardship and danger? *Nobody* does that. Nobody *ever* does that. Everybody chooses an easy life!'

' "Danger is the pathway from cowardice to Fame!" ' hinnied Hercules, too busy racking his brains for more sayings to pay much attention. ' "Folly is the fool's choice!" '

'Pompous little brat,' said the woman in red, and turning to the other she said, 'So you've won one at last, Virtue. Good riddance, I say.'

The woman in grey seemed equally surprised. Her

108

sharp, precise voice bobbed with delight. 'How very heartening. Still, you can't say I wasn't due for a win. Nobody has chosen a life of hardship and suffering for two hundred years now. Come along, Vice. Fasten your fastenings—and do at least braid your hair: you look a real slummock. Don't dawdle now.'

Together they strode away through the trees, Virtue and Vice. Hercules called after them: 'Hey! Where are you going? Anyway—who are you?'

The women linked arms and looked back at him quizzically. 'Don't worry,' said the woman in grey cheerfully. 'Your wish is granted. You shall live a life of struggle and suffering. Fame, danger, pain, work—all of those. I'll see to it. Extraordinary . . . ' (She turned back to her companion.) 'I really expected this one to choose you, Vice.'

And Hercules was left standing on one foot, his finger still pointing foolishly at the sky, his face gradually losing any likeness to old Rhadamanthus. Even the strange, haunting music faded away, and the birds rediscovered their voices. Hercules tried to remember the tune . . .

Inside the house, Linus, the music teacher, was crouched over his lute. A vague, short-sighted young man, he had difficulty remembering what time of day it was. When Hercules arrived for a lesson, Linus always supposed it must be time to give one. So when Hercules ran into the room humming loudly, and sat down at once, and took a lute on his lap, and picked at it, Linus stood up.

'Good morning, Hercules.'

'Shsshsh!'

'Don't shsshsh me, boy!'

'Shsshsh! I'm trying to remember a tune.' (He tried

to pick out the mysterious music on his lute, but could not find the right key.)

'It might help if you held the lute properly,' said Linus.

'Be quiet, can't you? I'm forgetting it! Mmmm . . . hmmmm . . . hmmmm . . . '

'*Wrist*, boy. How often do I have to tell you—keep that wrist arched.'

'Oh please! Quiet! Mmmmm . . . hmmmmm . . . hmmmm . . . ' But the haunting tune was dribbling out of his head like sand out of a fist.

'That fourth string is flat. Haven't I taught you yet? You can't ever play a lute till you've tuned it. Let me have it.' And Linus tried to take the lute out of Hercules's lap.

'Give it here!' protested Hercules. But already the tune had soaked away like spilled water and was lost everlastingly.

So unnerved was Hercules by his meeting with the two women, so lost was the piece of music, that Hercules's frayed temper snapped. Linus had hold of the body of the lute; Hercules had hold of the neck. With a turn of the wrist he wrenched the instrument away from his teacher and swung it like a club. His eyes were shut with fury.

He heard the lute crush like an egg-shell. He felt the broken strings coil back around his wrists and hands. When he opened his eyes, he thought that Linus must have run from the room in fright: he waited for the man's pale, refined face to reappear at the open door. Then he saw, at the other end of the slippery marble floor a heap of familiar clothes.

Hercules retreated to the other end of the room and sat down in a corner. Strangely enough, he could remember the ragged tune perfectly now. He was still humming it when the king came into the room. 'What are you doing there, boy? Aren't you supposed to be with Chiron doing sports? Where's Linus? I need a lutenist tomorrow at dinner. There are visitors. Important visitors . . . Hercules? Boy? Answer me.'

Hercules looked up and showed the stump of his lute still festooned with curling, broken cat-gut. 'Why am I so strong, father? Why? Other boys aren't so . . . I killed him, father. I didn't mean to. But I killed Linus.'

2

Broken Promises

They told Hercules that Linus was not dead at all—only stunned—and that when he came round, he was so angry that he had taken ship for Syria.

Hercules would have liked to believe them.

They told him that no boy of thirteen could kill a man with one blow of a lute. He wanted to believe them. He wanted so much to believe them that, by the following night, he almost did.

Only when the important visitors arrived (King Eurytus of Oechalia and his daughter, Iole), and the king asked Hercules to play his lute, did the boy hold the instrument on his knees and weep.

Princess Iole came and stood in front of him. 'What's the matter?' she asked in a whisper, purposely placing herself between Hercules and the adults so that they would not see him crying.

'Nothing . . . someone died. Someone I knew.'

'I'm very sorry. I hope they had a good life first.'

Hercules looked up. Princess Iole was about twelve, with sand-coloured hair scorched gold on the crown by

112

being out in the sun. 'Which do you think is best? To live a life of comfort and wealth or struggle and heroism?' he said.

'Who for? Best for whom?' said Iole, screwing up her eyes. 'Comfort and wealth are best if you've got children or elderly relations,' (and she waved a hand in the direction of her father), 'but personally I'd prefer a little adventure, even if it meant sleeping in cactus bushes and eating worms.' Hercules's jaw dropped.

Hurriedly he wiped his face with his sleeve. 'Whatever must you think of me?'

She did not even pause for reflection. 'I think you have lovely hands, but you're an odd shape. Look at you—you're as wide from side to side as you are from head to foot: you're square.'

Hercules stood up and looked down at himself. 'You mean I'm fat?'

'No. Just square. And you don't look a bit like your father or your sister.'

'That's because he's not my father. He's my stepfather. And Megara is my stepsister.'

'Is she more important than you? Is she older?'

'She'll be queen of Thebes one day. I won't because I'm not the king's true son.'

'Was your real father square, too? Who was he?'

'I don't know. I don't know who he was.' Her questions swooped at him until he felt like a berry tree stripped bare by the birds. But Hercules was not offended. Nobody had ever shown such an interest in him before.

Iole was not square. She was long and rounded, rather like a lute. He wanted to pick her up and find out what music came out of her. She did not take after her father, either. King Eurytus was long and thin with nobbles here and there, like bamboo. He giggled a great deal: the more wine he drank, the more he giggled. Seeing Iole and

Hercules still talking an hour later, he giggled uncontrollably. 'Looks like an alliance is forming between Thebes and Oechalia,' he snorted, pointing rudely. 'Why not? How about it, Amphitryon? Your stepson and my daughter. Let's make a royal match of it.'

'Aren't they a little young for such things,' said Amphitryon quietly, seeing Hercules blush.

'When they're older, then! My word on it! If he wants her, he shall have her!'

Later that night, Hercules still sat plucking his lute in the deserted banqueting room. His mother, passing the doorway, saw him and came closer. 'I hope you've put that other matter right out of your head,' she said, stroking his hair.

Hercules had. His mind was full of Iole. He said, 'Can I marry her? I want to marry her. She's lovely.'

It was his mother's turn to laugh. 'Gracious! Such thoughts at your age! Your first love, eh? That's nice, dear . . . But King Eurytus had had rather a lot to drink. I doubt if he'll remember what he said, tomorrow.' And away she went, content because Hercules was not moping about the death of his music teacher. She did not hear Hercules say softly, 'But *I* will. *I'll* remember.'

As Hercules grew, there was no concealing his phenomenal strength. There was no denying the likeness to his father, the king of heaven, whose arms, since the start of time, could strangle every snaking river, buckle the interfolded hills, and shoulder the sands of time into dunes of history. Not that Hercules knew who his father was. In fact he found it rather embarrassing that clothes stretched round his square frame looked like washing draped on a mountainside to dry, and that the lute strings broke beneath his fingers like thread. He said goodbye to old

Rhadamanthus, and Chiron his sports-master left Thebes as well. While he grew, he nursed the secret certainty that he would one day marry Iole. Then they would leave Thebes and travel the world in search of adventure, sleeping in cactus bushes and (if need be) eating worms. After all, his present life promised no hardship or suffering.

As Hercules grew, Thebes seemed to shrink. Once, its stone city walls had been his furthest horizon; now he could judge it for the small, vulnerable muddle of houses it was, with its belt of low stonewalling and few prosperous farms. When the young men of neighbouring Menia had been drinking, they galloped across the plain, across the carefully tended fields, and threw lighted brands over the wall. An alarm of clanking fire buckets woke the town and set the women screaming.

What began as drunken vandalism grew into a sport. The young men of Menia would dare one another to greater and greater mischief. Young Theban women were kidnapped. Theban wagons outside the city were stoned and looted. Dirty slogans were daubed on the city wall. The crops in the fields were put to the torch. Never a night went by without some wanton act of destruction, some flurry within the town. The citizens protested daily to the king.

Amphitryon protested to the king of Menia, but got the impression that he was rather proud of his wild young men. The next night nobody said so, but everyone knew, that the boys of Menia were coming in force for a pitched battle. Thebes closed its gates.

When they came, they were carrying shields and long staves which they banged against the shields with a taunting rhythm. They speared the ground with firebrands, and the grassy area in front of the gates was as light as day. Then they brought out a battering ram. The boys of Menia meant to take the town.

A new kind of panic gripped the city. Its army was small. It was too late to send for help. Hercules, watching from the high windows of the royal house, could see the commotion in the streets and hear the cries of panic.

Walking slowly down to the gate-yard, he watched the bending and splintering of the big wooden doors. Soon they would buckle inwards in front of the Menian battering ram. Sorry to see damage to a perfectly fine pair of gates, he opened the small, pedestrian side-door to the left of the barred gates. Looking over his shoulder at the mustered army of Thebes, he said, 'Well? Are you coming?'

Have you ever stood up to your knees in a cold sea, wishing you had the courage to go deeper, and had some stalwart soul wade past you, thigh-, waist-, chest-, neck-deep with not so much as a gasp at the cold? That was the kind of envious admiration the men of Thebes felt as seventeen-year-old Hercules waded in among the Menian rabble, one-deep, five-deep, fifteen-deep and was quite lost from sight. Only his fists now and then showed above the mob. Pricked with shame, Amphitryon's few soldiers went after him.

Have you ever watched an ebb tide strand the sea on a beach and shred the water into larger and larger holes? That was how the attacking mob from Menia fell to pieces at the hands of Theban Hercules. With one man lifted up and flung over-arm, he flattened a row of ten more. With one shield snatched from the hands of a lout, he sliced through a row of shields. When he heard the ominous scrape of swords being drawn from their scabbards, and saw an archer taking aim from the platform of a chariot, he put his shoulder to the chariot and left the archer sprawled beneath it like a turtle under its shell, the horse scattering the swordsmen.

They fell back. They called on the gods for protection

from 'this bull', 'this tyrant', 'this barbarian!' They ran, full of such terror that they outran the Theban men and left them to hurl stones and laugh abuse after them. Hercules simply turned away and walked back into the city, deep in thought. It surprised him when his stepfather, sweating and panting and sword drawn, fell on his neck and kissed him. 'You were magnificent, son! Magnificent! You left nothing for us to do! You swatted them like a swarm of flies!'

'They were so puny,' said Hercules with an embarrassed shrug.

'You struck terror into them, that's why!' Amphitryon was dancing round him, almost drunk with delight and pride. 'There's only one reward befitting a show of manhood like that. There's only one way I can show you how *grateful* I am . . . She's yours. Megara is yours. I give her to you—and with her the right to wear the crown of Thebes when I'm gone!' He looked for Hercules's face to light up, and saw it drop instead.

'But what about Iole?'

'Where? What's Iole?'

'Princess Iole. Of Oechalia. I can't marry them both!'

Amphitryon saw his daughter coming. He was anxious to tell her the good news. 'Zeus! I had no idea you remembered that plain little thing. Don't trouble yourself. She's already married, just this last month. Eurytus married her to some potentate. No, your way is open to take Megara—and may you live out your days in contentment and prosperity here in Thebes!'

Megara caught these last words of her father's and looked her stepbrother up and down with startled alarm. 'Me? Marry Hercules? But he's . . . he's . . . ' and her eyes rifled him up and down in search of a suitable adjective.

'Square,' said Hercules feelingly, and offered his stepsister his arm.

117

As any sister would, she slapped it.

They were not unhappy. They liked each other . . . as brother and sister can. Their family grew—a new baby every year, another room filled with crying in the royal house—and Thebes shrank still further in Hercules's eyes. Sometimes it felt like a chain round his chest that stopped him taking a deep breath.

Still, Megara was a decent girl even if she was not Iole. And his children were a wonder to Hercules. He would play with them for hours, and watch their fists rend feebly at their toys, and love them for their fragile helplessness. Whenever he walked about the grounds, festooned in clinging babies and toddlers, he knew that the two peculiar women in the forest were utter liars: this was not a life of hardship and suffering.

It was simply a matter of making time one day to kill King Eurytus for breaking his promise.

One day King Amphitryon was bitten by a snake. Not a large snake or a deadly one. He drank some wine to dull the pain, and by dinner time showed no ill effects but for a little tetchiness. At dinner, he raised a toast: 'To Thebes—may we all live and die here!' He noticed, with some vexation, that Hercules did not drink the toast.

'You know I don't drink, father,' said Hercules. 'I promised Chiron I would never . . . '

'Not drink a toast to Thebes? Just because you weren't born here!'

Hercules said, 'It's not that at all. I'll drink it in water if you like. Chiron told me . . . '

'Drink a toast in water? You may as well not drink it at all. It's an insult, an affront.'

118

'Just a little wine,' whispered his mother to Hercules, 'for the sake of good manners.'

'Manners before principles?' Hercules whispered back.

'Don't be pompous,' whispered Megara on the other side of him. 'Look how you've upset father.'

'Why father won't drink wine?' lisped the oldest child loudly.

'Because he's obstinate,' said the queen.

'Because he hates Thebes,' said Amphitryon angrily chafing his bitten leg.

'Because some old nag told him not to,' said Megara waspishly.

Hercules's temper snapped. 'Very well, I'll drink! I'll drink if you insist! To Thebes! May I live and die here in soggy prosperity!' and he emptied his cup. 'What if I did give my word to Chiron? Who keeps promises? Even kings don't keep promises. Take King Eurytus . . . ' He reached across and drank Amphitryon's wine as well. 'Though why a man should want to live and die in one place I don't know. How is the world better off for that? And why a man should marry his own sister for the sake of it . . . ' He spilled some of Megara's wine in snatching it out of her hand to drink. It made a large red stain over her heart.

The wine tasted good. It warmed him. He thought that if he drank enough, it might dissolve the hard, painful knot of anger in his stomach. But instead of dissolving, the anger swelled.

The little snake that had bitten the king still lay curled in a corner. But for the noise that followed, you might have heard it whisper, *'How long you made me wait, Hercules, for your destruction. But now I have you. Now!'*

Hera, queen of the gods, did not wait to see the result of her plotting but slithered out through a crevice into darkening night.

3

Hera's Doom

Hercules drank every cup of wine laid out along the table and demanded more from the servants. The walls began to heave and melt, the floor to lurch under his feet so that he fell against the table. The table dared to bruise him, so he picked it up and tore off its legs one by one. The doors of the room seemed to gape foolishly, like dumb mouths. He hurled chairs and stools into the stupid holes, and gagged the laughing windows with rugs torn up from the floor. It felt as though he was running through a long tunnel filled with cobwebs that caught round his head and made his eyes dimmer and dimmer, his ears deafer and deafer, his mouth full of sticky threads: he had to drink more wine to be rid of the taste.

Unable to focus, he was maddened by shrill little voices all around him: like whining mosquitos, they maddened him. He struck out to be rid of them, and kicked out at the soft, clinging demons that seemed to be dragging at his knees, trying to trip him up.

Who was that sitting in Amphitryon's chair, shrieking 'Stop! Stop! Stop!'? Eurytus? When had Eurytus been asked to the dinner?

'You know what I'm going to do to you, you shyster?' said Hercules, though his mouth seemed to be full of stones. 'I'm going to push your promises down your lying throat. Die, you lying scum!' And he trampled over unseen barricades of soft, hard, and unidentifiable objects, his feet and fists crushing everything that came between him and his revenge.

Perfidious Eurytus—he ducked away at the last moment, and let Hercules crash headfirst into the wall. A bloody blackness trickled down out of his hairline and swamped his brain in darkness. Hercules fell in a heap amidst the rubble of his own making.

When he came to, he was still lying there, and Amphitryon—it wasn't Eurytus at all—was still in his seat, though his head was bowed down as far as his knees. Dead on the floor lay two servants, Queen Alcmene, Megara, and, huddled round her like little broken boats smashed by a storm, all his six small children.

At the sound of Hercules's cry, Amphitryon started up in his chair and snatched up a copper ladle to defend himself. But when he saw Hercules's face, he laid it down again.

'What happened? Who did this?' said Hercules, on his hands and knees.

'Who did it? *Who did it?* You did it, Hercules. You kicked and pounded everything and everyone here into the Realm of Shadows. You trampled on your daughters, you pulled up your sons like weeds and threw them away. You murdered my wife and you murdered the wife I gave you out of my own flesh and blood. When the servants tried to restrain you, you broke their necks. Only the gods reaching out of heaven put a stop to your massacre. They hurled you against that wall—and I wish they had thrown you all the way to the Underworld.

121

You're not human, you. You've got more strength than a man and less pity than a beast . . . And I'm as bad as you. Because I made you drink.'

'Chiron told me . . . '

'I know what Chiron told you. But something drove me to make you break your word to him. Now I'm punished for it. Now I must keep the promise I made to your mother the day I married her. I swore always to protect you, life and limb. Protect you? Ha! What executioner could lay hands on you anyway? Protect *you*!'

Hercules stared at his two hands as though they were trusted friends who had unaccountably betrayed him. 'I *want* to die. I want it. Send an executioner now! My guilt is crushing me like rocks and boulders! If you won't punish me, I call on the gods to condemn me!'

A beam of light, as thickly bright as a column of solid brass, broke through the deep windows of the room. It bleached the floor where it touched, and a solar wind howled around the room.

From the slopes of Olympus, the king of the gods stared at the royal house of Thebes until, like a snail beneath a burning glass, it started to writhe. The lesser gods and goddesses stood silent, at a distance, half-turned away out of embarrassment. Fancy the king of the gods showing such distress over the fate of a mere mortal man. Justice surely demanded that Hercules should die. How long would Zeus hesitate before he struck the young murderer down?

A convulsive shiver shook his huge, blue-robed frame, then Zeus sat bolt upright on his throne. 'Can he help it if he has my strength in his arms? Or my fire in his core? It's a burden too great for any poor boy! Only a god could bear it . . . The drink was responsible, not Hercules!

Amphitryon was responsible, for making him drink! Hercules shan't die! My son shan't die!'

The gods murmured among themselves and shot nervous glances at Hera, knowing that the queen of the gods loathed and detested Hercules. But to their surprise, Hera showed no irritation when Hercules was spared. Toying affectionately with the faithful little snake in her lap she listened then coughed politely. 'You are right, of course, my love. What purpose will it serve to strike Hercules dead? Or to lock him away in prison? Bind him in service instead, to . . . to whom? I know! Bind him in slavery to his cousin, the king of Argos. Slavery will save Hercules from the sin of pride, and the world will see that he has been punished for killing those few paltry people.'

Zeus cast on his wife a look of grateful love such as she had not seen for many earthly generations. She blushed, and the little snake squirmed away among her clothing. 'That's a fine idea, Hera! That *shall* be Hercules's sentence! See where I carve it in fire on the walls of Thebes: *Hercules is bound in slavery to the king of Argos, that the gods may be praised. Let him serve and obey!*'

And the lesser gods and goddesses saw Hera roll her head on her beautiful, snake-like neck and smile as the cobra smiles. 'Die long and die hard, Hercules,' she whispered, 'at the hands of that *little* man. Let it never be written that the finger of Zeus struck you a glorious blow, nor that you died young and painlessly. *Suffer*, bastard. *Suffer*, you child of damned Alcmene! SUFFER!'

When Hercules read his doom written by fire on the walls of Thebes, he left at once for Argos. He took with him nothing but the clothes he wore, and would gladly have left those behind, because they were stained with his children's blood.

* * *

King Eurystheus of Argos was in every way a *little* man. His little head lolled between narrow shoulders and his small eyes kept secret his little thoughts. He prided himself quietly on the slenderness of his wrists from which his small hands drooped like unripe fruit. The walls of his palace were so thick, and the rooms inside so cluttered with ornaments, that he picked his way through narrow canyons of furniture and was overshadowed with lamps. When beggars begged at his gates, they got little charity. And when the people of his realm pleaded for his protection from the dark forces of the great World Beyond, they got small comfort. His heart had shrunk for want of love inside it, and he belittled the achievements of everyone but himself.

The only things about Eurystheus that were not small and mean were his coffers of treasure, his cowardice, and his vicious, inventive cruelty. He prayed to the goddess Hera for relief from his boredom . . . and she sent him Prince Hercules as a bond-slave. 'Excellent goddess!' He was only sorry that his new toy would so soon be worn out and broken. 'Have that criminal crawl to my throne on his knees!' he crowed. Hercules obeyed.

'So! Slave! What can I find for a drunken child-murderer to do in my spotless realm? Your hands are too bloody for you to stay inside *my* palace.'

Hercules crouched on one knee, his head bowed.

'Not so big as I expected,' said Eurystheus. 'I thought they said you were a strong man. You're quite squat really.'

'Square,' said Hercules.

'Don't you dare to open your mouth in my presence, *serf*!' piped Eurystheus, startled by the size of Hercules's voice. 'This morning I did you the honour of thinking

124

about you briefly. And I have thought of a fitting task for a butcher like you. The people of Nemea—one of the least significant towns in my realm—keep whining to me about some little lion. Apparently it's taken to killing children . . . A relation of yours, perhaps, ha ha ha! Kill it. What are you waiting for? That's all. Kill it.'

Hercules stood up and moved towards the door.

'Ah, but cousin!' called Eurystheus. 'Don't trouble to burden yourself with a sword or spear or bow or anything, will you? I hear the creature's hide is too thick to cut. It's killed two hundred hunters already.'

Hercules nodded without turning back to face the king, and strode out of the palace.

'He'll run away,' said Eurystheus with a snort of disdain. 'The goddess Hera didn't think of that. He'll run and hide himself. That squat oaf won't be back.'

The lion of Nemea turned over his latest kill with a large velvety paw. He did not do as other lions do, and haul his dead meat up into the safety of a tree. For the scavenger had not been born that dared to rob the Nemean Lion.

A new scent tingled in his velvet nostrils—a smell of warm meat salty with sweat: a salt that longed to be licked, a meat that asked to be eaten, a smell that begged to be tasted. He stood on top of his kill, and looked about.

The square, two-legged creature that he saw did not stir the lion's slow-pumping heart. A small meal. But the strange way it was standing excited his curiosity. It was leaning on a massive club of wood, one foot crossed casually over the other, and its eyes fixed on him. It *looks* at me, but it surely cannot see me, or it would tremble, thought the lion, and went closer, closer, and closer still. In fact he prowled tight round the legs of the two-legged creature, curling his tail around its shins and snuffing up the peculiar smell. Always before, these man-beasts had smelt of acrid, delicious fear. This prey only smelt of porridge and soap and milk and the sweat of a long journey.

'Raaow!' said the lion, and his cavernous mouth opened as wide as the stocky shoulders of his prey. But the shoulders did not flinch. Instead, the creature set whirling the club in its fist, making mesmerizing circles in front of the lion's eyes, and brought the club down with titanic force on the lion's velvety skull.

The Nemean Lion was thrown half a league by the blow . . . but landed on all four paws and came back at a run—a level-leaping run that ate up the ground. It launched itself at Hercules's head, all teeth and gullet and reaching claws.

Hercules ducked.

The lion writhed in the air and landed, rampant, in a bed of cactus. Once again it rushed at Hercules and, opening its jaws, received the unexpected meal of a club of wood rammed into its throat. It chewed and spat and swallowed.

Fed with meat and wood, dazed with clubbing, and burning with cactus needles, the Nemean Lion turned for its cave, thinking to gather its strength. But as it ran, Hercules ran after it, right to the mouth of the cave, and beyond. He braved the stench, he braved the bones, he braved the sudden dark. The lion shrank to a glimmering pair of green eyes; its noise swelled to an earthquake that threatened to burst the hollow cave. But Hercules did not slow his run until he felt his face collide with pelt, his hands tangle in the long-haired mane and his knees clamp shut around the glassy hindquarters.

Half strangling, half hanging on, he felt the gigantic

artery beat in the beast's foam-flecked neck. He felt the spinal cord through its beastly hide. He twisted and he wrung and he ground and he pounded until the lion—the terror of Nemea—flapped like a rug, and its flexing hide gave off a cloud of dust and fleas.

He skinned it and he scraped the skin. He tore off his own clothes, spattered with his own children's blood, and he put on the lion's pelt instead.

A city guard stared down from the wall of Argos and called timidly, 'Who goes there? Man or beast?'

Hercules silenced him with a scowl, and hurried on into the king's palace. Over his shoulders hung the velvet forepaws of the Nemean Lion, and across his forehead snarled the jawless, velvet nose. Its tasselled tail dragged in the dust behind him, and the pelt rippled across his back as he moved. The hind paws of the skin were knotted around his waist and dangled past his knees.

King Eurystheus was just finishing his breakfast when the door opened and a lion, walking rampant on its hind legs and wearing a human face, strolled in on him. The head lunged forward: Hercules was bowing.

When the servants found King Eurystheus, they could not persuade him to open the wardrobe door for fully half an hour. His little voice piped through the latch, 'Tell him to go away . . . Tell him to go and . . . Tell him . . . ' The latch clacked back, and Eurystheus's snub nose wiffled through a tiny gap. 'Tell him to go and kill the Hydra!'

4

Two Heads are Better than a Hundred

'We all know what Hera is doing,' said Hermes, in a hushed but angry voice. He was sitting cross-legged on a brush-covered slope of Olympus, surrounded by others of the Immortals who looked sulky and peevish. The cloud layer which screened the topmost peaks of the mountain from being glimpsed by earthly mortals, fumed and churned above their bent heads, and the air was clammy with water vapour. The gods were hiding.

Well, perhaps they were not exactly hiding, which would not have been dignified, but they were holding their meeting well out of sight of the queen's eyes.

'It's cruel,' said Athene.

'It's uncharitable,' said Apollo.

'And it's against a son of Zeus-the-Almighty,' said Hermes, 'which is more to the point. All in all, I'd rather be on the side of Hercules, if Zeus finds out what his wife is up to.'

'It's malicious,' said Athene.

'It's spiteful,' said Apollo.

'And it puts us gods in a poor light if the mortals hear

about it,' said Hermes, 'which they undoubtedly will. If Hercules kills the Hydra, it will be the talk of the world.'

'Well, I'll give my archer's bow,' said Apollo.

'And I'll give my sword,' said Hermes.

'And I'll give my helmet,' said Athene. 'He's got the skin of the Nemean Lion to protect his body.'

So softly, silently they went down to the base of Olympus, and furtively placed the weapons on Hercules's path to the Hydra's lair. Well, perhaps they did not do it furtively, for that would not have been dignified.

But when Hercules found the helmet and sword and bow, and looked up at heaven with a beaming smile, and bawled, *'Thank you, my lords and ladies!'*, all that came back was a startling buffet of breezes: 'SHSHSH!', and a creaking in the trees that sounded like, 'Hera will hear you! Hera will hear!'

The Lernean swamps writhed with the roots of drowned trees, and things squirmed unseen underfoot in the black mud. 'I don't like it,' said Iolaus.

Hercules had called in on his friend, Iolaus, who lived not very far from the lair of the Hydra. It had occurred to the strong man of Thebes that he might well meet his death in the Lernean swamp, and he did not want it thought that he had simply run away—disappeared out of cowardice. 'All you have to do is to watch, and report back to Eurystheus . . . if I . . . if the Hydra gets the better of me.'

'Gets the better of you?' squeaked Iolaus, his eyes bulging with horror. 'Have you ever *seen* the Hydra? Do you have any idea what you're talking about? It's . . . it's . . . it's so horrible that people fall down and die at the mere sight of it! Cut off one head and two grow in its place. It must have twelve heads by now, at least! I've lived in these parts all my life—it's safe enough outside the swamp—but I've seen the "heroes", so-called, piling in here to do great battle—all set to be famous.' He reached out and clutched his friend's arm. 'They none of them came out again, Hercules! I heard the screams. I heard the Hydra whistle. And every time, the whistle gets louder!'

Hercules slapped at the mosquitos which swarmed up off the water in clouds. 'Now, now, Iolaus, don't take it so much to heart. You know I'm not chasing fame. I'd rather be at home in bed. But the gods bound me to serve Eurystheus, and Eurystheus told me to kill the Hydra. So. Here we are. Don't let me down. Who was it used to eat spiders and keep a pet ragworm when we were young? Don't tell me you've grown squeamish all of a sudden?'

Beyond the next tree, Hercules almost trod on a sleeping head of the Hydra.

Like a gigantic python it was, though many of its teeth protruded through the thick, scaly lips. Without a second thought, Hercules drew his new, unblooded sword, and cut through the reptilian neck.

Instead of blood, a resinous gum welled in the wound—welled and swelled and formed a skin like scalded milk; swelled and healed and formed a green-pointed fork; welled and swelled until the forked ends bulged like rosehips with two new, born-blind heads. Both heads snarled. In both mouths, the teeth were already grown. And a spine-chilling whistle came from the nostrils on every outward breath.

Many more heroes must have fought the Hydra since Iolaus calculated the number of its heads. For now it had at least a hundred—a wilderness of swaying tendrils, and on the end of every tendril a vile, reptilian head. Like a squid or a great, fronded sea-plant disturbed by a turning tide, the Hydra quivered, and all its eyes opened.

The swamp in which it was rooted was clogged with rags and bones and hair, as the grass is below an owl's tree—the regurgitated waste from many, many meals. The heads ducked and weaved: it was impossible to count them, for they all looked alike, and all gaped mouths with banks of needle-sharp, thorn-black teeth and pulsating, soft, red palates. The whistle grew almost deafening.

The mouths lunged at Hercules. He was slow to jump backwards, and two pairs of jaws closed on his body. But the teeth could not penetrate the thick hide of the Nemean Lion. They stayed clenched in the fur when he cut through the necks with his sword. Four new heads were soon swaying among the forest of heads. He cut off six more. Twelve new heads were soon darting at him, and the fur of his lionskin was bitten bald. He backed away, stumbling in the quagmire, and joined Iolaus behind the shelter of a tree. The whistling and the tendrils pursued him, but the jaws could not reach so far.

Iolaus stared at him: 'You're alive! Pick up a head or two, stuff them in a sack and take them back to Argos. The king will think the Hydra's dead.'

Hercules, panting and leaning his back against the tree, looked shocked. 'But that would be dishonest! I couldn't hide the truth from the gods, could I? The gods would know. No, no, it's all right . . . I have a plan. Light a fire.'

Difficult as that was in the middle of a swamp, Iolaus looked on fire-lighting as simplicity itself compared with killing the Hydra. He scurried about, piling twigs into a hollow tree, and raised a fire as big as a beacon, thinking that Hercules wanted to summon help.

Not a bit of it. Into the fire Hercules thrust his massive club which was cut from such dense, massy wood that it glowed white hot and charred without burning up. 'Now. Every time I bring you an end, seal it with the club.'

'What!' shrieked Iolaus. But Hercules had gone. He was in among the thrashing Hydra's hundred and fifty heads like a man embroiled in octopus, reaching for the air and drowning . . .

But Hercules did not drown. Nor did the Hydra's heads chew him into a quid of lion fur, hair, and sandal. Its heads flew like the ears of corn under a flail, and two-at-a-time Hercules heaved the cut tendrils away from the rest. Like a stevedore drags the massive cables of a ship to the bollard, he hauled them to where Iolaus stood holding the glowing club.

'Well, don't just stand there, man! Seal the ends!' And Iolaus shut his eyes and held out the club (which took all his strength). There was a terrible noise of sizzling, and a smell of roasting lizard. The whole Hydra writhed and whistled.

But the cauterized necks did not grow new heads, and little by little Hercules hacked his way through the beast like a woodsman through a thicket: hacked and branded, hacked and branded, until the Hydra stood, like a pollarded willow beside a stream, stock still.

The whole swamp seemed suddenly to be shrinking, as if its putrid acres had sprung directly from the foot of the Hydra. A million slimy creatures from out of the mud were exposed to the purging heat of the sun.

One creature lay still as a stone. Very like a stone it was, with its rosy-white, hinged back. And while its legs were still submerged beneath the swamp, anyone might have trodden on it for a stepping stone. Hercules was about to do just that, in his haste to get back to Argos with the news of his conquest. He was not cautious about where he trod.

'Look out!' It was Iolaus who spotted the huge, serrated claw rising out of the water and the eight hinged legs. It was a huge land-crab.

Hercules drew back his foot. The crab sank down beneath the last layers of muddy water. But its two stalked eyes still waved in the air, watching him. With undreamt-of speed the eye-stalks moved through the fetid water as the crab scuttled in to bite. It was not to be robbed of its meat.

So Hercules plunged his club, still glowing hot, into the swamp, and the water round about it again steamed and hissed. Blushing pink with the heat, the crab bobbed up to the surface and escaped by scuttering sideways up a tree trunk. When it was on a level with Hercules's head, it flung itself at his throat, pincers gaping.

Iolaus squealed and put his arms over his head. Hercules swung his club and hit the crab in mid-air as though it was a bowled ball.

It cracked like the fossilized egg of some prehistoric monster, and something akin to its yolk dribbled out where it landed. The plants round about sizzled and burned with the foulest of smells, and both men covered their faces against the smoke. The land-crab's great claw clutched and wavered once, then fell.

Naturally curious to study such a huge specimen, Hercules went and poked at the dead crab with one of his arrows. The arrowhead went quite black before he put it back into its quiver.

'It's been good to see you again after all this time,' said Hercules to Iolaus. 'Thank you for your help. Don't let's leave it so long until we meet again.'

Iolaus looked back to that muddy spot where he had stood fully expecting to die. 'Well, Hercules, old friend, you know me. If ever you need anyone to help you out like this again, do me a favour . . . *ask someone else!*'

* * *

When they told King Eurystheus that Hercules had been
sighted from the city wall—and with helmet, sword, and
bow—he ran three times round his throne. 'Go and fetch it!
Go and fetch it now! Go and fetch my box!' he jabbered,
and his slaves ran from the room. They could be heard
struggling down the corridor with some very great weight.
'Set it down! Set it down! Set it down!'

They were only just in time. Hercules was at the door
before Eurystheus slammed shut the lid of his newly
wrought, great brass chest.

'Hail, master and cousin. The Hydra is d—' Hercules
stopped and looked around. The king did not seem to be
in the room.

'Dead, you say? Don't believe it!'

Hercules looked again round the room, but there was
no sign of the king. An embarrassed slave jerked his
head once or twice in the direction of a huge brass chest
standing beside the throne. Two slits halfway down, and
in the slits the glitter of two eyes, revealed the presence
of King Eurystheus. Hercules looked to the slave for an
explanation, but the boy only shrugged as if to say,
'Don't ask me.'

Unsure of the correct protocol for addressing a king
sealed up in a big brass box, Hercules sidled up to it with
some embarrassment, and knelt down respectfully on
one knee. Like that, he was on a level to peer through the
slits. The eyes inside blinked, and a little whimper
escaped the trunk.

'The Hydra really is dead. Send someone to see,' said
Hercules in a friendly way. 'It's easy to find what's left,
now that the swamp has dried up.'

A sigh of vexation echoed round the chest. 'Wait
there, slave. I'm thinking.' The eyes disappeared from the

slits, and the flicker of a candle licked yellow. There was a rustle of vellum documents, and pause enough for Hercules to look about. He noticed that there were charts and maps stuck to every wall of the throne-room with wax. He got up and went to examine them. Cerynia . . . Erymanthus . . . Elis . . . Crete . . . Stymphalus . . .

'I have another task for—Where have you gone?' said the box. Hercules ran back and knelt in front of it. 'I have another task for you, slave. Fetch me the Golden Stag of Cerynia.'

'What, dead?' said Hercules rather sadly. The Hydra and the lion had been one thing, but to kill the beautiful Stag of Cerynia seemed an awful waste.

Eurystheus, thinking to make the task even more impossible, said, 'No! Alive! Bring it to me alive!'

'Oh that's all right, then,' muttered Hercules with relief, and was immediately gone, leaving the brass chest delivering a pompous speech to no one at all except for a shuffling, uneasy slave.

5

Big Game and Sore Losses

For a year he trailed through the forests of Cerynia without ever a sighting. Sometimes he thought he heard its bronze hooves clatter against the dead branches that lay like snares under the fallen leaves. But it was only a woodpecker hammering at a tree. Sometimes he thought he caught sight of its golden antlers rattling the branches. But it was only the glancing rays of a low sun glimpsed through the crooked tree-tops. Sometimes he ran after its dappled hide only to find that he was chasing the spotted sunlight across the forest floor. And once he dreamt that a velvet lip nuzzled against his face, and woke to find spoors and hoofprints. But the stag had gone.

So finally he fetched salt from the shore of the sea, and carried it to all the pools of the forest but one. And he poured the salt into the pools until their taste was brackish and foul, and little frogs scuttered away through the green woods.

Only one fresh pool was left, and beside it he sat down with his back to a tree and his net in a bundle beside him, and he waited. For three days he waited, and the animals of the forest all came by him, panting for fresh water after drinking saltwater elsewhere. Squirrels and wild cats, roebuck and birds, rats and boars all brushed past him, some cautious, some reckless, but paying him no attention at all until their thirst was quenched. Hercules nodded and dozed.

There was frost on the ground when it came, and there was no mistaking the sound of its coming. All the other animals had drunk and gone, drunk and hidden from the cold. The pool was deserted. Its bronze hooves clashed on the frozen water with the sound of cymbals, and its golden horns rang as they shook the frozen reeds. Its hide sparkled with frost.

Having drunk at one of the salted ponds, the Golden Stag was parched for fresh water. It kicked and trampled on the ice that encrusted the water, and half-fell, half-leapt knee-deep into the shallow pool. Hercules opened his eyes the merest flicker, and his heart beat fast at the sheer beauty of the stag. But he did not move so much as a finger, for fear of frightening it away. He could see the sparkling throat gulp down the icy water and its warm breath turn to steam. Hercules's right hand crept towards his nets, like a spider crawling towards its web.

The creature heard the little grunt driven from Hercules's throat by the effort of the throw. It might have bounded, straight-legged, out of the far side of the pond but for the treacherous ice. It stumbled a little, and that was enough for the whistling net to overshadow it, then fall over the golden antlers and the glittering rump. Hercules leapt into the icy pool, and drawing close the rim of the net round the stag's knees, he bent his back and lifted the animal, his arms encircling all its four spindly legs. Like a stoop of golden corn he held it up high, and felt it tremble in his arms as he waded and slithered up the icy bank again. His own body began to tremble with the cold. Deer and man shook as though they were one beast.

Now at last Hercules could see that the antlers were not metal at all, but coated in a golden sheen of blooming velvet. In spring the gold would slough away. And the hooves were not made of bronze. They were only stained to a bronzy ochre by the oils of vetches and fleshy daisies it had trampled underfoot. The precious glitter of its coat thawed in the heat of fear, and ran down over Hercules's arms: water.

The stag was the most beautiful creature in the Cerynian Forest, but once inside the treasure house of a king it would be no more than a square of vellum, a pot of glue, a meal or two of venison.

'I shall take you to Eurystheus,' said Hercules softly, into one of the swivelling, flickering ears, 'but I'm afraid you'll be a sorry disappointment to him.'

'Take him to Eurystheus, will you? Not *my* deer you won't,' said a woman's voice. A pack of dogs bounded barking into the grove. Hercules shifted the stag this way and that in his arms and twisted his head round until he could see who was speaking. And he saw a woman, dressed in a doeskin tunic, holding a bow at full stretch, its arrow aimed at his back.

Hercules sighed. 'Does this fellow belong to you?' he asked, rocking the deer in his arms. It had ceased to struggle, and rested its jaw on the top of his head to look at the woman out of its golden, blinking eyes, through the mesh of the net.

'Why wouldn't he?' snapped the woman. 'Aren't I Artemis, immortal goddess of the hunt?'

'Oh. I see. Do you want me to let him go, then, madam?'

Artemis did not answer questions. She asked them, pouncingly, like a cat asking a mouse whether it wants to play. 'Explanation! What's your explanation? Who are you?'

'I'm Hercules of Thebes. I was sent to catch the Stag of Cerynia by my cousin, King Eurystheus.'

'You? Why you? Explanation!'

'Because I'm his bond-slave . . . Look, you put down the bow and I'll put down the stag. The gods set me to these labours, and if a goddess takes my prize from me, I know it must be my fate. What's a wasted year?'

The dogs bounding and barking round Hercules and snapping at the Golden Stag, struck a new terror into the animal and it began to struggle and kick. Hercules stumbled to and fro, surrounded by swarming dogs, the deer's antlers rattling the tree branches overhead.

'Labours? Gods? Which gods? Explanation!' snapped Artemis, striding about, drawing and easing her bow. A quiver of arrows worn diagonally across her back, pinned into place a torrent of red-gold hair longer than her tunic. The arrows were fletched with the feathers of birds Hercules had never seen. He heaved a weary sigh as he thought of Eurystheus's gloating spite when his bond-slave returned empty-handed. He had failed, after a year's patient effort. Surely Artemis, as one of the Immortals, knew of the doom carved by fire in the walls of Thebes. He was loath to tell the story of his crime again. But she insisted.

'I am Hercules, son of Alcmene and foster son of King Amphitryon of Thebes . . . '

By the time he finished, the goddess Artemis was sitting on a heap of panting, tail-wagging dogs, her chin in her hands, gazing up at Hercules who was still holding the Golden Stag. 'Go on,' she said, when he paused.

'There's nothing else to say. King Eurystheus commanded me to kill the Nemean Lion and the Hydra, and now he wants the Golden Stag of Cerynia.'

'That's the saddest story I ever heard,' said Artemis,

and tears streamed picturesquely down her suntanned face. The dogs whimpered obediently. 'I haven't been back to Olympus recently. I didn't know. I think someone up there must really hate you, and I can guess who. I mean I've only got to look at you to see whose son *you* are. He's a little bigger, of course. Almighty Zeus is a bit bigger.'

The stag had gone to sleep in Hercules's arms. It flinched and stirred as Hercules burst out laughing. 'Oh yes! Very likely! Me, the son of Zeus! And who's to blame for my sufferings except me? *I* drank myself to a madness, didn't I? *I* slaughtered my wife and kin, didn't I? No punishment is bad enough for me. I wonder what Eurystheus will do to me when I go back without the stag.'

Artemis looked at him with her head on one side. 'What strange creatures you mortals are. If we gods had to pay for our crimes, we'd spend from now till the end of time breaking rocks on the bottom of the sea. Off you go. The stag's yours—just so long as it's set free afterwards. But you know, its antlers aren't gold. And its hooves aren't bronze.'

'I see that,' said Hercules, hitching up the burden in his arms. 'I'm sure when my cousin sees that, he will be perfectly content for the beast to go free.'

Artemis wiped the tears off her face with a length of her hair. As she got up off her couch of dogs, they bounded madly this way and that, and woke up the stag again and sent Hercules stumbling to and fro with its struggles. When he looked round next, Artemis and all her dogs had gone. All the ice had melted off the pool, and primroses had burst into flower among the tree roots.

King Eurystheus was not impressed with the Golden Stag

of Cerynia. Confronted with a large, nervous stag, taller than his throne and clattering its oily feet on the marble floor, he climbed into his brass chest again and shut the lid.

Hercules waited for a time, and when the king did not come out again or shout any instructions through the slits, he went and referred to the maps on the wall. In the centre of a map of the province of Erymanthus, he saw a picture of a huge pig with tusks. 'Should I go after this next?' asked Hercules loudly.

The boy-slave in attendance by the throne could not keep silent. 'Oh yes! Please do, Hercules sir! My family lives in Erymanthus and the boar is the terror of the world. If anyone can kill it, you can! We all have faith in you! Oh please go there next!'

The lid clanged back on the brass box, and King Eurystheus poked out his head. 'Where's Hercules gone?' he demanded to know.

'He's gone to kill the Erymanthean Boar, sir,' said the slave-boy, dropping to his knees.

'Oh. Oh good. Good . . . Is it *very* dangerous?'

'Desperately dangerous, sire.'

'Excellent. Be sure to tell me if he gets killed. Now take that worthless hoax of a deer and turn it into venison. Look what it's doing now!'

They led it away, its bony antlers rattling the lamps overhead. But, without warning, it sprang through a high window, and disappeared amid the damp sheen of the gardens. Later it could be seen sometimes at the far end of a promenade or behind the fruit trees, its antler-velvet glistening like gold and its oily hooves shining like bronze, and granules of frost glistening like gems in its winter coat.

* * *

When Hercules crushed the giant land-crab in the swamp of the Hydra, the squelch was heard in heaven. Hera, lying full length along a lintel of lazuli, gouged at her couch like a cat sharpening its claws. 'Oh you villain, Hercules. You blood-thirsty, heartless wretch. What have you done to my Cancer, my darling little crab, my purveyor of poison, my deliverer of death? What, little one, are you dead and your work not done? One scratch of your poisonous claw would have sent Hercules screaming to his grave! Should I forgive you for failing me? No, you worthless object. But see what a funeral I shall give you.'

And she sent an eagle to fetch the crab's body from the swamp. She toyed with the dead thing for a moment, then hurled it over the horizon into the night beyond. As the sun sank, and night wheeled over the tree-tops to take possession of the sky, there hung the crab, cut out in stars, for all eternity. Falling stars dropped from between its spreading claws; like green drops of venom they drip-drip-dripped on to the Earth, though no one could say where they fell.

'Dear Cancer! Your venom is black on Hercules's arrowhead,' whispered Hera. 'Now let the sweet droplets of your revenge fall on his head and on the heads of those he loves. You shall hang in the sky for ever as a mark of my hatred for Hercules!'

6

Poisons

Hercules hoped for an easy conquest over the Erymanthean Boar—not because it was any less fierce than the Nemean Lion, but because its territory was the homeland of the centaurs. He resolved to go and visit his one-time games-master and ask his advice. So he approached their mountain home across the wintry plain, calling Chiron's name until he was half-hoarse. But he saw neither hide nor hair of his friend.

Then at last he caught sight of him, in a break in the trees, on the brow of Arcadia's hills. Hercules raised his hand and waved—and Chiron shied away on to the far side of the peak. There was no catching up with him.

The centaur's strange behaviour cast a bleak shadow over Hercules. He was bitterly cold; it was starting to snow, and he had not slept indoors since he began his bondage to Eurystheus. The prospect of another night under the frost-sharpened stars, curled up on the frost-sharpened ground, seemed suddenly insupportable. So he searched the hillside until he found a cave and, announcing his name on the threshold, he ducked inside, into the warmth of the centaurs' hearth.

'Greetings, Hercules. We have all heard a great deal about you. Come in, come in. Eat with us tonight, and sleep in the warm.' The only occupant of the cave was Pholus, whose hooves were large and hairy, and whose upper body had a fat, round belly as pink as onyx. He was cooking a meal of peas and beans in two large cauldrons. The other centaurs were still out on the hill, hunting or competing in games, keeping a wary look-out for the Erymanthean Boar which had killed seven of their number already.

Hercules sat down. 'I think I saw Chiron earlier. Will he come back here this evening?'

Pholus dropped his spoon with a clatter, and took a long time retrieving it. He was clearly embarrassed. 'No. I don't suppose so. Not if he knows you're here.'

'But he's an old friend! He taught me sports, you know. I'm a pupil of his . . . '

'Oh yes. He's told us all about you, Hercules. We know all about you. I'm an easy-going old hack, myself. But Chiron . . . well, Chiron's different. When he heard what happened at Thebes, he just . . . well, he just somehow . . . '

'Of course! He knows I broke my promise!' Hercules clapped his hands to his head and groaned. 'I must speak to him. He has to forgive me! You must help me to find him!'

Pholus tasted the dinner and stared thoughtfully at the roof, clearly struggling to find the least offensive words. 'I'm sure he forgives you, Hercules. It's just that he's *afraid* of you, you see.'

'*Afraid?*'

'We try to tell him it was a silly mistake. One silly mistake. But all he ever says is, ''A man who drinks once will drink twice.'' So, you see, I don't think Chiron will come in tonight.'

Hercules was stunned. He was choked with sorrow; he was furiously angry. Could Chiron seriously think that, having lost a wife and children because of wine, Hercules would drink again? Did he really trust his pupil so little? Hercules was wounded. 'Does he think that he has more will-power than I have? He doesn't drink! I won't drink!'

'*Chiron not drink?* Whatever gave you that idea,' said Pholus with a hinny. 'He *tries* not to. But every so often—when he's really down—back he goes to the vat. We centaurs are all alike. Drink's in our blood, and when we drink, there's a thousand years of civilization washed away in the flood. We chase women, we fall off mountains, we walk on to the tusks of the Erymanthean Boar. Centaurs will always be centaurs, no matter how much Chiron would like us to change.'

Hercules's head sank lower and lower between his knees. He had come to the centaurs' cave for comfort, and now he was more wretched than ever. Chiron drink? Chiron afraid of his own pupil? The hero of his childhood suddenly seemed small and flawed—a disappointment. All he had ever taught Hercules was thrown into doubt.

He brooded and brooded, and while he brooded, Pholus set a splendid meal of hot peas and beans and a whole loaf of warm bread at the guest's feet, along with a jug of milk.

'What, no wine?' said Hercules sarcastically.

Pholus blushed. 'Ah. The wine's not mine to offer, sir. It's the property of the centaur tribe. On the feast of Bacchus we do take the odd . . . '

'I want some!' said Hercules, pushing his face into Pholus's face. 'Now! Chiron says, "If a man drinks once, he'll drink twice".'

Then Pholus blenched. 'No, sir. Chiron's a fool, sir. You mustn't take to heart what he says. He's never

145

spoken a sensible word in his life. We laughed at him. We threw crusts at him. "Hercules is wise now," we all said.'

Hercules caught him by the beard. 'Are you calling my old friend a fool? Let me tell you something! I used to love Chiron like a brother. He was clever. He was fit. He was wise. If he says I'll drink a second time, then that's what I'll do. And I'll do it now. *So give me some wine!*'

'No!' said Pholus. 'No! No! No! I won't bring wine to you. We all know what happened last time!' And he cantered out of the cave, a paunchy, ungainly beast snorting down both nostrils.

Hercules walked up to the vat and smashed a hole in it with one blow of his fist. A geyser of wine struck him in the face, and he had only to open his mouth to drink.

It was made from fruit grown on the foothills of Paradise, but it tasted bitter, because he was drinking to get even with Chiron, and because he loved Chiron, and for a host of angry reasons in between. The vat spewed its contents down his chest and legs, and flooded the floor of the cave.

Meanwhile Pholus ran for help. He shouted, 'Come quick, the strong man is here! Chiron's Hercules is drinking the wine! Someone! Come quickly! Hercules is drinking! Chiron! Hercules is drinking again!'

Chiron, who had been creeping closer and closer to the cave in the hope of seeing his pupil once more from a distance, lost all fear at the sound of Pholus's voice. He only knew that he had to stop Hercules—that something terrible would happen if Hercules ever again allowed wine to wash away his senses. Through the thick, evening undergrowth he bolted, no slower on his feet than when he had taught steeplechasing to the Prince of Thebes.

146

But he was too late to stop Hercules from drinking. By the time he reached the cave, the stars were sparkling overhead like the bubbles in a dark, rich wine, and in the doorway of the cave Hercules stood swaying, his Olympian bow and arrow clutched like a lute, his eyes bloodshot like wine-fermented cheese.

'Hercules! Ho there! It's I!' cried Chiron.

Hercules peered through a darkness thickened to syrup by the fumes of drink, and saw a low tossing of the undergrowth. 'You, eh? I've been looking for you these five days past.'

So Chiron hurried on towards Hercules and stretched out his arms by way of greeting and apology. He was only a few paces away when Hercules raised his bow and fired.

Chiron leapt. The champion of the high jump leapt straight up into the air, twisting his head away and drawing up his long, slender legs. But the arrow struck him in the fetlock, and he fell on his side, and his tail shrouded the bushes with strands of silk. Pholus saw it all.

'There!' said Hercules. '*He* won't be troubling you any more. I've killed the Erymanthean Boar for you. Saw it. Shot it. Just like that. Piaow!' And he slid down the cave wall and slumped along the ground, insensible with drink. The last thing he saw, as he rolled over and his mouth fell open, was the constellation of Cancer the Crab dripping its starlight on to the hill of the centaurs.

Pholus ran to the side of his brother centaur. 'Chiron! Chiron! Let me help you! Let me see that wound!'

Chiron had his two hands clutched below his withers, and his legs twitched and kicked in agony. Pholus knelt down and pulled out the arrow. Its head was not shiny, but black and corroded. He tested its sharpness against his thumb and cut himself. For a moment he stared at

147

the little cut, and then he clutched his upper arm and said, 'Always clumsy. Always clumsy and stupid, that's me.' He gave a little sob, then rolled over, with his head in the angle of Chiron's body, and died.

Next morning, Hercules's head felt like a foul and overheated kitchen, where pots and pans hung from the ceiling and clattered and banged against each other. A scream came howling through the kitchen, setting the pans swinging and banging, swinging and banging. Hercules opened his eyes.

On the hillside, the whole tribe of centaurs was ranged in a ring around Chiron and the body of Pholus. Chiron was standing on his hind horses' legs, pawing the air with his front hooves and tearing at his mane of hair with both hands. Then he flung himself down on his back and clutched his wounded leg, and thrashed his hind flanks and heaved his upper body along the ground as though he were trying to pull man from horse. He called over and over again on the gods.

The centaurs would hardly make way for Hercules. They landed furtive kicks on him as he pushed his way through to Chiron. His sports-master stared at him with rolling eyes: even his upper body was creamy with sweat, like a horse. 'Well, boy, and who taught you to poison your arrows?'

'Poison? Arrows? Chiron, what have I done to you?'

'You've condemned me to everlasting torment, boy! Pholus was lucky—he wasn't an immortal like me. But me! I can't die! I can't be rid of the pain that's breeding and multiplying inside me like a million horseflies! Did I deserve this? For telling you the truth? Oh, Hercules! Pray to the gods to let me die like an ordinary mortal!'

Then Hercules saw the black-headed arrow and remembered the swamp and the Hydra and the land-crab and the hanging constellation oozing starlight. 'Me? Pray?' he said. 'Why would the gods pay any heed to a man who kills his friends?' and he embraced the half-man that was Chiron. When he broke free again, he turned his face to the sky and howled, 'If it's true, what Artemis said in the woods of Cerynia—if it is true that Almighty Zeus is my father, I ask one thing and one thing only for my birthright. Take this my friend, as someone took that foul crab, and scatter him in stars on the night sky as a glory to his race. And make him of stars so bright that they will prick my eyes each night and make me weep!'

Seizing the centaur by its horses' heels, he swung and loosed him like a folded sling, and hurled him upwards into the sky. The clouds shook with howling. And the lesser gods, who had been watching all the time, caught and carried him far out into the fields of night where other beasts graze on the periwinkle stars. And there they parted him, as the sun's rays are parted, when they strike the sea, into scattering drops of light. And there, in the cold of space, the droplets froze, each containing the essence of Chiron, his energy and intellect and wild centaurian fire.

Not until the following night did Hercules see his friend rear up over the hill of the centaurs, with a bow of moonlight and a quiver of meteorites, as though he were hunting constellar beasts across the night sky.

Pholus he buried in the hillside, in frost-hard clay, in a grave that was instantly covered by falling snow. During the blizzard, Hercules picked up his weapons and left. The centaurs did not see him go.

He followed the tracks of the Erymanthean Boar quite easily; the snow was as deep as the beast's bristling underbelly and it picked out a laborious path. He found it sleeping, and wrapped it in a net. Then he took it back to Argos, hog-tied, and set it down in front of Eurystheus's brass hidey-hole.

'You see what a kindness I've done you, cousin Hercules,' piped the king shrilly. 'The world talks of nothing but Hercules and his great labours. Not a word about your master. Not a word about *me*. I'm not sure I ought to give you any more of these opportunities to show off. I'm not sure I shouldn't lock you in a dungeon somewhere until the world forgets that you were ever born. I'm not sure a child murderer deserves such fame. I hear you've been killing centaurs this time. Another friend of yours dead, eh? It hardly benefits a man to call himself your friend, does it? I'm glad I can only claim to be your master, your owner, your better . . . '

'You are what you are,' mumbled Hercules, grinding his teeth. 'I am obedient to whatever work you give me. But I beg you, cousin, let my next task be more of a hardship and less of a glory, and let it be work enough to make me sleep at night. I have things in my head that don't bear remembering.'

The box gave a gulp. 'Well, take that pig away and have it roasted, and then be on your way to Elis. The smell of the place begins to offend my realm. There'll be no glory to reap from *this* labour, just work enough to keep you labouring for ten years, and filth enough to bury your pride. I'm lending you to Augeas to clean out his stables!'

An eerie laugh trickled in at the threshold. And though panic-stricken servants set about it with brooms, to sweep it out again, it got in behind the furniture, and came out at night, like mice, to gnaw on the silence. *'You have done well,'* Hera's voice whispered to Eurystheus from behind his curtains as he undressed. *'This labour is much the best of all, my little man!'* And a clammy hand touched him in the small of the back before he could pull the covers close round him.

7

Mucking Out

King Augeas had farm animals more than he could count. When they were loosed into the meadows they blotted out the landscape as far as the horizon—a great landmass of goats and bullocks and horses, overhung by clouds of flies. At nightfall, they were driven, with whips and whistles, into a stable that stretched for mile upon granite mile, over the horizon and beyond. They were sent as tributes by the kingdom's frightened neighbours—bribes offered in the hope of sweetening his barbarous temper. But nothing could sweeten the stables themselves.

Once Augeas had sent his slaves into the stables in droves to clean out the dirty straw, but the animals' trampling hooves and close-squeezing flanks had crushed them, and their bones lay lost beneath fifty years of dung.

To walk into the smell was like walking into a wall. All the beasts were diseased, and their ribs stood out like whip-weals, and their eyes were ringed with madness at the neglect that had blighted their lives.

King Augeas moved his bed further and further away from the stables, to the backmost rooms, then the leeward gardens, until at last a broad mountain stood between him and the stinking valley. He no longer troubled to loose the animals into the meadows, but left them penned up, day and night. The squalor disgusted even him.

Eurystheus did send a messenger ahead of Hercules. But as the messenger came up the valley and caught wind of the stables, he gave one sniff and ran away. So Hercules himself had to explain the task that had been set him. The king's couch was resting now between banks of hydrangea bushes with an awning to keep off the rain. He was dressed in a loose robe which had once been thickly embroidered with gold thread. But since he never troubled to undress by night or change his clothes in the morning, the garment had grown worse than shabby. It looked like a fisherman's net hung up to dry with a few ragged fish still dangling in the mesh. Night and day he lay reclining on his couch and eating, and vultures perched on the bedhead and ate his leftovers off the covers.

When he heard why Hercules had come, he rolled on to his back like a dog, and laughed chokingly. The honking giggle caused him great discomfort because of the wedges of wax he had used to stop up his nose against the smell. 'I'll make a wager with you, boy. Never mind Eurystheus. Never mind slavery. If you can clean out my stables, you can keep half the beasts yourself. And that's the word of a man who's never given away so much as a cold in the head.'

'I accept, Augeas. I accept your wager,' said Hercules. 'Now, if you could show me the stables?'

'Show you? Huh! I'm sure you can nose them out yourself. I'm not stirring a step in *that* direction.'

Hercules could see a thundercloud of flies hanging beyond the mountain. He could hear their buzzing. As he walked down into the valley of the stables, it was snowing flies, hailing flies. His feet sank into the boggy moss of the mountainside and at once swarms of flies gathered to drink the water that filled his footprints.

If the flies were thirsty, the animals were parched. A little choked stream which trickled alongside the stables kept alive those that could reach it, stretching their scraggy necks through the holes in the stable wall. Others, hollow-eyed, were dying of thirst. When Hercules threw open the doors, they had hardly enough strength to stumble out and jostle for a lick of water. League upon league of fly-blown creatures came wading through years of dung, out into the valley meadows. The light troubled them. The flies persecuted them. Hercules ached with pity. He threw down his pitchfork, and scratched the ears of a goat-kid that came and nuzzled his hand. The task was plainly impossible. A man could work a lifetime and still be ankle-deep in dung. In despair, he walked the entire length of the valley, and the little kid followed on behind him, until the sound of fast-flowing water tempted it away over a hill crest. Then Hercules followed the kid instead.

He found himself looking down at a raging river full of splintered tree trunks and scouring sand. Froth ringed all the rocks with a white and delicate lace.

'Water,' said Hercules. 'Clean, running water!'

At the water's edge on the far side of the river, crouched a young man scrubbing his body with a knot of wet grass. His skin gleamed and glowed, but his hands were red and wrinkled with being too much in water. Beyond him, a second, slow, green river made a meandering loop so as almost to maroon him on a dry spit of land between the two strands of water. He started at the sight of Hercules, and his twist of grass tumbled away downstream.

In a feverish burst of activity, Hercules set about

tearing up light rocks from the river bank and pitching them into the water: boulders and logs and whole trees and yet more boulders, until the debris washing down the swollen river began to pile up against his dam. The more it piled up, the more solid the dam grew, until the river began to spill over its bank and grope icily at Hercules's feet. The astonished youth washing himself on the far shore made a snatch at the river as though it were a coverlet slipping off his bed. But the river escaped his clutch. It was re-routing itself.

Hercules scraped a path for it with a tree branch. He rolled boulders out of its way. He diverted it into the valley of the Augean stables.

The beasts looked up from their grazing, from beneath their blanket of flies, and their eyes rolled with fear. For pouring down the valley came a rushing river, bounding and pounding across the mired grass and crowning each obstacle with foam. It chased them on to high ground: it washed their mildewed hooves.

It crashed against the stable doors and spouted in at the few small windows. It swirled through the stalls as dawn scours the sea-lanes with her first rays. It sluiced away the dirt like time sluices the present into the past.

Only when it was dangerously deep and threatened to sweep Hercules off his feet, did he wade against the current and throw down the dam he had built. The river returned to its usual course, roaring angrily like a beast disturbed from its sleep. Up on the hilltop, the young man was dancing and flinging his hands over his head and yelping with joy.

Dipping puzzled noses into the receding water, the beasts watched the water gurgle and suck and soak away. The stable building stood as white as the temples glimpsed on sunlit mountaintops. Its roofs were torn or sagging; the mangers were all piled up against the end wall where the water had swept them. Dispossessed flies teamed down the valley, mourning their comfortable dung, and here and there white stones gleamed like a trail of coins dropped from the pocket of a passing giant.

'It's done,' said Hercules. He had to say it twice before Augeas woke up.

'What do you take me for?'

'I tell you it's done.'

The king took the wax out of his nose and sniffed— gingerly at first and then deeper and deeper.

'Look for yourself,' said Hercules.

For an hour Augeas sat at the head of the valley and stared. No flicker of joy touched his unshaven face. At last he said, 'Look at it. The roof's all smashed.'

'That's soon mended,' said Hercules, rather taken aback.

'It's a ruin.'

'It was a ruin when I got here!'

'You youngsters. No patience to do a job properly. Always the quick trick, the slick trick. How did you do it?'

'He diverted the rivers, father! He drove rivers through there like a herd of horses. In half a day, he did it! Fifty years of filth in half a day!' It was the well-washed and shiny-faced boy from beside the river.

Augeas turned on them both a look of vilest contempt. 'Then the rivers did the work and not Hercules at all. I thank them heartily. I'll pay them a tribute of wine this afternoon. And I'll thank you, Phyleus, to keep to your washing and to speak when I permit it. Sons are a father's bane, Hercules. You did well to kill all yours when they were small enough.'

The young man blushed with outraged embarrassment. 'Father! May the gods punish you for saying such things. Pay your debts. If you promised Hercules anything pay

155

it to him now. He *has* cleaned the stables. Truly he has!'

For all his idleness, Augeas could move quickly inside his rags. He launched a kick and a push at his son that toppled the boy off the hilltop and rolled him down through thistles and thorns. 'Run away and starve. I've done with you and your treachery. I disinherit you,' and he bared his yellow teeth.

Phyleus tried to get to his feet. 'Disinherit me? Of what, father? This pigsty of a kingdom? A million flies waiting in attendance? You can keep it!'

Augeas drew a sword so rusty and encrusted that it looked like a stalactite wrenched off the ceiling of a cave. The cutting edge was blunt when he jabbed it into Hercules, but when he hurled it at his son, Phyleus fell, clutching his head. Hercules looked down at the graze on his chest and fingered the blood thoughtfully. Then he picked up King Augeas like something objectionable he had found in a mousetrap, and throwing him across the back of a goat, sent the animal scampering and skipping out of the valley and out of the kingdom.

'I regret, my lord, that you will have to wear the crown, now that your father has gone,' he told Phyleus. And he left the lad fervently washing his hair in the river so that his head should be deserving of a coronation.

8

Birds and Beasts

Eurystheus woke up with that accustomed quake of his heart and the usual question in his head: what impossible task could he find next for Hercules? Then he remembered the Augean Stables. That task would take tens of years, if indeed Hercules ever accomplished it. And the king lay back and wallowed in the thought of dung, more dung, and yet more dung. For several years he would be able to sleep in peace.

'Hercules is in the vestibule, my lord,' said the slave who came to wake him. 'Should I let him into the throne-room or do you wish to enter your chest first?'

Eurystheus gave a convulsive shudder, and he snatched the covers up over his head. 'Who? Where? Send him away. Lock him up! Offer up prayers!' Slowly, however, the king emerged again, white-faced but grinning. 'He's failed. The Augean Stables defeated him. I can sink him in a dungeon. He'll beg me to forgive him, but I won't! I'll send him back there to go on mucking out! You'll see! That's the way of it.'

The slave crept uncertainly out of the room, but stopped to listen by the door as the king's excitable voice started up again. 'You'll see! He's failed. He couldn't do it. You'll see!'

And a female voice replied, 'I think not, Eurystheus. You must try harder. Such a simple task I gave you, and you make so much of it . . .'

The servant peeped round the curtain that hung across the doorway. But he could see no one: only the king struggling into his robes like a man smothered by a collapsing tent.

Somewhere between the bedchamber and the throne-room, Eurystheus learned how Augeas had been turned out of his kingdom on the back of a goat and how Phyleus had been made king in his father's place. The idea so outraged Eurystheus that he forgot his fear, forgot his bronze hidey-hole and burst into the throne-room shaking his fists with fury. 'Is this how you serve a master? Is this how you humble yourself to the will of the gods? What gives you the right to be a kingmaker?'

He was confronted by the sight of an excitable crowd of women, their backs turned on him and their faces towards Hercules who sat on the steps of the throne listening to them. They did not even notice Eurystheus.

'Huge they are—wings as wide as this!'

' . . . with legs like cranes, and beaks . . .'

' . . . oh, beaks as sharp as cuttle and claws that rip . . .'

' . . . They steal the sheep!'

' . . . They strip the trees!'

' . . . *They eat our children*, Hercules!'

Hercules nodded sadly. 'I've heard of such birds. But what do you want the king to do? Send an army?'

'No! How can anyone fight an enemy in the sky? An army would be torn to pieces!'

' . . . No, we want to come here, Hercules . . .'

' . . . We need somewhere to live! The birds have torn

158

the roofs off our houses to steal us out of our beds! Ask him for us. Put our case to the . . . '

One by one, the people in the room caught sight of the king and fell to their knees. He looked them up and down, eyes bulging and cheeks puffed up with rage. 'Well? What have you to say to me, Hercules of Thebes?'

Hercules went and knelt, in all humility, at the king's feet, and pressed his forehead to Eurystheus's thigh. 'I humbly beg a favour on behalf of these people, your subjects from the region of Stamphylia.'

Eurystheus snatched his robe away as if it were on fire, and shrieked, in little staccato bursts, 'No! No! They *can't* come and live here. They *can't* live anywhere except where they belong. I forbid it. They can all go back where they came from. And you'll go with them to deal with these *birds*. If they eat you—well, that's the will of the gods . . . And good riddance!'

Turning his bowed head, Hercules caught the eye of a Stamphylian woman and winked. 'I humbly thank my master for your graciousness. You grant my favour without me even having to speak it.' And he hurried out of the room, ushering the women ahead of him like a brood of chickens. The taste of triumph in the king's mouth turned so sour that he spat.

The mucous fish of the sea softly slip out of the hand. The beasts of the land are wrapped in fur or hide, and the birds of the air are commonly the softest of all, carrying flakes of the sky beneath their downy feathers. But the bladebills of Stamphylia are not soft. There is no tender frailness in their skin-webbed wings. The brittle skeleton is razor-sharp and the bones barely cushioned by flesh. A bladebill flies like a rattle of thrown sticks, and its claws sink deep into its prey. At the touch of yielding meat, its head begins to saw and its beak to slash and its claws to close in an ecstasy of greed, and it shreds and tears and scatters; and a tongue as long and thin as an eel flickers about for the blood. A cow staggers under its weight; a straw roof buckles, and a man can do nothing but sink to his knees and die.

When Hercules arrived in Stamphylia with the babble of women, they were met by the sight of towns torn down, markets stripped bare, vines trampled into the purple ground, and villages in ruins. Slashed black trees wept sap through their wounded bark. The bladebills were mustered in the topmost branches of the black trees, stepping from foot to foot, groping the air with their claws and peering across the bare countryside.

At the sight of fresh meat coming, they took off, three, four, five at a time, and covered the sky. Like hide tents blowing across a desert they flapped slowly, noisily, piercing their own flapping with occasional blood-curdling shrieks. When their 'food' found shelter in a cave, they scratched vilely on the stone cliff outside and jabbed their beaks in at the door for a while before rattling back into the sky.

The cave was already crowded with people chased there by the bladebills. They looked up now, with hollow cheeks and haunted eyes, and covered their ears against the sound of the bladebills flying. The only food they had salvaged—sacks of flour—was mildewy with damp, and a greedy fire in the centre of the floor licked up whatever wisps of fuel they fed it. To the people in the cave, Hercules was just another empty mouth, and he looked like a man with a big appetite. They were not glad to see him.

Their fears were confirmed when he said, 'Make dough! Make bread dough out of all the flour you've got.'

'Do as he says,' urged the women who had fetched

him. 'He killed the Hydra! He caught the Erymanthian Boar! Do what he tells you!'

Water was scarce. They had to wait for it to drip-drip off the roof into the bowls of flour: it was two days before the flour was a solid mass. 'There's no oven to bake it,' protested the Stamphylians, 'and look at the mould—it's not fit to eat!'

'All the better,' said Hercules, dragging the dough towards the mouth of the cave, tub after tub after tub.

The bladebills ambushed him whenever he stepped outside. They swooped and tore at him. But the Nemean Lion's skin defied their talons, and the sword of Hermes lopped off their trailing legs. Like craneflies on a summer night, more and more came rattling out of the sky. Hercules fended them off with Apollo's arrows so they soon turned to eating the dough instead.

Some plunged in their beaks and could not pull them out again. Some tore off lumps and swallowed them. The dough stuck in their gullets, or weighed them down, until their wings could not lift them. In some, the mildew poisoned them like lead in a swan; it turned their grey throats green and their brains an unruly purple, and they thrashed about, wounding the other birds.

Once blood was drawn, the birds overhead folded their wings and dived out of the sky as cormorants plunge on fish in the sea. They did not fall on the dough or on to Hercules's sword but on to their fellow birds. And while they gouged and fought and intertangled their spiny wings, Hercules waded in amongst them, and notched the blade of Hermes's sword on their sharp bones, their wire-sharp sinews.

Just once, he felt a plume of feathers brush his cheek and, when he looked up, thought he saw a sandalled heel treading the air near his head. But then his vision was filled by a skin-webbed wing as big as a sail, and a spread claw snatched at his face. Afterwards, nobody watching from the mouth of the cave mentioned seeing a god at Hercules's side.

They bathed his cuts and groomed his lionskin and disentangled the claws of bladebills from his hair. They turned their eyes away from the carnage around the baskets of dough . . . and they said nothing, not a word—as if the air was better empty, even of words. Not a sheep bleated; not a cow lowed: there were no sheep or cows. There were no chickens either, nor horses, nor goats nor songbirds nor geese. There was not even the rustle of grain filling the fields. Stamphylia was stripped bare. The bladebills had eaten it all.

'You only had to wait,' said Hercules when they tried to offer him payment in bits and pieces of gold. 'I did nothing. The birds would have turned on each other for food sooner or later. Destroyers always destroy themselves. Do you know the kingdom of Elis? No, don't shudder like that. Augeas has gone now, and the stables don't smell. If you send your shepherds to his son, Phyleus, and tell him you've come for Hercules's share of the animals, he will give you half of all the goats and horses and cows in the Augean stables. They should help to re-stock Stamphylia.'

Then a clamour of cheering and clapping and laughter burst from the people and rose up over Hercules's head. It followed him all the way to the borders of Stamphylia, like a flock of seagulls following a ship.

Poseidon the Earth-Shaker, the Earthquake-Maker, the god of the oceans, sat in the blue shallows of the sea and watched a flock of seagulls fly over. From beneath the sea's surface, they looked like small white fish swimming, but even through the filtering foam their raucous voices were audible. It seemed to Poseidon that they were shouting, 'H-erk-culee! H-erk-culeee! H-erk-culee!'

The world was noisy with talk of Zeus's mortal son. The sea, flaking gossip off the shores of the world, washed it in at Poseidon's ears; it filtered down to him like water-shrimp. Soon even the sea god's kingdom would be awash with news of Hercules's feats of strength and heroics.

On Olympus, Hera slammed the doors of heaven while lesser gods conspired on the staircases. Zeus, thinking he was unobserved, and resting his head nonchalantly on one hand, took sidelong glances down at the sea-encircling world in the hope of catching sight of his son. Once, when he saw Hercules overrun and outnumbered by a flock of vile birds, he had whispered in Hermes's ear, 'Help him! Go on!' and Hermes had flown to the rescue. But then Zeus had wrapped himself in cloud and fingered his beard and sworn that matters were out of his hands. Hercules must suffer the fate allotted to him.

'Hercules is a common murderer,' Hera would snarl imperiously. But when she was gone, the gods would scamper to the parapets of heaven and watch the continuing Labours of Hercules. 'Twelve years!' they would whisper. 'If he survives for twelve years, he's no ordinary mortal.'

And hearing this, Zeus banged the arms of his throne and whispered to himself, 'If he survives for twelve years he shall be one of the Immortals. By my head, he shall!'

All this was known to Poseidon, the sea god, although the news had to drift to him on the tide. For no one thought to visit his oceanic realm while there were the Labours of Hercules to distract them. 'They'll be calling him a god soon and building temples to him, you mark what I say!' But there was no one there to mark him. Every ship that sailed overhead was filled with sailors talking about Hercules. Every giggle of naked girls that bathed in the surf was sighing for a sight of Hercules. The sea grew muddy with Poseidon's vexation.

Only King Minos, monarch of Crete, was too busy making daily sacrifice at the sea god's temple to take an interest in the stories of Hercules. Poseidon had great hopes of King Minos.

'I'll give them all something more worthy to speak of than *Hercules*,' muttered Poseidon. And he made, out of the shining hide of the ocean, a bull. He stuffed it with krill and gave it hooves of coral. Its eyes were Elmo's Fire and its horns were the shed tusks of the narwhal. It stood twenty hands high and was as placid as a summer sea. 'Minos shall sacrifice this blue beast to me, the Bull-Maker, the Earthquake-Maker, the Sea-Shifter . . . and the whole world will cast its eyes over the sacrifice and remember to fear Poseidon!'

The Cretans found Poseidon's blue bull wandering on the sea shore. People ran down to the beach and up to the palace. 'Lord king! Lord king! The gods have sent you such a bull!'

And when Minos saw it he ordered garlands to be made for its neck and said, 'Such a bull! By the gods, such an animal! Poseidon sent it. Yes, that's the truth of it. The great sea god desires a fitting sacrifice. A whole herd of prime bullocks wouldn't make as fit a sacrifice as this. Sound the horns! Summon the people! Offer up the beast on the altar of Poseidon! I shall make the cut myself!'

Heralds whose brass horns coiled around them like rampant pythons blew the summons. And from every small mountain sheepfold, every fishing village on the southern shore, every cattle farm, the people of Crete set off to see the king's latest devout sacrifice.

'No, wait,' said Minos to his High Priest. 'I want to

164

look at it for a while longer. See how it steps! See how it brandishes its horns!'

'But the people have been summoned, lord king . . . '

'Then sacrifice a dozen bullocks out of my own corral. Tomorrow the blue bull. Tell them tomorrow. I just want to look at it for a while longer.'

And as he looked, Minos began to question whether Poseidon had indeed sent the bull. 'Perhaps one of the other gods sent it. What a blasphemy it would be to sacrifice it on the wrong altar! . . . Or perhaps it was a present. Perhaps Poseidon was *giving* it to me in return for all my sacrifices. Perhaps he wants me to breed from it. Perhaps . . . ' And the more he speculated, the less he wanted to cut the throat of the blue bull. 'Perhaps it just wandered up out of the sea. Perhaps Poseidon doesn't even know it's here. Perhaps if he saw it, he'd want it for his own herd. And what would he do to me if I'd made the mistake of cutting its throat. Perhaps I ought to keep it by, until the facts are more plain. Perhaps . . . perhaps if I build a corral with high enough walls, Poseidon won't even hear tell of the beast and I can keep it . . . Oh!' Minos clapped his hand over his mouth to stop himself speaking any more blasphemy out loud. But in the secrecy of his head, he went on thinking it. He was now absolutely determined that the blue bull should not be spilt on the altar of the sea god. He would keep the animal hidden away where he could gaze at its beauty day and night.

The High Priest came and said, 'The people are still assembled at the Temple, lord king. Will you set an hour for the sacrifice of the blue bull?'

'Blue bull?' said Minos. 'What blue bull? What are you talking about? Send them home. No more sacrifices today. Blue bull? Don't know what the man is babbling about. What blue bull?'

'WHAT BLUE BULL?' cried Poseidon, and the veins in his forehead made channels of a different blue in the seething ocean. 'WHAT BLUE BULL?' And he scrabbled together the phosphorescence of a tropical night and hurled it at Crete. '*That* blue bull, you blasphemous dog!'

Encamped around the Temple of Poseidon, the people of Crete were disappointed. They had seen the blue bull being led up from the beach and wanted another glimpse of its glossy blue hide and the sweep of its ivory horns and the glow of its eyes.

They were starting to settle down in the sand for a night's sleep when they saw, all of a sudden, their own shadows cast black as daytime, and a comet of incandescent light burst over the western horizon. A faggot of phosphorescence spun slowly over their heads as though the air was syrup-thick. Poseidon had hurled a thunderbolt. But at what? At whom? The people leapt to their feet and stared. For there, between palace and beach, stood the blue bull.

The knot of light hit it on the side of the head, bursting on its serrated horn and splashing like mercury into its eyes and nostrils. Its mouth dripped phosphorescence. Its hide shuddered. Its wits shattered. Sweat dripped from its hide like rain.

At first, the people on the beach were transfixed by the beauty of the beast shrouded in dripping light. Even when it began to paw the ground and bellow, they did not think to run. Only when it came ploughing down the beach, its horns rooting up gouts of sand to right and left, did they run for the sea, run for the dunes, run for the boats. The blue bull smashed the boats and sank them. It smashed all the fishermen's shacks and the beach groynes. It turned back to the palace and crazed the ceramic walls with its iron skull. It maddened itself in ropes of clematis and vine torn down off the trellises. It threw the carts in the palace yard over the sea wall, and gouged its letterless name in the great oak doors.

Buttresses fell away. Plaster was flayed off like skin, and left the timbers of the building exposed. High up on the roof, King Minos howled his terror. 'Kill it! Kill it! Someone kill the beast!' His army ignored his commands and cowered alongside him with their arms over their heads.

'What must I do? *What must I do?*' yelled Minos at the oil-black sea.

But Poseidon had no advice to offer. Smug in his revenge, he turned his back on Crete and strode towards his dark deep-sea caverns.

So the people answered Minos instead. They called back up at the roof of the palace, *'Send for Hercules! Send for Hercules!'*

Poseidon stopped in his tracks and put his hands over his ears: 'That name again!'

On the roof, Minos said, 'Who? What did they say? Send for him! I don't know who he is. I've never heard of him. But send for Hercules!'

Poseidon curled his lip. 'Very good. Let them send for him. My blue bull can split him and spill him on my altar for a sacrifice. Then we'll hear the last of Hercules!'

9

Poseidon's Pride and Joy

The prayers of King Minos and the people of Crete hung over the island like a haze of heat. And the murmurings of Poseidon reached Hera, too, where she sat on the parapets of heaven, sulking.

So it was not long before the queen of the gods was slipping ghostlike to Eurystheus's bedside to whisper in his ear: 'Send Hercules to tame the mad blue bull!'

Hercules listened to the king's command and nodded. His face had taken on a strange illegibility, like the carvings of a lost civilization, half overgrown with creepers. A wild tangle of beard obscured his mouth. Eurystheus thought there was something very bull-like in the figure crouched in front of his brass trunk, and though the streets outside his palace were lined with citizens of Thebes grizzling and tearing their clothes in sorrow at the dangers facing Hercules, Eurystheus feared more for Poseidon's bull.

The roads of Crete were lined with people, too—caravans of carts and wagons moved families, households, whole villages from one end of the island to the other in an effort to escape the blue bull. But though the beast returned often to the rubble of the king's palace to throw down another statue and buckle yet more pillars, its frenzy would take it from the north coast to the south, from the east to the west. Over the mountains and through the olive groves it raged, with a hunger for devastation that was never filled. As the rocks of the sea are festooned with the wreckage of ships, so its horns dangled ropes, garlands, and torn cloth. Its hide was stained morocco red with blood, and flies followed behind it like the scavengers who follow an army to pick over the battlefields. People knew when it was coming, not only by the trembling of the ground and the cloud of dirty dust but by the canopy of vultures that circled over its spoil. In their terror, the people of Crete came to believe that the bull was not mad at all, for it destroyed with such a terrible methodical efficiency. Not an acre of island dry-land had been spared by its pounding hooves.

But inside the bull's head were far worse scenes of devastation. Not a thought remained that was not splashed with burning phosphorescence. Not a view came into his eyeball but it was struck through with fork lightning. The night seemed as bright and shadeless as noon. The world burned round him like an incandescent cage. So even when exhaustion griped at him he went on and on destroying.

So when he saw a bearded, thick-set figure ride into the royal harbour on the prow of a fast-moving ship, the blue bull was filled with the need to destroy both man and ship. His crescent slash of horns burst the ship to fragments, and the mast fell groaning and impaled the sea. But when the bull shook off the spars and sheets of the shattered ship, he saw that the man was ashore now and stood, arms folded, on the quayside. A great roar of voices echoed in the bull's ears: 'Hercules! Hercules!'—a

169

thunderous migraine of noise that made the beast roll its head on its neck.

Still Hercules did not move.

'Fight it, Hercules! Kill it! Cut it to pieces!' bawled the fishermen cowering among the ruins of the sea wall. 'You killed the Hydra didn't you?'

But Hercules did not move.

'Sacrifice it to the sea god! Cut its throat on Poseidon's altar,' King Minos called feebly from the broken parapets above the beach. But Hercules did not move.

The blue bull pawed the ground, lowered its head, grated the tip of one horn on the stone quay. But not until its flank twitched and hurled it forwards did Hercules turn on his heel and run. He ran and the bull ran after him. He dodged between the rubble and splintered bollards, but the bull cannoned through all obstacles and gained on him quickly. On the sand, both feet and hooves sank in. But on the marble steps of the promenade the beast's hooves skidded, and Hercules saved himself from the slash of the horns. Through the main street, through the ruins of the pounded palace, through its flowery yards and sweet-smelling places, Hercules fled the bull.

'Shame on you for a coward, Hercules!' shouted the cowering crowds. 'Stop and fight!'

But Hercules went on running. He ran the bull up hills until its blue lungs heaved. He ran it down hills till its hind quarters quaked, and he ran it through coppices of tightly packed trees. He ran it through briars till its flanks bled blue brine. He ran it over bare white rocks in the heat of the day, till its withers steamed salt sweat. And last of all he ran into the sea, and the blue bull followed him, bellowing through its upturned nostrils, its legs continuing to run even when it could no longer touch bottom.

From inside its head, the blue bull looked up at the

agonizing brightness of the sky and the cutting edge of the spinning sun. Waves broke into his breathing passages; waves broke into his eyes. The great weight of horn on his head dragged like the ice on a masthead that overturns an arctic ship. From somewhere overhead came the sound of rasping breaths, and as the bull's blue face sank beneath the surface, he realized that the rasping noise was his own breath and that he was drowning.

Hercules swam on, even though each arm felt like lead as he lifted it out of the water. He swam until he heard a bellow behind him suddenly cut short by a gurgling gulp. Looking over his shoulder, he saw the blue bull sink. The phosphorescence of its eyes glowed through the water: as he swam back, he could see its great bulk drifting immobile between surface and sea bed.

Diving down, he groped for the great sweep of horn, and drove back up towards the surface: climbing through the water felt like climbing a rungless ladder. But at last he broke surface among the floating debris of garlands, ropes, and cloth that had washed off the bull. He set off for the shore, swimming on his back, and beached the bull on the gentle slope of a sandy bay.

Side by side they lay, the hot sun steaming out of them every last desire to move. The bull stopped snorting and choking, and breathed in big, noisy sighs. Hercules tugged gently at its flicking ears and combed vinestalks and seaweed out of its blue hide with his fingers. For several hours the bull lay slumped in the warm sand, sunbathing. Hercules was wondering how to get it to its feet again when a groan (such as a volcano gives before it erupts) sent a veil of sand shimmering down all the dunes. A man waded down towards Hercules through the hot sand.

He was a tree-like man. The bones of his shins splayed into his shambling feet like trunk into roots. His green hair spread out like a leaf-canopy over his head, shoulders, and back. His mouth was big enough to harbour a barn owl and all its chicks.

'So you're Hercules. To think a brat so small could grieve my father so sore,' he said, grinding the words to pieces between his teeth. 'I am Antaeus, son of Poseidon, and you are an offence in his eyes!'

'I am? An offence to Poseidon. The gods forbid it!' Hercules went towards Antaeus, his arms outstretched in apology. 'I'm sure I never meant it. Have I failed to make sacrifice? Have I missed a festival? I've been so busy, you see.'

Antaeus took hold of his arm, wrist, and elbow, and thrashed Hercules bodily against the ground. The blue bull scrambled to its feet, bellowing resentfully, but Antaeus picked it up and threw it into the shallows, where it wallowed, winded. Thinking that the element of surprise had been his downfall, Hercules got up, adopted the stance of a wrestler and said, 'Come on, then: the Erymanthean Boar was bigger than you!' The next he knew, the sky was wheeling past, full of little lights like fireflies; Antaeus was shaking Hercules like a rug.

Sprawled on the ground, his head in a bush, Hercules found himself looking at the great sinewy tendons of the giant's calf and knee, as once again Antaeus dealt with the charging bull: one-handed he up-ended it and bowled it back down the beach. With the exertion of the throw, each knotty varicose blood-vessel pumped and the veins in his braced legs swelled green, as if succour from the ground were rising up through his legs like sap through a tree. The feet were entrenched deeply in the sand, and over a large area round about the sea-pinks and couch-grasses were withering away. The magma of the earth and the vigour of every spring was feeding the giant with energy.

172

Hercules was still lying prostrate on the ground when Antaeus finished with the bull. He grinned at the sight of Hercules's ashen face, and came scuffing across the dune at a loping run. So inviting was the prospect of crushing Hercules, gut and bone, that he could not resist leaping in the air to stamp down with both feet on the vulnerable spine.

But Hercules met him in mid-air, curving his back and bending his shoulders to intercept Antaeus and carry him, at a run, along the shore. The giant slapped and champed at him, until Hercules thought his ears must have been torn off and all his hair rooted up. But, above his head, the raging voice rose to a higher and higher pitch and the jabbing of knees in his back grew less and less painful. Antaeus reached and strained to put down one finger or scrape one sandal along the ground. But Hercules only held him higher and higher—at arm's length finally. Poseidon's son grew limper and limper, like a dying tree branch.

'Stop!'

The sea gave a convulsive heave, and waves about to break on the shore arched their backs with dismay. Poseidon the Sea-Breaker, the Earthquake-Maker, came wading through the surf like a shepherd stumbling through a flock of sheep. 'Stop it, Hercules! Or by all the rents and tears I've made in the ocean bed, I'll wash Crete off the face of the sea. That's my son you're holding!'

Hercules took a deep breath and closed his eyes. He could feel the clammy presence of the sea god, like a wet sea-fret against his face. 'I know it, Lord Poseidon. I do know it's your son. And if I once put him down, he'll tear me to pieces: I know that, too.'

Poseidon ground his teeth. 'I see it now. I see the likeness. I see why they talk about you as if your throne were already carved on Olympus!'

Like an uprooted plant, Antaeus was wilting fast. He called out whimperingly to his father who hissed with exasperation: 'What price, then, Hercules? I'll give you one of my own sea-horses if you'll set him down!'

'Oh. Thank you,' said Hercules, genuinely and pleasantly surprised. 'I've always wanted a horse. But all I want is a promise. If I put him down, he won't tear me to pieces.'

'By your father's name, I swear it,' said Poseidon.

Hercules was so struck by the oath that he put down Antaeus almost absent-mindedly. Fingers and feet scraped feebly at the ground, then dug in deeply. The hairs on the nape of Antaeus's neck curled, and the sear autumnal yellow of his back throbbed green again. He seemed to swell, as buds and catkins swell. When he grappled Hercules to the ground, it was with all the strength of the jungle that tears down cities with its inexorable creepers. Antaeus bared his teeth to bite Hercules's throat across.

'Antaeus! Leave him! Come away!' snapped Poseidon. 'Would you make a liar of your own father? Look at you. You're a disgrace to me. Didn't you hear my words . . . ?' And mighty Poseidon, the Earth-Shaper, the Earthquake-Maker frogmarched his son, mumbling and muttering, all the way along the beach until they were out of sight.

The blue bull had gone, too. In the place where Hercules had last seen it stood a palomino horse, as golden as the sand and with a mane very like the surf. Even far away from the bright, reflective flicker of the sea that mane kept its strangely blue tinge.

Because nobody expected Hercules to be riding a horse, he was through the city gates and had dismounted in the palace yard before any message could be got to Eurystheus.

So the king was surprised while taking dinner with his children.

Hercules was surprised, too, because he had not realized that Eurystheus had children. He was covered in confusion, for fear his wild appearance might frighten the girls.

But though Eurystheus dived under the table as quick as a rabbit, the princesses of Argos lolled unperturbed on their couches and lobbed apple cores at Hercules. 'What are you doing down there, father?'

'I . . . er . . . dropped some . . . er . . . bread.' Eurystheus emerged in some confusion. 'Blue bull tamed, is it, bond-slave?'

'Tamed, cousin, yes.'

'Cousin? Is that what he calls you, father? Is he allowed to call you *cousin*?' said the oldest girl shrilly. 'You're too soft with the slaves.' She looked out of the window. 'Oh, what a horse! What a beautiful horse! I want it. Is it yours, slave? Slaves don't have horses. I want it.'

'It was a gift from the great sea god Poseidon, mistress,' said Hercules, expressionless behind his beard. 'It was given to me for sparing Antaeus, the Earth-Shaker's . . . '

'I want a horse,' said the child.

Eurystheus, who was hurrying from wall to wall of the room examining maps and lists, wagged his head from side to side impatiently. 'Give Admeta the horse, Hercules. It's hers. I confiscate it. Why are you back so soon? I haven't thought of . . . '

'Don't want *that* horse,' said Admeta piercingly.

'What kind of horse do you want, mistress?' Hercules was quick to ask since he was extremely loath to part with Poseidon's present.

The child bared her teeth at him in a travesty of a

175

grin, and stuck out her tongue. 'Want one of King Diomedes's horses.'

'I'll get you one,' said Hercules in a flash.

'All of them. I want all of them. They're such jolly creatures.'

'I'll get all of them,' said Hercules with a glance over his shoulder. His glance met Eurystheus's as the king cast a look of delight towards his daughter.

'Yes, yes. Get the horses. Diomedes is a barbarian. I never liked the man.'

Hastily Hercules left the room, rejoicing in having kept his beautiful horse.

'Is that the man who keeps you so busy, father? Is that the one you call "that damned Hercules"?'

'That's him, my darling girl. The gods placed a heavy burden on me when they put Hercules in my charge. Finding ways of keeping him busy—finding work that's a fitting punishment for a murderer.'

'Oh, don't you worry about that, father. I can think of *plenty* of tasks for him to do. I can think of lots of terrible torments.'

Her father beamed at her indulgently and settled to his meal again, pausing between courses to pat Admeta on the head. 'Tell me, my darling girl,' he said, 'I've heard about that barbarian Diomedes. But what's so jolly about these horses of his?'

Admeta shrugged and replied through a big mouthful of food, 'Well, they *eat* people, don't they?'

10

Queen of the Amazons

King Diomedes was fond of his horses. Or rather he found them useful. For he murdered and executed so many people that without his stable of hungry horses, the litter of dead bodies would have piled up. Diomedes's realm was spotless. His horses were fat and sleek.

So he objected to the idea of giving up his horses to the Princess Admeta. In fact he told Hercules in no uncertain terms, his sword half out of its scabbard, that he would feed him, live and kicking, to the horses and watch while they ate him. So Hercules accompanied Diomedes as far as the stables before picking him up, sword and all, and throwing him over the door.

First the horses ate Diomedes, then they ate his sword, and all that was left of the king of Thrace was a space in the market square after his subjects happily tore down his statue.

Admeta grew bored with her new pets when she was forbidden to feed them on the palace servants. Eurystheus took one look at their long, gnashing teeth, their malevolent yellow eyes, and shut himself in his brass box with the doors of the palace barred. He told Hercules to drive them to Arcadia and release them there, where the sun god's own horses grazed.

'If he takes them I shall want another present,' said Princess Admeta whiningly.

Eurystheus gnawed his lip. His daughter knew how to bully her father. 'Did you have something in mind, my darling girl?'

'Yes,' she snapped. She was not unlike one of the Thracian horses when her teeth were bared. 'I want . . . I want . . . I want the jewelled belt of the Amazon queen!'

The servant below the throne gave a low whistle, cut short by a blow from the king. Admeta's younger sisters gazed at her in admiration: they could think of nothing so desirable as the jewelled belt of the Amazon queen.

'I wouldn't want a war,' mumbled Eurystheus. 'They're very ferocious women, those Amazons. They're not as gentle and ladylike as you, my darling Admeta. I mean, they'll kill a man just for *being* a man. I mean . . . '

'You mean I can't have it,' said Admeta, nipping off the words with her sharp little teeth.

'Of course . . . if Hercules could fetch it without starting a war . . . '

Hercules's face behind its beard expressed nothing, nothing at all.

'I don't care how he does it, but *I want that belt*!' Something in the tone of Admeta's voice made a little shiver run down the king's spine: it was so much like that nagging little voice that scuttled from cranny to nook of his bedchamber and lurked at the foot of his bed when there was no one there to be seen.

'In the name of Hera—*go and get that belt*!' he stormed

at Hercules, darting towards him. But he ran away again, back to his throne, as Hercules got wearily to his feet.

Hippolyta, queen of the Amazons, was as black as oil—as black as the night sea that seethes unseen on to beaches of black sand. She was tall—taller than a totem mouthing magic under a jungle moon. She moved with the slithering, sliding pride of a black panther. Her eyes were dark—dark like the sun's eclipse at noon or the moon's eclipse at midnight. The smell of her oiled and corded hair was strange as the scent of the black orchid. And round her hips, like the cable of a treasure ship, hung a belt of intricate gold thread. Plaited and whorled and fastened by two clasped golden hands, its strands, like water twisting and turning through rapids, parted to right and left of precious gems then splashed in golden tassels to below her bare knees.

The commanders of defeated armies claimed that the belt of Hippolyta had magic powers, that it could dazzle whole divisions of men. But then war-worn male soldiers defeated by a band of mere *women* tend to make excuses.

Hercules did not make the mistake of underestimating the Amazons. He had heard the rumours of their warrior prowess, and he believed every word. He walked into the Amazon camp without a sword or spear or shield, his hands high above his head in surrender.

Out from their woven huts, out from behind trees, out of heaps of corn husks where they had been sleeping, Amazonian women uncurled like blackest cats. They took up their long, oval shields and short throwing-spears and beat spear on shield in a slow drumming that speeded up to a frenzied clatter. Their prisoners—the men they had set to mending baskets, washing clothes, and sweeping out the huts—crept away with their hands over their ears.

Closer and closer the circle of women moved, jabbing their weapons towards his face and stamping the ground in time with the drumming. The harsh, high shriek of their voices pecked at him. 'What are you?' 'Who sent you?' 'We'll find a use for you!' 'How small he is.' 'What a puny specimen.' 'Too weak to carry a sword, even.' 'What a cowardly weakling.' 'Speak. Admit that you're a worthless man too scared to carry weapons.'

'I am neither man nor woman,' said Hercules. 'I am a story-teller. I came to tell a story to the queen of the Amazons whose name is . . . '

'I know my name,' said a deep, reverberating voice. 'I do not like it to be held in the mouth of a mere man.' The crowd of women parted and there stood Hippolyta, taller than any there and more beautiful than the black-limbed ebon trees. 'Did I send for a story-teller? Did I ask you to come? What do I want with stories?'

'Then I shall leave and take my story with me, for I have no trade where I have no audience. I just thought it would interest you, since it concerns kings and queens and the gods themselves. But no matter . . . Good-day, lady.'

'Wait! Wait a moment.'

An untold story is like a locked chest without a key. It tantalizes. It tempts. From the icy lands of snow and whale to the sweating jungle shade, it is valued the world over.

'Maybe I've heard it,' said Hippolyta sceptically.

'Kill me if you have,' said Hercules. And a few moments later he was seated on a rug of zebra skin while Hippolyta reclined on a couch of spotted hide in the privacy of her cool, dark hut.

Hercules began to tell his own life story, and while Hippolyta listened, her warrior women sulked outside, swatting at tedious flies with their large, listless hands.

In the gaping holes between the tree-tops, the moisture from the humid leaves dripped like saliva, and the sweltering sun made a steamy rainbow that intertwined with the creepers and dangling vines. Down this rainbow came Hera, queen of the gods, her black hair close-cloaking her sallow body. She came down, hand-over-hand, so slowly, so silently that the dozing women thought they were dreaming her . . .

'So the worthless man was enslaved to this small and spiteful king as a punishment, and sent here and there across the face of the wide Earth to kill monsters and capture great prizes and do unpleasant tasks. He had no part in deciding the tasks, no right to refuse them. No profit or joy came to him by his Labours. To fail or refuse would be death. So he killed the Hydra, he cleaned the Augean stables, and he captured the golden stag of Cerynia. All might have gone well but for his last, most fearful and most wicked task. He was ordered to fetch—imagine it!—the belt of the queen of the Amazons for the king's spoilt daughter!'

He shot a glance at Hippolyta. Her hands moved involuntarily to her belt, then she raised herself along the couch like a lion about to spring. She reached for her throwing spear and lifted it over one shoulder. Then the purple shadows of her black face scattered in a laugh. 'Hercules! What gall! What a bare-faced, shameless trickster you are!' she cried, tossing her corded hair far down her back. 'But you lied to me.'

'Not a word, lady, on my life!'

'Oh yes you did. Don't deny it. You said that you were

unremarkable and you are nothing of the kind!' and she made a cat-like leap on to the zebra rug beside him. 'You're extraordinary. Quite outstanding, for a man.'

'Then you'll give me the belt?'

'I do believe I will—and afterwards I'll come and take it back and teach that spiteful little king not to make a plaything for his children out of a brave and noble story-teller!' She began to unclasp the belt.

Hera whispered softer than the sound of the caterpillars dropping through the trees, pressing her lips against the delicate ears of the warrior women. 'Stir yourselves! Since when did you let a MAN creep in to the royal hut of your beloved queen? Think! Ask yourself! What weapons did he have hidden beneath that lionskin? What poisons are smeared on those hairy arms? With his bare hands he murdered his wife and all his little daughters. And I tell you, Hercules has come here to murder your queen and steal her golden belt! What will become of the Amazons when their queen is dead? Will you let squat Hercules make you his slaves and dancing girls. Quick! Quick! Kill him quickly or Hippolyta is lost!'

Just as Hippolyta was about to lay the jewelled belt in Hercules's hands, the fibrous walls of the hut were ripped to shreds by axes and jabbing spears. The warrior women came through the walls, came through the reeded roof, crammed the sunny doorway, hooting and shrieking their bloodcurdling war-cries.

One leapt directly on to Hercules. All he could do to defend himself was to wrap both arms round her so that her hands were pinned to her sides and her body shielded him against the thrusting spears. The women hesitated rather than plunge their weapons through the woman's body. Seeing how his armful of Amazon protected him,

Hercules backed through the door. Then slinging the warrior across his back, he ran. He did not stop running until the shrieking of the deep-jungle parrots all around drowned out the shrieks from behind him.

'What's your name?' he said as he ran.

'I'll die before I tell you that!' The woman's voice came jolting out of her.

'What's your name? Do tell me.'

'Never! Now put me down,' and she bit into him.

'Ow! Stop that! Why did you all attack me back there? I meant no harm, I swear it!'

'No harm? Ha! You're a filthy assassin and a thief!'

'Says who?'

'Says . . . says . . . I don't know who says it . . . The Amazons say it. I, General Menalippe, say it.'

Suddenly, out of a tree, directly in his path, a long sinuous figure dropped down. It was Hippolyta who had outrun her women, outrun Hercules, outrun her good nature. 'My women say you were planning to kill me.'

'That's a lie.'

'Women don't lie. Men lie,' hissed Hippolyta.

Hercules stood General Menalippe down in front of him as a shield, one arm round her body, one arm round her throat.

'That's a dirty trick,' said Hippolyta. 'How typical of a man!'

'You mean women aren't afraid to die?'

'Absolutely not! We scorn death!'

The general wriggled in Hercules's arms, but he had tight hold of her. Hippolyta's jabbing spear could not pierce Hercules without killing Menalippe. He could feel the hostage trembling from head to foot. 'Do you scorn death, Menalippe?' he said in her ear.

'Let me go!' she sobbed.

183

'What is the life of an Amazon worth, madam?' he asked the queen.

'More than the life of a man.'

'More than a tin belt, then. That's all I ask. Give it to me and I'll let her go.'

Queen Hippolyta slowly unclasped the belt one-handed, the other hand still brandishing her spear. She lashed at him with the golden tassels and they wrapped around his arm and hand.

'You are deceived in me, madam. I never meant you harm. The story I told you was true. I hope one day you will believe me. Now, I shall take General Menalippe here with me and set her free when I reach the sea-shore safely.'

'Cowardly man.'

And as Hercules ran off through the trees with Menalippe slung across his unprotected back, he could hear Hippolyta's taunts following him. 'Cowardly man! Cowardly man!'

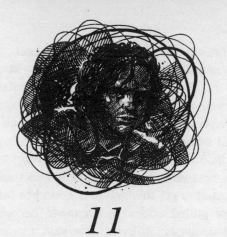

11

Holding up Heaven

'It's simple,' said Admeta, primping up and down in front of a mirror. 'It's so simple, I don't know why you haven't thought of it before.' The belt of Hippolyta, hitched up in both hands, was much too broad for her hips, and the weight of it pulled her robe out of shape. Its tassels trailed on the floor between her feet, though all the servants in Argos were quick to admire her finery. 'If you can't be rid of him, all you have to do is to set him an impossible task and then execute him for failing.'

'How "impossible"? I keep doing that,' whined Eurystheus.

'Well . . . *impossible*. I mean tell him to fly without wings, or walk on water, or climb up a sunbeam. Tell him to go to the Red Island by way of dry land . . . Look what your precious Hercules has done now, father! This nasty old belt has snagged my favourite dress!'

Eurystheus was peering short-sightedly at the maps on the wall. 'Red Island . . . Red Island,' he mumbled. 'Where is this Red Island, daughter dear?'

Admeta stamped her foot in irritation. 'Oh, *Daddy*! You're so *stupid*. The Red Island doesn't exist. That's the whole point! It's the place in the fairy tales where the giant Geryon and his two-headed dog guard the magic oxen. Everybody knows that story. Everyone knows the Red Island doesn't exist.'

Eurystheus looked crestfallen. It was a long time before the reasoning behind Admeta's plot sank in. 'You mean he *couldn't* get there so he's bound to fail.'

Admeta pulled a face which made her small features still more shrewish. 'Brilliant,' she said.

The king flinched under his daughter's rudeness, but only as the great bison flinches under the peck of birds. He sent for Hercules.

It was perhaps fortunate that Hercules had never heard the fairy tale of Geryon and his oxen. He did not know that the Red Island was the invention of mothers to frighten their naughty children: 'Behave now or Geryon and his two-headed dog will come and carry you away to the Red Island.' He set off willingly enough to fetch back the giant oxen, and he travelled south and he searched.

And he searched and he searched and he searched. And every time he asked for directions, people laughed at him but would not say why. At long last he sat on the southern beach, in the shadow of Mount Abyla, his reins over his shoulder, and he threw irritable stones at the tedious, crawling sea.

'Whaaa?' screamed the seagulls.

'I'm looking for the Red Island and the Giant Geryon!' called Hercules to the seagulls.

'Yeah, yeah,' shrieked the seagulls, darting out to sea along the blood-red line of the setting sun.

He shielded his eyes against the glare and saw that indeed the whole bulk of Africa spread out on the far side of the straits glowed red beneath the setting sun. Hercules was not fond of swimming. He considered the geography for some time—the tall mountain of Abyla behind him and the high profile of Mount Calpe on the far shore. Then, in order to reach the mythical Red Island, he did what men can only do in fairy tales. He leaned his shoulder against Abyla and he pushed. He pushed till the sweat stood in the pores of his skin and bellowed. He pushed till his muscles plaited and replaited. He pushed till the soles of his feet gouged deep gorges in the ground. He pushed till his eyeballs hammered on his lids. He pushed till the rocks of Abyla dented and grooved his flesh and cut through to the bone.

Abyla leaned over. It ducked its granite head which Hercules held down with his feet like the neck of a defeated opponent. Then he reached out with both hands and pulled on the peak of Calpe. He pulled until his shoulderblades stood out like the remnants of wings. He pulled until his spine bowed through the hairs of his back. He pulled until his handprints sank deep in the peak of Calpe. He pulled until the two mountain peaks clashed beneath him and an arch greater than any bridge in the history of Man spanned the Straits of Gibraltar.

No sooner was he across than a man with three bodies stumbled up the slopes of Calpe towards him. Geryon walked like a trio of drunken men leaning against each other for support. His six feet tripped each other up and his six hands waved to steady him. Behind him ran a two-headed dog of awesome size, though its need to smell each bush and tree with both noses made it lag far behind.

'People say I don't exist,' ranted Geryon, clawing his way up the hillside in a hysteria of rage. 'Now they'll see. Now they'll find a mangled body floating in the sea and say—no one could have done that but Gery—oh!' One foot tripped another, a third dislodged the stone four

187

of his hands were holding on to. The boulder overturned. Geryon fell backwards. As he scrabbled and fell, fell and scrabbled, he started a landslip that triggered an avalanche that swallowed up both ogre and ravening dog and stopped short only a few paces from a herd of glossy oxen grazing in the valley below.

Quickly, Hercules herded them together. The join between Calpe and Abyla was already groaning like the ice floes that split in spring. No sooner had he driven the cattle to the mainland, than the peaks sprang apart.

And those who saw it, or heard of it, told a new story to their wayward, sleepy children—'Bed now, or Hercules will come and do to you what he did to Geryon.' They renamed the twin mountains The Pillars of Hercules.

'But he doesn't exist!' said Eurystheus from inside his box.

'No, he doesn't any more,' said Hercules, somewhat confused, 'though I hope you won't believe what people are saying. I never laid a finger on him. He just fell.'

'But he doesn't exist,' said Eurystheus. 'Neither does his dog.'

'I'm sorry about the dog,' said Hercules, and utterly bewildered he left the audience chamber and the king of Argos in his brass hidey-hole muttering, 'Doesn't exist. Doesn't exist. Doesn't exist.'

Outside in the garden, a hundred and thirty-two giant oxen chewed on the flowers.

The obnoxious Princess Admeta was her own undoing. When Eurystheus was at his wits' end wondering what to do with a hundred and thirty-two giant oxen, she gave no thought at all to the problem. She was obsessed with a new idea.

'I know what Hercules can get me! I've been reading about them in religious education,' she said shrilly through a mouthful of shelled nuts. Just as the servants succeeded in mustering the cattle in one place, her piercing voice scattered them again. They startled the Cerynian deer out of the laurel walk and it leapt across a pile of terracotta pots, smashing them.

'What can Hercules bring you? Is it live?' asked the king wearily.

'No.'

'Is it dangerous?'

'No.'

'Is it big?'

'No!'

'Very well, then, my darling dear. You tell him. Only first tell him to come and take these oxen away.'

Admeta did not bother to tell Hercules to help with the cattle. She was in too much of a hurry to have her own way. 'Come and kneel here, slave,' she commanded, perched on the edge of her father's throne and pointing at the floor. 'You're to do everything I tell you from now on. Father says so. I command you to bring me the Apples of the Hesperides!'

'But, mistress! They belong to Zeus, father of all g—'

'Don't argue. I'll have you flogged if you argue.'

' . . . the goddess Hera gave them to Zeus on the day they were married!'

'Servants! Come here this instant and throw this disobedient dog out of the city, and don't let him back in unless he brings what I told him.'

Hercules looked around for the king, but he was out-of-doors, struggling with the oxen. There was nothing to be done—no one he could appeal to for common sense. 'Shouldn't I go and help with the cattle?' said Hercules anxiously.

'You're just trying to put off going. You're frightened of the dragon, aren't you? That's your trouble,' sneered the princess. 'Take your horrible person out of my sight this instant. You make my eyes dirty just looking at you.'

His face, behind his beard, showed nothing, nothing at all. But once outside the palace, Hercules leapt on to his sea-horse with a great savage cry and galloped all the way back to the Pillars of Hercules. He leapt the Straits of Gibraltar into distant Africa. He ploughed on beyond the land of the Amazons to the unmapped undercurve of the world's fat Equator.

There it was so hot that the sea-horse of Poseidon beneath him dissolved into steam and let him fall, on hands and knees, on to a desert plain. He lifted his hands in the air and cried: 'Oh, you gods, what can I do? Must I disobey the master you bound me to? Or must I steal from the gods themselves? Those apples are the property of Zeus the Almighty—his wedding present from Hera his bride!'

From very few points on the Earth's wrinkled landscape would the words of Hercules have failed to reach heaven. But now they came echoing back off the shoulder of a vast mountain. It was late evening. The shape of the mountain was hard to make out against the darkness of the sky. It was simply a shape bare of stars, a shape not unlike a crouching man.

'Quiet down there! A little peace and quiet, if you please. Take my advice and don't appeal against your fate to the gods. Reasonableness and pity are in short supply on the slopes of Olympus. I see the gods every day, squabbling, and gambling with the lives of men. My head is on a level with the highest terraces of Olympus, you see.'

'Who are you?' whispered Hercules as sudden tropical nightfall smothered him like a blanket.

'I am Atlas. Strange that you should bump into me, so to speak.'

'Atlas? The father of the Hesperides? The giant? But I can't see you! Where are you? It's so dark!'

'People mistake me,' said Atlas in a vague, baleful voice. 'They take me for a mountain. Earth and loam and rocks. Can you believe that? Earth and loam and rocks.'

Hercules's mind was whirling. 'Do you visit your daughters often?'

'Don't talk nonsense, boy! How can I go anywhere? I have to stand here and hold up the sky. You think *your* fate is hard? You should try this one day.'

'All right,' said Hercules, his eyes gradually becoming accustomed to the dark. 'I'll stand in for you. You deserve a rest.'

'You?' The ground rocked with laughter, and a star or two fell with green luminosity off the shoulders of the giant Atlas.

'I am Hercules, the son of Zeus.'

Jungle noises, whistles, screeches, and hoots filled up the very long pause. 'Are you? Are you, indeed?'

'Oh, but now I think of it, I can't. I must search out the Gardens of the Hesperides and ask for the golden apples that hang there.'

'Do you know where they are?'

'No,' said Hercules.

'Do you know what the dragon would do to you before you could pick the apples?'

'No, what? I'm not good with dragons. Are you? Do you know the dragon in question?'

'Oh, I knew him as a lizard, boy. He'd do anything for me. Splendid dragon. About this matter of holding up . . .'

'So you could pick the apples of Zeus without any difficulty. Unlike me.'

Again there was a long, cacophanous silence and then, 'See here, Hercules. What say I go and get these apples for you, while you hold up heaven for a while.'

'Done,' said Hercules, quickly sealing the bargain.

Rather than offend the gods in the twelfth and final year of his Labours, Hercules would willingly have lifted the Earth itself in his teeth and juggled with the planets. That was why he had offered to take Atlas's place. But as he crouched in the lee of towering Atlas and let the giant lower the sky's mass on to his shoulders, he did wonder whether the load would crush him to death on the spot.

The first touch of the sky was soft and velvety, though the stars' heat pricked, and meteorite dust blasted his skin like a sandstorm. It seemed bearable at first, but Atlas's hands were still taking the weight. As he let go, it was not like a weight but like a pushing, a pressing, a bearing down—like the force of gravity that pins men to the spinning Earth like a collection of butterflies, but doubled and redoubled and full of burning stars. Frozen comets ricocheted past his head. The muscles of his back plaited and replaited; the soles of his feet sank into the ground; his eyeballs hammered against his lids, and the sweat burst from his eye sockets. The blood roared in his ears; the branching blood vessels of his throat throbbed like serpents, and the vertebrae of his back ground together with the sound of pain. And all the while, the stars stubbed themselves out against his back like so many candles. Inside him, his big heart beat with such an agony of effort that far away on Olympus the gods thought a distant door had been left to bang.

Atlas went to the Gardens of the Hesperides—that realm of paradise beneath the setting sun, where a blood-red tide breaks against salmon pink shores. The

192

air is combed with fingers of rosy cloud, and the green flash of sunset leafs out the trees where hang the apples of Hera. A dragon scaled blue-green coils its sheen around the trunks of milk-white wood, and the sun and the moon hang at either end of heaven for ever and ever and ever.

He had no difficulty in taking the apples given by Hera to Zeus on their wedding day. His daughters and his dragon made no complaint, such was their delight at seeing him free of his burden of sky. His stoop straightened. His muscles eased with creaking noises like the graunching of icebergs, and for the first time in two thousand years, he looked around him at a landscape other than the sear African plain. Atlas stretched, arching his scarred back. A flock of birds flew past his head, wheeling and gliding for no purpose but to celebrate their freedom. The muscle-bound sea strained against its chaining tides. Atlas felt good to be free.

Holding the apples like two golden planets in the palm of one hand, Atlas went back to the central plains of Africa and saw the antelope herds bound tree-high, and the solitary jackals pattering over their limitless territories. He envied their freedom.

Hercules saw him coming, though his face was so clenched with pain that he could barely see or hear or breathe. His legs had buckled, his knees were resting on the sharp rocks and spiky shrub. The sky had sagged just a little, and there and here stars kindled the tallest trees of the highest mountains. Sweat soaked the skin of the Nemean lion and dripped off its snout. Asteroids thudded into his head and chest. Hercules held his life between his grinding teeth and thanked the gods in his heart for the sight of Atlas coming back.

'I've given the matter some thought,' said Atlas, sitting down in front of Hercules and studying his face with a mixture of contempt and pleasure. 'I've lost the taste for holding up the heavens. Since you've made such a fine job of standing in for me, I think I shall let you go on doing it.'

12

Digging up Hell

'I 'll deliver these apples to this little king of yours. I'm sure he'll find some way of rewarding me. It's the least I can do for you, after all.'

Hercules's tongue was so dry that it would not stir at first. His throat could only croak, 'Willingly. This is less of a burden than the Labours Eurystheus set me to.'

Atlas was startled. 'You don't mind?'

'Not at all. Pleasure. Easy work. Peaceful,' grunted Hercules in agony. 'One thing. Cloth. Cloth pad . . . across shoulders. Stars. Keep burning. Just lift . . . a moment . . . while I put a pad . . . ' All the major organs of his body seemed about to burst.

Obligingly Atlas folded a cloth pad out of his loin cloth. 'How shall we do this without dropping heaven?'

'You stand . . . beside. Take the weight . . . for a moment. Slip in pad. Roll heaven . . . back on to . . . me.'

So Atlas crawled in under the sagging skies, held a mere fathom off the ground by Hercules's cracking body. He took the weight, and Hercules took the apples out of his hands while he did so . . . then threw himself on his face and rolled out from under. 'I'm sorry, friend. I shall pity you till the day I die, but I am bound in service to King Eurystheus for another two days. I can't idle his time away holding up heaven. Each man to his own task.'

Atlas gave a great roar of outrage and agony, doomed to continue for a thousand years and a thousand more pinned between heaven and Earth. But Hercules had already run so far and so fast, clutching the golden globes to his chest that the giant's cry sounded in his ears like distant thunder rolling among the Atlas mountains.

King Eurystheus felt it at the foot of his bed as he woke— a hard, round shape like a pebble. 'Where is Hercules?' it said. 'Where have you sent him this time?' He pulled down the covers, but could find nothing there. He did not answer the question.

He put his hand into his pocket at breakfast time, and a small, slithering grass snake crept through his fingers. 'Have you failed me, Eurystheus?' it asked. 'Is he suffering?'

He cut open his loaf of bread, and out flew a crow bigger and blacker than a cat, and buffeted against his face. 'His time is almost up. Will you let him escape his doom alive? Will you rob me of my revenge?' croaked the crow and sat on his shoulder and could not be dislodged.

When the servants announced Hercules, the king tried to say he was busy, that he could not see Hercules, that he would see him tomorrow. But the crow sank its talons into his shoulder and whispered in his ear, 'Tomorrow Hercules's sentence is finished. He'll be free. He'll go back to Thebes alive. He'll escape, you fool!'

So Hercules was admitted. 'I have brought what I was told to bring,' he said.

'Good, good. Fine. Just keep them. I don't want them now. I don't have anywhere to put them . . . '

Then Admeta burst into the room. 'Hercules! Have you got them? Where are my apples? Give me my apples *at once*, do you hear?'

When the crow on the king's shoulder saw the golden apples—her own present to the Almighty Zeus on the day of their marriage, her rage almost split her in two. 'How dare you! What manner of man are you, Eurystheus? What manner of brat have you spawned?' She flew in his face and tore out his hair. He ran to his brass box, but it was no protection from the anger of the queen of the gods. She filled it to the brim with scorpions, and chased him round the room with fire. She sent ravens and bats to carry Admeta in their claws to the smallest and loneliest outcrop of rock in all the wide oceans, and muddied the waters all around it so that she might never see her own reflection.

His other daughters asked Eurystheus, as he sat with his threadbare head in his hands, 'What shall Hercules do next? Can he fetch something for us now? Tomorrow he'll be free. Won't you tell him to do anything else before he goes?'

The king smashed all the crockery off the table top, and the shards danced and spun across the floor. 'That name! Always that name! It haunts me! I never want to hear his name again, do you hear me? To hell with Hercules, I say. To hell with him!' Abruptly he lifted his head, and in an ape-like, humourless grin bared his teeth. 'Yes. That's it. That'll make him sorry he stayed alive all these twelve years. Tell the wretch to go to hell—to the Realm of Shadows—and fetch back the dog Cerberus who guards the gates of the City of the Dead. And have him swear to complete the task however long it takes.'

Hercules swore.

He cursed, too, and wept, and struck himself on the forehead with a clenched fist. 'So close to my time! So near to my freedom! If my cousin had been merciful he would have set me to this Labour first and not last. To go to the Underworld so weary and old! Oh, you gods, I would rather have gone a young man, to that place no man ever leaves! Now I shall be weary throughout eternity, and start my stay by antagonizing the king of the Dead and stealing his faithful dog.'

All day as he travelled down to the sea, all night as he sailed a fast, black ship single-handedly through the maze of sea-lanes, he wept aloud and rocked his square body on its haunches, and remembered the events that had set him on the path to the Underworld. And in the morning, when the dawn broke like an egg and filled his boat with yellow sunlight, he found he was not alone.

'Your doom is over, Hercules,' said Pallas Athene, tall goddess of the grey eyes.

'Your twelve years are completed,' said Hermes, messenger of the gods, reclining along a cross-tree of the mast.

'But I've sworn . . . ' began Hercules, unmanned by a sudden stab of hope.

'We know what you have sworn, Hercules. That's why we are here—to accompany you to the Underworld and speak to Pluto on your behalf.'

'Is there a chance, then? That he'll listen? I don't mind saying it: I'm more afraid of angering Pluto than any other god, since I have to spend all eternity in his Realm of Shadows.'

Athene blinked slowly. 'He has his good days . . . '

' . . . and his bad days,' said Hermes, folding his hands behind his head and gazing up at the sky. He kept from rolling off the spar with little flickerings of his winged feet. 'The thing about Pluto is that he's an inveterate gambler. You recollect the business with Orpheus and Eurydice? Pluto told Orpheus, yes, you can have your wife back from the dead if you can climb all the way back to the Land of the Living without looking back at her.'

'What happened?' said Hercules.

'Ah well . . . that was one bet Pluto won. Orpheus looked back.'

'Oh, now you've really cheered him up,' said Athene, jabbing her spear at Hermes in vexation. 'The less we dwell on Orpheus the better, I think.'

The Realm of Shadows has a thousand entrances—some gaping cave-mouths in the seashore, some ragged holes at the end of dark sea-lanes, some bottomless shafts concealed by heather from the unwary traveller, some gouged out by the feet of waterfalls. Hercules and his immortal guides approached by way of a giant wound in the flank of Mount Taenarus in Laconia. The passage was lit by the flickering of white bats which had lived for generations without ever finding their way out to the daylight. The tuneless music of water dripped from the high roof.

They paid the ferryman to row them, all three, across the great river Styx which flows between Life and Death and is neither land nor sea, bone nor blood, but dark cartilage twisting through the body of the Earth.

They disembarked at the cold wharf where all journeys end and none begin. And they reached the doors of Hades. There they could go no further, because a dog with three heads stood rending at the air with ravenous jaws. All the passageways and entrances of the Realm of Shadows met in this one place. Looking in all directions at once, Cerberus guarded the Underworld from all but the Dead.

Even Hermes would not go on. Even Athene came to a halt. When Cerberus saw them, he hurled himself to the bitter end of the three chains that bound his three separate necks. One snapped. One the dog bit through. The third he was grinding between jagged teeth when Pluto himself came patrolling. Such was the size of the god of the Dead that he took Cerberus by the scruff of two necks and held him pinned between his immortal knees. 'Sister! Brother! Why do you bring this mortal living man where none but the dead thrive?'

'To make a wager with you,' said Hermes quickly. 'This is Hercules, Prince of Thebes . . . '

'Ah! So! It is you who is responsible for this great pouring in of monsters and despots. These last twelve years they've trooped down to my dens with your name on their lips. What a slayer of giants you turned out to be! One day, when your time is done and you come this way with funeral pennies on your eyes to pay the ferryman, what earthquakes and upheavals there'll be! Your family, the people you've stolen from, beasts and monsters galore—all with scores to settle . . . ' This prospect of Hercules's fate seemed to put Pluto in an excellent mood. 'So you're the famous Hercules, are you? Small, aren't you?'

'Not too small to carry Cerberus back to the Land of the Living,' said Athene.

Pluto's face stiffened. 'You expect me to give him my dog? You're mad.'

'I don't want to keep him,' said Hercules quickly. 'I only want to borrow him. I can bring him back within the day . . . I bet you I can.'

'You and who else?' Pluto snorted with derision. His eyes gleamed. The temptation of the bet was working in his blood. 'All right, then . . . But you gods keep out of this. If this Hercules sprog can carry off Cerberus without help and without weapons and without harm, and fetch him back again, I'll let him. For the sport of it.'

Athene looked at Hermes uneasily. He shrugged. 'We've done what we can. Hercules must save his own skin now.'

The god of the Underworld loosed the chain on the third neck of the giant dog, and opened his knees just enough to let the beast slip out and lunge at Hercules.

Suddenly, a noise sweeter than the continual dripping of water through stone echoed hauntingly off every facet of the rocky Underworld. The six ears of Cerberus twitched. Its single tail thumped on the floor. Someone was playing a lute.

It was Linus, Hercules's music teacher, his body no more than a ragged shred of air, sitting at the head of a nearby passageway, poring over a lute strung with spectra of light. He had carved it out of the roots of trees grown down as deep as the Underworld itself. Round about him stood all Hercules's little children, no older than on the day he had killed them. None of them looked up: it was as if they were unaware of the intruders into their darkness. When Hercules called out to them, they did not lift their heads, but stared intently at Linus's hands, studying his skill.

The music confused and pleasured Cerberus, the giant hound, but not Hercules. He was overwhelmed by remembered sorrows. He lifted the dog, without caring whether or not it turned on him, and lumbered up the cavernous passageway. Not until the sweet tragedy of the music was fading far behind him did he begin to realize what he had done, and Cerberus to realize what was happening to him. The great hound of the Underworld stirred restlessly and snapped with its three giant heads at the walls of rock speeding by. Hercules filled his lungs and sang at the top of his voice all the lullabies his mother had ever sung, all the loud laments he had heard at funerals, all the shanties he had ever heard sailors sing as they hauled up sails cross-tree-high. Cross-tree-high, the hound of hell howled with all its three heads, then they reached sunlight. The dog's subterranean eyes had strained since puppyhood to see through the gloom of the Underworld. Now it gave a violent shudder and pulled in all its heads.

On the voyage from Laconia to Argos, it hung its three heads over the side of the boat and whined, and its six eyes turned a bilious green. It growled and trembled and had only just recovered its spirits when it reached the palace of Eurystheus.

13

A Wedding Gift

'Here it is, but I have to take it back,' said Hercules, opening the door of the throne room and loosing Cerberus into the presence of King Eurystheus.

When he opened the door again an hour later, the hound of hell lay sprawled on its side like a wrecked whale, its paws resting velvety on the dais. Cerberus filled the room. He lay very, very still. 'What's the matter with him?' said Hercules, panic-stricken. 'Eurystheus, what have you done to Pluto's dog? The gods help us both in the after-life if you've hurt Pluto's dog! Eurystheus?'

But there was no sign of Eurystheus, nor of his brass box, nor of his throne, nor his table set for dinner—nor the lamps nor the litter of furniture, nor the maps on the wall of Cerynia, Thrace, Nemea, and Elis. There was just Cerberus.

As Hercules knelt down beside the hound of hell, thinking to find its fur cold, its breath stopped, it gave a great sigh with two of its heads, whiffled its three noses and scratched itself in its sleep. Picking it up and carefully negotiating the door so as not to wake it, Hercules set off for Laconia once more.

Cerberus seemed strangely heavier on the return trip, and slept all the way. Hercules set him down again in the dank groove the dog had worn, over the years, with his clawing and lunging. He was just re-knotting the chains around the three necks when a young man came running. His feet made no noise of footsteps, because, of course, he had only the gauzy traces of his earthly body.

'Go quickly, Hercules! Go before Pluto knows you're here!'

'But I've brought back his dog—I wagered with Pluto that I could . . . '

'I know all that. Everybody here has heard about it. But don't you know how much Pluto hates to lose a bet? He'll never forgive you for succeeding—never forgive you!' Cerberus whiffled and stretched and barked once or twice in his sleep. 'Quickly! You must go! . . . But, Hercules . . . '

'What?'

'My name's Meleager. I have a sister in the land of the living . . . '

'What about her? Does she need help? I'll help if I can.' Hercules was barely listening: his mind was still running on the injustice of a gambler who refuses to lose a bet.

'Not help exactly, Hercules. She needs a husband. And unless I'm completely wrong in my information, you need a wife . . . No, don't interrupt. There isn't time. Ever since the rumours of your Labours began to blow round hell, I've been turning it over in my mind—you and she should marry. Our father is Aeneus—surely you've heard of him! It's a fine family, ours. And now I'm dead before my time, there's nothing I can do to keep my family name from drooping—yes, sir, drooping from fame to forgottenness . . . I know, I know, you think you'll never marry again because of what happened to your first wife. But just visit her, will you? Please just do me the favour of looking her over. She's followed all your exploits. She's always admired you without even seeing you! Don't say no! Don't say anything! Just go!'

A sudden noise startled Cerberus fully awake. Pluto came lunging down the corridors of the Underworld pointing a finger at Hercules: *'Where's my dog?'*

Cerberus jumped up, one head yelping with delight, the others snarling at Hercules and Meleager. It promptly fell over again with a brass-like clank.

'What have you done to my dog!' Pluto's voice climbed towards hysteria.

'Nothing, I swear . . . ' Hercules began to back away.

'Go,' whispered Meleager. 'You won't win an argument.'

'What have you been feeding him?' Pluto's voice echoed off a thousand rock faces.

'Nothing!' called Hercules as he ran. 'Nothing, I swear!'

Pluto pursued him a few steps, then turned back to attend to his dog. 'I can wait, boy,' he said over his shoulder. 'The faster you run, the sooner you'll be back here with me. Every mortal comes here in the end. I'll wait. I'll make a fitting reception for you when you come back with pennies on your eyes and a shroud in place of that lionskin. I'll teach you for shaming me in front of Athene and Hermes! I'll give you to Cerberus for a bone to chew on. My word on it but I will! *What's he been eating?'*

Hercules burst into the painful sunlight and threw himself down on the grassy slopes of Mount Laconia and tore his hair. Which way to go? To Argos? His twelve years of bondage were over. Why go back? Why go back to Thebes? His doom would still be written on the wall, and there would be no wife or children waiting there to greet him, nothing to do but grow old and await his certain appointment with Pluto. Why wander the world in search of adventure? One too many adventures would inevitably bring his brief, mortal life to an end. Whichever way he looked, Death grinned at him with as many faces as Cerberus and the Hydra put together. Despair griped at him: it was harder to bear than the weight of the stars had been on his back.

Then, at a distance, he heard a terrible scream—a scream that froze his blood and emptied his head of all its questions. He ran towards the sound, and found that not one day, not two days, but three days of running brought him to the source of the scream.

He could not make out the sight at first, for the spot ahead was seething with the jerky fluttering of birds which spiralled into the air as Hercules approached. Beneath their circling, a man lay spread-eagled across a rock on his back, chained hand and foot. The gaping wound in his side should have meant that he was dead. But the heaving arch of his ribcage and the kicking of his legs and above all that terrible repeated scream proved that Prometheus was still tormented with life.

'Who did this to you?' Hercules flailed at the repulsive eagles that hovered insolently beyond reach of his fists. From their beaks dangled red pieces of liver.

'It is my punishment,' gasped Prometheus, slumped in the momentary relief from pain. 'I who stole the secret of fire from the gods must lie here for all eternity and have my liver eaten out by eagles. Oh, gods! Never to die! Never to die! Never to be out of the blazing sun and the flies and the freezing night and the rending of the birds!'

An eagle dived impudently past Hercules's head and snatched a sliver of bloody purple from within Prometheus's side. The scream struck Hercules like a blow and made him stagger with grief. He tore off the

Nemean lionskin and engulfed in its folds all the bloodthirsty birds. He smashed the bundle against the ground and jumped on it and shook out the feathers.

Prometheus laid back his tormented head and laughed. 'More will come. The world has more eagles than you have seconds in your life, friend, but I thank you for pitying me.'

Hercules uttered a subhuman groan and, laying his hands to the chains which bound Prometheus he tore them out of the ground, snapped them off at the wrist, and hurled them so high into the sky that they were lost from sight. 'That for the doom of the gods! If they have no more pity than this, I defy them! I despise them! Their cruelty is worse than Diomedes of Thrace or the king of Elis or the Erymanthean pig! One day I must die and keep my appointed meeting with Pluto. But until I do, I'll find what joy there is in this world and defy all you vicious Immortals!'

Prometheus rolled off the rock and crouched beside it, shielding his wounded body with arms and legs made useless by a thousand years of immobility. 'Tell me your name, boy, that I may shame the gods with it wherever I go. How can you break the unbreakable? How can you end the everlasting? For my chains were unbreakable and my doom was everlasting. Who are you?'

'I am Hercules, son of Zeus—but never till today was I ashamed of my origins.'

All meekness, all penitence, all devout fear left Hercules on that day, and he moved under heaven like a scorpion, full of rage.

He no longer saw good cause to be unhappy, when the Underworld gaped with the promise of everlasting misery. So one lonely night he said to himself, 'Why not? Why not go and see Meleager's sister? Perhaps there's a little shred of happiness for Hercules somewhere on this Earth.' And he got up then and there and travelled to the ancestral lands of Aeneus.

None too soon. For he arrived on the day that Deianeira was to be married to a bull.

It was unfortunate, the matter of the bull. There were so many suitors for the hand of Deianeira—who was extremely beautiful—that it had been decided that they should fight for her. One of the suitors, a river god, had taken the unfair advantage of turning himself into a bull and had carried the day. When Hercules arrived, however, he wrestled the bull to a standstill, tore off one of its horns, and there he was—married to Deianeira. It was done without a thought, and none the worse for that, for who ever chose a wife or a husband by reasoned thinking?

This last-moment alternative to a bull came as a great relief to Deianeira. In fact there was no one on the whole wrinkled face of the Earth whom she would rather have married than Hercules. Hercules was famous. Hercules was the son of a god. To marry Hercules was a greater thing to the daughter of warrior Aeneus than to win the hand of a king. True, Hercules was more of a pagan than she had realized, and would not offer up a sacrifice in celebration of his wedding. But after the wedding, when she was alone, she waded into the brook where Hercules had thrown the broken bull-horn, and filled it with fruit and grain from the wedding feast, and laid it on the altar. 'Goddess of Plenty, I offer you this horn of abundance that my happiness may always overflow as it does today and as this horn overflows with good things.'

There was a clatter of hooves behind her, and she noticed that a centaur stood at the door of the temple watching her. Across its back hung a semi-circular blanket of fluffy white wool embroidered with gold. She smiled, and the centaur bowed from the flanks and slipped away. She did not see him again until later.

It was time for bride and groom to leave the wedding feast and travel to the solitude of old Aeneus's home on the far side of the River Evenus. High in the Olympian mountains, it had been raining, and the river was swollen—swollen so high that the torrent had carried away the only bridge. Deianeira was eager to swim across, but Hercules would not hear of it.

Suddenly the centaur was there again beside them. 'Permit me to carry your wife across,' he said. 'You, Hercules, who was taught by a centaur, know what strength there is in our legs.'

So Deiancira straddled the beautiful blanket, and the centaur lowered himself with great elegance into the rushing water.

'Now come with me, and I'll spill horns of plenty in your lap,' he said to his rider in a low voice full of sudden menace.

'No! Who are you?' said the bride in alarm.

'I am Nessus the centaur. I came too late for the competition, or I would have beaten your other so-called suitors. A woman doesn't need winning—she needs taking, and if she's already taken by another, then she must be stolen! I'll take you to the Hill of the Centaurs and make you brood mare to stallions and fighting men!'

'Hercules! Hercules, help me!' Deianeira hurled herself into the rushing water, but the centaur only scooped her up and rocked her in his two arms. 'Not willing? Then I'll take you there and persuade you after.' He swam with the apparent clumsiness and real efficiency of a horse, and his hooves were already gouging the mud of the far shore. Hercules was only halfway across, his hands full

209

of water, his bow slung useless across his back. He could only watch the centaur speeding away across the flood meadows.

On the far bank he knelt on one knee and took the bow off his back, an arrow from its god-given quiver. He took aim, his hands trembling so that the arrowhead bobbed on and off its target, first on Nessus, then on his wife. Her gauzy bridal clothes billowed and blurred the target. Nessus was getting away—it was loose the arrow or lose his bride. Hercules let the string slip from the crook of his fingers, and had stood up and was running before the arrowhead struck home.

It caught Nessus low down in the back—just above the tussock of hair that is a centaur's mane. His brain called to his legs to carry him onwards, but his legs would no longer answer and buckled and betrayed him. He spilled along the ground, with Deianeira pinned beneath him.

It was an age before Hercules could reach them—a full two or three minutes. The centaur twitched, and foam frothed from the corners of his mouth. 'Forgive me, lady. Love drove me to it. The gods have been just. They guided the arrow. My blessings on your marriage. Don't think unkindly of me, I beg you. Quickly—before he comes. Take a present from me in token of my shame. Take the robe off my back. Take it. It's all I have. Sew it into a robe for Hercules. And if ever . . . ' Approaching death rattled in his throat like the seeds in a poppy head. ' . . . if ever Hercules loses his love for you, give him the robe to wear and it will be rekindled . . . oh yes . . . rekindled . . . ' His hooves scrabbled once through the grass, then he turned his face against the ground and died. He did not have time to mention (if he had meant to mention it) that he was the brother of Chiron whom Hercules had killed.

* * *

Perhaps the threat of losing Deianeira made her precious to Hercules. He did not waste time on wondering whether he had married wisely. He simply loved her. And when no torments came raining down from heaven, he dared to hope that the gods had grown bored with him, or had lost sight of him among the trees and lanes of the mazy world.

They had three children, and if it were not for the dreams at night, Hercules might have been happy everlastingly.

14

Revenge and Forgiveness

He dreamed that he was running through the endless caverns of the Underworld pursued by centaurs, giants, hydras, boars, wives, servants and a multitude of dogs. And at the head of the pack ran Pluto, with Cerberus on a leash, shaking the chains that had bound Prometheus to the rock.

As Hercules ran, he searched—peering into the pitch black recesses, scrabbling through cobwebs, pushing aside boulders—without ever finding what he was looking for. He would wake tearing aside the bedclothes, his eyes straining blindly into the dark, and Deianeira would have to soothe him and reassure him and say, 'Who is it you're looking for in your dream, my dear? Who is it you hope you'll find?'

'I don't know. I don't know!' said Hercules, beating his forehead with his fist. 'When I see them, then I'll know.'

On the black cat-walks of night, Hera walked with her daughter, Hebe. Hercules was the furthest thing from her mind. The birth of a child to her had transformed the queen of the gods. No longer did her mind weave intricate plots of torment for mortal men. The fawning flattery of her serpents could not compare with the open, generous love offered her by her own little girl. What would she not have given to ensure that Hebe was always happy?

Already Hebe was a full-grown woman, for there is little childhood for the Immortals on Olympus. Mother and daughter were companions to each other, and gossiped endlessly about the other gods.

Only one niggling anxiety found room in Hera's breast. Every day, morning and evening, she saw her daughter lying along the parapets of heaven staring down at the Earth below. And Hera did not know—she simply did not know—what animal, what place, what person, what thing her daughter was searching for.

At last Hercules dreamed his dream through to the very end. His legs were failing, his breath was running short, the silent footsteps of the Dead behind were gaining on him, when all of a sudden a voice said, 'Here! Hide here, Hercules!'

The grey, bulging shape of a grotesque cactus grew out of the arid stone floor of the Underworld, with beckoning, spiny limbs. And perched high up amidst the needles sat Iole, the love of his childhood, the crown of her red hair bleached gold for all there was no sun overhead. She reached out her arms as if to help him up into the cactus, and it seemed that the needles were not thorny at all, but soft like the hairs on a peach. He had just taken hold of her hand when a great paw fell on his shoulder and shook him . . .

'Hercules. Hercules, my dear! Wake up. You're dreaming your dream again. Wake up!'

213

'Iole!' Before he was properly awake, Hercules roughly prised his wife's fingers off his shoulder.

'What's Iole?' asked Deianeira.

'A girl . . . someone I knew a long time ago . . . ' He struggled to break free of his heavy sleep. 'Yes! Now I understand what the dream was trying to tell me! There's a vow I never kept. That's what's been preying on my mind. I must go there. I must go now. The dreams will stop if I keep my vow!' His face, even through his beard, displayed a fierce frenzy of feelings, and he got up at once and pulled on the Nemean lionskin, knotting the paws around his waist. 'Kiss the children for me,' he said, and was gone, without shirt, without cloak, without weapon.

Deianeira's reaction was not unreasonable. Without explanation her husband had woken up in the night speaking a girl's name, and had left the house without a backward glance. First she cried, then she was angry, and then she said calmly to herself, 'Let's find out the truth here.' So she sent a letter to Thebes, to Hercules's stepfather, the lonely King Amphitryon. The letter simply said:

'Dear stepfather-in-law, pray enlighten me. Who is the Lady Iole?'

Amphitryon was getting old. But he racked his failing brains and after a time recalled the distant events of Hercules's childhood. He wrote back: 'Dear stepdaughter-in-law, I believe Hercules once felt himself bound to marry the Princess Iole of Oechalia. There are times when I wish he had. Permit me to beg an early visit from you both. Thebes is an empty place these days. Pray tell Hercules I bear no bitterness towards him.'

Deianeira could not read so far. Her tears obliterated the final words and she screwed the letter into a ball and threw it into the fire. 'So that's your vow, is it, Hercules? To marry Princess Iole. And what about your wife? And

214

what about your children? Oh, Hercules! Is this how the hero of the world behaves now that his Labours are over? No guilt? No conscience? No decency? No love left for me?' Her voice broke and she could not call her servant. She clapped her hands loud and long instead, and when the servant came, she bundled into his arms a rough and ready parcel of cloth. 'Take this robe to Oechalia. You'll find your master there. I hear it is cold there at this time of year. Beg him, for the love . . . no, say, for the duty he bears his wife, to wear this robe. Go! Now! Hurry!' The puzzled servant ran from the room, snagging a trailing corner of the white wool robe against the splintery door. 'Oh, Nessus! If only you were alive today! I could thank you for your present. Oh, I pray its magic is powerful enough to bring him back to me! Is any magic strong enough to mend a love that's broken?'

'No!' cried Hebe, and her hands clawed little pieces of plaster from the parapets of heaven: they fell as unseasonable snow. Quiet and still by nature, the daughter of Hera ran through the long corridors of heaven rending at the thin air as though it were dense undergrowth slowing her down. 'Mother! Mother! Don't let him put on the robe!'

Hera heard her daughter's voice and ran and caught her up in her arms and shook out of her a storm of tears.

'Don't let him put on the robe! Don't let him put on the robe!'

'Who, daughter? What robe? In the name of your father and all the gods, what's the matter?'

Hebe dragged her by the hand to the edge of a terrace and pointed frantically down towards the mosaic patterns of the blue-green earth. 'Hercules! Don't let Hercules put on the robe! Don't you understand? I love him! I love him! I love him!'

The name was like a slap to Hera. Her face emptied of expression. Her grip tightened on her daughter's wrist until the hand turned white and cold. Her lips thinned to a short white slit in her eternally lovely face, and her large, brown eyes narrowed. 'You *love* Hercules of Thebes?'

'Ever since I knew the meaning of the word!' said Hebe. Ignorant of her mother's hatred for Hercules, Hebe went on pleading, 'Don't let him put on the robe! Stop him! Warn him before it's too late!' She felt as if she was shouting at the deaf or shouting at the dead.

At last, after an eternity in the lives of the Immortals, Hera seemed to wake out of a deep sleep. Her mouth relaxed, her cheeks unstiffened, her brown eyes were replenished with affection. 'Tell me about the robe. I know nothing about any robe.'

It was true. She did not. The revenge of Nessus was all of his own devising.

It was cold. Deianeira sat gazing into the fire, murmuring prayers to the goddess of love. It took a long time before the persistent banging of the door in the wind disturbed her. She looked up—and saw that the door was unlatched. A fume of mist seemed to be creeping round it from outdoors. But then she saw that the door itself was smoking, glowing, charring, blackening. She threw a jug of water at it, but to no effect. A few white fibres of the robe were caught in the splinters by the latch and no water, no smothering would extinguish the fire. They had to chop down the door to save the house, and the wood burned to ashes and the latch melted to a shapeless mass.

'No!' screamed Deianeira. 'You gods in heaven, what

have I done? Don't let him put on the robe! Take my life, but don't let him put on the robe.'

'Iole.'

'Hercules.'

She had aged more than in his dream, but not much more. She wore her red hair up, so that he could not see whether the crown was still golden. But her shape was still as musical as a lute, and her eyes were still as green as the unripe pears of cactuses.

'I came here to keep my vow. I vowed to kill your father for cheating me out of marriage to you.'

She looked at him for a long time. She too had wanted that childhood marriage. At last she said, 'My father is already dead, Hercules. And I'm sure the gods would forgive the breaking of such an angry vow.'

Hercules was dejected. He was like a fighting ship suddenly becalmed. 'I no longer care what the gods want or don't want. I just wanted to keep faith with myself. I wanted to keep that vow and kill your father. I hope you understand.'

Iole took hold of his beard in her two hands and shook him gently. 'What kind of way is that to talk? You sound like a heathen. Not care about the gods? Your Labours are over, aren't they?'

'Yes.'

'And they've made you famous throughout the world, haven't they?'

'Yes.'

'And now you have a wife of good family and three lovely children, haven't you?'

'Yes.'

'And you can relax and be still the rest of your life. Would you want things any other way?'

'I would rather have married you, Iole, and travelled the world sleeping in cactus bushes and eating worms . . .'

'But I would have made you be a good, devout Greek and make sacrifice to the gods. What's all this about? It's not like you to be so stubborn.'

So Hercules began to explain about Prometheus and the bad temper of Pluto and the fate that awaited him through all eternity. 'Whatever I do—whether I honour the gods or defy them, they'll shovel me into that pit of darkness in the end, with all the people and beasts I've hunted or killed or offended. I'm afraid I can't see the use or the reason any more for saying my prayers—' He broke off when he saw his own house-servant running up the path towards Iole's villa.

Breathlessly the servant knelt down and presented a parcel of cloth to Hercules. 'Your wife begs you to wear this robe to keep you from catching cold.'

'How strange,' said Hercules, somewhat embarrassed in front of Iole. 'She knows I don't feel the cold.' He shook out the robe. 'Kind thought, but I really don't . . . Do you think I should make sacrifice to the gods, Iole?'

'To thank them for giving you such a considerate wife, yes,' said Iole firmly. 'To thank them for an end to your Labours. To ask them for a long, peaceful life and perhaps even their protection when you have at last to go down to the Underworld.'

'I will! I'll go and do it now—if you'll come with me!' The robe dropped to the ground, forgotten. 'Dear, sensible Iole. You always know best. I'm sure you're the wisest person I know. And you don't care whether I'm strong or weak, do you?'

'I just like you for yourself,' said Iole.

'That's why you were there in my dream, rescuing me . . . If only I had married you at the very beginning.'

218

'Shshsh.' She blushed. 'You can't go and make sacrifice dressed like that. You must wash and change.'

So Hercules laid aside the Nemean lionskin that had always protected his body, and he washed.

'You can wear this robe,' said Iole picking it up. 'It's a fine robe . . . and a token of love from your wife, I'm certain.'

'No!' cried Hebe from the parapets of heaven.

'No!' cried Deianeira as she rode into view of the villa and saw the white robe flash orange in the light of the setting sun as Hercules pulled it on over his head.

'When I make sacrifice, I shall thank the gods chiefly for you, Iole,' said Hercules, easing the shirt over his broad shoulders.

'No!' cried Hebe, covering her eyes.

'No!' cried Hera, seizing her daughter as she went to leap off the parapets of heaven.

'No!' cried Iole, seeing the hairs of Hercules's chest catch light and shrivel.

'NO!' cried Hercules as the robe cleaved to his flesh, every fibre meshing with the hairs of his body before trickling liquid fire through the pores of his skin. The deceitful centaur's revenge was terrible.

Iole ran for water to dowse the fire. She smothered Hercules with a blanket, but the fire would not go out. She burned her hands in beating at the flames, but the fire would not go out.

Though his body was blazing with a red more fierce than the raw sunset, all Hercules's mind could see were dark visions of the Underworld gaping, to swallow him up. An eternity of torment among his victims and enemies, under the peevish eyes of Pluto, under the reproachful eyes of his dead children, under the jaws of Cerberus, under the spite of the gods. The Hydra beckoned him, and Geryon clawed his way out of the ground. And all the while the robe burned without turning to ash and Hercules's body burned through to his soul, and still he did not die.

'Zeus take pity!' cried Iole. 'Let him die! Let him die!'

'Zeus take pity!' cried Deianeira.

'Zeus take pity!' cried Hebe to her father. 'Let him not go forever into the Underworld!'

'Husband take pity,' said the queen of the gods, dropping to her knees alongside her daughter.

But almighty Zeus hesitated, watching his son burn.

'*Zeus take pity!*' cried Hercules, reaching his hands towards heaven.

'It is done,' said Zeus the Almighty in that instant. 'That is all I wanted. Hear this, you gods great and small. My son shall not live out eternity in the Underworld. The mortal in him is purged away, and the hero shall remain, immortal, and live here among us. Wife—let the Earth's beasts and monsters and tyrants look up from every part of the blue-green planet and remember the Labours of Hercules!'

So, as a smithy takes up the white-hot metal in his tongs, Hera snatched up the blazing brand that was Hercules between two beams of the setting sun, and plunged him into the cold of the night sky—the black and sunless void of space spangled by the beastly constellations. The frame of his being was picked out in seven bright stars—shoulders, knees, and head between the centaur-shape of Chiron and the venom-drained Crab of light.

But his soul drifted, like constellar dust, out of the frame of stars and settled on the slopes of Olympus. There little Hebe pasted it together with tears into the husband she longed for, the husband she had longed for, for so very, very long.

Looking at the night sky, it seems that the stars which trace out Hercules are gradually expanding. Over the centuries, the constellation would seem to be failing, falling apart, disbanding as a party disbands when the music comes to an end.

But do not be deceived. The stars seem further apart only because the Earth is swinging in towards the centre of the constellation, pulled by the giant strength of gravity. One day, a million million years from now, the Sun's small family of planets will lose itself among the seven stars, and we shall be cradled in Hercules's arms. All of Earth's little gods, people, beasts, and children will fill that icy emptiness that presently lingers over his heart.

Theseus

1

The Oracle and the Sorceress

The singers sing of a time before Theseus was born. Then, men stood like candles on the table of the earth, and their lives melted quickly away. The wild and unkempt gods roared round the world, howling and blustering like the four winds, and with little care for the men they trampled, the candles that flickered and died. A man's life was soon forgotten.

A man's memory could only be kept alive by storytellers (and the memories of storytellers are small and overcrowded) or by his own children and by their children after them . . .

King Aegeus longed for a child—a son who could keep alight his memory in the windy halls of history, and inherit the crown of Athens, too. Oh, and a son to love him, as only a son can love his father!

But Aegeus had married once and his wife had died. He had married again, but after a time, his second wife, with her narrow waist and narrow eyes looked at him and shrugged. 'The gods clearly don't mean us to have children, my dear.'

Day after night he prayed to the gods for the gift of a

son. But still the only sound in his courtyard and streets was of other people's children, other people's sons. Without warning, without a word, King Aegeus got up one day and left Athens in a chariot, bound for Delphi.

There, where the earth had cracked open a little like lips cracked by the wind, wisps of smoke from the Underworld leaked out into a cave. The smoke was a sickly yellow. The smell was an acrid ache in the nose—a headache—a dizziness—a clouding of the brain. For carried in the fumes were words and numbers, nightmares and dreams. They stung the eyes. They muddled the brain.

Within the swirling smoke, seated on a three-legged bronze platform higher than a man's head, a girl sat rocking to and fro. Her head rolled on her shoulders and her eyes rolled in her head. And out of her mouth fell words as wild as nonsense. This was the Delphic Oracle, doomed by her gift of prophecy to sit in the foul vapours of the Underworld with a head full of visions. This was Xenoclea-Who-Knows-All-That-Was-And-Is-And-Will-Be. Her lids were shut. But inside her head lay all the answers to every question, and far more than Man dared to ask.

The floor was trodden hollow and the step in front of the tripod was pitted where a thousand knees had knelt. For a man could come to the Oracle and ask for knowledge only the gods should know. And the Oracle could see, with her closed eyes, clear into the future.

Aegeus, when he reached the door of the temple, almost turned on his heel and left. He had been so certain on his journey, so sure of his reason for coming. Here he might have an answer to the question that bored through his pillow each night to lodge in his brain. But now he wondered.

'They all hesitate,' said a voice from inside the temple. 'They all come as far as the door and wonder, "Would I

226

rather not know?'' You are right, King Aegeus. For all the good it will do you, you would do better not to ask, not to know.'

But Aegeus shook himself like a dog and ducked inside the doorway. 'Of course I must know! I'm a king, and unless I know, how shall I make plans for Athens? Will I ever . . . shall I ever . . . '

'Have a son? Ah, how many times have I heard that question? I am bored with it. Profoundly, boundlessly bored. Before I heard you coming, I saw your question written in the air. ''Will I have a son?'' The world's air is stale with that kind of question. ''Will I have a child? Will I have a husband? Will I have a crown?'' But *you*, Aegeus, *you* have a choice.'

'A choice? I don't want a choice, I want a son!' cried Aegeus, overbalancing off his knees so that his hands splattered the floor, wet with holy libations.

The tone of the Oracle's voice never changed. She did not even know what words spilled from her drooping, open mouth. Even childless kings could not move her to pity. 'The Sorceress Medea can give you the magic. But beware. Listen to my words, O foolish king, and let Theseus remain unborn. Accept the fate of the gods and do not bring yourself unhappiness.'

The king stumbled out of the cave, wiping his face with his dripping hands. His head was full of reechy smoke. His heart was jumping with amazement. But all the warnings rolled away and were lost. His brain was full of the name Theseus—'Theseus. Theseus! My son, Theseus!' he said, and knotting the long reins of his chariot around his waist, he whipped up his horses to a gallop.

It was all his outriders could do to catch up with him. 'To Athens, my lord? Not this road for Athens, surely?'

'No! To Corinth! I must see Medea the Sorceress.'

For the magic of a son, Aegeus would have ridden to the pit of the sea and prised it from the tendrils of an octopus. He would not have cared if the Sorceress Medea lived in the heart of a volcano and was as ugly as a sloth. Aegeus had never seen her and he was prepared for almost any sight—except for the one he saw.

Medea lived in a tower of pink stone, and her hair was braided with silver. Her white gown was tinged with the colours of sunset, and her hands were as white as the long wing pinions of a flying swan. She greeted Aegeus as though all her life had been spent waiting for him, and she gave him cakes and perfumed wine and the marinaded meat of turtle doves.

'And what service can I do my lord Aegeus to bring him joy?'

The king asked at once for the magic that would give him a son and heir. 'I have a thousand pieces of gold to pay you with, but if you need more I can pay you in yearly tributes of cattle and sheep and white ground flour.'

Medea held up her hand and smiled. 'You are welcome to my magic, my lord—more than welcome. All I ask is a welcome in your house if ever I should come to Athens. Now—show me yourself.'

Aegeus shuffled his feet awkwardly, spread his arms and looked down at the floor, blushing. He felt a shabby sort of a king, traipsing his dirt into the rosy drapery of her chamber. His sandals were white with dust. His tunic was sweaty. His breastplate was covered in fingermarks. Suddenly he leapt backwards as she flung a chalice of wine against his chest. It trickled down his armour, through his clothing, and dripped off his large knee-caps.

'Listen, King Aegeus, the very next time you hold a

woman in your arms, she will bear you a son,' said Medea softly.

'Oh, Medea! Oh, thank you! Thank you! I'm so very sorry—I'm dripping on your rug,' he said. Indeed he was not sorry; he would willingly have stood and dripped on her rug for ever. Because the longer he looked at Medea, the more beautiful she seemed. His body leaned forward from the ankles, his hands lifted from his side. He took one step towards her. Surely, one kiss was no more than he owed her for the favour she had granted him.

Medea, too, spread her arms, welcoming. Her fingers touched his . . .

Outside there was a clatter of metal against stone. The king's outriders burst into the room.

'Your chariot, my lord!'

'The horses are bolting!'

'We couldn't hold them, sir. They're out of hand!'

Aegeus ran outside to quieten his horses: they steadied at once, at the sound of his voice, and stood stock still while he wound their long reins once more round his waist. Medea came to the door to wave the king farewell. She was frowning a little.

In his longing to be home—to take his wife in his arms and give her a son—he whipped up the horses and left Medea's pink tower far behind him, dirtied by his flying dust. The sorceress, before she turned to go back inside, stamped her foot angrily and spat on the parched ground. She had meant that son to be hers.

It was a long journey from Corinth to Athens—too far by far to travel in one day. Aegeus decided to stay the night at the house of an old friend, in the village of Troezen. He was happy to the point of foolishness, hugging the servants and throwing his arms round his friend. 'Do you know what, Pittheus? Shall I tell you the most wonderful thing? No, it would be wrong to speak of it. My wife must be the first to know! Great news, though, Pittheus! The greatest news of all! The greatest news for Attica since that young bear Hercules was born! Hello, who's this young beauty?' Pittheus's daughter, Aethra, was standing at his elbow with a jug to refill his goblet of wine. 'Is it really little Aethra? By the gods, you've grown! Pittheus, she's *beautiful*! Have you found a good husband for her yet?'

Aethra blushed and hurried away to fetch more food to table, and while the wine flowed and Aegeus's hands waved as he sprawled in his chair and drew great cheerful shapes in the air with his cup of wine, the beautiful young Aethra watched the king through long, lowered lashes. She thought him the most lovely sight she had ever seen. When Aegeus finally dropped his cup altogether, in an excess of good cheer, she was the first to run and pick it up.

The first to run, the first to slip in the puddle of spilled wine, the first to fall and the first to be caught up in Aegeus's two arms to keep her from falling.

He set her on her feet again and smiled, his eyes loose in his head from drinking and his lids heavy. Suddenly, all the bleariness left his eyes, like a sky blown clear of clouds, and the lids parted wider and wider still. 'I didn't, did I? I couldn't have.'

'What, my lord?' asked Aethra shyly.

'Never you mind, girl. Never you mind. I didn't . . . No, of course I didn't.' His mouth gave a small, anxious tug to one side, and very soon afterwards he said his goodnights and went to bed.

He slept heavily. His good mood was restored in the morning, and he climbed into his chariot, looped round with the end of his reins as happy as the crack at the end of a whip. At the last moment, he caught the eye of Aethra and whispered teasingly over the side of his chariot, 'I have left a present for you. At least, it's a present for your son, if you should ever—one day, you know—in the future—have a son. He'll find my sword and sandals under that rock—when he's man enough to lift it.'

Aethra cast bewildered eyes at the rock he pointed out—a boulder so huge that an oxen team could hardly have moved it. She shook her head, meaning that she did not understand his joke or why he should make fun of her. As he rode away, however, she still thought he was the most beautiful sight she had seen since she had seen a forest fire ravage the crown of a wooded hill and set all the wild birds flying.

As soon as Aegeus arrived home, he opened his arms to his wife and clasped her to his breast. 'Your armour's hard,' she complained, and pushed him away.

A few days later, she caught a fever and died.

Aegeus was too disappointed to be angry. He simply supposed that the Oracle at Delphi had made a mistake. Or perhaps the sorceress's magic had splashed off his hard breastplate.

More years arrived at the gates of Athens, one year after another. Years raced through the streets, through Aegeus's palace, and trampled over him like stampeding horses, leaving a sprinkling of grey in his hair, a network of lines on his face, a stoop.

Then Medea the sorceress arrived one day from Corinth, in a chariot drawn by two winged serpents. Aegeus thanked the gods for sending her. All she asked for was a place to shelter, out of the wind and sun. But Aegeus took her into the shelter of his palace, even into the shelter of his bed. He married her. And there was more magic: she gave birth to a little boy—a prince for Athens . . . and called him *Medus*.

2

The Club and the Sword

'Where do you want me to put the basket of bread, mother?'

'Oh, in the middle of the table, I think, Theseus, where everyone can reach it. Though Hercules will eat it all, of course, as usual. When your cousin Hercules comes to dinner, nobody else gets much to eat.'

Theseus, who was seven years old, could not wait to see his cousin for the first time. People said he was the strongest man in the world. 'If I asked him, would he teach me how to wrestle, mother?'

The lady Aethra frowned. 'Fighting! Must you always be talking about fighting?'

'Does he have a sword, mother? Does Hercules have a sword?'

'No he doesn't. Just a big club.'

'How big, mother? As big as me?'

'Every bit as big. Now go and get washed. Do you mean Hercules to see you looking like the floor of the Augean stables?'

Before Theseus was washed, his cousin arrived—a man so laden with muscles that his body seemed to be

coiled round with snakes. He wore for a cloak the skin
of a lion he had fought and killed with his bare hands—
not just the fur, but the head, too, with gaping jaws and
staring eyes and creased, velvety cheeks. Hercules flung it
over a stool where it happened to fall paws downwards,
the head lolling towards the door.

'Come on! Come on! He's here! I heard him arrive!'
cried Theseus to all the other children who lived in the
house at Troezen. They came running from every
direction, and all bundled through the door together.

They took one look at the lionskin—they took
another—then they scattered. Screaming and shrieking,
they ran for the stairs, they ran to the kitchen, they ran
to their mothers and hid their faces and howled in terror
that there was a lion in the dining hall. All except
Theseus. He looked at the lionskin; he looked at his
cousin; he looked at his mother, and then he backed
towards the door—slowly, slowly. Between unmoving lips
he whispered, 'Don't panic. Stay perfectly still.' After he
had closed the door, his sandals could be heard pelting
along the corridor.

Hercules laughed out loud, and all the goblets on the
table trembled. But he stopped laughing when the noise
of sandals came pelting back again. The door opened and
in strode Theseus, dragging an axe almost as big as
himself.

'Don't worry, mother. I'll deal with it! Shame on
you, cousin, for letting a lion walk so close to my
mother!' And he swung the axe with all his might.

Hercules thumped the table with his fist. 'By all the
gods, boy! You've killed my cloak! And that stool will
never walk again! Aethra, what a little Titan you've got
there! Introduce me at once.'

So Theseus picked himself up off the floor (where the
weight of the axe had thrown him) and shook hands with

his cousin, the mighty Hercules. 'You have your mother's eyes, boy, but where do you get your fire from? Your father, maybe?'

Aethra dropped the plate she was holding. 'Haven't got a father, sir,' said Theseus cheerfully. 'Don't need one. I can look after mother well enough.'

'Theseus! How often must I tell you? Don't brag. I'm sorry, Hercules, but there's a streak of pride in the boy that the gods would frown on if they saw it. *You* speak to him. Tell him there's more to life than fighting and killing and having strong arms.'

Hercules plucked at his beard thoughtfully and slowly nodded. But his mind was somewhere else, and his eyes peered into Theseus's face. 'I've seen this face before. There's a certain noble gentleman in Athens with just the same face. When do you intend to tell the lad exactly who he is, Aunt Aethra?'

'When he's big enough and sensible enough,' said Aethra crossly, covering Theseus's two ears with her hands and hustling him out of the room.

Theseus nagged her every day, after that. 'Who am I, mother? What did Hercules mean? Do I have a father, after all?'

But Aethra only said, 'Soon enough. Soon enough you'll leave me. Soon enough there will be *real* lions lying in wait for you. Be content. There are more good things to be harvested from this world than what you can reap with a sword.'

In the days when Theseus was young, the world was young, too. Only a few ships were sprinkled on the world-encircled sea; only a few houses had grown up along its shores and river-banks. And what houses there were, were bare and barely higher than a man's head. Beds sprawled legless on the floor, and the grain and grapes rattled by in two-wheeled carts, pulled by small and pale-eared donkeys.

Men, too, were slight and lean, with narrow shoulders, and hips like hunting dogs—quick to look behind them, and narrow-eyed with looking out to sea.

Theseus, too, was lean as a boy. His ribs circled his chest like fingers, and his legs were as thin as grass. But as he grew up, the muscles plaited along his bones and his chest filled out like a ship's sail, and his neck grew from his chest like a thick-rooted tree. His hair shone like an otter's fur, but curled long and loose to his shoulder blades which were as smooth as the bronze plates of a prince's armour. And his eyes were such a turbulent blue that the superstitious peasants of Troezen said, 'There's the sea itself in those eyes. Poseidon the sea god must have fathered that boy!'

When Theseus was about seventeen, a sudden silence fell over Troezen—not the silence of people sleeping soundly in their beds, but the silence of people holding their breath in terror. They could almost hear the thump, thump of each other's hearts.

A monstrous man called Periphetes had come to the district—a man hunched over like a bear. As he walked, he left the splayed print of his left hand in the earth, and from his right hand he trailed a huge, bronze club. His head was the shape of a club; his nose was the shape of a club; even his brain was club-shaped, so much time did he spend thinking about clubbing.

Up and down the Corinth road Periphetes roamed. When he broke into a shambling run, he could keep pace with a horse and club the rider out of the saddle. He would smash down a roadside house and block the road with the rubble. Then when a cart was forced to stop, he would sneak up behind it and shatter the cart and squander the load and leave only the white-eyed horses to run off between their shafts. He clubbed cows and dogs; he clubbed fences and barns; he clubbed trees and wine vats. But chiefly he loved to club men and women who passed along 'his' road.

Word of Periphetes spread until nobody dared to travel from Corinth to Troezen, from Troezen to Corinth. 'Perhaps now he'll get bored and move on to a different place,' said the people of Troezen.

Periphetes did get bored when no one came along his road, when there was nobody to ambush and nobody to club. 'Betti moob on,' he thought with his club-shaped brain. 'Waygo nowbut? Corinff? Oober yonder-sider Troezen?'

Slowly, like a drip forming below his club-shaped brain, Periphetes formed an idea. 'Ohah! Clubben Troezen Igo! All de walk clubben, ander all de mennen, ander all de roof-underplaces, ander cartes ander animoos—ander prettiladies, ander babys, ander childer—yuck, Periphetes verihate childer.' And delighted with the idea of destroying Troezen brick by brick and bone by bone, the revolting Periphetes gambolled down the road towards the rooftops of the little village. As he ran, he left a groove as deep as a cart-rut, dragging his huge, bronze club.

The first Pittheus knew of the attack was when terrified peasants came hammering on his door. 'Let us in! Let us in! Periphetes is coming! Periphetes is destroying the town!'

They watched him from the roof, pounding the sheep-folds to pieces and pulverizing the cottages. The earth under the vines ran purple with their spilled juice, and the dry-stone walling tumbled in avalanches round the feet of Periphetes.

'Even if we bar the door, he'll club his way through

the walls!' whispered Pittheus. 'Aethra, hide yourself and hide the boy. Nothing will keep Periphetes out!'

But when Aethra went looking for Theseus to hide him from the club-man, she could not find him. Suddenly she heard her father calling the boy's name too, but urgently, distractedly: 'Theseus! Come back here! *Theseus!* What's he doing out there? What does he think he's doing?'

Theseus, his thumbs tucked into his cord belt, was scuffing his feet across the courtyard and out into the sunlight of the road. Past the gate he went, past the lemon tree, past the limes and into the yellow sunlight that dazzled on his tunic. Then he stopped, cocking his head on one side. He called out, 'Periphetes! Be off with you. You're not welcome here.'

'Greep! A verifool childer! A nearlidead bore! Comen closeup, bore! Periphetes grimpen ander grumpen yooz. Heep-eep-eep!' The club-man tossed the handle of his club from hand to hand and bared his teeth—curved as talons—at Theseus. Then he began to throw the club high into the air—higher each time—like a juggler. The sun flashed on the bronze. He caught it first with his right hand, then with his left, and now and then he caught it in both and smashed it down on the ground till there was a long shallow dent in the earth. 'Bed for bore. Make-I bed for veridead bore!' And he flung the club higher than ever into the air.

Theseus put down his head and charged. Like a bull he covered the ground, his arms doubled over his head to protect his skull from the jolt. As he rammed Periphetes, dust burst in clouds out of the giant's clothing and he let out a little, breathless grunt and sat down, hard. His massive club reached the zenith of its flight and began to come down again, still whirling. Theseus reached into the air and, with both hands, took hold of it. Once, twice, three times he brought it down on Periphetes's head.

It was not enough. The giant rocked from side to side, to and fro, but he did not fall over on to his back. In fact he drew up his knees as if he was about to get to his feet, and his two eyes struggled to focus on Theseus.

Theseus threw aside the club and seizing hold of a big boulder nearby, he raised it off the ground. As long as the span of his arms, it was, but he lifted it, clenching his teeth and bending his knees. And he half dropped, half threw it at Periphetes's head.

After that, Periphetes's head was no longer the shape of a club. Nor was his nose. Nor was his brain. And no thoughts of clubbing ever passed that way again. Periphetes was pretty much dead.

When he saw what he had done, and how easily he had done it, Theseus gave a great leap in the air and spread his hands towards heaven, as if to say, 'Did you see? Were you watching?' But there was no roll of thunder from the mountains of the gods, and behind him, the people of Troezen stood white-faced as if, all of a sudden, Theseus frightened them.

Then Pittheus began to stammer out congratulations and praise. He said he was very proud of his grandson, very proud indeed. The peasants and servants began to cheer and jig, whirling Theseus up in their dance. Only Aethra stood to one side, her face the colour of chalk. She called Theseus sharply to her side, took hold of his wrist, and led him away from the house, as if to scold him in private.

She led him back to the spot where he had lifted the boulder to throw at Periphetes, and she pointed at the ground. There was a shallow trench, and in it lay a sword and a pair of sandals.

'It is time to tell you. These were put here, under the rock, by your father. They're yours now, since you were man enough to uncover them . . . Don't interrupt. It is time for you to go and show yourself to your father. He'll be glad to see you—I'm sure of that—though he doesn't know yet that you exist. But you must be careful. Your father has more to give you than most fathers, and other people may grow to envy you.'

'You mean he's rich, mother? Or famous?'

'He is the king of the city-state of Athens, boy, and his name is Aegeus. Will you leave tomorrow? A boat will carry you all the way to Pyrrheus harbour: that's the safest way to go.'

'Then *I* shall go by road!' exclaimed Theseus, tipping back his head in that arrogant way that irritated his mother so much. '*I* never hankered after *safety*! My father has waited seventeen years to see me. He can wait a few days longer. Yes, I shall go to Athens by road, and maybe do a brave deed or two on the way that will make the gods stand up on Olympus to clap me.' And he flourished his father's sword so that it flashed in the sunlight and dazzled his mother and the others.

He kept the bronze club of Periphetes—a souvenir of his first victory.

3

On the Road to Athens

The air trembled in the heat of the sun. It looked as if the countryside ahead was melting. The trees wavered in the shimmering haze, and watery mirages puddled and evaporated on the roadway.

Theseus, his long hair hanging dark with sweat between his shoulder blades, was watching the horizon wrinkle like damp paper when, all of a sudden, he saw an extraordinary sight. Two huge trees were not just wavering in the heat haze—they were bending down, like two men bowing to each other, bowing from the waist. Their tips almost touched, then the trees went on bending and bending until they were hooped right over—arched like a greyhound's back. Then they righted themselves with a noise of lashing branches and a shriek that stopped Theseus in his tracks. Two black shapes rocketed across the sky in opposite directions, as though the trees had tossed their hats in the air.

'So far from home, and the trees themselves have heard tell of my fight with Periphetes! Are they really bowing down to me? Cheering me?' The sight so amazed him that he did not notice the man who stepped out on

241

to the road ahead of him. Theseus walked straight into him. 'Sorry,' said Theseus irritably.

Then two hands took hold of his shoulders and lifted him up and threw him—ooff—across a shoulder, as if he were a sack of sand. 'Where's your permit, stringbean? Where's your authorization to walk along my road?'

'Who are you? What permit? Whose road? Put me down, I demand it!'

'Oh-ho! Demand away, little spring onion. In the meantime, the trees are waiting.'

'Take care, sir! I am Theseus, prince of Athens, who took the bronze club of Periphetes and beat him with it! Do you want to suffer the same fate?'

'Who? Never heard of him. Never heard of you. But I'll warrant you've heard of me, little beetroot. I'm the Tree-Bender of the Isthmus!'

They reached a clearing among tall cypress trees. A rope hung down from the tallest tree on either side of the glade. Setting Theseus down beside a sapling, he buckled his huge belt round both Theseus and the sapling, to hold him fast. Then he hauled on one of the ropes, his muscles bulging like the crust of a plaited loaf. The tree wagged, then began to bend, until its top was pulled right down into the clearing. Trapping the topmost branches under his huge heel, the Tree-Bender began to haul on the other rope, until the tree on the other side of the glade had also bent itself in two. He cracked the two rope-ends in Theseus's face.

'Now! This end goes round your *left* ankle, and this end goes round your *right*. Then when I let go—*schrrquwczzz*—two one-legged men and both of them called Theseus! One in the eastern provinces and one in the west. Won't you just split your sides laughing, eh, little cabbage! And what a deal of squelching blood there'll be. I like blood and gore, I do. Nobody likes it more than me.'

When both trees were fully bent, the Tree-Bender held them down with his two huge heels while he unfastened his belt and freed Theseus—and held him upside down by his feet.

Theseus's head dangled down. He twisted and writhed, but the Tree-Bender held him fast with one elbow, while knotting one rope-end round Theseus's left ankle. The king's sword and the bronze club of Periphetes lay out of reach beside the sapling . . .

There were coils of slack rope heaped to either side. Theseus picked up a loop in both hands then, squirming round, sank his teeth into the giant's leg. It was no more than a gnat sting to the Tree-Bender, but he lifted his toes just for a moment. Theseus twisted the other way, bit the other ankle. The giant just laughed at his struggling—but he did lift his toes for a moment with the pain. It was long enough for Theseus to slip a loop of rope round that foot, too. The next moment, like an acrobat, Theseus swung himself between the giant's legs, reached up and caught hold of the Tree-Bender's belt, then launched kicks in every direction, until the Tree-Bender was forced to let go.

Irritably, the giant dropped Theseus on his head and raised one foot to stamp on him . . . The bent pine tree escaped from under his heel and sprang upright. The Tree-Bender flew into the air. There was hardly time for screaming before the left-hand tree straightened up and—*schrrquwczzz*—the Tree-Bender left in two directions at once.

When Theseus saw what he had done and how easily he had done it, he gave a great leap in the air and spread his hands towards heaven as if to say, 'Did you see? Were you watching?' But there was no roll of thunder from the mountains, no roar from the sea.

Just beyond the Isthmus, Theseus came to a village where the houses were all built on stilts. He was hungry, and would have asked for a meal, but no one was out working in the fields, no one at all. 'Hey! Hello there! Anybody! Where are you all?' And he rapped on the stilt of a house. A rope snaked past his face.

'Quick, boy! Climb up, you reckless fool! Don't you know the boar's about?'

'What bore?' said Theseus, disdaining to climb up the rope.

The woman of the house looked down at him from the threshold of the hut. 'The Crommyonian Boar, of course!'

'The what?'

'The Crommyonian Boar.'

'A big bore to warrant such a long name,' said Theseus.

'Oh, vast! Enormous! Huge! It's driven us out of our own fields and killed more than a dozen men who went to hunt it! Before we built our houses on stilts its tusks came smashing through the walls—right in the middle of supper!'

'Oh, *that* kind of a boar,' said Theseus, grinning. 'A little wild pig, you mean.'

The woman's eyes shifted from Theseus's face and across his shoulder. The platform on which her hut rested began to tremble. So did the woman. 'Look out! *Look out!* It's the Crommyonian bo—'

The name was so long that by the time she had said it, there was no time left for climbing the rope. Theseus turned and saw a boar as big as a rhinoceros, its tusks crossed over its nose like two great sabres, and thundering towards him so fast that its legs were a blur of movement in a blur of dust.

Theseus put two hands to the rope, jumped and tucked his knees up to his chin. The Crommyonian Boar trampled by beneath him, and the bristles of its back brushed his shins. It collided with one of the stilts of the platform, and brought the hut tumbling down on its head with a noise of splintering wood. The woman of the house, a baby clutched in her arms, ran shrieking towards the sea. The Crommyonian Boar got up and shook itself: its thick, short legs bowed outwards under the massive weight of its furious body. It lowered its head to charge.

Theseus too picked himself up from among the wreckage of the hut and snatched up the bronze club he had taken from Periphetes. As the boar came on, he lifted the club two-handed over his shoulder. As the crossed tusks rattled in his face, he swung the club—and he knocked the Crommyonian Boar—like a batsman striking a ball. Hoof-over-horn the Crommyonian Boar cartwheeled through the air and landed insensible in a patch of sea-pinks. It was only a matter then of taking hold of the monstrous white tusks and snapping the beast's neck. Painlessly he delivered the big pig into the safe-keeping of the goddess Artemis, who tends the spirits of all dead boars.

When he saw what he had done and how easily he had done it, Theseus gave a great leap in the air and spread his hands towards heaven as if to say, 'Did you see? Were you watching?' But there was no roll of thunder from the hills, no roar from the sea—only the timid clapping of the Crommyonian villagers as they lowered themselves down from their huts-on-stilts and stood about, wide-eyed.

Beyond the village, the path grew narrow—a gouge cut in

the side of a steep cliff, with beetling rocks rising to the left and a precipice falling into the sea on the right. Theseus paused to admire the view. A sharp wind was piling up waves against the rocks below. But the pathway ahead showed up like a white, zigzag scar on the face of the cliff. Screwing up his eyes, Theseus caught sight of another traveller ahead of him on the path. After two days of walking, he hankered after some company, and quickened his steps to catch up with the man.

He was only a little out of hailing distance when the man on the road ahead stopped. His way was barred by a human creature as round as a boulder.

Theseus had to pick his way carefully for fear of falling over the cliff-edge. He could not hear what words passed between the two, but the traveller all at once leaned down as if to fasten the other's shoe. In one quick and practised movement, the fat ambusher seized hold of him, belt and collar, and flung the unwary traveller over the brink of the cliff!

The scream was carried away by the gulls. But one thing heard it. Down in the sea, a ring of white foam spread where the traveller had plunged headlong into the water. Alongside it, another ring formed, as though a rock was drying out as the tide ebbed. It was round and hard like a rock as it rose out of the water. But a rock does not have a head at one end and stumpy cylindrical legs to either side. A great grey turtle reared up out of the surf, bigger than a rowing boat, bigger than a cow, bigger even than the Crommyonian Boar.

It chewed at the water, its gaping square head like a box, opening and closing. It devoured the traveller and cast a pebbly glance up the cliff face, as though it was accustomed to the treat.

The loose chalk trickled from under Theseus's sandals and over the precipice. He picked his way very carefully along the path to the place where the fat man sat barring the way.

'You! Small fry!'

'Who? Me?'

'Where do you think you're going?'

'To Athens, sir,' said Theseus courteously, although the hairs on his neck were beginning to stir, as the hackles rise on an angry dog.

'Not without paying the toll. I'm Sciron—the Guardian of the Highway.'

'Not much of a highway,' said Theseus, kicking some chalky scree into the sea below.

'Well, it's *high*, isn't it? And it's the *way* from where you've been to where you're going. So. Are you going to pay the toll or go back where you came from?' Sciron was a one-eyed man with shoulders so wide, a back so short and a head so flat and neckless that he was the same shape as the boulders round about him.

'What is the toll?' asked Theseus.

'You must tie my sandals for me. I'm too fat to reach my feet.'

So Theseus laid down his bronze club and twisted his sword so that its blade was out of the way. And he stooped down in front of Sciron and took hold of the loose sandal straps.

With fingers as quick as a conjuror, he bound the ankles together with three overhand knots, then, with interlocking hands, he made a stirrup for the fat man's foot and pitched him, heels-over-head off his boulder and over the edge of the cliff.

The great grey turtle had not eaten so well for a long time.

When Theseus saw what he had done and how easily he had done it, he gave a great leap in the air and spread his hands towards heaven, as if to say, 'Did you see?

247

Were you watching?' But there was no roll of thunder from the mountains, no roar from the sea—only the champing of the great grey turtle in the sea below.

Athens was already in sight when Theseus passed a troop of soldiers on the road. He was still wearing his sword down behind his knees, and his club was inside his long cloak. The soldiers, their arms round each other's necks, called out, 'What's a pretty girl like you doing out here on your own?'

'By the gods, you're a buxom wench and no mistake!'

'Big enough for two husbands, eh!'

Theseus twisted his sword back on to his hip and spread his cloak so that they could see his bronze club; they stumbled off with a howl of laughter, laughing at their own mistake as much as at Theseus. He did not trouble to pick a fight with them. But, watching them go, he did see that it was not the way of Athenian men to wear their hair loose down their backs. He thought, I must make myself presentable. I can't have my father thinking he has a daughter instead of a son!

So he knocked at the first house he came to, a fine, expensive villa cloaked in vines and with horses grazing outside. The owner was most hospitable: 'Come in! Come in, young lady! Oh dear, I *am* sorry—what a foolish mistake! Can I offer you a bed for the night, young sir?'

The man, whose name was Corydallus, took Theseus to a clean, comfortable room, brought him a basin of water and several candles, as it was getting dark. When Theseus asked his advice as to how to wear his hair, Corydallus told him, 'You must plait your hair behind and crop it really short in front. That way your opponent in battle won't be able to catch hold of your forelock while he cuts your throat! Here are the shears, young friend. When you've done, I'll show you to your bed. But you'll excuse me now. You're not the first traveller to stop at my house this evening.'

Theseus set about plaiting his long hair and then cutting away the golden curls that had coiled across his forehead for fully fifteen years. As the curls dropped down, it was like seeing his childhood fall to the floor, or the petals of a rose drop when the hard hip ripens. He paused in his snipping to pick up a handful of hair.

As he stooped down, his ear came close to the wall. His sharp hearing picked up the sound—there was no mistaking it—of a man choking. He crossed quickly to the window, stepped through it into the garden, and moved along the wall to the window of the next room.

There, Corydallus was putting two young men to bed—for ever. One was tall, the other short. The beds he gave them were of a standard length, but it was the rule of this gruesome house that every visitor must fit his bed exactly. So, when the one was too long for his mattress, Corydallus lopped off his head. And now he was stretching the little man to fit his bed. Theseus turned away and shut his eyes.

He wondered whether to slip away then and there, and tell his father, when he reached Athens, to send soldiers to arrest Corydallus. But then he drew his sword and, by the light of the moon, looked at his reflection in its blade. The face looking back at him was an angry, unfamiliar, and fierce face, with no golden curls across the forehead to make it gentle. He climbed back through the window of his room and waited for Corydallus to show him to his bed.

'This way, this way!' said Corydallus cheerfully, bowing a little with every word. He showed Theseus to the selfsame bedroom: there was no sign of the two young men he had murdered. 'You're a tall gentleman, aren't you, sir? I fear you may find my humble bed a little uncomfortable.'

'Bed? What's a bed?' said Theseus, smiling wide-eyed at Corydallus. When he was shown the two beds in the room, he shook his head in bafflement. 'Yes, but what do you *do* with them?'

Corydallus scratched his head. 'Zeus, what a peasant you are, boy. I suppose you sleep in the hay at home. Town folk sleep on *beds*.'

'Sleep? What's sleep?' said Theseus, grinning excitedly.

Corydallus began to be vexed. '*Sleep*. You know, zzz zzzzz!' And he snored loudly and shut his eyes and rested his head against his hands.

When he opened his eyes again, Theseus was still gawping at him, and seemed to be trying to imitate a snore. 'Oink-oink?' he said. 'Like a pig?'

'Well! I'll go to the foot of Olympus, I never met such a stupid young bumpkin! Everyone *sleeps*. Look—like this.' And Corydallus lay down on the nearest bed.

'Looks to me as if you're a little short for that bed,' said Theseus and, taking hold of both ends of Corydallus—hair and feet—he stretched him until he was a *much* taller man. 'Oh dear. I seem to have over-stretched you, sir. Now you're too long for the bed. No matter. I have a sword here to put that to rights . . . '

Next day, Theseus shut the door of the house behind him and walked the last mile into Athens. His hair was plaited and the plait hung down to the base of his shoulder blades. But the front was cut short to show that he was a fighting man and an Athenian.

250

4

An Assassination Attempt

I n the morning sunlight, a hundred tiny emerald lizards were basking on the white walls of the king's long, low palace. A little boy was throwing stones at them, trying to squash them or knock them off one by one. They scurried and scattered, but Medus was a very poor shot.

'Can you direct me to the king?' asked Theseus. He had already asked the servants, but they were too busy to answer, rushing to and fro with panniers and baskets, preparing for a feast.

The little boy said, 'Do you really expect me to speak to you? Do you know who I am? I'm the Prince of Athens! I'm Prince Medus!'

Theseus smiled tolerantly. 'So. I have a brother, and I didn't even know.'

'What did you call me? I'll have you torn to pieces between four chariots. You're not my brother. Haven't got a brother. Go away or I'll tell mother.'

Theseus was tempted to thrash the boy soundly, but instead he only patted Medus on the head. 'And just who is your mother, child?'

Just then, Medea came to the door to call her son. At the sight of Theseus she dropped the bowl she was holding, and black olives rolled about her feet. Medus let fly with his fists, and pummelled Theseus in the thigh. 'Look what you've done! Mother! Mother! He says he's my brother. Have him hung, mother! Have him fed to the catfish in tiny little pieces!'

'A dear child,' said Theseus politely to Medea.

'Medus! Stop that. Shake hands with your brother. My dear stepson. I knew at once who you must be. You're the very image of your father—a little taller, perhaps, and your eyes are bluer, but I can see for myself who you are . . . Medus, don't eat those, there's a good boy.'

The little boy was squatting on his haunches, eating the spilled olives off the ground, one by one, spitting the stones at Theseus, and muttering with his mouth full, 'Not my brother. Haven't got a brother.'

But Medea made Theseus as welcome as if he were her own son. She took him indoors and gave him breakfast, then showed him all the rooms of the palace (except for the king's). Theseus was too well-mannered to show his impatience, but his eyes were all about him as he went, hoping to catch a glimpse of his father.

Suddenly, Medea rested one hand on Theseus's arm as if an idea had struck her. 'Oh, such a joke! It would be such a joke! Will you do something for me, Theseus?'

'Madam, anything.'

'Then don't let's tell Aegeus who you are. Let's see if he can recognize you for himself! Come to the feast tonight as a stranger—and see if he can spot his own likeness in you. I'll make him pay a forfeit to you of a hundred golden pieces if he can't! Oh say you'll do it— for the sport of it.'

'Madam, I've waited seventeen years to meet my father. I can be patient until tonight, of course I can!'

As he left, intending to spend the day exploring the city and its sights, Medus tripped him up in the doorway, and ran grizzling to his mother when Theseus slapped him. 'Get rid of him, mother! Don't like him. Got more hair than me!'

His mother spread her skirts and wrapped them round Medus and hugged him close. 'If only that were all, my darling boy. Don't you understand? He was born before you were. That makes *him* the true heir to Athens. He'll disinherit you, boy. And I shall have to watch another woman's son take the throne ahead of you . . . Come with me, Medus—*and stop grizzling!*'

King Aegeus was kept busy all day with preparations for the feast. Whenever he caught sight of his wife, he saw her anxiously gnawing her lip. When at last they sat down alongside each other, at the head of the table, he leaned on the arm of his chair and asked, 'Is something troubling you, my dear?'

She too leaned on the arm of her chair and her head bent close to his. 'Spies, my dear.'

'Pies?'

'*Spies*, my dear. *Spies*. Athens is full of them, of course, but I never thought your enemies would dare to send a spy into the palace itself, in broad daylight. The gall! The treachery!'

Aegeus started up out of his chair. 'Where? Who is it? Who told you, Medea?'

Medea laid her finger to her lips. 'No need to alarm your guests. I have my arts, haven't I? I can see into a man's heart. I can see when he's plotting assassination.'

'Assassination!?' spluttered Aegeus.

'And I know how to stop a man's heart beating for ever,' said Medea. 'You see the youth there with blond hair cut like an Athenian fighting man—the one with the blue eyes. I've heard him speak, and he's no Athenian. He's a boy from the country, and he's here in the pay of that Cretan villain, Minos. And he's wearing a sword under that cloak.'

It crossed the king's mind that most of his guests were wearing swords and that many came from outside Athens. But his wife had magic powers and, after all, why should she lie to him? When you are married to a sorceress, it is all too easy to say, 'What must I do now, my dear?'

'It is all in hand,' said Medea. 'I have told the servant to poison the assassin's wine. Look. The beaker has just been set down beside his hand. Watch him drink and die.'

Theseus caught Medea's eye and winked. He fingered the metal of the wine beaker set down beside him. His mother, Aethra, had told him to avoid strong wine, gambling, and strange women. But his mother was in Troezen, wasn't she? He had a good mind to drink it down in one swig and call for more. He wanted his father to see him for the grown man he was. He picked up the beaker.

But when he raised it to his lips, the reflection of his own face so startled him that he hesitated and sat staring into the wine at his newly shorn forehead and curl-less cheeks. Then his father's voice addressed him.

'Young man. Yes, you. Why don't you make yourself useful and carve meat for us all?'

Medea ground her teeth. 'What are you doing? He was just about to drink!' she hissed.

'I like to see the man I'm killing,' whispered her

254

husband smugly. 'Look at the size of him, and the muscles on his arm. I'm glad my enemies didn't insult me by sending some weakling to assassinate me. What is he waiting for? Why doesn't he carve?'

Theseus was in fact gazing at the roast lamb that stood on the table in front of him. He had never in his life carved a joint of meat. He had never even watched with interest his mother or grandfather carve at table. Did his father already recognize him that he drew special attention to him? Did he want Theseus to make a fool of himself in front of all these people because he could not carve? Besides, he had no dagger. What should he use for a carving knife? Nervousness made him thirsty. A sip of wine and then he would make an attempt on the meat. No, his father might think he needed the wine to steady his nerves. For the second time, Theseus put down his cup.

A sudden idea came to him. If he could not carve well, at least he would carve with panache. And, drawing his sword, he flourished it dramatically, meaning to chop the roast lamb into a hundred pieces . . .

'At my own table he draws his sword to kill me!' stormed Aegeus, knocking over his chair as he leapt up. 'Guards! Cut him down! Show this assassin how the court of Athens rewards treachery!' Beside the king, his queen clutched her son to her bosom as if to protect him from the flying blades. But there was a smug smile on her lips, and little Medus was grinning. He stuck out his tongue at Theseus who was gaping in amazement at Queen Medea. Twenty armed soldiers closed in for the kill.

Theseus shook himself. 'Well, if that's the way of it!' he cried, and leapt on to the table, his sword raised in front of his chest to deflect the first blows.

'WAIT! WAIT! WAIT!'

King Aegeus too had leapt on to the table. He held both hands in the air and his face was blue with the exertion of shouting. 'He's got my sword. *He's got my sword! And my sandals, too!*'

'Thief! Thief!' bawled the soldiers, and they began to rain blows on Theseus's parrying sword.

'No! No! STOP!' bellowed the king, tearing his hair and lunging in among the clashing blades at great danger to his life. 'He's no thief! I *gave* the sword and sandals to him before he was ever born. Stranger! No one could have lifted that rock except one boy—and he with the help of the immortal gods. If you are that boy, then you are the one the Oracle promised! You are Theseus! *You are my son!*'

The feast broke up in disorder. In all the jostling and pushing, Theseus's beaker was spilled, and raised large, blistering burns on the surface of the table. Medea and Medus tried to creep away in the confusion, but Aegeus glimpsed them climbing through the window, and sent his guards to fetch them back. 'Soon enough you may go!' he told them. 'Soon enough you may take the clothes you are wearing and a chariot from the stables and leave Athens for ever. You are banished, Medea, and your spoiled brat is disinherited. This is my real heir, and his mother shall be Queen of Athens. Theseus, put my mind at rest this instant. Is your mother's name Aethra of Troezen? Yes? I knew it! Somewhere sewn into the seams of my heart I've carried the thought of your mother with me all along. Come down, son. I have a kingdom to give you. But first you shall finish carving the meat so that everyone here can feast in your honour!'

So Medea and Medus left the city-state of Athens in a squeaking chariot and a cloud of dust, like shame, that hung over them all the way to the horizon. Watching them go, King Aegeus thought, This is why the Oracle said my son would bring me grief.

Theseus was declared Prince of Athens, and wore round his shorn forelocks a plaited band of white gold that shone almost as brightly as his eyes. Aethra was brought from Troezen to be Aegeus's queen, and after that the king began to doubt the wisdom of the Delphic Oracle. There was little grief in having Theseus for a son. In fact, if it were not for the matter of Minos, King of Crete, Aegeus would have been the happiest man alive.

5

The Bull's Child

In the days when Theseus was Prince of Athens on the shores of the sea, Poseidon the Earth-Shaker, the Earthquake-Maker, the sea god himself ruled the oceans. And in the paddock ocean which stretched from the shores of Hellas to the island of Crete, he grazed his great blue bull.

Wherever Poseidon's bull roamed, men who looked out to sea, or sailors who gazed over their ship's rails on a stormy day, said that they could see the arch of its monumental neck and hear it bellowing out a challenge to the fishes of the deep. Its legs were the bent pillars of waterspouts, and its feet were splayed spray, and its head had a certain terrible beauty, too.

There was one person who looked out to sea more often than most. Forced by her marriage to the king of Crete to live out her life on the island, the lonely Queen Pasiphae often stood on the beaches and watched for Poseidon's bull. She made garlands to hang around its horns, and it learned to come looking for the haystacks of field flowers she set out on the shore. And as the bull ate, Pasiphae would stand hem-deep in the lapping water, and stroke her hand over its blue neck.

At last it grew so tame that she was able to straddle its back and ride the length of the long, deserted beaches. As she did so, she whispered into its flickering ears until it strode into the sea and tumbled her in the thrill of the surf. Sometimes it came to her with the ropes and spars of wrecked ships trailing from its horns, and then she would praise its strength and ask how many men it had drowned, and the bull would beat out the reply with its pacing hoof. In short, Pasiphae loved the beast with a love she had never shown to the king of Crete. And when a child was born to Queen Pasiphae, it bore no likeness to the king.

It had the chest and arms of a man, with the whitest of white skin and muscles as huge as the ruts of a cart-track. But its head and hips and hooves were those of a bull calf, and it grew to the size of a man in one year. Full grown, it stood horn and dewlap taller than the king himself, and its shoulders were hunched like the keel of a rowing boat. It crunched and ate the servants who brought it food.

When King Minos saw his wife's 'son' he knew well enough what had happened. He had a tower built as a prison for Pasiphae, and he had a pen made, too, for her bull-child. He tried to keep its birth a secret, but rumour spread from end to end of Crete that the queen's monster was chained up beneath the palace, and at night people could hear it bellowing.

Summoning to Crete the inventor-genius Daedalus, King Minos said, 'Build me a new palace—a palace worthy of a king who commands the sea-lanes of the world. I want a building so tall that by standing on the roof I can see a mile out to sea. And I want a cellar—a big cellar—bigger than the palace, and twisting like a maze. It doesn't need windows or steps or ladders or exits—just a grating here and there where meat can be pushed through—oh, and a trapdoor large enough to drop a man through. Its corridors must wind and weave so much that someone could wander for a year and never find his bearings. And at the heart of the cellar I want a cell with a manger and a mattress and a cake of salt . . . They call it the Minotaur, Daedalus, isn't that right?'

'I don't know what you mean, sir,' said the inventor nervously.

'I know what people are saying, man. They call it the Minotaur—the beast of Minos. But it's no son of mine. I never want to lay eyes on it again. I'll keep it, even so. I'll use it to make myself the terror of the empire. When people on the mainland talk about Crete, they'll lower their voices and say, "That's where the Minotaur lives in the king's cellar and eats human flesh!" Do it, Daedalus—and build quickly. The beast gets stronger every week. It may break free any day . . . '

So Daedalus went back to his room and worked night and day to draw up plans for the new palace and its maze of cellars. His young son woke up in the early hours, and asked questions, never-ending questions about the plans his father was drawing. But Daedalus would not answer. He only said, 'Be a good boy, Icarus, and go back to bed, or the Minotaur may come and eat you up.' At that moment, a bellow rang through the silent palace, and Daedalus and the little boy both shuddered.

When the great blue bull came looking for Pasiphae and could not find her; when there were no more heaps of drying flowers on the shore nor garlands for his horns, the beast grew angry and raged up and down the ocean-world, destroying ships, lighthouses, and breakwaters, undermining cliffs and shivering coral reefs into clouds of blood-red sand. Last of all, it vented its fury on the sea-wall at Pyrrheus—the harbour below Athens where Aegeus and the Athenian merchants moored their vessels.

The wall was high and curved, and the bull's horns glanced off its slabs of white marble until sparks flew up and were mistaken, out at sea, for lightning. The owners of the ships in harbour ran to the waterfront, thinking to make fast the ropes, or off-load their cargoes. But when they saw the bulging blue skull of the bull, and the scimitar slash of its horns rearing up over the sea-wall, they fled in terror, praying out loud to Poseidon. 'O mighty Earth-Shaker and Earthquake-Maker and Shifter-of-the-seas! Your sacred bull is smashing the world to atomies! Save us! Save us from the bull!'

Close by, at the temple of Athena, Theseus happened to arrive, to make his daily sacrifice to the goddess of Athens. But all the sacrificial birds were sold; there was not a stick of incense to be had, and all the white meal in the city was scattered on the altar of Poseidon.

'What nonsense is this?' demanded the Prince of Athens and, strolling down to the harbour at Pyrrheus, he walked the length of the sea-wall, pausing now and then as the great blue bull charged and shook it to its foundations.

A gaping cleft had been riven in the towering wall, and the sea spewed through with every successive wave. Theseus straddled the gap and taunted the bull: 'You blown dandelion! You puff-ball! You melting snowball! Is that the best you can do? Fighting walls is about your mark. It would be different if you had to fight an opponent with brains!'

Poseidon's bull pawed the sea into a turmoil of seething currents and raised a bellow which holed the clouds on its way to Olympus. Poseidon the Sea-Shifter cocked an ear to listen. Looking down from a terrace of the holy mountain, he

261

was amused to see his great blue bull charge on the harbour. Athena's city will be a sorry sight by the time my pet has trampled through its streets, he thought, laughing.

On came the bull, its breastbone raising a chevron wave that spilled over the wall and almost dislodged Theseus from his perch. Directly at Theseus the bull charged, the thick bone of its forehead showing yellow through its smooth, blue hide. It fixed its aim on the arrogant mortal straddling the crack in the wall, and it hurled itself at him.

High into the air Theseus flung himself, as if he were leaping the new moon and not just the crescent of huge, goring horns. The bull's head went through the crack in the wall. So did its throat. But the thick, hurtling body wedged in the gap.

It took only the weight of Theseus landing on the tossing horns to snap the bull's short neck. Outside the sea-wall, its gross body bobbed harmlessly on the lessening waves: dead.

When Theseus saw what he had done and how easily he had done it, he gave a great leap in the air and spread his hands towards heaven, as if to say, 'Did you see? Were you watching?' But no roll of thunder came from the mountains, only a groan from the sea and a jaundice-yellowing of the sky over Athens and a kind of smell on the wind.

With the help of cheering Athenians, who showered him with flowers and kisses, Theseus hauled the dead bull through the streets of Athens to the Temple of Athena. 'This morning there were no sacrifices on sale when I came to worship the goddess Athena: they had all been spent on the altar of Poseidon,' declared the prince, one foot raised on the lolling head of the dead animal. 'But now I have a gift for the grey-eyed Athena more fitting than a scrawny pigeon or a sickly whiff of incense. Here on the altar of Pallas Athene I spill the blood of a worthy sacrifice!' And he drew his sword across the bull's throat. Ice-flecked, purple blood stained the marble everlastingly.

The jaundice yellow remained in the sky all that month, and the smell in the wind, too. It was an acrid smell, as though the doors of a heavenly cattle shed had been left ajar. Then the same sickly colour crept into the faces of the palace servants, and the king's guard. Men and women began to fall down in the streets, and the sound of children crying could be heard all night long. There was sickness within the walls of Athens.

There was plague.

6

Flying in the Face of the Gods

There were no longer emerald green lizards basking on the walls of the royal palace. They had all been frightened into the eaves and crevices by the shouting mob hurling rocks. 'It's Theseus's fault! Theseus brought it on us! Theseus killed Poseidon's bull!' yelled the mob, and tore up the laurel bushes in the garden.

'Take no notice,' said King Aegeus to his son, inside the palace, as the guards boarded up the last windows and the rooms were plunged into darkness. But the shutters did not keep out the angry chanting: *'Theseus brought the plague! Theseus brought the plague! Theseus brought down Poseidon's curse!'*

'Perhaps they're right,' said Theseus, though his nostrils flared and his lip curled with disgust. Only a month ago the same mob had been cheering him for breaking the bull's neck.

'There's only one way to find out, son. I must ask the Oracle Xenoclea why the gods have poured down this plague on us. She may even know what we must do to be rid of it.'

'I'll go, then. I'll go to Delphi,' said Theseus, pacing up and down the dark room.

'No. You must stay here with your mother. She's so ill, and if it really is the plague, she'll want you here with her. But take care not to catch it yourself, son. It may be that the gods will demand my life in exchange for their forgiveness. Athens must not be left without a ruler.'

Theseus opened his mouth to argue, but what could he say? Could even he gainsay the gods? He sat down in the corner of the room and folded his arms over his bowed head to blot out the sound of the chanting.

So King Aegeus travelled once more to the temple-cave at Delphi with its floor hollowed by a million feet, the yellow, retchy smoke and the befuddled maiden balanced on her pedestal of bronze, seeing visions.

'O sacred Oracle, who sees the past and the future as the view from a window, my poor city Athens is riddled with plague. Why? What have my people done wrong?'

At first, it seemed that the Oracle would not speak. Her closed eyes stared through Aegeus, and her jaw sagged and her hair hung in tangles to the floor. Were the gods too angry even to show him a sign? When the voice came, it sounded all the more dreadful for its toneless, pitiless calm:

'You know full well why Athens is being punished. Your son, Theseus, killed Poseidon's blue bull. Did he expect to go scot-free? The bull has a child. The gods decree that the bull's calf must be fed.'

'The bull's calf? Where is it? I'll give it all the plains round Athens to graze on, and have a host of maidens weave garlands for its neck!'

'Silence, Aegeus. Even you and your Athenians have heard tell of the bull's calf. It is called the Minotaur and it lives on Crete where King Minos keeps it locked in the Labyrinth beneath his palace and feeds it on the flesh of maidens and men. Send seven young men and seven young women to Crete to feed the Minotaur, and Poseidon will lift his curse off the city of Athens. Such a little fine. Is the god of the sea not generous?' The slurred voice did not rise or fall one note. But as Aegeus turned to go, it pursued him into the daylight. 'Did I not warn you, Aegeus, that a son would bring you sorrow?'

'But have I not dealt fairly with you, man?' said King Minos. 'Have I not honoured our contract, to the letter?'

'Yes, yes. Of course. To the letter, my lord,' mumbled Daedalus. 'It's just that my conscience . . . My conscience, lord king.'

'Have I not supplied you with the finest materials, the best workmen? Have I not paid you in full and better?'

'Your majesty has been generous in everything. It's just that my conscience . . . ' The architect of the Labyrinth saw the patterns of the carpet on which he knelt squirm and writhe, as the monsters did in his nightmares, his many nightmares. Words deserted him. How was it to be said, without sounding critical of the king? And who criticizes a murderous king and lives? How was Daedalus to say that he hated the very thought of what he had done for King Minos. In designing and building the basement maze beneath the palace, he had become a party to the daily cruelty, the daily butchery, the daily waking nightmare. Daedalus had built the Labyrinth and now boys the same age as his own son were wandering its passageways. In his dreams he took their place, feeling his way through the dark, waiting for the moment when he turned a corner and came face to face with the Minotaur . . .

'Have I not housed you in comfort?' the king persisted. 'Has my hospitality somehow fallen short while you have been staying here as my guest? Do tell me, and I will make amends.' There was a sneer in his voice, a lack of interest in the queasiness of his hired man.

Daedalus confessed that he and his boy had lived in perfect luxury since arriving on Crete—a luxury unheard of in their home town of far-away Athens. He did not dare confess to the feeling that the tower-top room of theirs, with its gilded door and the soldiers posted outside, put him in mind of a prison. 'It's my conscience,' he said again lamely. 'It's just my conscience . . . '

'You do not like my Minotaur? If you had your way, you would starve it to death, I suppose. Did you never ask yourself, before you began work, what you were designing and to what purpose it might be put? No. No. I see you did not. The challenge of the project appealed to your inventor's brain. The originality of the assignment appealed to your architect's genius. Very well. You may go. I shall have your baggage packed for you. Go on! You are free to go. Let it never be said that Minos dealt unfairly with his hirelings.'

Hurriedly, barely able to believe his luck, Daedalus scrabbled to his feet; the carpet had left the imprint of its woollen pile on his knees. 'Your majesty is gracious—as ever—generous past measure! Thank you! Oh, thank you!' He turned for the door.

'Just one thing, Daedalus . . . '

'Yes, my lord?'

'I'm afraid I must insist that your son Icarus stays. My beast will be hungry again tomorrow. Your boy will serve to feed it.'

267

The inventor uttered a strangled cry and dropped all his parchment plans on the floor. He went down on his knees to gather them up, and stayed there, begging to be allowed to stay. 'You won't hear another word—not a word! Not Icarus! Not my boy! He's my whole life!'

King Minos smiled through his beard and nodded magnanimously. 'I am so glad I have managed to persuade you. Your lives will not be unpleasant here. I shall find many tasks for you that make use of your genius. It's just that you know the secret, you see. The solution to the puzzle. The answer to the conundrum. The map of the Labyrinth is locked within your brain, Daedalus. So you see I must keep you close at hand. You understand that, I'm sure. The secret of the map must be kept close at hand.'

Daedalus ran from the throne room. He ran down corridors he had designed himself and made beautiful with leaping lapis dolphins and scrolled sea patterns. The pictures were loathsome to him now; the dolphins seemed to leer and sneer at him, mocking his stupidity, saying, *Did you really expect the king to let you go? Ever? The map of the Labyrinth is in your brain.* Daedalus knew it all too well, for surely now, as he clawed at his hair and dragged his wrist across his drizzling eyes and nose, he could feel his very own monster rampaging and bellowing around the labyrinth of his brain: ugly, desperate, raging, detestable. Trapped.

As he reached the grid in the floor through which the Minotaur's food was dropped, he stumbled over his son, crouched in the shadows, peering down into the passages of the Labyrinth. 'Icarus, get up! Come away. How can you sit there hour after hour watching for that *monster*?'

Icarus protested at being dragged away from the grid. 'But I like to see it crunch on the bones, father! I like the way it picks them clean then crunches on them.'

Daedalus cast a despairing look at his son. 'There's no time to waste,' he said. 'Come with me. We're leaving.'

He dragged Icarus back to their room, and began tearing the shirt off his back and daubing him with a warm, white, thick, glutinous mess. All the while, the boy protested, 'I don't want to go anywhere. I like it here. What is this? Get it off me. It stinks!'

'It's candle wax. I've been collecting up the candle stubs after supper for six months,' said his father. Throwing open a chest in the corner of the room, he brought out, with reverent care, what looked like two dead eagles. 'I hoped it would never come to this,' said Daedalus.

Icarus was so startled by the beauty of the feathers when the wings were spread that he did not speak as his father plastered his own naked back with molten wax and struggled to mount a pair of wings. 'Well, don't just stand gaping, boy. Help me. It's difficult, behind my back.'

'You look like a duck,' said Icarus, chiefly out of fright.

'If I fly like one, I shan't mind,' said Daedalus, attaching a great drooping span of wings, each threaded out of thousands of feathers, to his son's shoulders. 'Now. These thongs on the leading edge are for your hands. Don't flap. Birds don't flap. Just leap, and let the hot air thermals carry you up high before you cross the coastline and move out to sea.'

Icarus took in none of this. He had just caught sight of his reflection in a bronze ewer on the table and was turning this way and that, with his wings spread, to appreciate the rainbow of oily colours in them. 'Above all, Icarus, above all, you must not fly too close to the sun. If we go now, in the cool of the morning, we shall be over the mainland by the time the sun's at its hottest.

269

If the gods had meant us to fly, they would have allowed the birds to share the secret of flight with us. But I've studied the birds. I've copied their wings. I've made what, till now, only the gods could have made. So keep low—out of reach of the sun's heat, or the wax will melt on your shoulders, and no god will reach out a hand to catch you as you fall.'

Icarus was at the window, gazing out in the direction of the distant sea. The new palace was tall and built on the edge of an escarpment, so that the drop below the window-sill made him dizzy with fear. A handful of busy sparrows hopped on and off the ledge, fluttering out over the drop; their tittering twittering was like an insult.

'I don't want to go. I like it here,' said Icarus, whiningly.

'Even though the king has said he'll feed you to the Minotaur? Now, jump, boy! Don't you want to be the first person in the history of the world to fly?'

Whether Daedalus unbalanced his son as he leapt past him, or whether Icarus jumped to stop his father going first, neither was sure. But after a moment's tumbling and an explosion of loose, ungluing feathers, the wind jammed under their wings with a bone-jarring shock, and they ceased to fall.

Air coming in off the sea and meeting the warm land, swept up the escarpment in columns, and on this hot air Daedalus and Icarus stalled and hovered. Their fists were white and their muscles knotted at first with unnecessary effort, but gradually they relaxed, and the island beneath them became like a carpet, a beautifully intricate carpet hung against a blue-painted wall of sea. They dipped a wing and turned away from Crete, out over the ocean, towards Sicily.

Daedalus was thinking, The seagull feathers are good. I shouldn't have bothered with the finches. Eagle

270

feathers would be best, of course—but so hard to come by . . .

Icarus was thinking, The first person to fly! That's what I am! What would the Princess Ariadne say if she could see me now. Look, a ship! I've a mind to sweep by their mast! They'll mistake me for the god Hermes himself. What? My wings are ten times the size of his! Ten times greater than a god! I don't need to squat on Olympus and bow down to Zeus every morning. I could fly straight over the peak of Olympus and pull Zeus's beard! I could cut the reins of the sun-god's chariot and send it careering all over the sky. What's to stop me? I could race the sun from horizon to horizon! I'll challenge him!

Down on the ship which Icarus had sighted, the Prince Theseus looked up and glimpsed the distant shapes of two birds against the bright sky. Too bright to discern what breed of bird, but one was much higher than the other, and spiralling higher still, towards the unwatchable sun. But Theseus's mind was on his destination and the thirteen companions who, with him, were being shipped as tributes to the king of Crete—as sacrifices to the hideous Minotaur.

'Not so high! Not so high!' cried Daedalus, though his son was already out of hailing distance. 'Remember what I told you! The heat of the sun, boy! *The heat of the sun!*'

Shreds of sound did reach Icarus, but ambition and pride had so swelled inside him—like dry bread inside a little bird—that he hardly felt the need of wings on his back. He felt he could have flown without them. The air was thin, too; it set his head spinning and stifled any common sense. It made him dizzy and hysterical.

*   *   *

Way, way above Icarus, the sun looked over the side of his blazing chariot and saw the tiny speck of a figure ascending. Not a bird—for the birds had long since learned that there was nothing to be gained from climbing so high—not another god, for none of the Immortals would have made himself look so ridiculous, daubed with wax and stuck with motley feathers. The sun reined in his chariot in a moment's astonishment, and sparks flew from around the incandescent wheel-rims. Heat pulsed and radiated from its blazing gold, like the ripples from a splash; the air throbbed with an unbreathable, searing heat. 'Little upstart!' snorted the sun-god, leaning out over the side of his chariot to keep Icarus in sight. The celestial horses paced and tugged in the traces, impatient to reach their stables below the western horizon. The chariot moved on, but still its waves of heat washed over Icarus's head.

There was no room in his lungs for boasting, now— only the thin, singeing air. There was no room in his heart for pride—only the pumping of terror. There were no wings on his back, either—only the larding trickle of wax as it melted and dripped and dropped.

Theseus shielded his eyes with one hand, against the brightness of the noonday sun, and saw a shape fall out of the sky and splash into the sea. A sea eagle diving for fish, perhaps. Another such shape was descending, in slower, sweeping turns, towards the settling spray. But the scar in the water had been already rubbed out by the incessant rolling of the sea. Theseus shrugged. His mind was on his mother who had died of plague because of him. 'Time to get into your costumes,' he said to his fellow sacrifices. 'Crete must be just over the horizon.'

* * *

Daedalus flew to and fro, to and fro until, at last, the body of his only son rose from the depths to which it had plunged. He scooped it from the water as a fish-eagle clasps a fish, and flew on to Sicily. A scorched and waxy pair of wings fluttered down a great while later, and washed about on the waves like a huge, dead bird.

7

Admiring Women

'I feel a fool,' said one of the young men. He was wearing a long, blonde wig and a gown stuffed out with sponge and cork.

'Better to look a fool and be a gentleman than to look a gentleman and be a fool,' said Theseus. Instead of seven men and seven maids, he had brought with him from Athens thirteen young men. He refused, Oracle or no Oracle, to allow young women to be fed to the Minotaur. 'Think of your sister and the fate you've saved her from,' he told the young man in the wig.

Theseus, in his pride, was not surprised to find King Minos himself awaiting the boat's arrival in the harbour at Heraklion. But Minos had actually come there in pursuit of his inventor, thinking that he must have fled the island by boat. Having found no trace of Daedalus or Icarus, the king was in a furious temper. He decided to comfort himself by gloating over the tribute from Athens. He would feed the first sacrifices to the Minotaur that night: the entertainment would take his mind off Daedalus. So there he was, on the dockside, when

Theseus's ship berthed. Standing at the prow were seven sturdy and buxom women. One had a particularly fine figure.

Daedalus and Icarus were suddenly forgotten as Minos tugged smugly at his beard and leered. 'You! Young woman! What would you say to a better fate than the horns of the Minotaur? Give me your hand and step ashore, won't you?' The young woman looked in panic towards Theseus, and stood rooted to the deck. 'Come on! Come on!' coaxed King Minos. 'Don't be frightened. I like to have big women around me. It's a stupid woman who turns down the chance to live.'

'Then Athens is full of stupid women, Minos!' cried Theseus. 'Our young women would rather die than lose their honour to a Cretan dog!'

King Minos's mouth fell open into a kind of fascinated grin. 'So! You must be Theseus. I heard that you volunteered to be one of the sacrifices. Such an honourable act deserves a just reward. What shall it be? I know! *You* shall be first into the Labyrinth!'

A young woman had been moving slowly along the waterfront, towards the king. She limped slightly, and carried her shoulders high in awkward nervousness. But she was dressed with the elegant simplicity of a rich woman and, as she walked, she nervously fingered a golden bracelet that snaked round her arm. Her eyes took in the Athenian boat and its cargo.

She reached the king's side at the moment he was taunting Theseus with the prospect of death in the Labyrinth; she fumbled at the bracelet and it fell to the ground and rolled into the deep harbour. King Minos turned furiously and slapped the girl. 'How careless, Ariadne. Clumsy and careless as usual. What are you doing here? Why aren't you at the palace?'

The girl blushed and her lip trembled as she stared

into the water. 'I saw the black sail . . . the Athenian ship . . . and I just . . . thought I'd just . . . '

'You wanted to see the famous Theseus, I suppose,' sneered the king. 'Well, take a good look. Famous broad shoulders; famous yellow hair; famous blue eyes. They say those eyes prove that he's the son of Poseidon himself! Tomorrow he'll be wandering through the Labyrinth, and the smell of him will be in the Minotaur's nose.'

'I am not the son of Poseidon, madam,' said Theseus loudly, 'but I'll fetch back your bracelet from the realm of Poseidon!' And in a gesture of great chivalry, he leapt over the side of the boat and disappeared from view.

It was a grand gesture, but once in the water, Theseus had not the smallest idea how to find the princess's bracelet. Instead of a firm, sandy bottom lit by filtered beams of sunlight, the harbour had a muddy bottom scattered with refuse and cloudy with fish offal. As he poked about with outstretched fingers, his feet flailing above his head, more and more silt swirled off the seabed, and the water grew more and more turbid. He swam straight into the loop of a ship's cable, and thought how ignominious it would be to hang himself accidentally, underwater, in some foreign port. He had a particular dislike of eels and crabs and starfish and all the other things that crawl in the sea's mud.

So when, in the murk, something soft pressed against his face, he loosed a cry of bubbles that almost emptied him of air. Then he saw that the softness was the flank of a grey-blue dolphin, and in its beak was the bracelet. But when Theseus took hold of its splayed tail, it dragged him not to the surface, but between a maze of boat-keels and out of the harbour mouth.

Just once it surfaced—long enough for him to gulp in air—and then it plunged down and down and down into a sea trench, to where the water was not warmed or much lit by the sun, and the only colour was the turquoise roof of the sea's surface far above. Under a canopy of barnacle-covered rock, tasselled with scarlet seaweed and hung with the sail of a sunken ship, sat the queen of the mermaids. She held a conversation, in clicks and squeaks, with the dolphin, during which the princess's golden bracelet dropped to the sand. But Theseus, whose eyes were bulging and whose lungs were collapsing for want of air, could only point to it and throw up his hands in a slow-motion helplessness.

After the mermaid kissed him on the mouth, it was as if he had taken three deep breaths in the dry sunlight.

She said very little that he could understand and her voice was dolphin-like, peppered with sharp clickings of her tongue. But Theseus quickly realized that she *approved* of him: 'Beautiful! Enchanting! Almost godlike!' Her tail encircled his legs like a tongue, licking. Languorously she wound herself around him, tail first and her long arms trailing. Her hair coiled about his head and neck. The dolphin thrust the bracelet back into his protesting hands and the queen of the mermaids thrust her crown on to Theseus's head. 'Delicious! Incomparable!' And with a clicking in her throat like the teeth of a comb, she went spiralling out of sight through a fountain of bubbles threshed from the water by her massive fins.

The dolphin stood on its tail, backing away from Theseus in a series of bows, like an obsequious courtier. It was beckoning him to follow and, catching hold of its tail again, he was swept back through the harbour mouth, back through the maze of boat-keels, to the weed-slimy wall of the waterfront.

When his head burst into the open air, Theseus could hear the sound of oars splashing, swords rattling and the double-quick march of soldiers running. His dive had been mistaken for an attempt to escape, and Minos was shamed by the prince's gallant return and the presents of crown and bracelet that he laid at Princess Ariadne's feet. The look on the girl's face was charming to see; her lips were pursed as if to open them would have spilled all the admiration inside. Her eyes shone.

But all the other Athenians had been bound with rope and loaded into an open cart, like provender on its way to market. Theseus was forced to join them.

The size of Crete astonished Theseus. As he had sailed into harbour, the island had reached out on either side as far as the eye could see. What people called an island seemed to Theseus like a continent, and more buildings perched on it than seagulls on a rock.

On the journey inland, it began to rain—a cold, persistent drizzle that soaked the prisoners through and through and saturated their disguises. They plucked at their plaits, nervous of being found out. But their guards rode heads-down in the rain.

At first, Theseus memorized each crossroad, each notable tree, each farm building they passed. But the journey to Knossos palace was so long that he soon lost his sense of direction. If he escaped now, he would not know which way to run for the sea. 'Still, it's an island,' he told himself. 'Whichever way I go, I shall find the sea.'

The landscape was strangely green compared with dry Troezen or sunbaked Athens. He resolved one day that Athens must conquer Crete and seize its fertile farms and fat cattle. But it was an arrogant hope. Everything on Crete was so new, so remarkable, that it was like stepping forward into a future time.

And when he saw Knossos palace, his confidence for the first time failed him. Here was a building the like of which he had never seen—so beautiful that even the young men doomed to die in its cellars were glad to have seen it. Its pillars were spirals of marble, and its walls shone with blue waves, like the sea itself, with playing dolphins and leaping acrobats, charging bulls and scroll patterns high and low. Most remarkable of all was the sheer size of the palace which was not (like the buildings of Athens) made up of four walls and a roof, but was three- and four-storeys high. Stairs—not ladders but stairs cut like terraces in a mountainside—climbed up to rooms balanced *on top* of the ones below! And stairs went *down*, too, into chambers and cells cut like caves out of the ground itself! There were not two corridors but a dozen, not four windows but forty. This fantastical palace, built with skills that were nowhere to be found in Athens, towered over Theseus and made envy stir in the pit of his stomach. To see all this and then to die without a chance to copy it? That would be too galling to bear.

'What made me think of that?' Theseus demanded of himself. 'What made me think of dying? I killed Poseidon's bull, didn't I? So I can cut its monstrous son into joints of beef, can't I?'

The high gutters of the palace spilled rainwater on his head, and he shivered convulsively. 'It's a wet day I'm having!' he called out loudly to his companions. 'A man could catch his death of cold!' The prisoners smiled wanly at him as they were jabbed and prodded with spears, and hurried through the huge doors, down stone steps and into the palace jail.

It grew dark outside without Minos sending for a sacrifice. A Cretan sailor had arrived at Knossos with news of Daedalus and Icarus. He had seen them, he said, *flying* towards the mainland, and had followed their flight for as long as he was able, in his caique. A short while after losing sight of them, he had found a huge pair of wings washing about in the ocean. One at least had drowned. From their cell in the cellars, the Athenian prisoners could hear the king laughing out loud—a hollow, sinister, echoing laugh that set the beast in the Labyrinth bellowing. And the bellowing went on all night. The Minotaur had not been fed, and it was hungry for meat and marrowjuice.

8

The Beast in the Labyrinth

Minos did not send for Theseus first, after all. In the morning, one of the young men was dragged to the door by the guards, kicking and screaming. He clutched at Theseus, who stood beside the door. 'You said *you'd* go first. You didn't say it would be like this. You said we wouldn't have to die!' Theseus shrugged and turned his face to the wall, and they heard the struggle continue in the corridor overhead—further on, the scraping of a grid, the thump as the boy was dropped through, the rattle of the grid sliding back into place. There was a sobbing and scuffle of feet as the boy ran, through the pitch black corridors, away—or so he hoped—from the Minotaur.

When Theseus turned back to face his companions, they were staring at him with pale, shocked faces. 'He was right. You did say you'd go first,' said the boldest of them.

'I wasn't sent for.'

'You could have offered.'

'Well, of course I could! But think! You're quick enough with your reproaches, but you're so slow to *think*! It's *morning*. If we're to escape, we need cover of darkness. It's no good my fighting the Minotaur until this evening.'

The boys nodded sheepishly; all except one who muttered, 'He could have killed the Minotaur and stayed hidden till evening.' They all put their hands over their ears as they heard the first sacrifice turn a corner and meet, in the blackness, the Minotaur.

At noon, the Princess Ariadne brought the prison guards their lunches. They were startled to see the royal princess in such a low part of the palace, but she explained that she wanted to make the prisoners beg for their lives: it would be fun, she said, to refuse them. Once outside the cell gate, she signalled urgently to Theseus and he went closer to the door. Ariadne said, 'Theseus, if I help you to escape, will you take me with you?—As your wife?' Theseus looked round sharply, but none of his companions had heard.

Escape. What a sweet sound the word had to it, all of a sudden! Escape! Then Theseus remembered the boy in the Labyrinth. 'I came here to kill the Minotaur. I won't go back until it's dead.'

She was taken aback, but after running her eyes up and down his body she said, 'You might. You just might. But what then? How will you find your way out of the Labyrinth without my help? Nobody does, you know. Nobody ever has. It's a maze, you see. Daedalus built it so that a man could wander up and down its passageways for forty years and never find his way back to the grid.'

'But you know the secret?' Now it was Theseus's turn to run his eyes up and down Ariadne.

He did not much like what he saw. She strongly resembled her father and she stood awkwardly, with one hip stuck out, so that both feet could rest flat on the floor. They were large feet. Her hair had neither the ambition to curl nor the weight to hang straight. Her eyes, which doted on Theseus, were pleasant, however. So was her mouth which, as his eyes lighted on it, opened and said, 'I love you, Theseus. I loved you the first moment I saw you. I loved you before, when I heard the stories they told about you. And I love you now.'

'And I love you, too, Ariana.'

'Ariadne.'

'Ariadne. Why else did I leap into the sea to get back your bracelet? Why else did I beg the queen of mermaids to give me her crown as a present for you? Why wouldn't I count myself honoured above all men if I could take you with me when I leave here. Now . . . what's the secret of the Labyrinth?'

'Open your hand.'

He opened his hand and, furtively, she thrust something into it—something harsh and small and round.

'A ball of string?' he said, with a look on his face that was something between disbelief and disgust. And what was more, she took it back!

The guards came, then, and warned the princess not to stand so near the grille, in case the prisoners took it into their heads to grab at her. She hurried away, bobbing as she limped, and lifting her dress on the stairs, so that her big feet showed. As she went, she glanced over her shoulder at Theseus. Crying made her mouth less pretty than before.

Theseus was sent for at suppertime—escorted to the king's chamber and searched thoroughly for any kind of weapon. The chamber was full of evening sunlight and beautiful women whose dresses plunged to their waists and were caught up between their legs. These were the bull-maidens of Crete, the acrobats who leapt the horns of charging bulls and rode standing upright on their withers. At the sight of them, Theseus was filled with a longing to live. If he, the prince of Athens, was to marry such a brave Cretan beauty, what children might come of it! The thought kept his mind off the bellowing in the cellar.

'I have seen him,' declared King Minos. 'I have looked my last on the mighty Prince Theseus and so has the world! Take him away and feed him to my beast!'

Theseus shook off the guards' hands and walked, of his own free will, back down the corridors to the open grid of the Labyrinth. He would not let them lay hands on him or throw him into the darkness, but hopped lightly down and landed on his feet.

'Don't worry!' he shouted out, knowing his companions would be able to hear him from their prison cell. 'I'll be back!' Then the grid rattled back into place over his head and he was alone in the Labyrinth with the darkness and the Minotaur.

But there was Ariadne's ball of string, one end tied to the grid, and the ball lying by his feet. All he had to do was hold it in one hand as he went, and let it unwind and ravel out behind him. Whenever he chose, he could follow it back the way he had come. 'Of course! Why didn't I think of that? So simple. A clever lady, that princess,' mused Theseus.

At every bend in the Labyrinth, there were two choices of passage. For every choice there were four more choices beyond. At first, Theseus knew when the prison cells were behind him, when the king's chamber was overhead. But after a time, he felt like a child that has been blindfolded and whirled round and round and round and left to blunder, hands outstretched, in search of someone to touch. Sometimes the ceiling was so low he felt he was suffocating. Sometimes passageways led off round him in eight different directions, and he felt he was lashed to the hub of a giant wheel that was spinning, spinning, spinning. When he fell over something in the dark, he scarcely knew which was the floor, which was the wall, which was the ceiling. His reaching hands discovered what he had fallen over. Yesterday it had been a young Athenian. Today it was no longer.

'*I am Theseus. Prince of Athens!*' He heard his voice, thin and high-pitched, dribbling away down the passages like water down a sewer. It came trickling back, distorted and redoubled, from the passageway behind him. The hair stood up on the nape of his neck. His scalp crawled. And he set off to run, colliding with brick walls, falling over mounds of bones, flaying the skin off his hands as he turned invisible corners.

One more corner, and he found himself dazzled by the meagre light of one torch jammed into a bracket on the wall. A figure—it seemed to be a man in hide trousers and no shirt—was bending over a manger of straw, his back to the doorway. As Theseus blundered into the core of the Labyrinth, the figure straightened up and turned to face him.

'So you have come at last. I have been waiting for you, Theseus of Athens,' said the Minotaur.

It was a soft, lowing voice, and the eyes which fastened on Theseus's sweating face were liquid brown and full of reflections of the burning torch. Huge, velvety nostrils rankled at the smell of him. The hinder hooves clattered on the paved floor. The string fell from Theseus's hand and rolled away, back into the darkness. 'You killed my father, and now you have come here to destroy me. Well. We shall see. We shall see.'

Theseus heard himself saying, 'Yes, beast—monster—murderer. Yes, we shall see.'

The beast spread his hands to either side of his darkly

285

haired body and shrugged. 'I am a man encased in the nature of a bull; I am an animal cursed with the vices of a man. I am a beast imprisoned for ever in the dark horrors of the Labyrinth. What is your excuse, young man?'

But Theseus, seeking the element of surprise, snatched the torch out of its bracket, and flung it at the Minotaur. It ducked aside, and the torch fell into the manger, where flames flared up with a deafening roar and threw fifty gigantic shadows of the Minotaur across the tiny cell. The beast reached out a calm, unpanicked hand and took Theseus by the throat, lowering its head to gore with one horn.

By the light of the blazing straw, they struggled on the floor of the cell, grappling for holds, biting and wrenching and kicking. They drove the breath out of one another in great sobs and groans. There was none of the skill or finesse of wrestling. There was none of the flourish of a bullfight—just a desperate, grappling mêlée of fists and hooves and horns and feet. Theseus could not get a grip on the shining hide. The Minotaur could not keep hold of Theseus for the quantity of sweat that ran down him. The beast had hold of his wrist, and pinned him to the floor; a horn tore open his shoulder. Theseus broke free and threw hot ash into the beast's moist eyes. He wrenched the red hot manger off the wall, and branded the Minotaur's hide so that the creature bellowed in torment and fell to its knees.

Then Theseus had hold of the horns—just as he had taken hold of the blue bull's horns—and wrenched them round and down. The bull-man was reaching over its shoulders, clawing for some counter-hold on Theseus's body. Suddenly it let its arms drop and said, 'You were always my fate. Oh! to be gone from here!'

Theseus threw his whole weight on the horns, and

the Minotaur fell dead beneath him, its neck broken and its eyes closed, as if in sleep. Large drops of moisture sparkled on the muzzle: the ashes had enflamed its eyes, Theseus supposed.

Presently, the last straw burned itself out, and utter blackness closed in. Theseus crawled about the floor of the cell, the breath sobbing in his throat, groping, groping for the ball of twine. What was that noise? Did the beast stir? Was it not entirely dead? Theseus swept his hands frantically over the paving slabs and, at last, brushed against the string Ariadne had given him. It rolled away from him, and it seemed hours more before he found it again. Clutching it to him, he began, on hands and knees, to wind up the ravelled string. It led him—along a route that defied all logic—left and right and round and round the maze of Daedalus's Labyrinth. It was more intricate than a spider's web, more complex than the blood vessels in a man's hand. It had as many tricks and turns to it as the cunning brain of its architect.

Then Theseus looked up and saw Ariadne's face above him, beyond the bars of the grid, holding the end of the string, and he burst out with joyful gratitude: 'I love you, Ariadne of Knossos! I love you!'

She was muffled up in her cloak, ready for the journey. 'Quickly! Quickly!' she kept saying. 'We must get away from here. If my father finds out that I'm gone, we'll never get off the island.'

But Theseus would not go without his twelve companions. He killed the sleeping guards and opened the prison gate. Together, all fourteen of them—as many leaving as had come—crept out of Knossos Palace to the horses Ariadne had stationed in readiness. 'I have a boat in the river estuary below Margarites,' she said.

'What colour is the sail?' said Theseus.

'What colour is the sail? What kind of a question is that? I don't know . . . brown, I think.'

'Then it won't do. We'll go back to Heraklion and leave aboard the boat we came in. There's a white sail rolled up under the decks. I promised my father the king that I'd send the ship home under its black sail if I failed, and sail it home under a white one if I succeeded. He'll be watching for a white sail, you see.'

So, despite the extra risk, despite the lights that burned in braziers along the waterfront and the coming and going of little fishing boats in the harbour, Theseus and his crew and the Princess Ariadne crept to the prow of their Athenian ship, and slipped the cables which moored it.

Then Theseus sent one youth to each of the Cretan fighting ships moored to the marble waterfront. On board each ship they left fuses burning—little orange glows in the darkness. As the Athenian ship under its black sail slipped out of Heraklion harbour, the glow of dawn increased and the orange glow of fuses in the fighting ships grew to a great inferno of burning timber and canvas and rope. Lights came up in the houses, too—the hundreds of houses perched like seagulls on a rock—and all the town came running to see the king's fleet sink in flames to the bottom of the harbour.

9

Ariadne

T here were no bounds to Ariadne's joy. Although she had left behind her mother, her father, and the island where she had been born, nothing could dim her delight. She wore it like the shining cloak that hid her twisted leg, her clumsy body, and her large feet. Tending to Theseus's wounds at the hands of the Minotaur, she felt she could just as easily have mended the rift in the clouds where the sun shone through. Preparing him a meal on board, she felt she could have made wine out of water and bread out of sand. Standing at the prow of his ship and looking out for a first glimpse of mainland Hellas, she felt she could have streaked there through the waves like a blue dolphin, guided by the stars. If Poseidon's great blue bull had come now, hurtling over the waves to smash the little ship to fragments, she could have cartwheeled over its back and ridden on its shoulders all the way to Athens—and better than any bull-maiden of Crete! She was loved, and she was overflowing with love herself.

It amused Theseus to see her standing there at the prow of the ship, leaning forward over the water while, below her, the ship shouldered aside the sea. But the crew sniggered and said, 'Seen prettier figureheads, eh, Lord Theseus?'

Into her cloak, Ariadne had stitched so many valuables—jewellery and money—that every hour she could produce some new and precious present for Theseus, like a conjuror producing birds. But the young men giggled as they whispered together. 'It's just as well she has got treasure inside that cloak of hers, because she hasn't much else to interest Theseus.'

Ariadne was an educated and sensible woman—she knew more than Theseus did about the lands beyond Crete. She amazed them all with stories of a nation to the East peopled by tall, swarthy women who waged war as warriors while their menfolk stayed at home to cook and tend the animals. But it only made the young men rub their hands eagerly and say, 'That's the kind of wife for me! I'll stay home and she can go out and do the work!'

Theseus, too, thought, That's the kind of wife I need—some handsome warrior-woman who would give me sons like Hercules and fight back-to-back with me against the enemies of Athens. Yes, I could be happy with a woman like that.

That was when he began to look at Ariadne out of the corner of his eye, to watch her as she moved about the boat, but without letting her see that he was watching. When she turned to look at him, he made a point of looking another way. He did not choose to meet her eye: something about the shortness of her lashes depressed him.

They put in at the island of Naxos for fresh water. Ariadne went and picked fresh limes to make a cordial for Theseus. She milked a goat and brought him the cream. She offered to scrub down his white sail which had got stained in the bilges to a dirty brown.

'These are not the pastimes of a princess,' said Theseus.

'No, but they are things I can do to please you, and that is why it pleases me to do them,' she said, and struggled down the gangplank, dragging the white sail after her.

But Ariadne did *not* please Theseus by fetching and carrying, by working and thinking of work to do. All his life he had imagined himself marrying a woman with all the regal dignity of the rising sun, with all the stately splendour of noonday, with all the beauty of sunset. He looked for pride in her, equal to his own pride. Hour by hour, since leaving the Labyrinth, he found that he loved Ariadne less and less. By the time they reached Naxos, he loved her not at all.

Their marriage bargain was still a secret. None of the young men knew what he had promised. Ariadne had picked up the ball of string at the mouth of the Labyrinth and said that he must carry it with him always, as a token of her love. 'You have entangled my heart in a maze,' she said, 'and in an endless cord of love.'

The young men were adamant: they would not sail back into the king's presence in the dresses and wigs of their disguises. So they ripped them into long shreds and ran howling and whooping into the nearest village to steal clothes from the local men. Ariadne, quiet and industrious, was down by the water's edge in a little bay near the harbour, but out of sight of the ship. Theseus leaned back from the waist and threw the ball of twine as far out to sea as his strength would let him. It hit the seam of the horizon that joins the sky to the sea.

When Theseus's men came running back from the village, they were anxious to get under way. Theseus had only to cut the cable and let the boat blow out to sea on a stiffening off-shore breeze . . .

When Ariadne saw it sail round the head of the bay, her hands hovered over the sailcloth she had been scrubbing. She could see Theseus standing at the prow, his face towards the horizon. She raised one arm to signal, and shouted his name.

But he neither turned his head nor looked for who had called. His name broke off in Ariadne's throat, like a fishbone that choked her, and she let her hand fall. The surf rolled over the white sail and washed it away from her, into deeper water. But Ariadne stood watching the ship move away. The further it sailed, the smaller it seemed to grow, and inside Ariadne's narrow chest, her heart shrank too, until it was only a small, black speck.

When Theseus saw what he had done and how easily he had done it, he dusted his hands together and grinned at his good fortune.

Then the thunder rolled among the mountains of the gods, and a soughing roar came from the sea. The smile froze on Theseus's face, and he looked over his shoulder, suddenly convinced that he was being watched.

The great black square of the sail flapped at him . . . like a fragment of night that had snagged on the mast as they sailed out of Heraklion harbour . . . like a fragment of nightmare.

'Where's the white sail?' he said, as the mainland came into view.

King Aegeus's advisers and courtiers tried to tell him that Theseus might be gone for weeks—months—that King Minos might keep him in chains for a long, long while before sending him into the Labyrinth. But Aegeus knew Minos's lust for blood, and the Minotaur's ravenous appetite. 'By the third day Theseus will either be dead or he will be sailing home from Crete,' he told them. Then he went and stood on the clifftops to watch for the returning ship.

Up there on the cliffs, with the sea below him and the sounds of the city drowned by the gulls, Aegeus realized how little he cared about being a king. His wife had died of the plague, and now his only son, his Theseus, was pitting his life against the terror of the world. Aegeus wished he could have been a farmer, with one or two sheep and a little son with thin arms and legs and not many brains, who stayed home from morning till night.

He prayed, 'O you gods, look down on Theseus wherever he is. Judge what a fine boy he is, and reward me with his safe return! It's not true what the Oracle said! He didn't bring me grief—not really—he never made me sorry to have a son. If he returns home to me, I'll give up my crown and trust Athens to his safe-keeping. O grant it, you immortal gods, and I shall be at peace for ever. *Send a white sail! Oh, please!'*

Over the horizon it came, like a small black tear in the seascape. Aegeus tried to tell himself that it was another ship, a different ship, not an Athenian ship at all. But the closer it came, the more certain it was: Theseus's ship was sailing home beneath a black sail. He had failed.

Aegeus sank to his knees and rocked slowly to and fro. His face was quite empty of expression. He said, 'Now it's true. Now. The Oracle did speak the truth. "If you have a son," she said, "he'll bring you sorrow." And here it comes—a ship laden with a cargo of sorrow enough to fill all the storehouses of Athens. You were right, Xenoclea. Rather than live through this moment, I would sooner have had no son. Well. Well, I'll not go down to the harbour and off-load that cargo of sorrow. No. Let Athens find a new king. There will always be kings enough to fill the world's crowns. There will never be another Theseus . . . And there will be no more King Aegeus.'

And raising his arms over his head, he let himself fall forward over the edge of the cliff, into the roaring protests of the sea's open mouth.

10

Hippolyta, Queen of the Amazons

E very officer of state, every general of the army, every lady-in-waiting and all the children of the palace were aboard the black galley which put out from Pyrrheus that day. King Theseus was at the prow, raised up on a gilded platform and standing knee-deep in flowers. They sailed along the sword-bright channel of reflected light that stretched across the sea from the rising sun, and when they had rowed ten leagues, the oarsmen drew in their oars.

'Because this sea holds my father's body, let it be called for evermore the Aegean Sea, in memory of him.' Theseus lifted a wreath of flowers off the platform and pitched it into the sea. Flower petals drifted away like the feathers of a drowned bird.

An approving murmur ran round the ship; statesmen nodded and said that it had been well done, very well done, and their ladies agreed with them. Then a child, who had climbed up the empty rigging for a better view, called out that there were sails to the north.

'And to the south, too.'

'And some behind us!'

'And more sailing out of the sun!'

They were beautiful, junk-rigged sails, woven in orange and flame-red, and worked with strange symbols. Each ship had eyes painted to either side of the prow which swept up like an arm raised in salute.

In his pride, Theseus thought that the news of his conquest of the Minotaur and his sinking of the Cretan fleet had brought this convoy from the far side of the ocean to pay tribute to his bravery. Only when the flotilla of gleaming ships had circled the black galley and they were turning in to ram her did he realize, too late.

'They're Amazonian ships!'

Beyond the shields that decorated the sails of the bright hulls, beyond the flash of spearheads, the hair of the crew was curled as tightly as the fleece of a black lamb and their bodies gleamed with oil. Tall they were— taller than all but Theseus, and their teeth flashed white in their black faces, and their armour flashed, here and there, where it was fastened with silver clasps.

Two or three aboard Theseus's galley were armed with bow and arrows. But they hesitated as they drew back their bowstrings, and the arrowheads wavered on their fists. 'They're *women*, my lord Theseus!'

'Yes—women in body, but lions inwardly! These are the Amazons! You gods on Olympus, were you *sleeping* to let heathens get the better of Athens like this? And *women*, too!'

'Have a care,' whispered his chief-lieutenant. 'The goddess Athene, guardian of Athens, is a woman in armour.'

Theseus opened his mouth in retort, but only snarled in exasperation as he looked around him. The ladies-in-waiting were shrieking up and down the galley. The children were crying. Officials of state were fighting each other over who should hide in the sail locker. The army generals had not loosed a single arrow.

296

On came the eyed ships, the high-prowed, high, proud, Amazonian ships, and the black galley lay helpless. Theseus drew his sword and waited for the splintering of wood that would come when they rammed him.

But the Amazonian ships carried brake-oarsmen— women of gigantic size who could stop the progress of their craft within three strokes of an oar. The warlike bows halted, with their painted eyes gazing over the rails of the funeral galley, and a woman's voice put a sudden end to the Athenian panic:

'Theseus! Prince of Athens! Surrender to an enemy who has you by the throat!'

Having no plan, and no hope of winning a fight, Theseus sought to delay his surrender. 'Prince? Your spies are slow to inform you, Amazon! I am King Theseus now! May a king not ask to speak with the leader of those who would rob him of his crown?'

There was a pause and then a woman as tall as Theseus himself and dressed in armour just as fine as his own, leapt the tall bow of her ship and landed on the stern deck, scattering a huddle of maidens. 'I am Hippolyta, Queen of the Amazons. Which is Theseus?'

The blood stirred in Theseus's veins when he saw Queen Hippolyta striding towards him down the length of the boat. She moved like the oily black water of an African river. Her arms were like the massively entwined creepers of the jungle, and her hips were as wide as the bole of a baobab tree. Her throat was as dark and inviting as the wine flowing from a wineskin, and her lips seemed swollen from eating succulent and exotic fruits. He drew in a sharp breath of admiration, and reached down a hand to help her on to the flower-strewn platform.

Looking up into his face, she missed her footing and fell against him as she landed, and he wrapped steadying arms around her. 'Queen Hippolyta, my shame is

297

deserved, since before now I neglected to invite the world's most beautiful woman to be a guest in the city-state of Athens.'

She leaned back from him, like a rearing cobra. 'So, you are Theseus, who slew the Minotaur and scuttled the Minoan fleet. Is it true, then, that your father was your so-called sea god, Poseidon?'

'Not a word. I am as mortal as you are!' and Theseus laughed.

'Can mortal eyes be so blue?' she said.

'Yours eclipse them with their darkness.'

'Or mortal hair so bright?'

'In the eyes of our gods, black lambs are a more perfect sacrifice than white ones.'

'Would you have put me to the sword, then, like a lamb, if you had conquered me in battle?'

'Lady! I slew the Minotaur and Sciron and the Crommyonian Boar. But what kind of a fool would I be to cut the brightest star out of the sky? My sword would sooner have melted.'

'Oh, Theseus!'

There was a long silence full of glances and sighs, before Theseus took the queen's fleecy head between his hands and kissed her on the mouth.

'Empty the boat,' she murmured, and when Theseus was slow to respond, she pulled out of his arms and shouted to her women, 'I want this boat empty! Ferry the Athenians home safely and allow them to give you food and drink and entertainment.'

Her warrior maidens were astounded. 'But Queen Hippolyta! We have them at our mercy. Shan't we stick them with our spears?'

'No! I have surrendered to King Theseus. He is the victor, I tell you. Deliver yourselves into the hands of his generals. I command it. And empty this boat.'

So all the officers of state, the generals in the army, ladies-in-waiting, and children of the palace were lifted over the gunwales into the Amazonian ships and ferried ashore. Amazonian and Athenian were each as astonished as the other, exchanging suspicious glances. Theseus and Hippolyta were left drifting in the black galley, in the heart of the Aegean Sea, amid flowers, and under a blazing sun. It was three days before they re-entered Pyrrheus harbour below Athens.

Hippolyta sent her women home. She gave away her crown to her sister, saying that she had no more heart to live by fighting, and that the Amazons had a new queen now.

'But what will become of you?' asked her sister.

'I shall stay here with my Theseus.'

'But are you to be married? We'll stay for the wedding! Shall you be queen of Athens? We'll ally ourselves to these Athenians and fight by their sides in war!'

'In time. All in good time,' said Hippolyta smiling the distant, thoughtful smile that was new to her. 'What marriage can there be? In front of which altar would we take vows—he in front of the altar of Pallas Athene and I in the sight of my ancestors? I consider that we are married already—since I am going to have his child.'

So soon there were only two black lambs left among the white flocks of Athens: Hippolyta and her baby son, Hippolyte. They brought as much beauty to the city as a verse of poetry written in black ink on a scroll of white paper. When she shed her armour and wore Athenian robes, the people stopped trembling at the sight of her and began to admire her graceful movements, her graceful dealings, her graceful words and laughter. And as Hippolyte grew up, there were those who greeted him in the streets with the words, 'Hail to the prince of Athens.'

Hippolyta was like Theseus's shadow, always at his heel in the morning, and dancing when the lamplight flickered in the evening. Her love was as edgeless as the night. And just as a man ceases to notice his own shadow, Theseus hardly gave her a thought.

Oh, she was a pretty enough ornament in his palace. And Hippolyte, at two years old, was life itself to Theseus. His skin was the colour of acacia honey, and his hair was like the Golden Fleece. But his mother was nothing to Theseus, who thought of her as a prize he had won in battle—a trophy awarded him by the gods, out of admiration.

In his pride, Theseus did not notice that his own bright hair was greying, that his own tanned skin was lined with age and that heroes, when there are no monsters left to fight, grow old like ordinary men.

And ordinary men fall in love.

Love. All his life Theseus had seen it in the eyes of women. If anyone had asked him, 'Theseus, do you know what love is?' he would have shrugged and said, 'Of course. Women have loved me all my life.' And who could blame him? Until Phaedra came to Athens, Theseus had never been in love.

Phaedra was . . . Phaedra was as lovely . . . Phaedra was as lovely as a woman can be (except those like Hippolyta who are lovely in nature as well). She did not sigh at the sight of him. She did not tremble at his touch. Her eyes did not linger lovingly on the back of his head after he had passed by. Little by little, this strange behaviour—quite unknown to Theseus—fascinated him. Finally he spent all his days wandering about Athens in the hope of catching sight of Phaedra.

He invited her to eat at the palace whenever she wanted, and once in a while she did. But whenever

Theseus sat down beside her, she lowered her eyes and left her food uneaten.

In the end, his passion grew to such a heat that he seized hold of her in the street and shouted, *'Why don't you like me, Phaedra?'*

Phaedra lowered her eyes and straightened her robes. 'My lord, you mistake me completely. Why should I not like you. I, not like Theseus? The glory of the world?'

'Well then, why don't you love me?'

'My lord, what love can there be between a king and an honourable maiden, without injury to her honour?'

'I'm not married. *You're* not married. Why shouldn't we marry? I'll make you queen of Athens!'

'What about Hippolyta?' asked Phaedra softly.

'What about her? I never married her exactly. She's a foreigner, isn't she? She's black. I won her in time of war . . . But you would have to take Hippolyte for your son. I want him to rule in Athens after me. Does that upset you?' He gnawed his lip in terror that Phaedra would refuse him.

But she raised her face, looked deeply and earnestly into Theseus's eyes and said, 'My lord! I would have it no other way. Hippolyte is a dear boy.'

When Theseus saw how he had won Phaedra, how at last he had won her, he gave a great leap in the air and spread his hands towards heaven as if to say, 'Thank you! Thank you, you immortal gods!' He did not even notice when the breeze set all the doors in the street banging, and brought up from the harbour the noise of tinkling shackles in the ships' rigging—a noise very much like laughter. Neither did he notice that Phaedra's eyes were different from the eyes of other women.

They were empty of love.

A band of musicians with curling horns went ahead of the bride and groom, and the route to the temple of Athene was strewn with flowers though the hot sun had shrivelled them by noon. Priests and priestesses chanted in harmony, and plumes of fragrant smoke rose from every altar, like the spiral columns of Knossos Palace. Dancers capered about with masks on poles in front of their faces—dolphins and mermaids, horses and lions—ducking and weaving between the guests.

The ruler of every petty province, the general of every military garrison in the region, the wife of every man of rank was there to see the wedding conducted with due ceremony. In fact everyone who could be paid or commanded to attend was present in the procession. Only the townspeople showed some unwillingness to go to the temple, but stood just inside the doors of their houses as the bride and groom went past. Few seemed to smile. The occasional voice shouted out, 'Hippolyta! Where's Hippolyta?'

Neither did little Hippolyte go to the wedding. Too young, said Theseus. Too little to remember it.

The dancing stopped. The hubbub was still. Phaedra and Theseus faced each other in front of the high priest. 'In the sight of Almighty Zeus, father of the gods who took Hera from among the ranks of the Immortals to be his wife, I, Theseus, king of Athens, take Phaedra to be mine, being an unmarried man and she an unmarried . . . '

'Is *that* what you are?' said a voice almost drowned by the banging-to of the temple doors. Hippolyta, dressed not in her Athenian robes but in only the skin of a lioness and carrying a clutch of spears, stood with her back to the door. First there was a craning of necks, then a murmur of astonishment and dismay, then a pushing and shoving as the congregation made way for Hippolyta. Phaedra, too, slipped her hand out of Theseus's hands and moved away into an angle of the wall.

'What do you want, Hippolyta?' said Theseus, and was surprised to find that his voice shook.

'What do I want?' said Hippolyta. 'What do I want? Justice. What do I want? Revenge. What do I want? My son. What do I want? Blood!' And she hurled one of her spears directly at Theseus's head. He ducked one, but to avoid the second he had to fling himself to the ground, and roll under a bench to shelter from the third.

'Someone give me a sword!' he yelled. 'What, are you all paralysed? Somebody give me a weapon!'

But there were no weapons worn in the temple of Pallas Athene, and the guests stood blinking and helpless.

On his back Theseus lifted the bench that was sheltering him, and hurled it at Hippolyta so that she was forced back down the centre aisle.

'What have I done, Hippolyta?' he said, trying to struggle to his feet. His sandals slipped on the marble and he did not succeed. He had nothing left but words to deflect her spears. 'I never thought *you* would turn on me like this!'

'You never thought? No! When did you ever *think*, except about Theseus? Theseus's glory. Theseus's victory. Theseus's happiness. Theseus's wife! I was a queen once—as powerful and victorious as you. But I *thought* you loved me, and I know I loved you. And I thought that that made you my husband and me your wife. I thought when Hippolyte was born that I was all the wife you would ever need. But no! You *thought* Hippolyta was a trophy you had won with a kiss and a string of clever words. Shame on you, Theseus! Shame on you for a spoiled child!'

She came on, lifting her black feet as she had lifted them once over twigs and stones and adders remorselessly stalking her prey. Her outstretched spear touched Theseus's collar-bone, the tip pressing then piercing the skin. Theseus looked down in astonishment at the tiny trickle of blood. 'You've wounded me, Hippolyta!' he said in disbelief. 'I'm bleeding.' He struggled to pull away from the pressure of the spear. 'I thought you loved me. I thought everybody loved me!'

'Ah, but love is a hawk, my darling Theseus. Love is a hawk you carry on your wrist. It will fly for you, kill for you, and come whenever you call. But only while you feed it and speak to it gently. If you leave it to starve, can you be surprised if it turns on you and *tears out your blue eyes*!'

Putting both hands to the end of her spear, she raised it to strike Theseus dead where he lay. But in that moment, a sunbeam wandered across the floor of the temple and shone on the grey-gold of Theseus's hair and on the tears starting into his eyes in terror. Hippolyta felt love stir one last time in her heart, and before she could thrust it back down, it had betrayed her.

Theseus's creeping fingers found the first spear she had thrown lying on the floor, and he snatched it up, kicked her feet from under her, and caught her on the spear-point as she fell on top of him. 'Treacherous Theseus . . . ' she whispered, then died.

They say that when there is something evil afoot in the jungles on the distant shores of the ocean, all the birds stop singing. In the temple of Pallas Athene, there was not a sound, not a voice, not a murmur, not a cry. The congregation melted away through side doors and passageways, and Theseus and Phaedra were left to walk back alone along the route of the procession: king and queen, man and wife.

11

The Gods Reward Theseus

*M*y dear Hippolyte,
*On this, the occasion of your twentieth birthday, I
send you my greetings and pray to the gods for your
happiness and prosperity. Although I am not your true mother, I
feel just as tenderly towards you as your father, the king. And the
whole world knows that Theseus loves you more than life itself.
Death holds no fears for him, knowing that you will inherit the
crown of Athens and rule after him.*

*However, the gods will not permit me to let this day pass
without telling you one small secret which your father has kept
from you. I would not be doing my duty as a stepmother if I did
not tell you.*

*You must often have asked yourself: who was my mother? It
is time to tell you. Your mother was Hippolyta, Queen of the
Amazons. You do not remember her, do you? So beautiful. So
popular. What became of her? Now, when you read this, I must
beg you not to upset yourself, not to feel you have a duty to
avenge her, not to think any worse of your father. He felt it
necessary—and who but the gods can say he was wrong?—to
MURDER your mother. He stabbed her with a spear, in the
temple of Pallas Athene.*

Please do not let this spoil your birthday. I remain your affectionate stepmother, Phaedra.

Queen Phaedra rolled the letter, sealed it with wax, and sent her messenger with it to Hippolyte's bedroom. When the servant had gone, she sat in front of a mirror, pressing her cheeks with the back of her fingers. They were burning with the thrill of what she had just done. 'Now die, Theseus. Die at the hands of your own son.'

Hippolyte stifled a cry and then ripped the letter in two. For a minute he stared at the two pieces, then held them back together and reread the letter twice, three times.

It was not true—the part that said he did not remember his mother. He did have a few shreds of memory, like a torn picture, of long, dark fingers and a smiling mouth, and eyes as black as his own. He had simply not realized that the woman he remembered was his true mother. That much he was willing to believe. But murdered? By his own father? By Theseus the Hero?

All Athens knew Theseus to be the bravest, most renowned, wise, and just monarch on the shores of the Known World. The story of how he had killed the Minotaur and Poseidon's great blue bull had spread throughout the continent: princes would come just to sit at his feet and copy the clothes he wore, the way he cut his hair, the way he buckled on his sword. During his reign, the city of Athens had been graced with buildings more beautiful than any elsewhere in Hellas. People spoke of history as 'the time before Theseus'. Kill a woman? Kill his own son's mother? It was unthinkable. It was a lie.

Phaedra had meant, like a god prising open a volcano, to spill the boiling lava of Hippolyte's rage. Hippolyte's revenge would erupt and engulf Theseus.

She succeeded in loosing Hippolyte's temper, but instead of swearing revenge on his father, he leapt to his feet and roared along the corridors of the palace to Phaedra's own chamber.

Hippolyte smashed open the door and saw Queen Phaedra, her half-fastened hair tumbling down out of startled hands. She backed away from him.

'Why? Why did you send it? What did you think I would do? Did you really suppose I would believe you? Theseus—the legendary Theseus of Athens—a murderer of women?'

'But it's true,' said Phaedra lamely, and her voice failed her. Her plot had gone awry.

Or had it? Already footsteps were running on the stairs and landing. Help was on its way. Theseus would very soon arrive to witness the scene. 'Very well,' said Phaedra drawing herself up to her full height and tossing her head. 'I wanted you to kill Theseus. What are you going to do about it? All these years I have waited and plotted, plotted and waited. All these years I have waited for you to grow strong and Theseus to grow weaker. Theseus is getting old. I can twist him to my purposes. So what will you do about it?'

With a roar like a volcanic eruption, Hippolyte gave vent to his temper. 'I shall kill you myself!' he vowed, and putting his hands round her throat, he forced her backwards across the bed. Her fingers clawed at his face, but his thumbs were on her windpipe, and no sound came from her but a clucking like a hen whose neck is being wrung.

Then a hand like a vice rested on Hippolyte's shoulder and his father's voice said in his ear, 'What? Would you murder my queen? You have condemned yourself to death, you treacherous dog!'

'Not me, father! She slandered you! She wrote me a letter . . . she . . . ' He let go of Phaedra, unmanned by the

307

look in his father's eyes. Never had he seen such anger: it equalled his own, except that his own had suddenly deserted him. He felt ashamed and foolish to be found on his twentieth birthday throttling his stepmother. Phaedra wriggled free and into the protection of Theseus's arms. 'He tried to murder me, Theseus! I don't understand! Unless . . . I didn't tell you . . . I didn't want to hurt you. But last week Hippolyte begged me to stab you as you slept—said he was old enough to have the crown, and that if I killed you, he and I would reign over Athens together! I wrote him a letter telling him I wouldn't—that I loved you too much. The next thing I know he comes bursting in here! And he put his hands round my throat and I thought . . . I thought . . . oh, Theseus, my darling! I thought I should never see you again!' Tears flowed freely then from Phaedra's eyes, and Theseus hushed and soothed her.

Hippolyte began to speak—'It's not true . . . she said . . . she wrote to me that . . . '

'You black spawn of a foreign viper,' Theseus snarled, the spittle foaming round his mouth. 'You unnatural, murderous abomination! You stain on the world's mud. With my bare hands I'll kill you!'

'Oh no, father,' said Hippolyte peaceably, holding up his two hands as if to lay them on the king, even in self defence, would be a traitorous act. 'We must not ever fight, you and I. Let us never put to the test which of us is stronger. I'm twenty, father. You're getting old. I won't fight you, father. Don't make me fight you.'

'Aaaaaaaah!'

Every soul in the palace froze at the sound of the king's cry. His son stared at him in appalled fascination. 'Aaaaaaaah! You gods on Olympus! Listen now to the man they call Poseidon's son! Listen to the slayer of the Minotaur! Listen to Theseus of Athens. It is true! This tapeworm I have fed with my love, this weevil I have sheltered in my heart, this traitor I have entrusted with all my hopes—look how strong he has grown! *Revenge me, then!* I am waning like an old moon. My muscles are stiff, and the gore the bull-man gave me aches when the wind blows. Look down from Olympus and do not suffer the scum of the world to overwhelm the glory that was Theseus! *In the name of all I have ever done: revenge me and strike Hippolyte dead!'*

Hippolyte, white with horror and trembling with dismay, reached out one hand and touched his father's mouth as if to stop the words being said. It was like reaching towards the jaws of a mad dog. *'Cursed?'* he whispered. 'Have you truly cursed me, father?' Then he leapt over the bed and out of the window, touching the ground only a few yards from his own chariot. In blind panic, he jumped aboard it, winding the reins round and round his waist as he whipped the horses to a gallop.

Out of the yard, through the streets of Athens and along the road to the coast the chariot thundered, and behind it a cloud of dust rose up so high that it was visible from the peak of Olympus.

In the halls of heaven, against the walls of heaven, the gods reclined on their couches and looked at one another with eyes full of eternal boredom. Around them, like motes in a ray of sunlight, the ash from sacrificial fires drifted up from altars on earth. Wishful prayers, like the sound of a draught through a small and unsealable crack, whined continually around the legs of their couches. And now and then, like a door banging in a wind, came the words of a curse uttered on earth in the name of the gods.

'Well?' said Zeus the Almighty. 'We all heard Theseus

curse his son Hippolyte. Are we to answer his prayer and throw down our doom on the boy's head?'

Dionysus crushed a peach in his fist so that the juice ran down into a beaker, then drank. 'It's the first time he's ever asked for our help.'

'He's got by well enough without us before,' said Hermes, preening the wings on his helmet.

'I remember how his mother used to pray for us to forgive Theseus his terrible pride . . . but that was a long time ago,' said Hera, threading a needle while, at her feet, the Fates were cutting out a black robe, with sharp pairs of scissors.

'He slaughtered my bull and my bull's calf,' said Poseidon. 'And people call him my son when he's nothing of the kind.'

Only Pallas Athene stood by the vaulting door of heaven and, resting her chin on the end of her spear, looked wistfully down at the white sprawl of Athens near the coast of the blue sea. 'The boy Hippolyte doesn't deserve to die,' she said. 'He's done nothing wrong.'

'But Theseus deserves it,' said Zeus with a note of finality in his voice. 'Let us vote on the matter of Theseus's curse.'

Lazily, indolently, the gods each raised a hand: the right hand for yes, the left hand for no.

'It is decided,' said Zeus the Almighty. 'Poseidon, I think I can safely leave the matter with you.'

Hippolyte turned his chariot on to the coast road, the cliff-top road. He glanced continually up at the sky, expecting at any moment a thunderbolt to hurtle out of the clouds. But there was no roll of thunder and only the scrape and rattle of pebbles where the undertow of retreating waves rolled them down the beach. No one

310

followed from the city. At last, Hippolyte slowed his horses to a walk. 'The gods have seen how father mistook me. They turned a deaf ear to his curse. The gods are just. What was I thinking of to run? I should have stayed and made him listen to the truth about Phaedra. I shall write to him from Corinth. I must make him believe me. It's not as though he doesn't love me: he's loved me for as long as I can remember . . . until now.'

Out at sea, the undercurrents moved with silent power beneath the lilac sheen of surface water. Like sheets of different colours, Poseidon the Sea-Shifter, the Earthquake-Maker, tied them with an overhand knot, and the steady rhythm of the sea's rise and fall was briefly interrupted.

Hippolyte looked out to sea and saw that a dyke of water was heaping itself across the mouth of the bay—a barrow of water—a fold of glassy sea piling up cliff-high—a tidal wave. Hippolyte flicked the reins of his chariot, but thought, Surely up here on the cliff . . . surely they would not send the sea when I'm way up here . . .

The wall of water began to move inshore, the seabed lay exposed ahead of it, looking bald and littered. The wave itself was clean—clean like a glacier. Only one small black shape was balanced on its summit. Faster and faster it moved, always forming a crest but never breaking. Sea and land were set to collide—the cliff of water with the cliff of rock.

They shattered in a white explosion of chalk and spray that soaked Hippolyte to the skin. The wave also delivered up, on to the land, off the crest of the tidal wave, a massive, black dog-seal.

It was vast and ebony, and gleamed like a slug. And when it opened its mouth, the bark that came out of it was like a pack of hounds. It raised itself, on angular flippers, and heaved its black blubber over the gravel of the roadway. The horses in the chariot screamed with terror and bolted. Hippolyte spread his feet wide and braced his knees against the sides. Every time the wheels went over a rock, he was tossed in the air, but managed to keep his footing . . . until the wheel-hub hit a tree stump and shattered.

The chariot rolled, the horses shattered the shafts. They galloped on with renewed speed now that they were rid of the weight of bronze—and had only the weight of the driver to pull.

Hippolyte, tied round with his reins, was dragged face-down along the rocky cliff-top path until the exhausted horses stumbled over the edge and into the sea below.

No trace of Hippolyte was ever found, except for a smashed chariot, a place where the hoof-marks stopped, and another, further back, where some damp, flippered beast had dragged itself along the roadway before diving back into the sea.

News was carried to Theseus while he was still comforting Queen Phaedra with kisses and soothing words. He turned the colour of cold volcanic ash and whispered, 'Why, Hippolyte? I loved you more than life itself. You and Phaedra were the whole world to me.'

But the news brought quite a different colour to Phaedra's cheeks. She broke free of Theseus's arms, threw back her head, and laughed out loud. 'It's done! It's over! I'm free!'

'Free?' said Theseus, already afraid.

'Free of *you*, Theseus. Free of twenty years of pretending to love you and being the dutiful and devoted queen. It's not as I intended, of course: I meant for Hippolyte to kill you. But this is better: he was *more* than life to you, and I made you curse him to his destruction. My revenge is perfect!'

'*Revenge?* But what have I ever done to you?' Theseus

stammered, shaking her by the shoulders. 'You're the only woman I ever loved . . . I never wronged you!'

'No. But you wronged my sister. You did her a grievous injury, then boasted to gods and men about it.'

'Your *sister*?'

'Yes, my sister—Ariadne of Knossos—the girl you promised to marry and then deserted on lonely Naxos. You broke her heart and in return I've broken yours!'

Grief gave way to anger. 'I'll kill you. I'll kill you, Phaedra!'

'I expect so. But then the people of Athens will never forgive you. You brought about the death of your father and mother; you killed beautiful Hippolyta and cursed your son—who was more glorious than ever you were. One more killing, and the legendary Theseus will be shamed for ever in the eyes of Athens.'

It was true. When Phaedra was executed in the market place, no crowds gathered to watch. The people stayed at home and muttered among themselves or crept out after dark to daub insults and crude bulls in paint on the palace shutters. The shutters were never opened any more.

One day, King Theseus dressed before dawn, took a caique from the harbour and sailed out to sea—to an uninhabited island close by Naxos. There he sank the caique and built himself a verandah out of the wreckage, in front of a cave where he slept at night.

Sailors passing by in ships sometimes saw him sitting beside a fire on the beach, and hailed him and waved greetings. But Theseus was rather too proud to wave back.

Odysseus

1

The Land of the Lotus-Eaters

'When will father come home?'

Queen Penelope turned away from the bright window to look at her son. 'Soon, Telemachus. Soon.'

'But the war has been over a long time now,' said the boy, fingering his father's golden spear and quiver of polished satinwood.

'Troy is a long way away—the other side of the world-encircled sea, on the far eastern shore. If there are no winds in his favour, his men can only row. It would take many, many months to row from Troy to Ithaca.'

Telemachus tried to lift the huge sword that stood in the corner of the room, but it was too heavy for him. How much more must the king's sword of gold weigh that his father had worn when he went away to war!

'Why don't I remember his face, mother?'

'Child! You were only a baby when he sailed for Troy. The siege lasted for ten years. I can describe him to you—how his hair curls forward from the crown—how he wears his beard trimmed to a point—how his tan is darker than the mainland Greeks who never sail between

317

the sun and the sea. And his hair is almost the colour of his bronze helmet—ah, I forget, you never saw his warrior's helmet, or his blue eyes looking out. I can describe him to you, child, but I wish there were someone to describe his son to him—or that he were here to see you for himself.'

'But you say he'll come soon, mother?' said Telemachus.

'As soon as the gods allow. This island of ours, this Ithaca, it's his home. It's his kingdom. And what use is a king without a kingdom or a kingdom without a king?'

And her eyes returned to the sea below the palace— to the brimming ocean whose waves were always arriving, always beaching, on Ithaca's rocky shore.

In the prow of his boat, Odysseus stood and gazed ahead at the grey swell of the sea, which seemed always to be moving but never arriving. And he longed for the rocky shores of Ithaca and for his dear wife, Penelope, and for a sight of the son he had seen only as a baby.

For ten days the wind had torn white spume off the wavetops. It scudded into the clouds and mixed sky with sea so that there was no horizon. Odysseus's twelve ships had been driven aslant across the heaving water, and his sailors had lifted their oars for fear they be smashed like twigs. Not even the seamanship of their captain could steer them where they wanted to go or tell them where the storm had brought them.

Somehow, the twelve boats had stayed together. Somehow none had been snatched down by the sea. And now they were sailing in unknown waters, and the exhausted men lay slumped over their oars. The twelve sails hung in strips, slit from top to bottom three, four times. And Odysseus was at the prow of his ship watching for some friendly sign of land.

There! A cluster of birds, rising like ash from a bonfire, hung in the sky over a yellow coastline.

'Look and praise the gods! There's rest and food and fresh water for you. Lean on your oars and let the first crew ashore be the first to go foraging!'

In each ship the oars rattled home between their thole-pins, and forty-four wooden blades sliced white slits in the creamy ocean. The lead ship moved forward with such a leap that the cockerel on the stern—Odysseus's own mascot—was unbalanced, and spread its speckled wings and threw back its scarlet comb and crowed with all its might.

The shores of the island were turquoise where the sea spread transparent skirts over soft white sand. The ships slipped ashore with such ease that the weary sailors could simply step over the sides and throw themselves down on the warm white dunes, beneath the shade of palm trees. Most fell asleep then and there. But the first crew to step ashore were eager to press inland to find what lay beyond a green clump of palms.

'Be careful,' said Odysseus. 'Find out what people or beasts live here. They may be unfriendly. They may be frightened by five hundred strangers on their shores. Tread carefully.'

So the foraging party agreed to take care and to return by nightfall with news of the land's people and animals and plants. On the beach, Odysseus lay down and waited.

As the sun went down, and the low light poured thick as honey through the sea-lanes and dry-land pathways, he watched for his crew to return. Night fell over land and sea alike, and a million stars cascaded. But the crew of the first ship did not come and did not come and did not ever come.

'Do you think they've been ambushed, lord?' asked Polites, captain of the tenth ship. 'Or maybe wild animals

319

have eaten them or trapped them somewhere in the darkness.'

'Bring your crew and we'll go and see. But let us be stealthy. Remember how we had to fight the Circones in Thrace when they had us outnumbered. I don't want to lose more good men, fighting.'

So without helmets or swords to clatter, the second party crept off the beach and inshore, through thickly and more thickly wooded pathways. They could hear the pretty tinkling of fresh water. In the darkness, they could smell the thick, sweet smell of coconut. And as they felt their way, the plush skins of hanging fruit brushed their hands and faces, and over-arching blossoms dropped petals in their hair.

All at once, dawn stood in the sky and let fall strands of golden light, like curls of hair. Odysseus and his company found themselves on the edge of a beautiful clearing where a glistening pool lay full of early morning sunlight.

Stretched out on its shores, in their dark and gleaming skin, lay smiling men and women. And in among them—their swordbelts unfastened and their helmets full of fruit—sprawled the crew of the first boat. Raucous laughter flew back and forth across the pool, and the light flashed on the rims of bronze bowls piled high with succulent fruit. A girl was picking still more from the overhanging trees. So soft and ripe it was, that the juice ran down her arms. She carried it to the sprawling Greeks who crammed it into their mouths and threw the stones— plop—into the centre of the pool.

In his hiding place, Odysseus was speechless with amazement. But Polites leapt forward into the clearing and called out angrily, 'Why didn't you come and tell us about all this? Did you want to keep it all to yourselves?'

The idle soldiers grinned and waved their hands. The dark-skinned strangers smiled, too, and hurried to bring a bowl of fruit to the newcomers. But Odysseus (who was quick of hand but quicker still of wit) took the bowl and held it in the crook of his arm, untasted. 'Stir yourselves, men! We've got a long day's rowing ahead of us.'

A dishevelled soldier flapped one hand at Odysseus. 'What? Leave our friends, here? For what? To heave some wooden hulk over the lousy sea? Sit down, why don't you? Have some fruit. By all the gods on Olympus, it's the most delicious stuff you ever ate in your life!'

The soldiers behind Odysseus were anxious to taste the wonderful fruit and jostled forward. But Odysseus held up his hand and continued speaking in a loud, good-humoured voice. 'Not as good as your wife's goat stew, surely, Stavros—and nothing to compare with the first cup of cold wine your daughter will bring you as you beach on the shores of Ithaca?'

The soldier picked up another fruit and bit into it and let the juice run down his chin and chest before answering. 'Ten years we've been gone from Ithaca. My wife will be old and fat by now. My daughter—she'll be married and good riddance. This is the life for me.'

The man next to him sniggered and scratched his head. 'I'm beggared if I can remember if I'm married or not. Seems to me I did have a wife once. Ach, who needs one? I'll live on fruit and friendship till I die!'

Polites and Odysseus exchanged glances. 'I know that man,' said Polites under his breath. 'He has nine children waiting for him at home. What spell have these devils put on him?'

Odysseus showed the bowl by way of reply. 'Have you seen what they're eating? The fruit of the lotus tree. By tomorrow they won't remember Ithaca itself, let alone their wives and children. Tell your men, and warn them on no account to taste the fruit. When I give the word, let two good men each seize on one poor fool and carry him back to the boat. Something tells me it won't be easy, either: I've heard tell of these Lotus Eaters.'

The dark-skinned strangers were pressing close round Odysseus now, with smiles and outstretched hands, full of fruit. 'Rest! Eat! You're welcome to everything we have!' they seemed to say. But Odysseus slipped free of their juice-sticky hands and, with a shout, seized on Stavros and flung him over his shoulder. His soldiers fell on their companions—two on to one—and hauled them to their feet, belabouring them with reproaches: 'Think of your wife! Think of your children! Think of Ithaca!'

But the lotus-eating Greeks only clung to their precious fruit, and cursed and struggled. As they were overpowered, they begged to be allowed to stay. They implored Odysseus to leave them, forget them. Then they began to cry and sob pitifully. Stavros beat with his fists on Odysseus's broad back, and howled, 'Please don't make me go! This is my home! This is where I belong! Don't make me leave my friends. The fruit! At least take some fruit aboard! I'll die if I don't have more fruit!'

Closing their ears to the wailing, Odysseus and Polites led the way back to the beach, calling ahead for the boats to be made ready. The juice-sticky natives followed on for a time, clinging to their Greeks, wheedling and pleading and all the time smiling. But they would not be parted long from their beloved trees, and began to drop off like contented leeches, and patter back towards the clearing.

On the shore, five hundred men sprang to their feet. Masts were lifted, rooted in the deep sockets of the boats' keels. Sails were raised. Oars were run out.

'Put them aboard and lash them under the thwarts!' commanded Odysseus. And the writhing and wriggling

322

lotus-eaters were stuffed under the seats like so many furled sails, and bound there with strong rope. The dismayed crews heaved their boats off the soft and clinging sand, into the surf, then leapt aboard and leaned on their oars. And in every boat, forty wooden blades sliced white slits in the creamy ocean. The lead ship moved forward with such a leap that the cockerel on the stern unbalanced and spread its speckled wings and threw back its scarlet comb and crowed triumphantly.

2

Polyphemus and the Man Called No Wun

All at once, dawn stood in the sky and let fall strands of golden light like curls of hair. Odysseus's fleet lay on the open sea. The gentle water was dinted like hammered gold, and rowing was easy. In time, the madness of the lotus-eaters died in their hollow stomachs, and they took their places, shamefaced, at their empty oars.

At the stern of every boat, great amphoras of blood-red wine were rammed into heaps of sand, to keep them upright. Odysseus had looted the wine from the Circones in Thrace, and though the enterprise had cost him six good men out of every boat, they now had wine enough for the journey, however long it proved. The wine was so strong that they drank it diluted ten times over with water, for fear of falling insensible over their oars. No, drink was not lacking, even when the sun hammered day after day on the dinted golden sea. But there was not a morsel of food in the boats. They had to find land and sustenance quickly.

There! A spire of dust and choir of bleats hung in

the air over a craggy, wooded island. As the boats drew closer, the men could see shaggy, long-horned goats watching them from every ledge of the cliff-ringed shore.

In each ship, the oars rattled between the thole-pins and forty-four wooden blades sliced white slits in the brazen ocean. Odysseus stood at the prow, with his cockerel on his arm and, as the ship leapt forward, the cock's talons sank in and drew blood as red as the comb on its head. It gave a squawk that chilled the sweat of those that heard it—even under the brazen sun.

The little island was uninhabited except for the goats. But from the top of its single pointed hill, Odysseus could see across a strait to fertile dry-land. Terraces of vines and olive-trees plumed grey-green above the shore— and there was a harbour guarded by elegant, swaying, black poplars, like Trojan sentries in their plumed helmets.

'This time I shall go and reconnoitre, myself,' said Odysseus. 'Eleven ships will stay here. I and my men will go across the strait to scout about.'

On the far shore, Odysseus chose just twelve of his best men to venture further inland. All they carried with them for baggage was an amphora of wine to offer as a gift to the king of the country. At the very top of the slopes, huge arching cave-mouths embellished with vines showed that men lived here. But Odysseus did not have to climb so far before finding a cave with a walled yard in front of it, ripe with the smell of sheep. No one was inside.

'Look, captain! Cheeses! And look at the size of them!' cried a soldier, trying to lift a cheese as big as a millstone. 'Let's take these before the owner comes back. They'll last us all the way to Ithaca!'

'Where's the hurry?' said Odysseus. 'I've a mind to see what kind of a man builds walls this high and makes cheeses like these. The laws of hospitality will oblige him to give us food and presents: we might get better than cheese to take away with us! And since when did Greek fighting men have anything to fear from a shepherd?'

So the scouting party went inside the cave, and settled themselves down to wait for the shepherd's return.

The sun sank down, and the low light poured thick as honey through the olive grove, vineyards, and the mouth of the cave. All round the cave walls, between the heaps of dung, pans of milk were settling into curds and whey. From the size of the pans, the skimming spoon, the firewood, and a great club lying on the floor, Odysseus knew that the owner must be a giant of extraordinary strength. But nothing prepared him for the creature who came.

A herd of sheep and goats, huge as cows and horses, clattered down the slope and into the yard. Behind them came a hill—an overgrown hillock of sinews and rolling flesh. Hairy skin, with pores as big as rabbit holes wrinkled over the muscle and bone of a breathing, walking mountain: Odysseus might have called it a man, but for the one giant eye that stood in its hideous forehead, above the cavernous nostrils and the pothole of a mouth.

The moment the ogre had chivvied the last of his animals inside, he rolled across the gateway a boulder so huge that twenty Greeks could not have rolled it away again. Then he kindled a fire, and yellow light washed over the floor and up the walls of rock.

'Well, well, well. And who have we here?' said the one-eyed giant.

'Ha-ha. A dozen poor, unfortunate Greeks sheltering from weariness and hunger in the hospitable portals of your charming home,' said Odysseus, walking forward jauntily, and greeting the ogre with a wave of his hand. 'Ha-ha, we might have been scared out of our skins by your . . . your ample size. But we are the servants of Great Zeus, father of all the gods, and of course we know that no god-fearing man would do harm to a fellow servant of Zeus.'

The ogre squatted down with his hands spread over his grinning mouth, and peered at Odysseus with his one great rheumy eye. 'Is that so? Is that so? Well, and surely you aren't all alone on the big ocean? Just the . . . eight . . . ten . . . thirteen of you? Are there no more? Where's your boat, good sir?'

But Odysseus (who was quick of hand, but quicker still of wit) said, 'Brother! I'm appalled to have to tell you that our boat was wrecked on that promontory beyond the beach—smashed to pieces. We are the only survivors. Still, we count ourselves fortunate to have found our way here, to your delightful home. May I have the honour of knowing your name?'

The ogre's mouth gaped in a laugh as noisy as falling trees. He reached over Odysseus's head, picked up two of his crew—the fattest ones—and smashed them head-downwards on the floor. He ate them then like men eat slivers of honeycomb trying not to lose a drop of the juice. And he said, while his mouth was still full, 'So, you think Polyphemus ought to be frightened of old Zeus, do you? Huh! You ignorant little worm. Why should a Cyclops give a spit what Zeus thinks? Least of all Polyphemus, son of the great god Poseidon who just now smashed your boat like an eggshell. My father stands in the ocean trench and chews on the clouds. Poseidon has the better of Zeus, as Polyphemus has the better of . . . what did you say your name was?'

Most of the crew were huddled together against the back of the cave, weeping at the terrible death of their friends. But Odysseus said, 'I didn't tell you my name. And why should I tell it to an unholy monster like you? I shall keep it secret now, till I die!'

'Oh, don't be like that! You're my guest! Tell me your name. Go on. Tell me. I'll grant you a favour if you tell me.'

'Oh, very well, then,' said Odysseus. 'My name is No Wun. Now spare the rest of us if only because we are your guests!'

Polyphemus picked his teeth. 'No Wun. What a stupid name. All right, No Wun. Because you're my guests, I promise I won't eat another man . . . until breakfast time! Ha! ha! ha!'

Delighted with this joke of his, the hideous Cyclops lay down beside the fire and went to sleep on his back so that he snored all night long.

At the sound of the first snore, Odysseus's men drew their swords, ready to stab the creature in its knotty neck. But Odysseus held up his hand and whispered urgently, 'Don't be so rash! If we managed to kill him, how would we shift the boulder out of the doorway? We'd be trapped in here like prawns in a pot until the other giants came looking. A mouth for every man of us, I dare say.'

'What then, Lord Odysseus?' said the youngest man of all, trying to hide his helpless tears. 'The goddess Athene made you quick of hand and even quicker of wit. So save us from being eaten!'

Towards morning, Odysseus was standing looking at the giant club or shepherd's crook that lay in one corner of the cave. 'There might be a way,' he said. 'For all but four of us.'

At dawn the Cyclops grunted and opened his one bleary eye. Quickly Odysseus kicked dung over the crook. All night long they had sat blunting their swords on it, hacking off splinters of the hard wood. As Odysseus nonchalantly scuffed dung over the hiding place, his men embraced each other for fear Polyphemus had wakened hungry.

None too soon did they say their goodbyes. The Cyclops reached out one lazy hand and then another, and chose two thick-set men for his breakfast. He bit into them like apples, and spat out their belts like pips. Then rolling back the stone in the door and shooing out his sheep and goats, he fixed his malicious eye on the Greeks. 'Until tonight, honoured guests,' he said, grinning; and ducking outside, he rolled the stone back across the mouth of their prison. The sound of the bells round the animals' necks grew more and more distant.

Horror and misery paralysed the poor, trapped men. They looked into each other's faces and wondered, 'Will it be you or will it be me for supper?' All day long, as they faced each other across the massive shepherd's crook and hacked at it with their blades, they wondered, 'Will it be you or will it be me?' Sooner than they wanted, they had their answer.

Polyphemus unsealed the cave and drove in his goats and sheep. There was no chance of a dash to freedom before the stone was in place again. Choosing two of the crew, Polyphemus nibbled them like skewered lamb, then crunched on their bones for the marrow.

'I brought you a present—before I knew you for what you are,' said Odysseus as the Cyclops wiped his mouth on his forearm. 'It would have gone down well, too, with that miserable meal of yours.'

'Oh, give it me, No Wun! I like presents! I'll tell you what: give me my present and I'll grant you all the honour due to a guest of mine. Is it a bargain?'

'A bargain,' said Odysseus. He and two others crawled

into the darkest recess of the cave, and fetched the amphora of wine. Polyphemus's one bulging eye gleamed. He grabbed the great stone jar, lifting it without the least strain, and drank a greedy swig.

'No Wun, this is delicious! Nectar! A drop of liquid sunlight. I have vines of my own, but my wine tastes like vigenar compared with . . . like nivegar . . . like givenar . . . oof! This stuff is strong, No Wun!'

'Before you drink it all, you owe me a favour,' said Odysseus tartly.

'Thasstrue. Very droo! How troo-oo-oo!' slurred the ogre, wagging one drunken finger. 'Tell you whassit to be! I'll eat you la-la-lasht! Ha! ha! ha!'

Overjoyed with this joke of his, and hiccupping happily, he keeled over on to his back and fell asleep beside the fire.

Throwing aside the clods of dung, the Greeks unearthed the crook they had sharpened to a point with their swords. This point they hardened in the hot embers of the fire until it glowed red hot and was on the verge of bursting into flames. Humping it on to their shoulders, they ran at the Cyclops's lolling head, lifted the wooden shaft—and plunged it into his one, closed, flickering eye—right through the lid.

The scream deafened them, like the clap of a bell deafens a man with his head inside it. They scattered to all corners of the cave, holding their hands over their ears to dull the re-echoing, redoubling roar. Frightened sheep lumbered up against them. Polyphemus's hands groped for them . . . and the rest of the night lay ahead.

Giants from the caves higher up the hill heard the agony of Polyphemus, and were roused from their beds. Their gigantic feet could be heard displacing rocks as they slithered down the steep paths in the darkness. 'What's the matter, Polyphemus? What's the matter?'

'My eye! My eye! I'm blinded!' screamed Polyphemus from inside his cave. 'Help me!'

'Who did it, Polyphemus? Who has done this terrible thing to you?' they shouted back.

'No Wun! No Wun did it! No Wun blinded me!'

There were grunts and disgruntled noises from the outer darkness. 'An accident, maybe,' said one voice.

'Struck blind by the gods, maybe,' said another.

'In that case, his father can help him. Let's not cross the gods by interfering.'

'Too dark for dressing wounds, anyway,' said a voice growing smaller as the speaker climbed back up the hill.

All night stars cascaded in the sky. But Odysseus and his men, sealed in the cave, did not see them, and Polyphemus would never see them again. He groped and scrabbled about for the Greeks, but felt only his animals and their udders fat with milk. When morning came, the animals wanted to be out in the sun, with grass and leaves to eat.

Still groaning and grinding his teeth with agony, the giant Cyclops crawled to the boulder blocking the entry. He rolled it away, but immediately sat down across the doorway, with his hands barring the gap to either side of his hips.

'Try it! Just try to escape!' he taunted his prisoners. 'I'll swat you like flies and eat you slowly, slowly, slowly.' The goats stumbled forwards and he fumbled furious fingers over each one before letting it pass by and run free.

Odysseus was too busy to tremble. He was dragging together the giant sheep and lashing them, three by three, side by side, with rushes from the matting on the floor. Beneath each middle sheep, a member of his crew clung on to handfuls of fleece. The sheep bleated forwards towards the doorway, and Polyphemus fumbled furious fingers over each back, side, head, and tail. But of course he could not feel the man slung beneath each centre sheep. Soon only Odysseus remained and only one sheep. It was the biggest animal of all—a ram with coiled horns and clumps of fleece that overhung it like snow overhangs a mountain-top.

Odysseus crawled underneath the ram and clung so tightly to its fleece that his arms and legs were smothered in wool. The big ram headed for the daylight which crept in round the giant shape of the Cyclops. Polyphemus stopped it with his right hand.

'What's this, Woolly? Are you last of all, today?' said the ogre, recognizing his ram by its coiled horns and wealth of wool. 'You're usually first away—first out to eat the green grass. Oh, Woolly! I'll never see it again, that green grass! I'm blind! Blind, Woolly! Blackness. Nothing but blackness between now and forever. Dear, handsome Woolly, how will I see to pick the burrs out of your fleece, now? Oh! If you could just speak! Just for a moment! You could tell me where they were hiding. You could direct me to those repulsive little Greek ticks so I could stamp on them one by one. You'd do that for me, wouldn't you, old friend? If you just had the wits and the words. Go on with you. Go on. Leave me in my blackness. But come back soon tonight. After I've killed the Greek lice, I'll be lonely here in the darkness.'

The great woolly ram trotted off, slowly because of the weight of Odysseus hanging in its fleece. Not until he was a sunray's breadth from the cave, did Odysseus let himself drop, and lie on the stony ground enjoying the sight of the blue sky.

His men mustered round him. They ran helter-skelter down the goat paths to their solitary boat, and their six paltry oars sliced six white slits in the ocean. But under the quarter-deck and thwarts were lashed a dozen giant sheep for their meat.

To reach the island where the other ships were waiting, they had to sail right below Polyphemus's high-arching cave. From its perch on the stern, Odysseus's cockerel crowed into the face of the sun, an arrogant, piercing crow. They saw the ogre cock his head and turn towards the sea, his one empty eye-socket staring. Pride welled up in Odysseus, and he too crowed like the cockerel: 'Hey! You with the blind eye! Do you see what comes of scorning Zeus? Great Zeus and the goddess Athene—she of the *two, beautiful, grey and shining eyes*—sent us to teach you humility! So much for the son of Poseidon!'

Polyphemus gave a bellow of anguish, and knelt up—his frame cast a shadow over the whole length of the boat. He picked up the boulder from the doorway of the cave and hurled it in the direction of Odysseus's voice.

It fell just ahead of the prow, and a huge wave pitched the boat backwards for twice its length—almost smashing it against the shore. The crew only saved it by heaving on the oars with all their might.

Odysseus laughed crowingly, and wagged his fists in the air. 'Missed, Polyphemus! Don't you wish you had your eye now?'

'Sit down, captain! Sit down, please!' his men begged him. 'One more boulder like that and we are dead men, for all your cunning and wit!'

But the cruelty of battle welled up in Odysseus, such as he had not felt since he saw Troy burn. He cupped his hands round his mouth and yelled, 'Know this, Polyphemus! That it was Odysseus, King of Ithaca, who blinded you and stole your woolly sheep. That is my true name, and darkness is your true fate for ever and a day!'

This time Polyphemus did not let out a shout. He rose silently to his feet and stretched out both arms towards the sky he could not see. 'Poseidon! Hear me! Father and god who stands in the ocean trench and chews on the black storm clouds—look down from holy Olympus and see what Odysseus of Ithaca has done to your only son! Blind! Blind as night, I am, for ever and a day. Reach up out of the sea! Reach down out of the clouds! And plunge him and all his boats deeper than the depth where all fishes are blind. Forbid that he should ever see wife or home again, since I shall see no such comfort! And let his doom be remembered on every shore that fringes the world-encircled sea!'

His swinging fists smashed a gobbet of rock out of the cliff face and, raising it over his head, he hurled it down on the sound of the ship's dipping oars.

It fell just behind the stern, and a huge wave picked up the boat and flung it, spinning on the crest, across the narrow straits, and drove it ashore on the beach of the desolate, uninhabited island. Startled goats scattered. But for a time no man moved from the oar he was grasping. For a time, no man breathed.

'Take out that huge ram of mine and roast it here on the beach! And let's offer it up to Zeus for our happy escape!' cried Odysseus.

The six remaining men looked up at him across their oars, and the sheep bleated under the thwarts. After a time, they did as he said, according to every rule of holy law. Afterwards they and the crews of the other boats roasted other sheep and greatly enjoyed eating them, washed down with Circonian wine.

But they did not omit to plant each of the six empty oars upright on the shore, and to call the names of their oarsmen three times across the mist-smothered sea, so that they might always be remembered.

Night fell over land and sea-lanes alike, and a million stars cascaded. From the top of a lonely summit, Odysseus looked up at them and saw huge navy clouds swell like pride, and blot out the stars one by one. At last only one bright star remained, awash in the night sky, like a shipwrecked sailor afloat in the world-encircled sea. The waves breaking on the shore of the little island seemed to whisper, 'Poseidon. Poseidon. Poseidon.'

3

A Parcel of Wind

Their holds filled with fresh meat and their amphoras with good wine, enough for any journey, the men of Ithaca rowed on across the brimming sea. Like slices of lemon they bobbed in the bowl of shining water where the gods dip their hands. And sail and tide and rowing brought them to an unmapped island.

There! A blinding flash of light signalled the sun's reflection off some shining shore. But the island that came into view had no chalk cliffs, no sand dunes, no scrubby green hills. It was encircled by a shining wall of golden bronze—without steps, without rungs, without even the heads of nails to give a man foot-holds to climb up. And as the ocean nudged it, the whole vast island rocked and yawed. It had no roots of bronze sunk in the ocean bed, and no anchor to hold it in place. The island of Aeolia drifted wherever wind and the tides carried it.

As the bulwarks of the twelve boats banged gently against the bronze, and the men laughed at the sight of their own reflections and combed their matted beards, Odysseus stood up in the prow and hailed the inhabitants of this colossal fort. He had no sooner started to speak than a withy basket, secured with four strong ropes, was lowered down. It was large enough for only one man and, without hesitation, Odysseus himself leapt in. 'Hold off your boats until I return,' he called. 'There may be presents for everyone from such a handsome realm.'

Odysseus was not disappointed. He was helped from the basket and escorted most courteously to the dining hall of King Aeolus. There seemed to be a feast in progress, for a long table was laid with bronze, silver, and golden dishes, with places enough for six on each side and for Aeolus and his queen at either end.

At the mention of Odysseus's name, the king knew at once what voyage the twelve ships were on. 'In drifting here and there, we have met with many a Greek ship homeward bound from Troy. And every storyteller aboard every ship had some heroic story to tell about Odysseus. They say the grey-eyed Athene gave you cunning hands and still more cunning wit. But why so long voyaging? Aren't you heading a long way round for your beloved island of Ithaca?'

Odysseus thanked the king for his gracious compliments and explained about the storms that had blown for ten days and beaten the fleet to the southernmost shore of the sea-encircling world.

'Ah! I recollect that storm! Poseidon, the Earth-Shaker, the Sea-Breaker, was restless and quarrelsome. Why do you flinch like that at the name of Poseidon? You have nothing to fear from him. Why, at present there's not a banner of wind flying over the ocean that I didn't hoist myself. Zeus entrusted the winds to me—as a lesson to old Poseidon for his surly bad temper. After our meal I'll show them to you. Now—fetch another chair and set another place for the heroic Odysseus, terror of the Trojans!'

Tempted as he was, Odysseus was unwilling to eat while his men went hungry down below. But King Aeolus saw what was in his mind and said, 'As much as we eat here I shall command to be lowered down to your ships. No honest servant of the gods ever comes to Aeolia and goes away unsatisfied.'

Just then the king's family entered, to the sound of music. Six handsome sons and six radiant daughters, all with hair the colour of bronze, took their places at table. And when Odysseus spoke of his travels, they listened as attentively as only islanders can, valuing the news of travellers.

Indeed, Odysseus thought that loneliness must be worse on Aeolia than for any man on his own islands of Ithaca, Cephalonia, or little wooded Zanthe. For there were so *few* of them. Aeolus and his family, with their few trusted servants, alone peopled the huge, bronze-fendered realm. From the white-elmwood of the hall's ceiling hung clusters of delicate shells, and as the family talked, their breath and laughter set the shells tinkling with a sound like the laughter of the gods themselves. Night fell outside, and a million stars cascaded, but not with a sweeter music than the tinkling of the Aeolian air.

'If your sons ever travel across the glossy ocean's back, they must come to Ithaca and stay at my palace, and enjoy what food and gifts I have to share with them,' said Odysseus. 'I'm sure they could not lay eyes on the maidens of Ithaca without choosing them for wives.'

King Aeolus seemed confused, his sons and daughters embarrassed. 'But we never *leave* this realm or travel (except where Aeolia takes us). Here we have everything we need—for each daughter a husband, for each son a wife, and for me as fine a queen as Penelope of Ithaca must seem in the eyes of Odysseus. You see, I married my sons to my daughters; my daughters to my sons. Now they need never step one pace away from Aeolia: everything they need is here.'

The lord Odysseus blushed at his mistake, and turned the conversation to stories of battle and heroic deeds, forged in the heat of Troy.

All at once, dawn stood in the sky, and let fall light like curls of golden hair. They had feasted the night away, and Aeolus had served every manner of delicacy, sending the same to the boats below.

Odysseus rose to take his leave, but it seemed there was to be one last present more magnificent than the rest. As Aeolus clapped his hands, four strong servants carried in a massive, cowhide bag. The drawstring round its neck was plaited out of strands of silver wire and white silk and, as it stood on the floor, certain of its folds unfolded, the creases creased and recreased.

'In this bag are all the winds but one. I've left free only the wind from the south-east, to sit in your sails as far as Ithaca. Your men can ship their oars and sleep. No one but the man at the tiller is needed. You'll be home in a matter of days.'

'Of all the presents any man ever gave me, none was more welcome than this,' said Odysseus, embracing the cheerful king. 'But how can I return them? Surely Zeus entrusted the winds to you? He'll look to you for their safe-keeping.'

'As soon as you're safely home, loose the cord and set free the other winds.—Be careful how you do it, or you may raise a hurricane! The winds will scatter and blow this way and that. But I and my sons can gather them up again as we float about the oceans. Now, be on your way, or that son of yours will be a grown man before you ever see him!'

A shiver shook Odysseus, though no draught set the

strung shells tinkling overhead. Delight soon took its place, however, as he watched the servants of King Aeolus hoist the great bag over the bronze parapet, and lower it down into his boat.

When Odysseus himself was lowered down, he found his men asleep in the bilges, asleep along the thwarts, asleep over their oars. The twelve boats bobbed against the bronze wall, chipping their bright paintwork, and the captain's noble cockerel was pecking on the dregs of the feast. A lively south-easterly breeze had already sprung up and was going to waste, with no sails to catch it. 'Stir yourselves, men! Look to your sails! Draw in your oars and prepare yourselves for your wives' nagging. I myself shall take the tiller. The wind's in our favour and Ithaca is waiting!'

In each ship the oars rattled inboard from between their thole-pins, and twelve mended and tattered sails flowered against their mast-stems. They filled with wind, and the fleet leapt forward—so fast that the cockerel perched on the stern made angry noises in its throat.

So Odysseus stood on the quarter-deck, his arm on the tiller and the great cowhide bag stowed beneath. He rested one foot on the knot of the silver cord. He was so eager for the first sight of Ithaca—its craggy green hills, its stony terraces of corn, the tall Mount Neriton rising from its heart—that he could not rest his back or close his eyes or lay down his head and sleep. For ten long days and nights he eased on the tiller, swung on the tiller, leaned on the tiller, and blessed King Aeolus and the great god Zeus for the lively south-east wind.

There! There were the green nodding heads of the trees on little Zanthe. And there beyond was the great black scowling brow of Cephalonia. 'If I close my eyes for a moment, then open them again, I shall see my beloved Ithaca. Easy to stay awake with the hope of my own bed

to sleep in tonight. Easy to stay awake . . . even if I close
my eyes . . . '

But when he rested his head on his arm, his arm on
the tiller and his back against the stern, he was soon
sound asleep, his foot sliding down off the bag's silver
cord . . .

'Thought he'd never sleep,' said Eurylochus to the
man alongside him. 'What is he guarding so carefully in
that bag? It doesn't say much for his trust in us that he
won't sleep for fear we steal it.'

'Have you seen how it moves sometimes?' said his
comrade. 'I reckon it's alive.'

'Nah: it's treasure from that floating treasurehouse,
Aeolia. That place is crammed from sea to sky with
jewels off the sea-bed. Why else does it have that great
wall round it and no way in for the likes of us? That
bag's full of treasure, and he thinks, since we didn't see
it given, we don't have to share in it. Well, let's see just
what our noble captain's keeping to himself, shall we?'
Eurylochus crawled forward, and twitched at the end of
the silver cord. One man pulled on one end, one on
another, a third man on the third loose end. Though the
knot had seemed intricate and difficult to untie, it
unravelled in a moment, and the neck of the bag fell
open like a gaping mouth.

'What are you doing, you fools?' Odysseus sprang to his
feet. But his mutinous men could not hear what he
shouted. Their arms were over their faces, and their hair
streamed backwards as a blast of wind hurled them
against the mast and wrapped them in the splitting sail.

First came a golden west wind—strong but milky soft
and heavy with the smell of Ithacan oleander. Next came
a ragged east wind, full of tattered sea birds that swooped
and screamed in their terrified ears: a green and nauseous
wind that pitched the boat from one beam end to the

341

other, then rolled them in sidelong troughs. Caught in its claws was the searing red south wind, full of desert grit that scratched their faces and loaded down the twelve wallowing boats. Next came the north wind, white and whining, grey and groaning. It clapped the boats in ice so that they hung lower and lower in the heaving water. In pulling down the rags of sail, their hands froze to hemp and canvas alike.

The cowhide bag was whipped up off the deck and flew, on a funnel of wind, towards the milk-white sun. It started an avalanche of cloud tumbling down the sky, while winds from every point of the compass whirled and cavorted as far as the far horizon, then swooped back to ransack the boats. One wind was full of rain, one of hail. One was full of flying fish, another of crabs off beaches. One was white with lotus blossoms, and one was noisy with the shouts of Polyphemus still calling on his father, Poseidon: *'Help me! Avenge me!'*

And one wind plunged and bubbled into the ocean then spouted up into the sky, hissing, 'Die, Odysseus! Down, down and drowning deep! Poseidon has spoken!'

It seemed a single moment later that his ship's heaving career through the mountainous seas was halted by a *clang*. The thwarts buckled and splintered, and the bulwark cracked in a dozen places as they were driven against a shining cliff of bronze. Odysseus saw his own face reflected there, the black-ringed eyes and the terror written in them. And he saw his twelve brave ships hammer against the bronze wall of Aeolia like hammers against a bell. Their crews beat on the shining wall with their fists and called out for King Aeolus to save them.

But they were there still when the winds subsided and the waves dispersed to the fringes of the blue carpeting sea and there was dead calm.

One head, and then thirteen more, looked over the golden parapet. 'So! It is you, Lord Odysseus of Ithaca,' said the king's voice.

'King Aeolus! Kind and generous friend. You'll help us, won't you? Gather up the winds, or lower down to us one gentle south-easterly breeze to carry us home! My men are exhausted. How are we to row such a way as the winds have blown us?'

But in reply, the king and queen and all their twelve children only tipped down the water from their washing bowls. '*Go away, you godless man.* This would never have happened if the gods were with you: if they wanted you to reach home. You've angered one of the Immortals on high Olympus, and I won't offend them by helping you.'

'But, my Lord Aeolus! I did just as you told me! It was only the foolishness of my ignorant men that brought this disaster . . . this accident!'

'Accident, my Lord Odysseus? This was no accident. Some voice has spoken against you in the halls of the gods. Get away from the walls of my bronze realm. You dull the shine with your ungodly breath!' And the king's head disappeared, behind his golden parapet, though his children stayed to spit the stones of olives down on the unhappy Greeks below.

The silence was broken only as, in each boat, forty oars rattled out between their thole-pins, and their wooden blades sliced white slits in the creamy ocean. For many days there was no sound but the creaking of wood and the drawing of weary breath, as the men heaved on their heavy oars.

When all their strength had gone and only shame remained to make them row, they looked up and saw the Land of the Laestrygonians.

There! A pair of breakwaters reached out like a pair

343

of loving arms, and between them a limpid harbour. Odysseus had his own boat hang back until all the others were safely berthed. Then, seeing there was no room for his vessel, he moored it by a single rope, outside the harbour mouth.

The green water was so clear that they could see every pebble, every weed, every crab on the sea-bed.

A tall young woman carrying a water jar on her head watched them from under her hand. She beckoned and waved her hand—a friendly girl and someone you could call beautiful if she were not so uncommonly tall. Odysseus felt sorry for her, thinking how the other girls must make fun of her, and how a boy will shun a maiden who stands head and shoulders taller than him. He walked along the breakwater and began to introduce himself and his men, looking up into her beaming smile. In such a hospitable anchorage, they could not have met a more hospitable native.

'You must all come up to my father's palace,' she said. 'You see it up on the hill? He does so love to have people to supper.'

Her father, she said, was King Lamus, and his palace was finer than any building Odysseus had ever seen. Its marble pillars stood taller than trees, its roof of porphyri spread out at the height where sea eagles stretch their wings, and curtains larger than sails blew in the upper windows. As the princess climbed the spiralling stairs of rosy onyx ahead of Odysseus, he laughed with delight at the magnificence around him and said, 'I thought all the gods on Olympus had forgotten me. Now I see that they were planning new delights for me and my men.'

His feet stumbled against the top step as the girl's mother came out on to the gallery. 'Well, Midget, and who have you brought home today?'

'Five hundred Greeks, Mama,' said the princess. 'Won't father be pleased?'

Her mother made the doorway she stood in look low. She could have dandled her little daughter on her knee, and if she had sat down on the shore, only a lighthouse could have saved sailors from shipwreck on her shins. Behind her came the king himself—eighty times bigger than Odysseus: the linen round his waist would have made tents for an army.

'Ah, supper!' he cried. For his daughter had spoken the truth. The king and all his kin liked nothing better than to have men to supper. Roasted or raw, cooked or still kicking.

King Lamus reached over the balustrade and grabbed up two men in the palm of one hand. Like the Cyclops, he savoured his food.

Back down the onyx stairs, out from under the porphyri roof ran the Greeks, scattering this way and that. But the Laestrygonians had heard how King Lamus had fresh Greeks for supper. They had seen the boats in the harbour, and were there on the waterfront, waiting.

Most of the Greeks reached their ships, dodging between the huge, sandalled feet of the giants, leaping their bulwarks and posting their oars with furious speed and deftness between their thole-pins. But the Laestrygonians simply took hold of each ship with finger and thumb, at the prow or by the anchor chain, and lifted it up, and tipped out its crew of shrieking men.

Each giant carried a fishing spear, and with these they killed and killed and killed the helpless swimmers in the limpid water. Though some dived deep, and some hid among the weed, the Laestrygonians could see them through the clear green water, and speared them with their long spears, and ate them off the prongs. The empty boats they thrust prow-down into the silt.

Not one half, not one third, not one tenth of the men threaded their steps between the giant feet and ran the length of the high harbour wall. Scarcely fifty men slipped between the darting prongs and leapt off the seaward side of the breakwater. There lay Odysseus's boat, moored only by its cable. And there Odysseus—last to flee—slashed the cable with his king's sword, and leapt the widening gap as his men hauled on their heavy oars. He clutched the high stern; he tumbled his legs over the bulwark, and he dropped down beside the tiller. As he did so, his cockerel pecked at him angrily, and put its head under its wing.

Forty-four wooden blades slashed white slits in the red ocean and Odysseus steered for the open sea. He did not look back, for he knew that the harbour, with its two reaching arms, was no longer limpid clear. Its waters ran blood-red with spilled Circonian wine from the smashed amphoras. And blood.

The sun went down, and the light poured thick as honey along the quiet sea-lanes. Night fell, and a million stars cascaded. But only fifty-two men of the five hundred who had set sail from Troy looked up and saw them.

4

And This Little Piggy . . .

The Dog Star hung in the sky by night, and by day
the bright discus of the sun flew overhead. But there
was no knowing what course they wished to lay by
either sun or moon. For Odysseus did not know where
disaster had brought him. He steered to the west, always to
the west, and northwards, hoping to see the friendly profile
of some Ionian isle. His men wept over their oars until it
seemed the bilges ran with tears. And sometimes rain, cold
and slighting, fell in Odysseus's face as if the gods were
spitting on him. Uneasily he watched the horizon, half
expecting Poseidon to shoulder aside the blue main and
shake his hair in the sky.

There! No, it was only the welling shoulder of a green
promontory, lying along the horizon. The rowers pulled
towards it with half unwilling oars, for fear that this new
landfall harboured some monster as ravenous as King
Lamus or the appalling Cyclops.

But the ridged sea delivered them on diagonal waves
on to the dark sand of a beach overhung by Alleppo
pines. The long, green bristles were so heavily laden with

cones that they looked to be full of birds. But there was no birdsong.

Odysseus said to his friend, Polites, 'I am putting half the crew under your command. Let's draw lots to see which half goes reconnoitring.' So they shook stones, one black, one white, in a bronze helmet, and Polites drew out the black. Odysseus threw the helmet aside and clutched his comrade in his arms. 'Take care, old friend. The stones themselves would shed tears if any harm came to you.'

He watched the party of twenty-four men climb through the steep, piny path, grunting with exertion, the green spines catching in their cloaks or woollen jerkins. Half of him felt torn away.

On the black sand, his half-crew sat beneath the slatted shade of their oars, and slept. But Odysseus, to shorten the waiting, went hunting and killed a stag to roast over an open fire.

The sun went down, and the low light poured thick as honey through the sea-lanes and dry-land pathways. Still Polites and his men did not return. At that very moment when the sun falls beneath the sea with a flash of green, Eurylochus stumbled out of the trees, his hair spiny with pine needles, and his face a picture of fear.

'Aboard! Aboard!' He tried to shout, but his breath was spent, and his tongue was rigid with terror. It clacked in his jaws. He fell headlong in the black sand, and clutched Odysseus's feet. 'Aboard or we're all pork, bacon, and brawn!'

Not until the sky was black, and a million stars cascaded did Eurylochus recover enough to say what he had seen.

'We came to a house—oh, a magnificent villa, with animal houses and vines and great curved doors hammered out of copper. We thought we were done for

348

when a whole pack of wild animals came tearing round the house towards us. Not just boars, I don't mean, nor wild cats, nor wolves, but lions and black-furred cats as big as lions, with yellow eyes, and great striped beasts— and golden ones spotted with black. We thought they'd tear us limb from limb! One of them leapt right up at me! . . . But they just pawed at us and licked our faces and rubbed their heads against our knees. I tell you, they were like little lap-dogs, the way they fawned on us! The relief! Imagine it! And then we heard singing inside the house, and Polites called out, and the big copper doors swung open . . . ' Eurylochus halted, his eyes empty, his thoughts lost inside the house with the shining doors.

'Go on, man! What opened the doors? A monster? A magician?' demanded Odysseus.

'Oh, she's beautiful. More beautiful than any mortal woman you've ever seen. Circe she calls herself. She wears her hair in plaits that swing down behind her knees, and she carries a silver rod in her hand, and she smiles and smiles . . . I don't know why I didn't follow the others when she beckoned them in. My legs were trembling so at the sight of her—and something inside me felt like a big brass anchor holding me back. As soon as they'd gone in, I regretted it. I ran up to the window to see what I was missing.

'She had a table laid already, and highbacked seats for every man—as if she was expecting us. She pulled out footstools for each one to rest his feet on. I saw her creaming feta cheese with oil and honey and oregano and wine in a beautiful transparent bowl. Something else she added, too . . . Something . . . something dreadful!' Eurylochus tore at his hair wildly. 'I don't know what it was. Some herb with little flowers. I saw Demos—my friend Demos—trowelling up the food with his fingers—

he's always a great one for his food, and it did look so *delicious*! Then I saw him flinch a bit when the woman passed behind him and tapped him with her rod. She tapped everyone. Suddenly I thought, What's the matter with Demos's nose? It was flat, like a boxer's nose—and then like a snout. His eyes sank into his head and the clothes fell off his back.—Agh! His back was covered in bristles, and his legs were too short to balance him in his chair. He fell off on to the floor—on to his hands and knees—I mean on to his trotters. He was a hog, sir! A swine! A great grunting pig, and all the rest were like him.'

'Even Polites?'

'Even him, sir. She drove them out through the back doors and into the sties. I'm telling you, we weren't the first sailors ever to come here. She has boars and pigs and hogs more than they had in all Troy! It's dreadful to hear them. You can tell from the way they squeal and the look in their eyes—they have minds still, but they're all wrapped up in pig. And who's to spare them living out their natural lives like that—eating swill? Eh? It's the most horrible way the gods ever thought to punish us! And it's all your fault!'

Odysseus had already looped his long bow across his shoulder, and was strapping on his sword. He stopped short and put his hand on the sword hilt, half drawing the blade. 'What did you say, Eurylochus? What did you say?'

'I said it's all your fault for angering the great Earth-Shaker and Sea-Shifter, Poseidon. Now take us away from here before we're all turned into sucking pigs!'

The blue veins stood out on Odysseus's temple, and his knuckles whitened on the sword. But he controlled his temper and, turning his fiery eyes on the rest, said, 'As soon as the sun is up I am going to Circe's zoo to rescue my comrades or to die in the attempt. Let follow who dares, and let all craven cowards stay behind!'

To a man, the sorry crew followed Odysseus up through the Alleppo pines. Even Eurylochus, afraid to be left alone, fell in behind.

The morning sun splashed against Circe's great curving copper doors and hurt their eyes with its brightness. Wild animals rushed out to greet them: leopards nuzzled them, a wolf wagged its tail, a tiger rolled in the path for its stomach to be tickled. And the hogs in the sties pressed against the gates, with heart-rending squeals.

Odysseus's men crouched alongside their bristly comrades, and tried to comfort them, though the smell of the swill alone was sickening.

Odysseus alone stood in plain view of the shining doors, thigh-deep in the fragrant herbs that grew in vast variety round about the house. Thyme and oregano, basil and rosemary, garlic and bay flourished all around. And twining in among them, the lovely but deadly delphinium and nodding mandragora. Odysseus looked down and, between his two sandals, a little white flower was peeping out. It was a moli flower. He bent down, picked it, and pouched it—petals, root and all—in his cheek. Just then, the great curved doors opened, and the sorceress Circe smiled at him.

She was as beautiful as the blue-trumpeted convolvulus that twines on Ithacan walls. Her hair hung down like the first rays of dawn, and her eyes were as clear and as green as . . . the harbour of Laestrygonia.

'Come in! Come in! You look weary. Look where I've prepared a seat for you, and a meal.'

Indoors, he let her lift his feet on to the footstool beneath his chair, and bring him a bowl of cheese creamed with honey and oregano and oil, and a cup of purple wine.

351

And he ate and drank it all.

Whap! She tapped him lightly on the shoulder with her slender rod of silver and, turning away, Circe said, 'Now get to the sty with your comrades.'

Odysseus sat back in his chair, crossed his ankles on the footstool, and patted his stomach. 'Ah, delicious!' Circe's footsteps faltered. She looked over her shoulder.

She just had time to fall on her knees before Odysseus leapt across the table, sword drawn, and raised it two-handed over her head. 'No! Don't strike, my Lord Odysseus! You cannot kill me; I'm immortal. And besides, my dear, dear lord, you have no reason to hate me. I *know* you are Odysseus of Ithaca, for it was written in my horoscope at the moment of my birth that I should be conquered in heart and body by Odysseus, the greatest of the heroes of Troy!'

Odysseus spat out the shreds of the little moli flower that had saved him from her magic potion. 'You ogress! You swineherd! You unnatural woman! How can I believe the words of a creature who defied all the natural laws of hospitality and made hogs out of my men? . . . Unless you swear by all the gods on Olympus to empty your heart of mischief.'

'I swear! I swear! By all the gods and goddesses who ever saw the face of mighty Zeus—my mouth is yours with all its kisses; my arms are yours with all their embraces and with all their strength to help you; and my love is yours—bottomless as the Lake of Avothres in your own realm . . . '

So Odysseus knotted his hand in her braided hair, kissed her on the mouth, and sheathed his sword.

She summoned five handmaidens—each as lovely as the stars in a constellation. And they brought wrappers of linen-lawn, ewers of water, jugs of wine, bowls of food, and music. Odysseus would have none of it—nor would he lie down on the soft white bed Circe offered him—until his men were released from their misery.

Circe went to the sties, from sty to sty, anointing each bristly back with oil. Gradually, snouts, tails, ears, and hog-hair melted away, and the pitiful Greeks found themselves kneeling in the muddy squalor of the pig-run. They burst into tears, wagged their heads and hands in gratitude towards the heavenly gods, then looked about for their captain so as to bless him for saving them. But he had already gone. He was already behind the locked doors of the white and fragrant room to which Circe had led him by the hand.

She laid him on pillows and lambskin, and cradled him in immortal arms.

Dawn, its tresses tumbling on to the bed, woke Odysseus. He sat up and looked out at the view. Beyond the herb garden were olive groves and orchards of lemons, apples, and limes. Vines entwined the marble colonnades, and hives shimmered with the early morning movement of bees. Tall, dark cypresses swayed like dancers, and the soft green of the pine forests was sprinkled with asphodels and orchids.

All he could see of the steely sea was a strip as long and narrow as a sword. Out there, the great Poseidon, Earth-Shaker and Sea-Breaker, who stood in the ocean trench and chewed the clouds with rage—out there he was waiting to cut off Odysseus.

I'll wait, thought Odysseus. Perhaps, in time, his anger will cool. And besides . . . this is a good place. It isn't Ithaca, but it is a good place. My men are tired and I am tired. We need to rest.

And though men said of him that his body was a strung long-bow and his wit the flying arrows, he unflexed the bow, and hung up the quiver of his cunning, and lay down again beside the sorceress, Circe.

5

The Realm of Shadows

The grape harvest came, and the olive harvest, too. The season of winds passed by in the sky overhead, but on Circe's island there was never more than a breeze and a sprinkling of rain to make the greenery tremble. Circe's garden flourished by magic, by the watering of bright springs which she conjured from the ground— one day here, the next day there.

'There are springs and rivers on Ithaca, too,' said Odysseus, 'but without winter rains, it would be a brown, dry, dead place.'

At the mention of his little, rugged island, a door banged somewhere in Odysseus's heart. The pages of his mind leafed over, and he glimpsed the face of his queen Penelope looking out to sea. But at the very first shadow of sadness, Circe kissed him with magic kisses, and his thoughts sank back into the soft pillows of her white and silver bed.

But when the thoughts of his men turned towards Ithaca, their wives and their children, they had only the delights of the island to distract them. After a year, the sweetness of the melons no longer amazed them; the tenderness of the meat no longer satisfied the hunger within them. One morning, when Odysseus came out to breathe the morning air, Polites was standing by the door. He said, 'Have you seen your men lately, my friend?'

'They always seem happy when I catch sight of them,' replied Odysseus.

'They have eaten so well that their armour will not fasten. Their muscles are flabby for lack of use—what exercise do they get but to play with the leopards and walk the wolves? Every night they drink more than is good for them and get mawkish, and sing the old songs, and start talking about their dogs and farms and children . . . They say you've forgotten Ithaca altogether—and Queen Penelope and your only son. They say you're happy to stay here in Circe's house till you die. I know that's not true. But how can I convince them? It's time to go, Lord Odysseus. It's time to go.'

Odysseus looked over his shoulder at the trestle where his king's sword lay tarnishing and his bronze helmet served for a bowl to keep figs in. 'You're right, Polites. I know it in my heart. Tell the men to make ready the boat—mend the sail, retouch the paint, rub the oars with linseed oil. Tomorrow morning we shall set sail for Ithaca. I'll go now and ask Circe to direct us on our way. With her magic arts, and the knowledge of a goddess, she must know where Ithaca lies.'

'Be careful, my lord. Don't let her tempt you to change your mind.'

'Polites, have a care. I am Odysseus of Ithaca, hero of Troy! If I decide to go, no woman is going to prevent me.'

And when Circe saw the look on Odysseus's face, she knew at once that his heart was set on going. 'With my magic arts and the knowledge entrusted to me as a goddess, I could tell you where Ithaca lies. I could teach you what stars to follow and where to keep the noonday sun as you steer. But I am forbidden. My heart forbids me, but more than that, the gods on Mount Olympus forbid it. And I cannot tell you what winds will blow. I cannot know what miseries Poseidon has in store for you. And I am forbidden to know whether all or any of you will ever reach home alive. Oh, Odysseus! Think again! Stay in the safe harbour of my two arms . . . No, I can see it's useless to speak of safety to a hero. Well—and are you hero enough to go where you must, for the directions you need? Are you? Because the man I'll send you to can tell you about more than your journey across the sea: he can tell you about your journey from birth to death: every second and syllable of your life.'

Then Odysseus trembled from head to foot, as he had trembled when he saw the great Achilles carried off the battlefield at Troy, an arrow in his heel and the astonishment of death in his eyes. 'There was a man—a soothsayer—everyone has heard of Tiresias of Thebes. If he were alive, you would have sent me to him. But he's dead long since. Who else?'

'No one else,' said Circe. 'Tiresias is the man I mean. You must look for him in Hades.'

His knees buckled under him, and Odysseus felt his heart clamour against his ribs. His vital organs melted in the sweat of terror. 'No living man in the history of the world has been down to the Realm of Shadows!'

'You have forgotten Hercules, my friend, who borrowed the great dog Cerberus as one of his Labours. And Orpheus who went there to fetch back his beloved Eurydice when the god of the underworld stole her away.'

'*But Orpheus failed!*'

'Then you must not fail. Oh, Odysseus, Odysseus, my love! You need not fetch anything or anyone *out* of the

Realm of Shadows. You need only the advice of old Tiresias. Do you have the courage for such a journey?'

Odysseus's men had prepared the boat to set sail, but then lain down for their afternoon rest, when their captain came leaping down the beach calling to them. 'To your oars, men! And bring aboard only one perfect ram, a black sheep, and food enough for three nights at sea!'

Bleary eyed, the men jostled on the beach. 'Where are we going, then?'

'Not to Ithaca?'

'A trial voyage for the boat, my lord?'

'They're sacrifices. Why are we loading sacrifices?'

'Where's Elpenor?' demanded Odysseus. 'Is he drunk again? Good-for-nothing waster. He moves as fast as a tortoise and that's too fast for his brain to keep up. They say he was so stupid in battle that the Trojans didn't know whether to shoot him or make oars out of him. We used to call him 'Elpless Elpenor. Where is he? Well, we'll sail without him . . . ' And by complaining ceaselessly, incessantly about the missing Elpenor, Odysseus managed to put to sea without answering their questions. Wooden blades sliced white slits in the creamy ocean. The boat leapt forward. But on the stern rail, the captain's old cockerel sat huddled in its cloak of wings and made not a sound.

They followed Circe's directions to the last syllable, taking for their pointer the sword which hung in the sky from the belt of starry Orion. Through the smooth and colourful sea ran a trough of grey, turbulent water: the current called River Ocean. Into and along this, the boat was drawn irresistibly. Their oars speeded them, but the River Ocean guided them, until mist from the cauldron sea

357

curled over their heads, and nothing was visible of the sky. There was a smell in the fog—half sea, half land—and a noise of waves breaking. The rowers snatched in their oars as the boat slid under a narrow arch of rock. They snatched in their fingers as the boat squeezed, with not a hand's breadth to spare, into a tunnel of clammy granite.

'What place is this you've brought us to?' demanded Eurylochus, and his voice boomed and re-echoed up and down the passageway.

'It's the sea-lane to the Underworld,' said Odysseus. 'Our solitary hope of finding our way home. If it had not been necessary, I would not have brought you here.'

Then Eurylochus fell on his knees in the bottom of the boat, and the rest of the men let out such a wail of despair that its echoes hammered in their heads for an hour after.

There was no need of oars: the flow of River Ocean carried them on. When they reached out their fingers in the darkness, they felt the slime on the walls, and sometimes a smoothness like hair, or the flinching softness of a face. Night was absolute, but no stars cascaded. Then the walls widened and the echoes of their crying soared into the vault of an over-arching cavern as high as the dome of King Lamus's palace.

In impenetrable darkness, the boat beached on drifts of decaying seaweed whose invisible ooze closed over the men's feet and ankles as they stepped out. A phosphorescent glow drew them to the mouth of a second sloping tunnel. It sloped so steeply that their leather sandals slipped: the sure-footed ram and sheep almost escaped them. At the foot of the slope, one man cannoned into another. Punches were exchanged. Then the sailors looked around them—and saw the faces of the dead, watching.

They were in a vast cavern—as high almost as the

dome of the sky itself. Night was absolute. But a million white faces teemed through the gloom, trooping towards Odysseus and his men, with outstretched arms and reaching fingers, their lips shaping words they had no breath to speak. They filled the cavern; they climbed down the uneven blackness of the walls; they hung like bats from the over-arching roof.

Snatching his king's sword from his thigh, Odysseus killed the black ram and the sheep with one stroke, and their blood made a phosphorescent pool on the cavern floor. Like jewels set in the solid darkness, a million eyes gleamed with delight. Far from falling back, the ghosts rushed forward with a noise like the sails flapping on a sunken ship . . .

'Stop! These beasts are sacrifices to the god Pluto!' yelled Odysseus. 'None may drink the blood who has not been invited to feast with me, the servant of Pluto and of mighty Zeus!'

The eyes of the dead remained on the blood—wistful and longing—and their sighs lifted Odysseus's hair.

That was when he saw Elpenor—not fat and grinning, as he usually was, but pasty-faced and solemn, standing apart from the rest. His limbs and armour and hair were frayed out to merest shreds: the suggestion of a body. And his head was twisted awkwardly on his shoulders.

'You're here ahead of us. How, Elpenor? You weren't in the boat. I know you weren't at your oar!'

'No, master. I was here already, sir. You see I was sleeping on the roof when you called us. I jumped up, and went to climb down the ladder. But I forgot, you see. I forgot where I'd put the ladder on the way up. Yes, comical, wasn't it? Over I went, and landed on my head. And my neck was broken. But nobody noticed. Nobody missed me. No one came looking for me. 'Elpless Elpenor, you all said, I suppose. And I'm there now. At least my name is—wedged inside my body. Nobody buried me, you see. Nobody called my name across the water. So I don't have one here.'

'You don't have a name?' said Odysseus. He wanted to reach out and comfort Elpenor, but there was nothing to take hold of.

'The spirits don't know my name, so they can't speak to me. And I can't tell them my name, because they can't hear me. Ha, ha! I'm No Wun, you see, Lord Odysseus. Just like you were in the cave of the Cyclops.' It was horrible to see a ghost laugh so joylessly.

'We shall bury your body, Elpenor. If we live to see daylight again, we shall go back and give you all the honours of a soldier and a sailor. I swear it, by the all-powerful Zeus, master of the gods.'

'If you would . . . if you would . . . ' The boy's voice seemed to come from the bottom of a deep well, and his face diminished, as he backed away, to the size of a pin-head. But in going, he led Odysseus's eye towards a woman.

Hard to recognize a woman after thirteen years. Even your own mother.

'Is it? Can it be you?' But the ghost's eyes rested not on Odysseus, but longingly on the pool of sacrificial blood. 'Come forward, Anticleia, daughter of Autolycus, wife of Laertes—and feast with your son!' called Odysseus, though his voice broke with emotion. The female ghost fluttered to the pool of blood and drank from it. 'Mother! Mother! Are you dead, then? Can it be true that you're not tending your lambs and sewing covers for the beds of Pelicata Palace?'

The ghost stared into Odysseus's eyes and lifted her hands towards his face but without touching him. 'How long can an old woman live on hopes and wishes, son? You did not come and you did not come and you did not ever come home. I didn't have the patience of your dear wife, Penelope. And I hadn't the courage of your dear son, Telemachus. My old heart broke with grief: I was so sure that you were dead . . . And I was right, too, surely—because here you are, in the Realm of Shadows.'

'But I'm alive, mother! I'm alive! I strayed into strange waters, and I'm here to ask directions from old Tiresias of Thebes. Oh, mother, couldn't you have waited for me just one more year, just a few more . . . '

'*Who spoke my name?*' A tall spirit—taller by a hand's span than any of the rest—parted the hosts of the dead as he bore down on Odysseus.

The other Greeks fell on their hands and knees and sobbed hysterically, saying, 'We'll never leave here.'

'Pluto will hull our souls like peas!'

'Who will call *our* names over the ocean? We'll be nameless for ever!'

'I, Odysseus of Ithaca, spoke your name, Tiresias—I who have braved the belly of Hell to ask your advice—I who was directed here by Circe the goddess whose hair is like the first rays of dawn and whose fate it was to help me! Come forward and feast with me!'

'Hmm. Achilles was right. He told me when he came here, white with the astonishment of death, that you were a . . . *remarkable* man, Odysseus.' When Tiresias spoke, his puckered, drawstring lips did not move. His voice seemed to come from the centre of his breast-bone. 'You are heartless, too, to disturb the immortal drifting of my spirit. Not since my days of flesh have I vexed myself with other people's lives, other people's futures. Well, well, what is it you want to know?'

'From Circe's magical isle, how must I steer to reach Ithaca?'

When Tiresias spoke at last, he spoke of stars and tides, of islands and shoals, of the singing Sirens and the

Wandering Rocks, of Scylla Six-Headed and Charybdis the Hole. And last of all he spoke of the Island of Helios. He spoke so softly that only Odysseus could hear. And he spoke secrets that might have been sold for diamonds to the sea-captains of the world. The hero's hair stirred in the nape of his neck when he heard of the dangers ahead, but he did not allow his voice to tremble when he said, 'Circe, maiden of the plaited hair, said that you could tell me more—more than the course of my voyage home over the world-encircled sea.'

'Did she? Did she?'

'She said you could tell me the voyage of my life, from birth to death: not just what's gone before, but things to come as well. Shall we reach home alive?'

The seer turned his face away. Still his voice emerged from the fumy regions of his ghostly back, but Odysseus could not see the look on his face. 'If you steer the course I have told you—if you take the precautions I have told you—above all if . . . '

'If! If! Shall I reach home or not?'

'There are choices to be made, young man. How can I know what you will choose in your foolishness, or what fate your foolish men will choose for you? If you do not let them slaughter the Cattle of the Sun, you will reach Ithaca again. Your wife will welcome you, your son will listen to your stories, and the suitors will be driven out of Pelicata Palace.'

'Who? What suitors? What are you talking about, old man?'

The ghost turned back towards Odysseus wearily. 'Even now, young men are beaching their boats in the three bays of Ithaca. "Odysseus is dead," they tell your queen. "Admit it and do not waste your beauty in waiting for a dead man. Marry one of us. Marry and make a king for Ithaca. For what good is a dead king to his kingdom, and what good is a kingdom without a king?" So say the suitors.'

Odysseus let fly such a roar of disgust that the spirits' diaphanous bodies fluttered in the draught. He drew his king's sword and wielded it round his head. 'I'll cut their blood from their flesh and their flesh from their bones!' he raged.

But dead men don't flinch at the sight of a sword's blade, or the fury of a living man. The host of ghosts began to drift away.

'Come, men! There's no time to waste. I must be in Ithaca before the next moon wanes! There are rats in my granary, and maggots in my vines! What? Haven't you seen enough of the Underworld? There'll be time enough to see every room of it when you're dead!'

His men needed no second telling. They fled, on skidding sandals, up the sloping passageway to the impenetrable dark, the water, and the smell of seaweed. They could not drift back the way they had come, because the flow of River Ocean was against them—down, always down—so they felt and pulled their way, sliding their hands over the slimy softness of the walls.

Against the flow of River Ocean they pulled their boat through, until it nosed out into the brightness of morning. Dawn was dancing in flowery cloth-of-gold against the eastern sky, and her unbraided tresses curled across the water. It was the most beautiful sight the men of Ithaca had ever seen. And if the rugged green of their little island home had rested then on the horizon, each and every man would have lived for ever.

6

Sorrow and Singing

'Oh, Telemachus!' cried Queen Penelope to her handsome son. 'Is he really dead and under the sea? Or in some distant land? Am I a widow and are you left fatherless? If I knew! If only I knew!'

'I'm sure he's alive, mother. I'm sure the gods will bring him safe home to us. Do please be patient for just a little while longer.'

'Oh, I have patience, Telemachus. More than the sea has that pounds on a rock to make sand. But how am I to drive off these suitors? They eat our food and drink our wine, and they tell me, "Odysseus is dead! Ithaca has no king. Marry me! Marry me! Marry one of us!"'

'I'll fight them, then, and drive them away—every last one of them! They only want father's crown and gold and palace and flocks, and to be king of Ithaca.'

Penelope stroked her son's hair (it reminded her so much of Odysseus's own brazen curls) and said soothingly, 'You're still only a boy, Telemachus, and they are looking for an excuse to kill you. You can't fight them all—there are thirty or more of them with their feet on the tables and their noses in the vats! If I must be patient, so must you.'

But Telemachus leapt up and seized his father's spear which stood against the wall. 'At least I can go and *look* for my father. Zeus knows, I was too young when he left to remember his face, but someone somewhere must know what has become of him. I'll travel to the mainland—seek out the men who fought with him at Troy. If I have to, I'll climb Olympus itself and ask the gods what has become of him! Perhaps I'll come home with good news. Perhaps I'll even come home with Odysseus himself to save you from these *sandflies*!' And he was gone, all at once, to muster a crew of the few good men he could trust, who tended their sheep in Ithaca's wild places.

'The goddess Athene go with you!' called his mother after him. 'And may she guide you to my dear Odysseus!'

The hero's name echoed down the empty corridors of the palace, hollow and lonely and sad. And Penelope turned back to the window. The little harbour below was full now of brightly painted boats. With every tide another arrived—but never the king's ship. Only more suitors to harry her with threats and wheedling. Perhaps it was true what they told her—that Odysseus would not come and would not come and would not ever come: that his soul was already pining in the Realm of Shadows. And now her only son was setting off across the heartless sea whose waves were always arriving, always coming home to the shores of Ithaca, but always with empty arms.

From the mouth of Hell, Odysseus returned to moor his brightly painted boat in the harbour of Circe's magic island, while the pine-scented air was thick as honey with the low light of evening. They found the body of Elpenor, sprawled in the shadow of the house, with a gentle panther keeping watch beside him and brushing off the flies with his long, black tail.

His comrades buried him in his armour beneath a mound of earth, and honoured him with all the rites of death. Odysseus himself dragged the heavy oar that was Elpenor's from the ship to the top of the mound, and drove it into the soft earth. And Odysseus himself called the man's name three times over the striped and brimming ocean:

'Elpenor! Elpenor! Elpenor!'

When he climbed down, Circe stood waiting, with a cup of wine and meat. 'Well? And did Tiresias answer all your questions?'

'He told me the terrors that lie ahead. But nothing can equal the sights of the Underworld itself. Whether I stand or lie down, whether I fight or run, whether I stay here or try to reach Ithaca—one day I must dwindle down into a flag of mist, and live in the dark for ever, and my name be forgotten on the Earth. What terror can compare with what I've seen?'

'Then stay here with me, Odysseus, and I shall keep you from death for a hundred years.'

For a moment Odysseus hesitated. Then he shook himself, and the fear flew off him as the water flies off an otter's fur. 'I must set sail. I've a mind to hear the Sirens' song in the morning.'

'You reckless man, Odysseus,' said the goddess bitterly. 'Do you think, because Athene gave you a body taut like a bow and a mind as quick as arrows, that you can listen to the Sirens and live? For as long as ships have sailed, the Sirens have sat on their rock and sung. A bare, bald rock it is, heaped up with the bones of sailors. Each one of those sailors has heard the singing of the Sirens and leaned on the rails to listen. First he has thought, "What a sweet sound." And then he has thought, "I must hear more." And then he has thought, "What a waste of my life not to have spent it here, listening!" And then he has thought, "I'll die if I leave this singing!" And then he has died—long and lingering—his ship foundering on the barren rock and his body sprawled at the feet of the Sirens, starving in his ecstasy and parching in his rapture, and loathing himself for his foolishness. You think you and your Greeks are different, but mortal men are all the same when it comes to the Sirens' singing.'

Odysseus held up his hands as if he surrendered to her greater wisdom. But in his eyes she saw the gleam of mischief.

'Oh, you self-willed, headstrong man, Odysseus! Go to my beehives and take the wax from the combs. Knead it and slice it and seal the ears of all your men. Then have them tie you to the mast with rope. And tell them when you beg to be released, to tie you tighter still, and with more rope. Now, say goodbye, and let it never be said by gods or mortal men that I did not help you all I could!'

Then Odysseus kissed her and laughed out loud, and said, 'When they sing my story on Ithaca, I'll have them call you the goddess of magic powers, whose hair hangs down in golden braids like the first rays of dawn; wise as the bees and as sweet as honey. I shall remember you, Circe, whenever my hives are overflowing!'

He boarded his brightly painted ship and stood at the prow, his cockerel on his arm, and four dozen wooden oars sliced white slits in the creamy sea. The sail hung down, hungry for wind.

* * *

367

Warily he kept watch for the Island of the Sirens. There!
Was that birdsong or human voices drifting towards him?
Either way, a sweet sound to hear at sea. He kneaded the
wax: the heat of the morning sun made it soft. He stopped
up the ears of his men, one by one, and all the while the
music grew louder.

Too quiet, too low. I must get closer, he thought, and
stood with his hand to his ear, on the dipping prow. It
was Polites who roped him round and round, and tied
the rope ends to the mast.

'What are you doing?' said Odysseus irritably,
mouthing the words at deaf Polites.

'Only what you would have commanded me if it had
not slipped your mind, my lord. I heard Circe's advice.'

> *Come, my sisters, come and see*
> *How the world-encircled sea*
> *And slow tide of purple time*
> *Have brought, at last, the one sublime*
> *Fast vessel we*
> *Have longed to see—*
> *The Odyssey . . .*

'Circe lied. She said the island was bare and barren.
But it's covered over in flowers—orchids and lilies and
bougainvillaeas . . .'

> *See how his head is crowned with curls;*
> *See how his sail, all unfurled*
> *Hangs empty out of pity—*
> *For though some call us pretty,*
> *Loneliness*
> *Tortures us*
> *Odysseus . . .*

'Everyone lied! They said the Sirens were harpies, with
the bodies of vultures and the heads of women. But
they're lovely! Lovelier than the orchids or the lilies or
the bougainvillaeas . . . Lovelier than Ithaca. How would

my crabbed, ageing wife look alongside them—their shoulders so white, their eyes so imploring. Poor ladies! What manner of man would I be to spurn them? Polites, untie me!'

> *Ah! When the world pronounced your name,*
> *Why did they not speak of the flames*
> *Of glory that around you wreath?*
> *The gods forbid that you should leave.*
> *What happiness*
> *Remains unless*
> *You swim to us,*
> *Odysseus?*

'Polites! Can't you see? Circe lied to us? Let me go this instant! I command you!'

But Polites's shoulders were hunched over his oar: he could not hear, and if he looked up, his eyes did not linger on Odysseus's twisted mouth. 'Polites! You'd better do as I say or I'll kill you afterwards for defying me! Untie me!'

But Polites turned his head away so as not to look into Odysseus's face on every backward pull of the oar.

'You other men! Listen! The man who frees me can have Polites's rank! Any of you—look at me! Whoever frees me can have Ithaca. Take it. How can I rule Ithaca when I'm needed here. Don't you hear what they're saying? They've waited centuries just for me! Men! Look up! TAKE THE WAX OUT OF YOUR EARS! Cut me free, I beg you. Look! The distance isn't so far—I could swim across! You go on if you must: take the boat: I shan't need it. But cut me free and let me swim.—Look, the distance is getting wider. For the love of all the gods— have pity on me! *Someone!* What are you? Pieces of rock? Does it please you to see the hero of Troy reduced to tears? Don't you know what pity is?'

Then Polites leapt up from his thwart and, with his

eyes turned away from Odysseus's face, he fetched another coil of rope and wound it round and round and round both man and mast, from ankle to throat, from throat to ankle. All the while, Odysseus begged, pleaded and sobbed, pulled grotesque, piteous faces, plunging from rage to craven tears as the weather alternated between lightning and drizzling rain.

When he had done, Polites sat down on the heaving deck: only one gap in the coils of rope allowed the king's right hand to reach and claw at him. Polites took the hand in his, and held it, though Odysseus's furious grip squeezed like a vinepress. Deafly he watched the silent mouth contort, and he watched the veins beat in his captain's temples in time with the strokes of the plunging oars.

At last the grip relaxed. Odysseus's head fell forward on his chest, and large tears splashed down on to Polites's hair. Over the starboard quarter, the Island of the Sirens dipped out of sight below the brimming horizon. Polites took the wax out of his ears, and fetched a knife, and cut free Odysseus whose body was ringed round with the marks of the hempen rope. In a small and faltering voice he asked, 'What did you see, Polites?'

'Three hideous vultures with horny talons and the heads of women. An acre of jagged rocks where nothing grew except white trees of bone that used to be good men. What did you see, my lord?'

But the question was never answered. For a headwind brought a fine grey spume and the sound of distant roaring.

'Unstop the men's ears, Polites, and let the tillerman take an oar. I'll steer, myself.'

'Why? What is it, my lord?'

'If Circe and Tiresias spoke the truth we are about to see the greatest terrors of the undiscovered world.'

7

Snake-headed Scylla and Charybdis the Hole

Four dozen tapered and polished blades splashed into the troughing sea as the men dropped their oars. The sea was a dark, slate grey, like the tiled roof of some endless ocean palace. Somewhere beneath that roof, Poseidon sat.

'Don't give up, men!' cried Odysseus, cheerfully striding the length of the boat, up and down between their slumping shoulders. 'This is not like Laestrygonia or the Land of the Cyclops! We aren't flying like sparrows into traps! I *know* what lies ahead. Didn't we travel to Hades for the knowledge? Tiresias told me! Ahead of us on the port side are the Wandering Rocks. No ship has ever passed under their shadow and sailed out again. No speed of rowing, no following wind could drive us through with speed enough to escape destruction. So? A simple choice, then! We must keep to the *starboard* side of the channel—hard by the smooth-faced cliff . . . '

'We're sailing towards Charybdis—Charybdis the Hole!' cried Eurylochus, his jaws clattering with fright.

'Yes, and if we time our passage carefully, we shall pass Charybdis when it's full of sea. Courage, men! Aren't we loved by the goddess Athene herself? And didn't we row down to the Underworld to prepare us for this trip? What must I do to put the fire back into your hearts? Must I put on the armour I wore at Troy? All right. Here! The golden breastplate and the brace of bronze. And here! The bronze helmet on my head, so that the gods will see the sun dazzle on it and know where we are! Now split the ocean with your polished oars so that the gods may stand in admiration of your speed!'

Between every thole-pin the oars rattled, and four dozen wooden blades sliced white slits—white trenches—in the creamy ocean. But Polites said under his breath, 'My lord, Tiresias warned you that no armour and no sword would stave off Scylla.'

'Did you hear the words he spoke, then, Polites? Did the others hear them?'

'Only you and I, my lord. And you are right to leave the men in ignorance. If they knew that Scylla was waiting, no words or whips would drive them through this channel.'

The words between them were washed away by salt spray, and wisps of smoke smudged the sparkling air. A noise of avalanches reached them through a screen of smoke and, little by little, they could make out a movement.

For a moment it seemed that the sea was solid and only the land was moving. Travellers speak of reaches in the sea where ice floats mountain high, always cracking and rending itself, while palaces of snow slide into the water down rivers of frozen sea. History speaks of the earth splitting open and bleeding molten fire through its wounds, blacking out the sun with ash and drowning whole kingdoms in fire. But no one could have put words to the sight that greeted Odysseus and his men.

Towers of rock sky-high writhed shoulder to shoulder for as far as the eye could see, grinding together their crags and precipices, striking sparks from the flint. Boulders big as bullocks stirred and rocked—as loose as an old man's teeth—then overtoppled and bowled down the cliff face to shatter the sea. Gouts of lava spouted from every crevice, snatching seabirds off the wing and dissolving all trace of them. Along the cliff's stony roots, the sea boiled blood-red. The channel was peppered with dead and dying fish. The hull's timbers began to bow as it furrowed through the boiling water. Steam condensed on scalded faces and ran down like sweat or tears.

Hard over to starboard they rowed; hard over as far from the Wandering Rocks as they could go; so hard over that their starboard oars clattered against the base of the opposite cliff. A sheer, smooth cliff it was, as smooth as the walls of Aeolia, as smooth as the forehead of Athene herself. Not a ledge, not a crevice, not even a tuft of grass to give a man footholds who began to climb up. The top was out of sight. But higher than an archer could shoot an arrow, they could glimpse the dark mouth of a cave . . .

'Are we close to Charybdis yet, captain?' asked one of the men. They dared not look over their shoulders to see the way they were going. They could already hear the crashing of water.

'Not yet, not yet. Not till this smooth cliff drops down lower and a fig tree juts out—that marks where Charybdis opens its mouth. Courage, men! Sound carries . . . we're not close to Charybdis yet.'

His men's eyes were on him. They saw Scylla first, reflected in the bronze of his helmet. He saw that they had seen her and said, 'Bend your heads to your chests and row! Whatever you see, whatever you hear—just look to your oars and *row*!'

Odysseus drew his king's sword, thinking to defend his men or die in the attempt. But when she came, there was no defence against Scylla.

Liars tell of monstrous squid that rise from the ocean trench to wrap great ships in their embrace and drag them down to devour them, in lairs of water and bone. But no liar could have invented the beast that came out of that cave.

Above their heads she snaked her six necks. She cast a shadow like a many stranded whip, each knotted end the size of a fist. But the shadow grew—larger and larger—on the boat's deck. The Scylla's heads were not the size of fists. They were not the size of melons. They were not the size of drums. The Scylla's heads were larger even than the fist of King Lamus, who ate men out of his palm. Each mouth was the size of a slimy cave. And set in her jaws, like stalactites and stalagmites, were six rows of rending teeth. Her teeth were as many as the blood vessels in a man's body: vessels she loved to break, along with bone and muscle and heart.

With each head she lifted a man—pulling him from under his oar. Six heads, six mouths, six men calling on the gods for deliverance. Six heads, six mouths, and six sons of Ithaca weeping their last for their wives and children. Six heads, six mouths, and six dead men, each with Odysseus's name on his lips, begging to be spared. Six heads, six mouths, but not a limb or head or reaching hand or shrieking left, for the Scylla had devoured her catch and was coiling herself back into the bloody recesses of her cave to digest her meat. Though she had lived for centuries, her only purpose on the surface of the earth was to ambush and to eat and to sleep.

374

'Row, men, row! Shut your ears and your eyes and row till we are out of reach of the Scylla. Or she may strike again!'

Then Odysseus was glad of his king's helmet with its long nosepiece and cheeks of bronze. For it hid the pallor of his face, and the terror, and it hid his tears, too, which flowed like blood. He looked at his king's sword and the six blunted crescents in its shining blade where he had hacked at the scaly neck of the writhing Scylla. He shook his head; he plugged up his ears; but the voices went on ringing inside his head, even though they had been long since silenced: *'Save us, Odysseus! Save us!'*

Only the sound of Charybdis could drown out those voices.

Charybdis was a Hole. Charybdis was a mouth. Charybdis was a gill in the throat of the fishy ocean. When the ocean breathed in, water and air, flotsam and jetsam, weeds and waves, fish and birds were sucked into its gaping pit, and spun deeper and deeper than the deepest well in the world, whirled round in a spiral of sea. And when the ocean breathed out, water and air, flotsam and jetsam, scale and feather were belched out again in gouts of sea like the foam from a mad dog's mouth.

Twice in every tide the whirlpool sucked down every atom of water and floating morsel—as deep as the seabed itself. Twice in every tide it expelled all that it had sucked in, but for a perpetual litter which circled for ever in its vortex.

The first sight they had of Charybdis was the tall mast of a ship, circling, circling, circling—as though an invisible god were stirring the water with it. The noise was of ripping canvas and cataracts of sea, of the cowhide bag of Aeolus unfastened beneath the surface. They could not make themselves heard above it; they could not hear their own thoughts and when they breathed, they breathed in flying spray.

'Is the tide right?' they mouthed at Odysseus through the smoke of spume. 'Shall we be sucked down?'

'Row!' cried Odysseus. 'If the gods wish it, Charybdis will breath out and let us pass. If the gods don't . . . ' They could not hear him above the racketing of Charybdis. All they could see was the brightness of his eyes in the arches of the king's helmet, and the twisting of his mouth beneath the nosepiece. And they could feel the boat slip sideways beneath them, dragged towards the spiral trough of Charybdis. The six oars of the six dead men were sucked through their pins, and bounded towards the whirling pit.

Then—as it seemed they must surely glide sideways over the glassy rim—there was a sudden silence, a moment's silence, as in the mind of a dying man. The solid, glassy rim of Charybdis shattered and, with a gurgling confusion, the waters levelled. The broken shipwreck floating at its centre paused for a moment. They could see every open slat. They could see every gap in the ribs of the skeleton crew who sat at its oars.

The next moment the shipwreck began to swing the other way. The coil of Charybdis was rewinding. The other way. The waves spun and, at the centre of the coil, the water dipped like a saucer, dipped like a dish, dipped like a bowl, dipped like a trough.

'Row!' cried Odysseus, and they sped onwards with their polished oars flashing like beams of sun. '*Row!*'

Charybdis, breathing in, grew as deep as a cave, as deep as a well, but the boat of the Greeks was skimming beyond the reach of its centripetal pull. They were past. They were unwrecked. They were alive!

Beneath the bronze nosepiece of the king's helmet, they could see Odysseus's teeth flash white as he grinned. And when the noise of Charybdis died away, he was still repeating, 'Well rowed! Rowed like true men of Ithaca!'

As they looked beyond him, they could still see the tip of the mast of the dead ship spinning

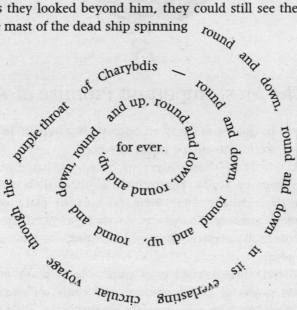

round and down. round and down. round and down in its everlasting circular voyage through the purple throat of Charybdis — round and down, round and up, round and down, round and up, round and down, round and up, for ever.

8

The Most Important Promise of All

T he golden sea was studded with jewels of sunlight too bright and too many to count.

Three times Odysseus called the name of each man eaten by Scylla. Three times he shouted their names over the sea. But there were no oars to plant on the shore in memory. There was no shore to plant them in, nor place to sacrifice Circe's black sheep in gratitude to the gods.

There! Their dazzled eyes were able to make out the grassy slopes of an island from the circlet of clouds on the horizon. Odysseus screwed up his eyes against the brightness. 'Tiresias of Thebes spoke the truth! We've reached the country of Helios!'

The men looked up and smiled ill-fitting smiles. Fright had changed the shape of their faces.

'I know what you're thinking,' said Odysseus, 'but put it out of your minds. You're thinking, here's a sheltered mooring for a night's sleep and a bite of food. But we won't set foot on Helios. I say lean on your oars and let's put it far behind us before sunset.'

A murmur of discontent ran along the boat. Reproachful

eyes scowled at Odysseus. The rhythm of the oars faltered and the blades halted in the air, like the feathers of a forlorn sea-bird. Eurylochus got up, his feet splayed across the keel of the boat. 'And I say we stop and rest. We're not all superhuman like you. We're not all heroes with leather for muscles and fire for blood. We're just poor mortals. *We* get tired. We get very, very tired and we need to sleep. We don't enjoy sleeping over our oars while you stretch out on the quarter-deck in half a mile of cloak. We don't relish waiting for a storm to come up out of the darkness like a fist, and smash us to splinters or shovel water over our heads. We don't care much for a man who *knew* about Scylla and chose not to tell us. Six of us have died today cursing the name of Odysseus who can't even spare the time to give them funeral rites. To put it briefly, *captain*, we don't *care* to row on past Helios. It looks like an excellent place to spend the night.'

Odysseus put his hand to the hilt of the king's sword, but the tiller swung and nudged him off balance as all the men stood up at their oars and began to stamp their feet. They were applauding Eurylochus.

'You foolish . . . What's it to me where we drop anchor? We can all walk home our separate ways to Ithaca, if that's what pleases you. I was just concerned, in case Eurylochus here was too weak-willed to resist the temptation of roast beef. Because, as you know, if any one of you so much as lays a finger on the Cattle of the Sun, we can all look forward to death and destruction.'

The purple veins throbbed in Odysseus's temples, but a hundred fingers were drumming on the oars of the ship. Insolent eyes glared at him. 'Captain,' said Polites softly, 'we have enough grain aboard to keep us in bread for a week—a black sheep, too, and honey from Circe's hives.

I think you'll find that the men can resist the temptation for just one night.'

Odysseus did not answer, but threw the tiller over sharply, so that the boat veered towards the Island of Helios. The cockerel on the stern rail reeled and reached out a grasping claw to keep itself from falling.

The surf was heavy: it slammed them down on the pebbles of the beach, and boiled around their chests as they pulled the boat up higher. The island had no lee shore, for it had no hill of any height, and the winds blew over it and set the grass tossing and rolling, shaking free seeds like the white spray from the crests of waves.

When the sun went down and light poured thick as honey along the sea-lanes, it found no dry-land pathways to wander in. The only branches were the branching horns of the sun god's beautiful cattle.

Their silken hides gleamed russet red in the sunset, and their great brown eyes blinked at its brightness. When the sunbeams stroked their backs, their withers twitched and their stocky legs stamped and their long tails swished seed-heads out of the white, autumnal dandelions. Their curving horns were as long as the king's bow.

Odysseus's men fetched the black sheep Circe had given them, and the sack of ground grain, and they ate roast lamb and doughy bread. Night fell, but instead of a million stars, rain cascaded out of the sky, and behind it came the wind.

'Where would we be now if we'd stayed at sea?' said Eurylochus smugly, and the rest agreed with him.

They overturned the boat on the beach and sat beneath it, chewing on their bread. Then they wrapped themselves in their cloaks and went to sleep—or lay awake and listened to the drumming of the rain and the lowing of the cattle trampling the wet grass into the mud.

Next morning it was still raining, and the sea hurled itself up the beach like a chained dog lunging with white teeth at an unwelcome visitor. The Greeks did not so much as put out their heads from under the upturned boat, though it was dark underneath it, and the sun's cattle chewed on the ropes.

Next morning it was still raining, and the lightning, like barbed Trojan arrows, wounded the sky and set it growling. The Greeks lay on their stomachs, chewing on their bread, and watched the raindrops quarry holes in the beach.

After a week, all the grain that Circe had given them was gone. They did not want for water. It trickled out of the bilges, it leaked between the boards, it condensed out of their steamy breath against their chilly skin. But all their food was gone.

Odysseus wandered the island from north to south, west to east, and returned with the leather of his skirt double its weight with water, his hair plastered to his neck with rain, the hairs of his arms darkly sodden and his shirt transparent over his streaming chest. But he had found nothing to eat but grass—grass or the succulent beef of the sun god's cattle.

After another week the rain stopped but the wind still gusted from the north-west—a gale fit to drive them back the way they had come, back into the mouth of Charybdis and the six jaws of Scylla. Odysseus took his old cockerel, his mascot, and wrung its neck and boiled it in sea water—beak, claws and all. The stew tasted of sand and sinew, and it was as tough as bridles and sandals and bowstrings. They ate in silence, sheltering under the boat from the clouds of sand that scudded ahead of the wind. Towards the end of the frugal meal, the boat began to rock. It toppled over, and loose oars clattered down on top of the men: they scarcely had the strength to protect themselves. It was not the wind that had blown the boat over: a large cow was scratching its fat hide against the wooden hull.

Forty-five pairs of eyes looked askance at Odysseus. Forty-five hearts brooded. This is a glorious end, they seemed to say, for men who survived the Trojan Wars.

'I shall go and pray to Athene of the grey eyes, and to great Zeus, father of the gods,' said Odysseus sharply. 'We were not saved from Charybdis and the six-headed Scylla for the skin to fall off our bones in the company of cows.' He walked away slowly; his brains were dizzy and his eyesight smudged with hunger. Some friendly cows fell in behind him and followed him to the other side of the island where, like priests in attendance, they watched Odysseus make his supplication to the gods.

'O Athene! Goddess of War! Can nothing but the flame of battle fire your grey eyes? Is it of no interest to you that your champions in war are jointless with hunger and their bones are hollow and empty of marrow? Was it for this that you strung the taut longbow of my body and armed it with arrows of cunning? The bow-string is frayed almost to breaking and the arrows have no more strength to fly! Plead my cause in the Halls of Heaven— or distract Poseidon for an hour so that we may creep out from under the shadow of his anger! You alone know what sacrifices I would make to you and to almighty Zeus if ever I reached Ithaca alive. You whispered in my ear the secret of Circe's potion; you planted the little white moli flower at my feet; you filled Charybdis's gaping mouth with water as we passed by. For what? For us to scatter our shining bones among the sun's cattle? *To die among cows?'*

A little brown bird fluttered past his head and, in turning, Odysseus saw the bird light on the bristles of a prickly cactus. And there! in the heart of the cactus was a prickly pear—flame orange and peppered with black spines. He wrapped his arm in his cloak and reached in for the pear, rubbing off the skin against the ground. It was a miserable fruit: spines still found their way into the roof of his mouth. But to a man who had not eaten for two weeks, except for a mouthful of chicken broth, it filled him like roast meat and left him with nothing but the longing to sleep. He lay down in the shelter of the cactus. Just as he began to doze, he realized that the wind had changed direction.

He dreamed of making grateful sacrifice to the gods, on the shores of Ithaca, and he woke with the savour of it in his nose . . . the savour of roasting beef. The wind had changed, as he had prayed it would. But now it brought on it a smell that choked all happiness in his heart.

Leaping up, arms flailing and sandals slipping, he ran back across the island. The smell grew stronger in his nostrils. The dreadful certainty grew stronger in his heart. He reached the beach in time to see Eurylochus scraping an empty hide with his battle-sword. The skinned beef rolled on a spit. The other cows stood round at a distance with large, sad eyes, uncomprehending.

'You fools! You godless fools! We are all dead men!' cried Odysseus picking up Eurylochus by collar and belt and flinging him bodily into the surf. Then he turned on Polites, who was sitting cross-legged in the shingle, his head bent over a fistful of meat. 'You! Even you! Why didn't you stop them? Does it taste good, the taste of death? I hope so, because it's the last meal you'll ever eat!'

Polites looked up at him, closing one eye against the brightness of the sky. He spoke quietly. 'I know it, master. But there was truth in what Eurylochus said, for all he's three-parts fool. He said that it was better to die on the ocean, fighting the gods, than to die inch by inch of hunger and be mourned by a herd of cows.'

But Eurylochus had changed his tune: 'Acchh, the sun god will never miss one cow. And if he did, would he begrudge one cow to starving men? If you don't want yours, captain, we'll eat it for you. There's enough emptiness in my belly for the whole herd!'

Odysseus fell on his knees, groaning, and beat his forehead on the ground. The smoke from the fire and the blackening baron of beef was carried by the wind up into the sky, across the very path of the sinking sun. Into the silence that had fallen over the crew came one mournful bellow. They looked around them, but all the cows had walked off and were out of sight. Their eyes came to rest, every man's, on the smoking carcass roasting on the spit, and the whites of each man's eyes showed in sheerest terror. The carcass bellowed again.

'To sea! To sea!' cried Odysseus, jumping to his feet. 'When the sun drives overhead, he'll look down and count his cows. Then he'll melt the brains in your head and the bones in your limbs if you're still here! If we set sail now, we shall have all night before the sun god can take his revenge.' Odysseus barely believed his own words, but his men were eager to believe. They carved themselves hunks of cooked meat from the spitted roast, righted the boat, and each man posted his shining oar between its thole-pins. They launched energetically, their strength renewed by the food, their speed redoubled by the danger. Odysseus would not eat one mouthful of the meat, and he boarded the ship with his brain still dizzy, his eyesight still smudged with hunger.

The mast was raised, the mended sail flowered against its mast-stem. As the Island of Helios dropped below the horizon, the sun god soared over their heads, dazzling bright in his shining chariot, dropping down towards the rosy arch of the sunset. There was a flash of green at the moment he disappeared from sight.

Night fell, and a million stars cascaded, like pebbles hurled down on the unloved—like sparks of white-hot anger. As morning approached the men grew more and more silent. Only Eurylochus was noisy in his confidence: 'We're safe now. The sun god won't trouble himself about one dead cow.'

But when the sun rose next morning, there was a ridge of dark cloud above it like a scowling eyebrow over a glaring eye. Sunbeams searched the ocean: they lighted on the lonely boat bobbing on the brimming waves and a wind sprang up in the west that was like a voice calling over the sea: 'Poseidon! Poseidon! *There* is Odysseus!'

The sea writhed. The smooth swell flexed like muscles. The sky lowered, and the sea rose as if it would crush the ship between. Then strings of water, like the stringing saliva in the corners of a mad dog's mouth, joined sea to sky, and waterspouts stood all around: a forest of waterspouts, a colonnade of pillars, as though the surface of the sea were a palace and the sky its roof held up with columns of water. And from down in the sea's cellar, the king of the palace was coming . . .

Odysseus held the tiller. Polites stood up, although the boat was rolling and pitching. His abandoned oar was tugged out through its slit and floated away as he walked the length of the deck. When he stood face to face with Odysseus, he said, 'Farewell, master. Remember my face when we meet again in the underworld.'

'Farewell, old friend,' Odysseus replied, as they embraced. 'I would call your name across the ocean myself, but my voice cracks at the thought of parting from you: the spirits might not hear me.'

So Polites faced the heaving ocean and cupped his

hands around his mouth and called his own name across the twisting sea-lanes. 'Polites! Polites! Polites!'

An arching wave as dark as the walls of the underworld itself reared up over the boat. Beneath them was water, beside them was water, above them was breaking water. Then the wave crashed down on the boat, smashing the mast so that it fell on Eurylochus, instantly killing him. As the wave withdrew, it dragged with it the mast and sail and, tangled in the ropes, the body of drowned Polites.

There! Shoulders of green water ruptured the melting sea, and tangled locks of foam shook in the sky. *'Let each man call his own name across the ocean!'* cried Odysseus into the teeth of the wind, and those who heard him cupped their hands to their mouths and called across the thundering sea, 'Demos!'

'Stavros!'

'Nicoliades!'

'Georgi!'

'Platonis!'

All the shining oars were snapped off short, like the legs of a beetle pulled off by a child. Some of the oarsmen were run through with their own, sharp-ended oars. Some were seized from their thwarts by snatching waves. The sea had sixty-thousand jaws, and each as hungry as the mild-mannered Scylla. The wind went about, and carried them back past the island of Helios. The sun god drove his bright chariot to the top of Noonday Hill, and poured down molten heat between the tempest clouds. He blistered the skin of the rowers, and dried up the marrow in their bones. But then Poseidon, jealous of his revenge, blotted out the sun with pitch-black clouds, so that he might kill Odysseus in the privacy of darkness.

9

An Eternity

'*B*reathe in, Charybdis, and swallow down Odysseus
and all his hopes!'* Poseidon's voice hissed in every
spume-frayed wave. The forked lightning of his
trident jabbed one prong to the right and two to the left of
the hull. The water that broke over the ship was hot now,
and the air was full of ash from the fires of the Wandering
Rocks. The sea was a bowl where dead fish stewed. And
Charybdis was breathing in.

Faster and faster the surface layers of the sea were
slipping towards the Hole. The mast of the death ship
was still at the centre, still stirring the cauldron
Charybdis. Some of the remaining crew leapt overboard
and tried to swim, seeing that the ship was doomed to be
swallowed. The undertow snatched them, sure as sharks,
under and down. The rest clung to the lurching boat in
the hope that Charybdis would breathe out and halt its
whirling for long enough to spare them. But the downward
spiral was only just beginning, and Charybdis the Hole
grew deeper and whirled faster by the second.

Poseidon's angry breath sped them towards it. All the
litter of the sea—splintered spars, the fins of whales,

barrels washed overboard, broken breakwaters, rafts of weed, fishing pots, and drowned sailors—washed against the hull with thuds and bangs. Then it was gone—over the glassy rim of Charybdis, and the ship was flung by its speed out over the empty well of the whirlpool, enshrouded in spindrift and spray.

From the aft deck, Odysseus flung himself into the air. His hands clawed over his head. He grabbed the twisted branches of the leafless, salt-blasted fig tree that overhung the abyss of Charybdis. The earth at its roots shifted; pebbles fell away into the swirling water; the branch sagged under the weight of Odysseus. But it held.

Had he not gone hungry for weeks on the Island of Helios, had his thick-set body not been reduced to ribs, pelvis, and wasted shanks, he would have wrenched tree and root out of the cliff, and fallen with them into the gaping whirlpool. But he clung, as thin as a grasshopper clinging to the underside of a blade of grass, and beneath him his ship plunged down to destruction.

Joint parted from joint, plank from keel, tiller from stern, hand from broken oar, fingertips from wreckage, prayers from lips, breath from lungs, life from body, as the *Odyssey* and its crew plunged to their doom in Charybdis's dismal abyss. Not one cry climbed through the roaring spray to Odysseus's ears, but the sound of the sea itself was like the screams of a thousand drowning sailors, the wailing of a thousand widows, the breaking of a thousand hearts.

The sun went down, but inside the tent of spray that canopied Charybdis, Odysseus could not tell night from day, evening from morning. Night fell, while a white hail of spray cascaded over him: every breath was like drowning. The thighbones burned in his hip-joints; his arms groaned in their sockets; his sinews unwound from his bones, but still he clung to the fig tree, and Charybdis raged beneath him—so steep-sided that pieces of his brightly painted ship were embedded in the glassy spiral of water, like a frieze on the wall of a temple. The Hole was so deep that the sea-bed itself was dry at the base. There! A dim gleam came from the king's golden breastplate and the bronze helmet he had worn to dazzle the gods. Quivering in the sand stood the king's sword—until water washed over them and clattered them together like tin pots. They did not float: they were lost from sight under the rising water. Charybdis was breathing out!

Slowly, slowly the vortex of the whirlpool grew shallower—as deep as a well, a cave, a trough, a bowl . . . Fragments of painted wood that had once been a boat as bright as the spring flowers, jostled each other on the boiling eddy. Odysseus let go his grip on the fig tree and fell the short drop into the lava-warmed sea. He grasped the keel of the *Odyssey* as it swirled out of the sway of Charybdis. It was the only fragment of flotsam he recognized from his own boat. Even the death ship they had seen spinning intact for the space of a tide or two was shattered to sodden black shards.

Lying on his face, and paddling with arms that weighed like lead in their sockets, he floated away from those dreadful straits.

For nine days the sun, still hot with anger, raged on his unarmoured back. For eight nights the white moon's reflection swam beside him in the sea. Salt whitened his hair and wrinkled his skin, until his own wife would have called him an old man. And just as a grape dries and shrivels into a wrinkled raisin, Odysseus's heart shrank inside him; he let drop the last of his youth into the bottomless ocean where nothing lost is ever found again. When the ninth night fell, clouds swallowed all

389

the stars but one, which floated like a shipwrecked sailor in the edgeless, pitch-black sky.

But the world-encircled sea is not without shores.

There! A heap of blackness like the shoulder of some great sea-beast stood out hard and shineless against the slick black ocean and the cloud-soft darkness of the sky. Odysseus was too weary to move his hands which hung down through the water and were brushed by unseen fish. But the current carried him closer and closer to the dark outline of the island, and soon his dangling fingers touched sand, and the paintless keel of his broken boat rolled him on to his back. He looked up and saw the one last star dimmed by morning, then sleep swallowed him entirely.

When he woke, someone was singing. The song was so sweet that he thought for a moment that the sea had carried him back to the barren roost of the singing Sirens. But when he stirred, he could feel a down quilt under him, and a blanket of lambswool over him. His eyes were puffed up with saltwater, and he could not see, but small, soft hands were stroking his hair and forehead, and a sweet foam of warm honey was trickling past his lips.

He tried to sit up. 'I am Odysseus, King of Ithaca and ruler over . . . '

The singing ceased. 'I know very well who you are, Odysseus, for you are ruler of more than Ithaca, Cephalonia, and little wooded Zanthe: you are ruler of my heart. And because you have been chosen by an Immortal, you shall be immortal, too.'

'Circe? Is it you?'

There was a tinkling of silver as his nurse dropped the spoon. Some of the softness went out of the voice. 'Circe? What's that pig-farmer to you? Beside her, I'm the day-star beside a candle.' A cool tissue wiped his eyes, and he was able to open them. Leaning over him was a woman dressed in green and yellow, like the spring, and her breath smelt of honeysuckle. She leaned across him, and her hair hung round him like a curtain as she covered his face with kisses.

This is a good place, thought Odysseus. It's not Ithaca, but it is a good place. Besides, I'm weary. I must rest. He said: 'Madam, what's your name and who are your people?'

'My name is Calypso, and this is my island—Ogygia. There is no one here but me—you and me, my love.' She crept under the lambskin blanket and dozed in the angle of his arm.

Little by little, the strong longbow of Odysseus's body grew pliable again, restrung with courage and cunning. His thoughts and plans bristled like a quiverful of arrows worn high on his back, and he put out of his mind Poseidon the Tormentor.

But he could not put out of mind Ithaca or his queen or his son—or the words of Tiresias about the suitors who were swarming round his hives. 'I must get home as soon as I can,' he told Calypso.

But she only shrugged her white shoulders and stroked his brown arms and said, 'I have no boat to give you.'

Calypso was a nymph, and her house was a sand-carpeted cave hung with woollen rugs and scarlet drapery. It looked out on an arcing bay of white sand and mauve water through a paling of aspen and cypress trees. The land was dappled like a leopard with leafy shade, and white-headed grasses, like the manes of horses, tossed in the jasmine-scented air. Passion flowers, white and purple and open-mouthed, entwined the entrance to the cave, and here Calypso had her loom. The warp and weft were as fine as spider's thread, and her golden shuttle flew as fast as a sharp-nosed yellow hornet, to and fro, to and fro, while she worked.

But after Odysseus came to Ogygia, Calypso rarely spent time weaving at her loom. She trailed like a shadow at Odysseus's heel, and whenever he turned, he found himself beached in her white arms.

Her kisses tasted like the fruit of the lotus tree; they had the power to make a man want more. For a time, Odysseus became a lotus-eater in Calypso's arms. But as week turned to month and month to year, he tired of her admiration. Whenever he said, 'Today I shall go fishing', she replied, 'Don't go. I love you. Don't you love me?'

Whenever he said, 'Today I shall practise my archery', she replied, 'Silly bows and arrows. Don't you love me any more? Stay here with me.'

Whenever he said, 'I'm getting fat and my muscles are weakening', she replied, 'No matter. I love you as you are.'

When he told her stories of Troy, he could not speak three words before she interrupted him with sighs and exclamations: 'How wonderful! No wonder I love you!'

Even when he did not speak to her, she would repeat, 'I love you, I love you, I love you.' It was not conversation as he remembered it. He remembered sitting under his vine-arch with Penelope and discussing affairs of state.

'I don't care about politics,' said Calypso. 'I only care about you.'

He remembered how Penelope had told him stories to while away the winter evenings.

'I don't know any stories,' said Calypso. 'Besides— you tell stories so much better than I ever could.'

He remembered how wise Penelope had been in matters of history—how they had walked along the headlands of

Ithaca and imagined how the world had looked when no one but the gods played on its open places.

'Why look to the past?' said Calypso when he told her. 'The present is all that matters—that and our future together—you and me for ever and ever and ever.'

He remembered how, as they had walked on those summer evenings, Penelope had pointed out all the little flowers to him, naming them by name and making up poetry about the birds and the sea. 'I want to walk over the headland, Calypso,' he said.

'Walk? Why walk when we can lie down and kiss? How can I kiss you when you keep *talking* so.'

Odysseus gave a sudden groan and hurried out of the cave. He walked and walked, while there was light left to see by, and then he sat down on a cliff, overlooking the sea, and wept bitterly, his knees pressed into the sockets of his eyes and his body rocking to and fro, to and fro. 'Oh, Penelope! Penelope! What will become of you and your son, with me a prisoner on this mound of sugar? O you gods, who sent me here to eat syrup off a poisoned spoon—remember me! Remember me! Remember me!'

'Have you forgotten?' said Queen Penelope to the suitor Eurymachus. 'I am a married woman and my husband, whose food you are eating, is Odysseus, hero of Troy.'

Eurymachus wiped his mouth on his hand and grinned at her. 'Forgotten, lady? Forgotten great Odysseus? Of course not! He's the hero who drowned on his way back from Troy and left a widow and no one to rule over Ithaca.'

White-faced, Penelope plucked at the weft of her loom with nervous rage. 'No one to rule? He left his son, didn't he? He left Telemachus! He'll come home soon with news of his father—or perhaps with Odysseus himself.'

Eurymachus stood up. 'No, lady. I told you (and you knew already in your heart of hearts) your worthy husband died long since. What? He could have walked barefoot from Troy across the sea-bed by now, if he was still alive. Choose a new husband. Look! There are plenty to choose from here in your own palace! Take a young, handsome husband who'll give you some fun in the years to come. Your boy, Telemachus, may have fallen into the hands of pirates or been swallowed in the sea like his father. Or maybe he's fallen in love with some pretty face a thousand miles away. And if he returns? What then? He's only a boy—years from manhood. How could he hope to hold the island states of Ithaca against . . . against those who would take them from him? Your palace is charming. Your food is excellent. But all this *waiting about*—it gets on a man's nerves. I strongly advise you to choose one of us for a husband—before anyone *unmannerly* thinks of helping himself to the crown.'

'Are you threatening me, Eurymachus?' whispered Penelope, trembling so with fury that she dropped the shuttle of her loom.

'Me, madam? Your devoted admirer and slave? Your ardent lover whose very heart waits on your permission to beat? Me, threaten you? Never!'

'Then, if you are my slave, tell this to the other suitors and pay heed to it yourself. On this loom I'll weave a wedding veil. When it's finished, I'll wear it in marriage to one of you. Then Ithaca will have a king again. Tell them, will you, Eurymachus?'

'Lady! Beloved Penelope! I myself will fetch you a veil woven by fifty maidens out of cobweb if that's all that's keeping you from marrying!'

But she held up her hand and succeeded in smiling with all sweetness. 'You ask me to admit that my dear

Odysseus is dead. Very well. Give me this little while to mourn for him while I weave. It's only fair, Eurymachus.'

The suitor bowed with a great show of respect, but behind his hand he was grinning, for he believed he would not have long to wait before the crown of Ithaca was his. Outside the room he caught the sleeve of Antinous, another of the suitors, and led him aside into a dark corner. 'The old girl is weakening. She's weaving a bit of lace and when it's done she'll marry. Now—about Telemachus. If he gets any older, he'll start thinking of himself as heir to the crown. I think it would be kinder if we let him know the true situation—keep him from raising his hopes unduly. Don't you agree?'

'I see what you mean,' said Antinous.

'Let's take a few men out to Asteris, to meet him on his homeward voyage. Ships always put in there for the last night. Then we can . . . *discuss* things with him.'

'Slit his throat, you mean?'

'Antinous, you're so crude sometimes,' sighed Eurymachus. 'Yes, slit his throat.'

When the suitors heard the news—that Penelope would marry when her veil was woven—they hacked open a particularly large barrel of wine—from the cellars of Pelicata Palace. Then they drank themselves merry and stumbled upstairs to the room where Penelope's loom stood in the daylight of the window. They stood around and watched her shoot the shining shuttle to and fro, to and fro.

'Be done in no time,' they whispered.

'A month at most.'

'Let's take bets on how long she takes—I've got a better idea! Let's take bets on who she chooses. Ha! ha! ha!'

Later, much later that night, when the suitors were all asleep, with Pelicata wine on their chins and their dirty sandals under Pelicata's white blankets, Penelope got up from her royal bed. She crept along the corridors, past the tall grey squares of window and the view of the moon-silver sea, to the room where her loom stood. In her hand was a pair of scissors. Stitch by stitch, she undid everything she had woven that day.

'This veil of mine shall be longer in the making than all the reefs of the sea built up from the tiny lives of shellfish. It won't be finished before Telemachus comes back. It won't be finished before my hair is as white as salt and my skin as wrinkled as the sea. It won't be finished before my dear Odysseus comes home—even though he doesn't come and doesn't come and doesn't ever come. O you gods! have you lived so long up there in the cold, thin air of Olympus, that your hearts have died within you? Or have you forgotten what it is to be in love?'

10

The Quarrelsome Gods

I n the east the sun gleamed on the greening copper
domes and palaces of black-skinned princes in
barren, stony kingdoms. In the west, the sun was
just rising on shivering barbarians blue with cold. In the
north, dark-haired gypsies were still sleeping where they
had fallen down with weariness from dancing under the
moon. And to the south, the sunlight caught on the
golden shuttle of Calypso the nymph as it flew to and fro,
to and fro across her loom. From the far side of her
island, smoke was rising from a sacrificial fire.

From the highest terraces of Mount Olympus, the gods
could see every mortal and lowly immortal under the
sun. The goddess Athene stood on one such terrace and
sniffed up the sweet sandlewood fragrance of Odysseus's
fire. Around her the lazy gods sprawled in ones and twos,
on silver cushions lined with cloud. Their late sleeping
irritated her. The perfection of their line-free, egg-shell-
smooth faces irritated her. The heady scent of roses
irritated her. Tipping her warrior-helmet back on her
head, she banged the base of her silver spear on the
ground.

'You're vexed,' said Hermes. He lay on his back on a couch, his hands under his head and his blue cover slipping on to the floor. 'What do you see that vexes you so much when you look over there?'

'I see a good man making sacrifice, and his smoke pouring past the gods' nostrils without raising so much as a sneeze! Does religious devotion count for nothing any more?'

Hermes lazily lifted his head. 'Ah. You mean Odysseus. You always liked these hairy-faced mortals with their black-wool arms. He puts me in mind of a sheep—all that wool and bleating.'

'He's been held captive on that island for *seven years* now, weeping and breaking his heart—and what do we do to help him?'

'Held captive? On Ogygia? With Calypso? That's one prison where most men would pay to be penned up. I call it most ungrateful of Odysseus to spend all his time beating his head on the floor and weeping: worse things happen at sea, so they say!' Hermes laughed and wagged his heels in the air. 'Your trouble is, you're jealous!'

'*Jealous?* Of *her*?' The goddess of grey eyes tossed her head, threw back her shoulders, and strode purposefully into the Hall of Heaven. She had determined to speak to Zeus while his mind was uncluttered. Already prayers had begun to rise up on the thermals of morning air; soon the prayers of worshippers from all over the sea-encircling world would be racketing about the quiet corridors of Olympus. And Zeus would find it all too easy to brush aside her request.

'Zeus! Father! Mighty father of all the gods,' she began briskly as she entered the blue marble hall. Her sandals slapped the ethereal pavement. 'Has Poseidon's foul temper poisoned all heaven that we no longer show mercy to a faithful worshipper—a man who makes sacrifices every day and libations of saltwater tears? Is a lowly sea nymph to be allowed to imprison one of *my* champions—one of those I crowned with fame on the Trojan battlefields?'

The father of the gods sat among the swathes of his train which creased and interfolded like the foothills of the Pindus Mountains, topped by the snowy whiteness of his hair. He had a young man's face, but his eyes were as old as the lakes that sit in the remote craters of extinct volcanoes. 'We all know your feelings, child Athene, on the subject of Odysseus.'

'Feelings?' Athene bridled, her nostrils flaring beneath her grey eyes. 'I am the goddess of war! My *feelings* are those of a commander who sees one of his men mistreated!'

'Yes, yes. Of course. Naturally. But warrior Odysseus did blind Polyphemus, son of Poseidon. And his men did eat one of the cattle of Helios—the sun god's pride and joy. Must they have no revenge?'

'Is seven years not punishment enough?' retorted Athene. 'Polyphemus broke all laws of hospitality, and ate Greeks like apples, and spat out their souls like pips. No beef passed Odysseus's lips, and the guilty men are washing about in the cold sea, with dogfish gnawing on their bones. Is seven years' imprisonment in the cave of Calypso not punishment enough for any mortal? The years Odysseus has lost will never come again.'

'Imprisonment? On Ogygia? That's one prison where most men would pay to be penned up. And I hear tell that Calypso has offered Odysseus *eternal* life if he will love her in return,' said Zeus in slow, measured words.

A frisson of anger shook Athene from head to foot. The base of her spear cracked against the celestial pavement so that hail fell on to the places beneath. 'That meddlesome strumpet! That presumptuous nymph! If we are going to let her make *gods* of all her lovers, heaven will soon be full to overflowing. Are we to jostle shoulder-to-shoulder through eternity with mortals trooping continually up to Olympus's gates saying, "Calypso sent me." "Calypso made me immortal, let me in!"'

'Enough!' Zeus held up his hand. The smallest contracting of his brows sent thunder rolling round the horizon. Athene's words froze on her lips in awe. But her bold eyes still rested on the father of the gods. He said, 'It has been in my mind for some time to let Odysseus leave Ogygia. It pleases me that he has rejected Calypso's offer of immortality. Besides, his wife's prayers rise up on every puff of wind, and his son's too. The name Odysseus seems never to be out of my head. For the sake of my peace, I will send Hermes to command Calypso to let him go . . . But since he *is* mortal, he must use mortal means to reach Ithaca's shores. No galleys of cloud. No rainbow bridges. No silver dolphins to carry him over the waves. Only a wooden raft made with his own hands. And one of the gods must keep old Poseidon busy with talk, and his back turned, because I won't forbid the old Sea-Shaker his revenge.'

'But why, father Zeus? Why? Why? *Why?*'

'Because, my daughter, I look at you and I ask myself how *I* would feel if some small, braggartly mortal put out *your* two grey eyes with a white-hot stake of wood.'

Hermes strapped on his golden sandals—the ones with wings at their heels—and leapt over the parapet of heaven to begin his downward flight. Men looking up thought that they glimpsed a sea-eagle stooping over the fish-silver ocean: the sight was too bright for mortal eyes to see his golden cap and plaited rod of serpents.

He landed outside the cave mouth of Ogygia's nymph, beside her loom. It stood abandoned, the shuttle hanging down by a gossamer thread. Inside the cave, Calypso's voice was loud and shrill:

'I tell you, you *shan't*! Must you be forever asking? You *shan't* go. I love you—and in time you'll learn to love me. What, more tears? There'd be tears enough if you had to change me for old Penelope. It's twenty years since you saw her. Don't you realize how age twists a mortal woman's face and melts her figure into a shapeless . . . '

There was a sharp crack. Calypso came running to the mouth of the cave with the red shape of a hand burning on her cheek. She was startled to see Hermes, who stood quietly listening, with a look of amusement on his face. 'What do you want?' she snapped.

'I have a message for you from great Zeus, father of all the gods . . . You have to let him go.'

Calypso grew still paler, and the mark on her cheek grew brighter in contrast. 'Is this your doing, Hermes? Can't you bear to see one of the Immortals in love with a mortal man?'

Hermes spread his hands with a look of injured innocence. 'I'm just a messenger. This is a command from Zeus.'

'It's *her* doing. It's Athene's doing. She's jealous of me. That's what it is. Well, I won't let him go—I *won't*! She shan't have him: he's *mine*!'

'Calypso! It would seem he's nobody's, this warrior sea-captain with the shaggy arms. No one owns his heart—unless it's his Queen Penelope and the island he's pined for these last seven years. Seven years and he hasn't learned to love you yet. Is he so slow to learn, this man whose cunning is likened to the arrows from a bow?'

'Yes!' cried Calypso, furiously rubbing her cheek. 'Yes, he's stupid and obstinate. He wants nothing but to build a raft and put to sea.'

'Then give him an iron axe and tell him which trees he may cut down. Find him rope and a sail—and then cast your eyes over the ocean for a new lover.'

Calypso took up the shuttle and jabbed it angrily into the weave of her tapestry—a tapestry picturing a man dressed in a golden breastplate and a plumed helmet of bronze with a long and shining nosepiece. She said bitterly, 'You idle Olympians. You have nothing to do but look over the parapet of heaven and make mischief. In time he would have loved me. I know it.'

Hermes kicked up his winged heels and sprang into the air. Men looking up thought they saw an albatross riding on the thermal columns of air as he spiralled into the sky. But he did not fly back to Mount Olympus. He flew from atoll to atoll, using the islands like stepping stones. At last he sighted a brightly painted ship trailing behind it a wake of white water. He dropped down, down to the pitching deck of Telemachus's boat. Men looking up thought they saw a gull stoop on a fish. But Telemachus looked over his shoulder and found the dark, Levantine face of a sailor close to his. A heavy brown hand rested on his shoulder. Hermes had disguised himself as the ship's first mate.

'Shall we be mooring at Asteris on this voyage?' the mate enquired.

'I shall moor there tonight,' said Telemachus. 'It has a deep-water bay in the north . . . perfectly placed, and there's fresh water. People who sail from Samos to Ithaca always moor there on the last stretch of the voyage. It's only a day from Ithaca, and the water is always running low on board by the time we reach it . . .'

The Levantine nodded and said, 'Just so. Hmm . . .
May I make a suggestion, captain . . . ?'

Eurymachus and Antinous, those murderous schemers,
dropped anchor in the northernmost bay of Asteris. Spiny
with swords and bristling with arrows, they and a band of
suitors thirty-strong rowed ashore. Some hid by the spring;
some watched from the promontories; some dug a deep pit
and lined it with thornbushes and covered it with leaves;
some ranged themselves, bows strung, round the pretty,
sheltered bay. Their ship was moored out of sight. No one
arriving from the sea would see that others were already
there, lying in ambush. Pots of oil stood ready to light when
the moment came, so that the archers could shoot flying
flame into the sails of Telemachus's ship. Whether by
knife, sword, arrow, fire, or drowning, Telemachus must
surely die.

Only one fear remained in Antinous's mind. 'Supposing
he has found his father. Supposing we snare the bull as
well as the calf in our trap?'

'What? After twenty years? The man's dead. When I
said it the first time, I didn't know or care if it was true.
But after all this time, the man's dead for sure. And if
he's not dead he's forty years old, which is as good as
dead. Do you expect me to tremble at the thought of a
grizzle-bearded forty year old and his beardless son? If
they both come, we'll kill them both. Right? Of course,
right. The only chore is the waiting.'

There! As the sun declined, and evening light poured
thick as honey through the sea-lanes and dry-land
pathways, a brightly painted boat came into sight. The
murderers crouched low in their places. They wore no
piece of metal for the sun to glint on. They had blacked
their faces with mud for fear Telemachus glimpse them

403

among the bushes and suspect an ambush. They lay perfectly still, testing the sharpness of their knives against their thumbs, laying arrows across their bows. In a minute or two Telemachus would sail into the arms of the bay and drop anchor for the night—drop anchor for ever. And from overhead a hail of arrows would hurtle on to him and fill him as full of spines as a hedgehog. Then he would roast beneath his own canvas when it fell, burning, from the mast. Eurymachus licked his lips, which were dry with excitement. Afterwards he would hurry home and break the sad news gently to the queen— how Telemachus had died in a storm at sea. Ah, how comforting he would be! When the veil was finished and the grieving queen was ready to marry, she would surely choose the suitor who had comforted her in her hour of grief . . .

The brightly painted ship was only a furlong from the island—almost within range. Antinous eased his arrow on its bowstring. He would hit Telemachus right between his foolishly wide, blue eyes.

A cry came over the water—Telemachus calling instructions to his crew. 'Raise the genoa and lean on your oars, men! There's plenty of water to drink in Ithaca—and wine to go with it. We'll row all night with this fair wind.' And the brightly painted boat skirted the island of Asteris and did not drop anchor in the pretty, sheltered bay.

Antinous gave a great groan of dismay and stood up to watch the ship skim out of sight. Then he cursed foully and smashed his bow across his knee in a fit of rage.

Odysseus felled twenty trees and split the trunks length-wise. He roped them together and bored a hole to take the tall mast. All the while he worked, Calypso said nothing, but sat chin-in-hands, with pouting lips, and a frown between her eyes. But on the last day, when he had finished, she moved away up the beach, scuffing her heels, and returned with a tapestry folded over her arm.

'This may do for a sail,' she said. 'But it has no magic power.'

'Yes, it has!' cried Odysseus, kissing her. 'It has the power to encourage me! Thank you, Calypso!' The tapestry was of a cockerel, its head thrown back and its wings spread in crowing. Odysseus tacked it to the crosstree where it tugged and cracked in the breeze. He rigged a tiller from a forked branch and the keel of his broken ship, and built a wattle fence round the edge of the raft to keep it from being swamped. The nymph gave him food and drink for the journey, and for the first time in many years she seemed a most agreeable companion. He was even prepared to kiss her once more when the time came to say goodbye.

The tapestry cockerel swelled its breast as the sail filled with wind. The imprints made in the sand by the heavy logs filled with saltwater, like eyes filling with tears, as the raft was set afloat by successive waves. The tiller oar cut one white wound in the dark water beyond the creamy surf.

And Calypso stood on the white sand with one white hand waving, the golden shuttle in her fingers as though she were weaving magic in the salty air. She did not return to her loom at the cave-mouth until the cockerel sail of Odysseus's raft was crossing the horizon, and the figure of Odysseus was lost from sight.

The raft made good progress while the sea was flat. It twisted and rolled when the sea grew choppy, slapping the waves down and jarring Odysseus's knees. When the

405

sun god drove his flaming chariot up to Noonday Hill and across the sky, Odysseus rigged a canopy to keep off the scorching heat, and in case the god looked down and recognized him. But it was not the sun god who first recognized Odysseus.

It was Poseidon.

Slung in a hammock of cloud between the north and easterly horizons, Poseidon the Earth-Shaker and Sea-Shifter rolled over . . . and saw a speck of wood floating on the ocean. He might have taken it for flotsam from some shipwreck, but for the brightly woven sail flapping over it. Poseidon narrowed his eyes, to see better against the brightness of the water. His brows, purple as thunderclouds, puckered and his nostrils flared. 'ODYSSEUS!'

He summoned up, from the northern realms of the white sea, all the white horses of his herds and, with whipcracks of thunder, stampeded them over the wave-tussocked meadow of the sea.

Odysseus looked over his shoulder and saw the dark clouds rise up on the horizon, as dust-clouds rise up from under the hooves of galloping horses. He saw a mass of whiteness and heard the thunder of hooves. He just had time to drop his sail before he saw the manes of spray, the curved necks of over-arching waves, the pounding hooves of grey water that dropped in gouts out of the over-arching waves, and the whiplash thunderbolts driving on the stampede. He wrapped his arms round the mast as a child wraps its arms round its mother's knees.

Poseidon's horses pounded over the raft—great waves foaming at the mouth, sweating foam and snorting foam out of black nostrils. Their watery hooves splintered the beams of Odysseus's floor and broke the rope, so that the floor opened and sea rushed in between the logs. Then it was sucked back down again, and with it went Odysseus, through the boards of his raft and into the dark shock of the cold sea. When he surfaced, the raft had already been swept far away from him, a heap of firewood loosely lashed together with tangled ropes. The sail slipped to the bottom of the sea where undulating skates and manta rays swam over it, wondering.

Like a Laestrygonian, Poseidon fished for Odysseus with his trident, jabbing with pronged lightning, one prong to the right of him, two prongs to the left. The sea and sky turned black with bruising. But Odysseus swam with the speed of a darting fish after his raft, and clung to it, and got his legs astride a single log and slumped face-down, like a baron of meat on a spit. The rain drubbed on his back until he thought it would beat him senseless. Huge dark shapes seemed to swim up from the depths, in front of his exhausted eyes, and he thought they must be mountainous sea-creatures of the kind that sip shipwrecked sailors off the surface of the sea. At any moment a guzzling mouth might bite off his arms or legs as they dangled down through the water . . .

There! Something took firm grip of his thigh and almost pulled him off the log. A fishy tail writhed past his head. 'O goddess Athene! Why did you not let me die in Troy and have my armour shared out between the heroes and my name shared out among the world's storytellers? That it should be like this!—to have my body shared out between the fishes and my name swallowed by sea-beasts . . . ' He tried to call his name over the ocean for the ghosts to hear in the underworld. But seawater filled his mouth and half drowned him.

'Why call your name? I already know who you are, Odysseus, King of Ithaca. My name is Ido.'

He turned his head, and there, her hands around his thigh, was a sea nymph, flicking the silvery green scales of her tail, her hair spreading on the water around her sweet face, like the leaves around a water-lily. 'Take this scarf, Odysseus, and tie it round your chest. Then swim for land—over there. I and the other sea nymphs have been watching your game with Poseidon. It's most exciting. I'm so glad you've left Ogygia and started to play again. I shouldn't help you, I suppose, but Poseidon is *always* winning. It's tiresome to see him winning all the time. And truly he's not half as pleasing to look at as you, Odysseus. The other nymphs will be angry with me, but one little cheat—one little helping hand—how can it change the outcome of the game so very much? You're still so many miles from Ithaca . . . '

She gave a playful tug on his leg which overbalanced the log and spilt Odysseus into the sea, before she threshed her tail and dived back down through the seething sea. His leather skirt began to pull him under. He unfastened it and let it drop, kicked off his long-stringed sandals, and tied the sea nymph's scarf round his chest: it buoyed him up, and from the crest of a wave that threw him bodily into the air, he glimpsed the land of Scheria.

Its coast was as jagged as though, when the gods shaped the mainland with axes, this shard had flown up from their axes and wedged itself in the flesh of the sea. Jagged pinnacles lay offshore from jagged precipices—the rock so sharp that even the sea birds lighting there screamed at the sharpness. There was no beach, no bay, no harbour, no haven. Poseidon's mares hurled themselves against the cliffs and shattered into glittering walls of spray. But however many spent themselves on Scheria's shredding shore, there were always more let loose from the paddock sky to trample Odysseus and tumble him on towards the rocks.

11

The Stone Ship

Though the windows of Pelicata Palace looked out on three separate bays, and into each came the striped sea, always arriving, wave after wave, and though Penelope looked out every day as she sat at her loom weaving, Odysseus did not come and did not come and did not ever come. The harbour now was crowded with little boats as, with every tide, new suitors arrived to tempt her with their looks, their worthless presents or with flattery. But only one boat newly arrived in the harbour gave her any joy. Her son Telemachus had returned from searching for his father.

There he stood in the doorway, the shine of sun in his hair and sea salt on his skin. 'Well? What news?' said Penelope, hardly breathing as she spoke. 'Is he alive? Is he coming? Has he forgotten us? Or have the gods forgotten all of us?'

Telemachus laid down his spear and sword, and kissed his mother gently. 'I sailed to the northern shores of the ocean—to Pylos, Nestor's home. Nestor fought alongside father under the walls of Troy. I asked him if he had seen a shipwreck or heard of any accident.'

'And what did he tell you? Good news? Bad news?'

'No news at all. Nestor helped Odysseus set sail from the shores of Troy: twelve Ithacan boats he helped to carry into the sea. They put to sea together, then struck off in different directions, lost sight of each other by nightfall, lost the sound of each other's oars before morning.'

Then Penelope's heart sank like a little boat.

'But listen, mother! He's heard no *bad* news—no news of shipwrecks or pirates or wars. He told me to visit old Menelaus, who set sail that same day. So I travelled by chariot and horse, by donkey and by foot, across great dry seas of rocks and dust to Lacedaemon, to King Menelaus's palace.'

Penelope was impatient to know. 'What did he tell you? Good news? Bad news?'

'No news at all.'

Then Penelope's heart sank like a little pebble.

'But, mother! He told us not to give up hope. He travelled for years himself to reach home. He was shipwrecked in Egypt—*Egypt*, mother! on the southern shores of the world! But there he was, after all his troubles, alive and well and home. I'm certain my father is alive. And one day soon he will come home. The strangest thing happened as I sailed past Asteris . . .'

But his mother had turned and was looking out of her window towards the waves, arriving, always arriving, always beaching on the shores of Ithaca. 'I'm sure too, Telemachus. I'm sure that everything they said is true. But how long must I creep barefoot through my own halls night after night to unpick my weaving and save myself from marriage to one of these . . . these vermin? And when they've eaten every sheep, drunk every tun of wine, torn every blanket, and sold every brick of the royal palace, will he be grateful for what I've done? What kind of king will he be when this scum has frittered away his kingdom?'

Odysseus was hurled up against a rocky pinnacle like a prisoner thrown into a pit of spears to be pierced through and through. He wrapped his arms and legs round it as he had clung to the mast of his raft, and Poseidon's mares galloped over him. And as each wave retreated, it tried to drag him away from his handhold, filling his nose with water, prising at his fingers, tearing at his shirt. He would willingly have let go: the rocks were razor sharp and covered in grazing barnacles. But then the sea would only have hurled him against the cliff. When dark green, slimy weed caught round his legs and flapped, he thought it was his skin flapping from the bone. Scum creamed in his hair. He looked to right and left, but the cliffs seemed unbroken for as far as he could see.

There! A streak of lighter blue in the ocean showed where a narrow river was issuing out to sea to the east, mixing its fresh water with the brine. He put his bare feet to the pinnacle of rock and launched himself in the direction of the estuary. The sea shouldered him up against the cliff. But little by little, he edged his painful way towards the tiny estuary.

He swam against the current. He put down his feet and walked over mussels and limpets until he was wading in fresh river-water—though all the time the river tried to push him back out to sea. Climbing out on to the bank was like climbing Olympus itself to the weary Odysseus. He crawled into the cradle of a split olive tree that overhung the river, and went to sleep still crouched on hands and knees.

He woke to the sound of voices—so high and melodic that he thought they must belong to nymphs. Wrapped in anguish, he lay as still as a dead man and prayed. 'O fearsome Athene, goddess of the battlefield, whose only thoughts are of duty and war and manliness, forbid that yet another nymph should take a liking to me! If one more Immortal falls in love with me, I think I'll hurl myself off this island's cliffs and let Poseidon use me as he pleases!' Then he parted the leaves of the olive tree and said, loudly, 'I'm a married man and I have no time to spend in loving *you*!'

There was a squeak of surprise, and five young maidens hid themselves up to their shoulders in the river where they had been bathing. Their clothes hung like may blossom on the bushes all around, and the laundry they had brought down to the river floated downstream out of their startled hands. The tallest of the maidens recovered herself and said, 'I should think not, sir! I am a princess shortly to be married, and I can well do without you, you ragamuffin!'

A sorry-looking hero lowered himself painfully out of the tree—his skirt and sandals gone, his arms and legs etched with gashes, his beard white with salt and his eyes a fearful red with saltwater. When he saw his reflection in the river, he was ashamed to admit that no immortal nymph would have looked at him and sighed. 'I am Odysseus, King of Ithaca. My apologies and compliments, lady, but can you spare me a bite of bread?'

'Not until you turn your back and spare our blushes,' said the tallest maiden. 'But your sufferings, which must have been many, make you welcome on Scheria. On behalf of my father, King Alcinous, I greet you—whoever you are.'

They carried Odysseus back to the palace hidden beneath the laundry. 'Because it would hardly be fitting for unmarried maidens to be seen in the company of such a . . . *masculine* man,' explained the Princess Nausicaa, covering up his head with a damp sheet, 'especially a gentleman without skirt or sandals.'

The creaking and jiggling of the cart rocked Odysseus to sleep again, and when he woke, the princess and her maidens-in-waiting were nowhere to be seen. He was all alone in the laundry cart, in the yard of King Alcinous's palace. Out of respect for the ladies' good name, he presented himself at the door of the palace as if he had walked all the way from the shore by his own efforts.

The king greeted him hospitably enough, was sympathetic at the news of his shipwreck in the storm. But when Odysseus gave his name, the king threw up his hands in amazement. He called for a feast to be prepared at once, and summoned dancers, men and women, to dance in celebration. 'Praise be to the gods on Olympus that I should be given the honour of meeting you—even of helping you to a new boat! The stories of your part in the siege of Troy are known all over the world! A day's journey in one of my fast boats will bring you to Ithaca. But tell me, what voyage have you been on that has brought you to my ragged little island?'

Odysseus was startled. 'Why, I'm still sailing home from Troy, by way of death and disaster!'

'From Troy? From the Trojan Wars? You can't mean that for ten years and more you've been travelling without ever arriving? Have you been pining in some dungeon or tied to some Moorish oar for a galley slave? What became of the men in your company—the other men of Ithaca?'

Odysseus had just lifted from the bronze plate in front of him a succulent breast of chicken. Suddenly, as his eyes met King Alcinous's eyes, and he remembered the deaths and disasters of his long journey, he found he could not eat one bite. His throat was full of tears, as a pipe clogs with leaves when the autumn rains pour down it. He swallowed awkwardly, and began the story of his voyage.

413

When he began, night was falling and the light poured thick as honey along the sea-lanes and dry-land pathways. When he finished, night's million stars were cascading into a pale pool of morning near the horizon. All night, as he spoke, an old man sat in a corner and wrote. He had no need of daylight, firelight, moonlight, or the morning's plaited beams, for he was blind. But he cut single words with his right hand in a tablet of wax, and read them over with his left.

As Odysseus told his story, it was as if each man listening saw for himself the cruel monsters, the crawling sea, the spiteful gods, the beckoning islands. For a long while after, no one spoke.

Then King Alcinous cleared his throat. 'Odysseus, you've seen more on your travels than most men have even heard tell. You've suffered more than most men could bear without their hearts and bodies breaking. But your troubles are over now. Just beyond the horizon, Ithaca lies waiting for you. I'll give you treasure enough to return home in glory, and a boat and crew to carry you there. Now—here's food and drink to give you strength for the journey. And let's pray that at last the gods will give you safe passage home.'

Bronze and gold cauldrons, chests of linen and casks of wine were loaded aboard the finest, fastest ship in the king's fleet—for indeed, on the far shore of Scheria, there was a large harbour crammed with brightly painted, tall-prowed, tall, proud boats. The island's counsellors and statesmen feasted and fêted Odysseus all day long. Their kindness and generosity were worthy of King Aeolus, but their friendship was more gentle and forgiving. Kind as they were, Odysseus could not help but glance at the dawdling sun, hour by hour, and long for sunset when he could set sail across the last stretch of ocean for Ithaca.

When the crew took their places at the oars, Odysseus

414

curled up on the after-deck, on the mound of kingly clothing given him by Princess Nausicaa. He was asleep before the long, polished oars had slit the first white wounds in the creamy ocean.

For week upon month upon year, Odysseus the warrior, whose body was strung like a longbow and whose mind was as quick as arrows, had snatched sleep from between battles, from amidst adventures, and from under the shadow of danger or misery. Even on Calypso's isle, during seven years of idleness, he had slept as a horse sleeps, on its feet, an eyelid's blink away from waking, waiting for the unwelcome touch of Calypso's magical hands. But now he slept so soundly, so profoundly, that the tremors of an earthquake, the caresses of the Scylla, or the crash of a thunderbolt could not have made him stir.

But down in the pit of the ocean's stomach, the Earth-Shaker, the Sea-Shifter, the Earthquake-Maker seethed with anger. Poseidon saw the Scherian ship and in it Odysseus. And the sea god reared up so high that he pushed his blue-green face through the clouds of Olympus and bawled, *'Zeus! Father of the gods! I'm shamed for ever! The Scherians have made a laughing stock of me!'*

'Calmly, brother! Calmly!' said all-powerful Zeus. 'Nobody is laughing at you, nor ever will. Who would dare?'

'Then why is Odysseus sailing home to Ithaca with more treasure under him than he ever looted from Troy? Why are the Scherians helping the man who blinded my son? They're flouting my authority! They're aiding my enemy! They're thwarting my revenge!'

Now Zeus, who had long since formed a fondness for the daring, roguish Odysseus, drew back the clouds and glimpsed an early-morning cove on Ithaca where the waves broke in gentle diagonals over the pebbles. The Scherians rowing ashore leaned so hard on their polished oars that the elegant ship ploughed up the beach and left only its rudder afloat in the surf. Odysseus was ashore, safe from Poseidon's spite.

Even the beaching did not wake him, and the crew carried him, after-deck, linens and all, and laid him in the shade of an early-morning tree, surrounded by the presents of gold, bronze, and wine. Then they pushed their fast boat back into deep water and climbed aboard.

But Zeus's all-seeing eyes were set so wide apart that he saw, at the selfsame time, Polyphemus, the sea god's son, sitting weeping from his one blind eye. And Zeus pitied the pitiless Poseidon. 'What is it you want to do?'

Poseidon's black hair seethed and his anger frothed at his lips. 'I mean to blast that Scherian ship and to shovel a mountain out of the sea to wall up Scheria!' He scowled, and hunched his shoulders from which the tides swung. 'Will you stop me? Will you let these miserable mortals fly in the face of a god? Since Time began I've hemmed them in—these islands, these island-dwellers. Night and morning they've had me to thank for their wretched lives. Will you let them crawl as they like over my rippling back and forbid me to crush them?'

'Poseidon! Brother!' cried Zeus. 'These thankless Scherians have forgotten the honour and respect they owe you. Make an example of them, why not? Then every mortal who crawls upon the muscles of your rippling back will say, "Dare I anger Poseidon? No! Look what happened to the Scherian ship!" There is no need to weary yourself walling up Scheria.'

Poseidon was startled into silence. Swinging his cloak of tides across his face, he strode and waded round his maze of islands. And finding the Scherian ship at the harbour mouth of Scheria, he clutched it in both hands.

In the space of an oar's beat, the hull was fastened to the bed of the sea with a stem of granite, and the waves broke against it, and the sea-birds settled on it, crying. The planks and the keel, the rudder and its tiller, the mast and its crossbeam, the decks and their hatches, the Scherians and their oars were all turned to stone.

The faces of people who stood on the harbour wall turned rock-grey with fright. They ran to King Alcinous with the terrible news.

'We have offended Poseidon,' said the gentle, devout king. 'Kill twelve oxen and let's offer them up as a sacrifice to him . . . But afterwards, count the faces aboard the stone-ship and tell me if Odysseus too is turned to stone.'

'He is not, father,' said Nausicaa. 'The after-deck, the kingly clothing, and all the presents of gold and bronze are gone. Odysseus is safe home on Ithaca.'

King Alcinous nodded slowly and gave a sad smile. 'Home, yes. But safe? For every friend who laughs with joy to see him, a dozen envious villains will wish he had died in Troy or on the voyage home!'

On the night that Odysseus told his story to King Alcinous and his court, Queen Penelope went to bed early in Pelicata Palace. She left the suitors to drink themselves drunk by her husband's hearth and went to bed. But she did not sleep, for there was the veil to be unwoven, the sewing of the day to be unpicked. When the house fell silent, she wrapped a shawl round her shoulders and crept barefoot to the room where her loom stood in the window.

Though there was no starlight, she moved quickly. She was accustomed to finding her way round bench and table in the dark, to where the rug edges might trip her, to where a careless step might set the fire-irons clattering. Her bare feet knew the way: she held the scissors in her right hand.

Suddenly her shins collided with something soft and warm that grunted then rolled away. Against the grey square of the window, a man's shape rose up from the floor. 'So-ho! Polybus, fetch a lamp! We were right about our little spider. She was only weaving her web to catch out us poor men!'

A light flared up and cast wildly flickering shadows into the eyesockets and cheeks of Eurymachus. He took the scissors out of her hand. 'Shame on you, madam. And all this time I took you for an honourable lady.'

There was wine spilled on the floor. Eurymachus and Polybus had fallen asleep drunk, in front of the loom, trying to fathom out why the veil never seemed to grow. By accident they had found her out. Now their grinning teeth showed yellow in the lamplight. 'The waiting's over, dear lady. The time has come for you to make a choice. Why not choose me, eh? Then I'd never tell the others how Odysseus's grand queen crept in her night-clothes to trick her way out of a bargain.'

Penelope drew herself up to her full height, like a swan stretching its wings. 'Should I be ashamed, then, of loving my husband too dearly?'

'*Twenty years*, lady! That's how long your *dear* husband's been gone! No one can accuse you of being hasty if you remarry now! But will you keep to your bargain, now you've been caught out in it? Veil or no veil, it's time you were a bride again.' And he stood close up against her, menacing, and with triumphant eyes gleaming down into her face.

'How am I to choose? So many men, all of *equal merit*,' said Penelope bitterly.

'That's for you to decide, lady. But tomorrow. You must decide tomorrow. Choose looks or charm or wealth . . . But *choose*.'

12

A Stranger at the Door

When Odysseus finally woke, he could not think where he was. At first he thought it was Ogygia where, in seven years, he had slept away nights on many different beaches, with never an eye to their shape or features. Then he remembered the raft, and thought he must have drifted to the beach on that, for indeed he was lying on planks of wood. Then he remembered the storm and the island and Nausicaa and King Alcinous and the ship full of presents. And he looked for some sign that this small bay was a part of his own little kingdom. The water was full of reflections: a multitude of colours floated there like fruit in a bowl of mulled wine. But there are many such bays in the world.

The bay was guarded by prickly oaks, columnar cypresses, and small bushy olives. But there are many such trees in the world. He stood up and wandered among the shining presents of King Alcinous, running his disbelieving fingers around the rims of the bronze cauldrons. Perhaps the ship had brought him only as far as Cephalonia or little wooded Zanthe—the outlying islands of his kingdom.

But there! There was the head of Mount Neriton—a shape so familiar to his eye since earliest childhood that it fitted his hopes as a key fits a lock. 'I have come home to you, Ithaca,' he said. 'And when I have cattle and sheep to my name again, I shall sacrifice ten of the finest to Athene, goddess of the grey eyes, who gave me this moment.'

He hid the cauldrons, weapons, and other gifts in a cave at the head of the beach, thinking, Home, yes. But safe? For every friend who laughs with joy to see me, a dozen villainous suitors will wish I had died in Troy or on the voyage home. I must take care how I return to Pelicata Palace.

Telemachus, though he sat down at mealtimes with the suitors, spent as little time as he could in their company. Their insults set the blood frothing in his veins, and sweat formed on his brow when he saw how their fingers twitched on their sword-hilts at the sight of him. But it pleased him to see the bafflement in their faces. 'Who warned you?' said their eyes. 'Which god shielded you from harm?' They dared not speak a word of their cowardly ambush.

Caution advised Telemachus not to walk alone in dark places or to stroll along the clifftops when Antinous was close by. When he wanted peace, he went to the hilltop cave where an old pigman tended the king's boars and pigs.

The hungry suitors, with their liking for roast pork, had left the pigman fewer than twenty pigs to tend; he had no need to stray far from his cave, and he was always ready to talk to Telemachus about King Odysseus: he was a friend as much as a loyal and devoted servant.

But as Telemachus approached the cave that day he heard scuffling inside, and voices. Cautiously he ducked inside and saw, sitting with his back to the far wall, a fleece pulled round him and over his head, a man who was not the pigman. The stranger looked up, only his eyes showing as he raised food to his mouth. And he looked at Telemachus so piercingly that the boy was half alarmed, half affronted.

'Come in! Come in, my lord Telemachus!' called the pigman from the darker recesses of the cave. 'Meet my friend. He's . . . uh . . . he's . . . '

' . . . a shipwrecked soldier,' said the stranger. 'Crete's my home and misfortune's been my fate, ever since I set sail from Troy.'

'Troy? You were at the Wars?' said Telemachus. 'I suppose you saw Odysseus there, fighting alongside Achilles and Nestor and Menelaus?'

'I suppose I did,' said the stranger. 'And what's he to you?'

'A king, sir, and a hero and a father—and a man who would give you a ship to get you home, if he were able.'

'Why, is he poor, then, that he's got no ships in his fleet? I won't believe it! The harbour's full of ships, and that palace up there is not the home of a poor man.'

'Oh, but it is,' said Telemachus. 'It's the home of a man rich in honour but too poor to call one breath of air his own. I'm afraid he's dead, you see. Poor Odysseus is drowned, sir, or pining in some dungeon, or sweating over an oar in slavery.'

'Then you would be glad, young sir. Surely, a young pike is lord of a pond until the big old pike comes out from under the weed. You must be glad the old pike is gone.'

Telemachus did not hesitate in answering. 'Sir, I have no power on this island. I am a ball tossed to and fro between the hooligans who have taken over the palace.

But if I had all the power of a king and the magic powers of an immortal, too, I would only use them to wish my father home again, safe and well!'

Odysseus let out a great laugh and threw off the fleece that hid his face and body. Telemachus flinched at the sudden movement, then frowned angrily. 'What are you then? A god from Olympus? You have the look of one, though a god would surely show more kindness than to laugh at the misery of a fatherless son.'

Then Odysseus laughed again, at himself this time. 'What a fool I am! I thought you'd recognize me, but how could you? I recognize *you*, of course. Looking at you is like looking into an old mirror where my own reflection has been trapped for twenty years. I'm your father, Telemachus. *I am Odysseus!*'

Telemachus said nothing. The frown still crouched between his eyebrows, and he turned to the pigman. 'He is lying, isn't he?'

'No, lad, he's not lying. This is your own father. I know every feature of his face like I know Neriton Mountain.'

'But where's the king's sword? *Where's the king's bronze helmet?*'

'At the bottom of the sea, along with all my companions—along with every beam and shackle of the *Odyssey*. But I am not. Finally, boy, that's all I can say—I am neither drowned nor captive. I have come home.'

For weeks upon months upon years, Telemachus the prince had smiled, and reassured and comforted his mother with brave words. He had been brave—as brave as any full-grown man. Now he laid his forehead on his father's shoulder and wept out loud like a little boy.

As for Odysseus, the hero of Troy, his throat felt as choked as a pipe that the autumn rain pours down and

clogs with leaves. He blinked his eyes repeatedly, and
pulled the fleece forward again over his face.

Telemachus went back to the palace alone for dinner. He
seated himself at table with the suitors, ignoring their jibes
and the way their fingers twitched on their sword-hilts at
the sight of him. Queen Penelope sat apart, and ate alone,
in a gallery that overlooked the hall. She ate where there
were no knees to nudge her, no eyes to wink at her, no
winy mouths to blow her unwelcome kisses.

Out in the yard, the smell of meat reached the ancient
hound that lay by the door. Her mangy coat was brindled
with grey; her eyes were milky with blindness, and fleas
swarmed in her hackles just as the suitors swarmed over
the king's property. The dog, who received no kindness
from the suitors, sniffed once and twice, but had no hope
of a meal, and rested her head back on her paws with a
sigh. Then her nose twitched again. A smell reached her
which she had not smelt since, as a year-old puppy, she
had hunted Ithaca's rocky ravines. Ah, how she had
raced then, through the tall grass and scrub, as fast as if
her backbone were an arrow fired from her master's
bow! She had been happy then, in the days of that
smell!

Her ears twitched and her nose sniffed, but all her
old eyes could see was a blurred shape against the
sunlight. Tremblingly the aged dog rose to her feet on
shaking haunches. Her tail began to wag.

'Yes, it's me, Argos, my old companion,' said Odysseus
under his breath. 'But you are the first and last that must
recognize me just now.' He sat down beside the dog, his
back to the doorpost, and Argos laid her old head on her
master's lap and died. After twenty years, her long wait
was over. She was content.

When the suitors looked up, all they saw was a ragged and bent old beggar sitting propped in the doorway, nursing a dead dog in his lap. Telemachus called out to the beggar, 'Here, old man. You are welcome to come in and ask food from everyone at this table.'

The beggar pressed the heel of his hand into his eyes. Then, setting aside the dog's head off his lap, he got up awkwardly and shuffled to the table, with cupped hands, to receive whatever gifts the suitors would give him.

Antinous stole a glance at the queen. 'Oh no. Oh no. I couldn't possibly give you anything, you reeking old tom-cat. This food belongs to King Odysseus, hero of Troy. *We* are guests of his wife, the delectable Penelope. What kind of guests would we be if we made free with her food and gave it away to every stinking vagrant who crawled through that door? No, no. I know my duty towards Penelope and the unfortunate Odysseus.'

'You mean you want it all for yourself,' said the beggar starkly, and turned to the next suitor, with his hands outstretched. But Antinous was so furious that he picked up his footstool and hurled it. It struck the beggar between the shoulder-blades and knocked him flat, emptying his lungs of air. The other suitors burst out laughing. They threw things too, bones and plates and boots. Telemachus half rose from his chair, then, as if he had remembered something, meekly sat down again.

It was Penelope who called down from the gallery, 'Send the man to me and don't begrudge him a bite of food. My Odysseus may be stranded among strangers: I hope he'd receive kinder treatment at *their* hands.'

She should not have spoken. Her voice drew the eyes of the suitors, and the sight of her put out of their minds all thought of beggars and food. Eurymachus said, 'Lady! You have much more important matters to think about. We're waiting. We're waiting to hear your decision.

Who's it to be? Who'll sleep in your bed tonight and rule Ithaca ever after?'

'He's right, mother,' said Telemachus, much to the astonishment of Eurymachus. 'It is time. I was with the pigman today, and of all the great herds of pig that roamed this island when I was a boy, there are fewer than twenty left. Soon Ithaca will be ruined, and you will be too old to attract a new husband. Unless you want someone to take the crown by force, make a decision and make it now. What Ithaca needs is a warrior strong enough to defend her against all-comers. Set some feat of skill and strength, then rest your fate in the hands of the gods.'

All the while he spoke, Telemachus drew nearer and nearer to the gallery, fixing his mother with his eyes and defying her to interrupt him. Her jaw dropped. Her face was ashen white. But Telemachus went on remorselessly, 'There! Look, there is Odysseus's hunting bow—the bow he left behind when he took with him his warrior's long-bow. Let the man who strings it and fires it into a given target claim my mother and the whole island kingdom of Ithaca!'

Penelope plucked at her skirts, her head ducked forward in grief and confusion, and her cheeks flushed red. She searched her mind for the hardest target of all. Then she squared her shoulders and said, 'Very well. It shall be as my son advises . . . commands me. You see those axes hanging from the roof? Each one has, at the handle-end, a loop for a man's belt to pass through. Set up the axes along the table, handles uppermost. If any man can string Odysseus's bow and shoot an arrow through every loop, let him clutch my hair and call me wife. There. I have said it. And may the gods reward you, Telemachus, for this advice of yours.'

Telemachus seemed not to hear. He was collecting

up all the shields and swords and spears that belonged to the suitors, and giving them into the arms of the servant, Melanthius. When Penelope stayed standing in the gallery watching, her son said, 'Very well, mother. You may go to your room now. I'll tell you when the matter has been decided. Go, and lock the doors behind you.'

The suitors were amazed—so amazed that Melanthius had made several trips in and out of the room before any of them noticed him carrying away their weapons. Eurymachus said, 'What's he doing with those?'

Telemachus was quick with his answer. 'The smoke from the fire is tarnishing them. I hate to see good weapons ruined. I told Melanthius to polish them all . . . Besides . . . I'm afraid (since one of you will undoubtedly win my mother tonight) that the rest of you might start fighting, in your disappointment. That would be a fearful waste of noble blood. You—beggar!—lift down my father's hunting bow, will you? I'm not tall enough to reach it.'

But Polybus pushed the beggar aside and snatched the bow off the wall, with a loud laugh. 'Me first, I think.'

He put the bow-tip to the floor and pulled on the other end to bend the bow. But though he heaved and hauled and sweated, he could not bend the bow enough to string it. Another suitor snatched it out of his hands. But he could not bend it either. Eurymachus took the ends of the bow in his two huge hands and tried to arch it. But it was as unbending as the silver spear of the goddess Athene.

'Permit me,' said the beggar, taking the bow from Eurymachus.

Bracing it between his right ankle and left hip, he bent the bow and strung it with the yellowing gut that had hung loose for twenty years.

'Give it here,' said Antinous, and snatched the bow. The axes stood ready by now, their handles upward. He laid one of his own arrows to the bow and took aim along the row of loops. The bowstring hummed. The axes fell like skittles to right and left, and the arrow lodged in the wall.

One by one, the swaggering suitors enraged themselves with unsuccessful attempts to shoot an arrow through all the loops. Eurymachus, when he failed, hurled down the bow in fury, but when the beggar leaned down to pick it up, he snarled, 'Don't even think about it, tom-cat. This contest is for the hand of a queen.'

'Very well,' said the beggar mildly. 'I shan't shoot through the loops . . . though in my own country I've halls and cattle and servants of my own, and I'm better thought of than a beggar by my wife and son.'

They turned their backs on him scornfully, and called for wine to steady their hands before they began the contest afresh. The beggar gathered up the arrows that had buried their barbs in the furniture and walls. Then he stepped on to a chair and from there on to the table. He drew the bow back to its limit and loosed an arrow. It found its target instantly.

Antinous, who had just raised a goblet of wine to his lips, neither saw nor felt the arrow. As it passed through him, it carried away with it all life and breath and heartbeat. Antinous stood dead on his feet with a look of surprise in his eyes, then fell to the floor, and the spilled wine flowed round his head.

All eyes turned on the beggar. He had thrown off his rags and was naked to the waist, with a heap of their arrows at his feet. His greying golden hair curled across his forehead and deep into the nape of his neck, and the sinews of his arms were plaited like the strands of a great anchor-rope.

'Yes, it's my father,' said Telemachus, leaping on to the table alongside the stranger. 'It is Odysseus. Too late to regret your journeys here to Ithaca, you scum. Too late to call on the gods, you godless vermin. King Odysseus has returned!'

While Odysseus was still travelling, the story of his travels passed from mouth to mouth around the shores of the sea-encircling world. He had come face to face with the terrors of the Known World, and their reflections were in his eyes. When the suitors met his stare, they saw there the Cyclops, the Laestrygonian slaughter, the Scylla, the Sirens, the sea-shifting cyclones and subterranean spirits beckoning, beckoning them to subterranean shores and endless silence.

Odysseus, the hero of the Known World, was home now, and the world would know of it, come what may!

13

The Secret of the King's Bed

The silence was broken by Ctesippus throwing aside the bench that stood between him and Odysseus. He came on with his fists clenched to either side of his body, like a rolling, growling bear, and flung himself forward with such force that Telemachus's spear bent in his hands as he thrust it home into Ctesippus's chest. Then Odysseus's arrows flew. The suitors let out one roar between the fifty of them—a roar as loud as Polyphemus gave as he was plunged into darkness—as they reached for their swords and shields and spears, and found they had been tricked.

Melanthius heard the yell—Melanthius the servant who had played an unwitting part in the downfall of the suitors—Melanthius who had grown rich doing favours for the suitors—Melanthius who had been promised a golden chariot by Eurymachus if he won the queen. 'Melanthius! *Give us our weapons!*' yelled Eurymachus.

Two against fifty; fifty against two. Melanthius thought once, thought twice, grabbed up an armful of swords and spears, and ran to the gallery from where he flung the weapons down to the suitors below. A dozen were already sprawled face down, face up, spiny with arrows.

Telemachus saw the treacherous servant at the gallery rail. 'We're betrayed, father!'

Odysseus snorted with contempt. 'What? Did the gods preserve my life for twenty years—did they rob Poseidon of his revenge for a handful of wine-sodden wasters to cut me down in front of my own fire? No! I call on you, Athene, goddess of the grey and furious eyes, to shake your silver spear in the face of these *leeches*!'

The size of his voice was enough to strike doubt into the suitors as they struggled with one another for the too-few swords. But when a wind stirred round the roof, and smoke from the fire was forced back down from the ceiling and swirled in choking clouds around them, they were thrown into panic. Like sheep they panicked, one starting to run and another to follow and two more to follow the leaders. Round and round the table they ran, falling over the dead suitors, falling over the fallers, trampling on live and dead alike. And all the time the bowstring of the royal hunting bow twanged like the bass string of a harp striking the rhythm of a storyteller's poetry.

At the dark end of River Ocean, in the Realm of Shadows, the ancient spirits were jostled by a tumbling-in of strangers. White and ragged strangers somersaulted like acrobats into the halls of the underworld with the astonishment of death in their eyes. But no one greeted them. The ancient spirits drifted by without astonishment, nursing their own memories for all Eternity.

'Spare me, Odysseus!' cried a fat and wheezing suitor

throwing himself down at the king's feet and clasping his knees. 'I never did any harm! I always told the others that you'd be coming back! Here! Take my sword!'

Odysseus knotted his hand in the man's hair and, looking at his son, asked, 'Is it true?'

'He sailed to Asteris with the others to lie in wait for me. And he prayed to Poseidon for your death, while he butchered the finest of your bulls,' said Telemachus.

So Odysseus took the fat suitor's sword and cut off his head with one sharp slash.

'Spare me, Odysseus!' cried a thin and hollow-eyed youth, rolling from under the table to clasp the king's feet. 'I am only a bard, a storyteller in search of history and truth. I never did you any wrong! Look, I have no sword!'

Odysseus knotted his hand in the lad's hair and, looking at his son, asked, 'Is it true?'

'It's true. He's lived on grain gruel rather than eat your beef, and he sang laments when the suitors were too drunk to stop him, and he comforted my mother with stories.'

So Odysseus pushed the boy back under the table and, wielding the sword over his head, he leapt down to do battle with Eurymachus, hand to hand.

For weeks, upon months, upon years, Odysseus had suffered at the hands of giants, magicians, the lesser immortals and the greatest gods. Now his sword was as murderous as the hands of the Cyclops, the fish-spears of the Laestrygonians, the white fists of Poseidon. Eurymachus and every other suitor were hurled nameless into the Realm of Shadows. Only the traitor Melanthius he did not kill in hot blood . . . but afterwards, while his blood ran cold with fury.

Silence fell over the dining hall. Even the wind outside abated and the smoke rose in a clean column once more, through the roof. The only sound was of Telemachus and Odysseus breathing hard after the violence of the battle.

Telemachus saw his father's eye turn towards the gallery, beyond which Queen Penelope waited. The king went to the foot of the stairs, but halted and turned back and seated himself in a chair by the fire. 'You tell her, Telemachus. I've been gone for so long. I can't think what to say. I can't tell how she will feel about me. It's been so many years . . . '

Telemachus climbed the stairs and knocked on the locked chamber door of Queen Penelope. 'You may come out now, mother. The matter of the suitors is settled.'

The door opened a crack, and his mother's face, small and anxious, appeared. 'I heard fighting.'

Telemachus could not keep from smiling for another moment. 'Yes, mother! The suitors are all dead! *Odysseus* killed them. He's come home, mother! *He's come home!*' He waited for the laughter to break in her eyes, but she only blinked slowly and her lips narrowed.

'What nonsense is this you're telling me?'

'See for yourself!' cried Telemachus.

Penelope looked over the gallery rail at the figure sitting hunched in thought beside the fire. Telemachus saw her fingers tighten on the rail and her knuckles whiten, but still she did not smile. Sadly and slowly and with queenly poise, she descended the staircase and picked her way between the bodies of the dead suitors. Odysseus rose to greet her.

'Sit down, my lord. You must be weary,' she said quietly, and seated herself on the other side of the fire, her back erect and her eyes on the flames. Odysseus sank back into his chair. 'I shall send a waiting woman to wash your feet, and have a bed prepared for you,' said Penelope.

Odysseus bit his lip and said timidly, 'I would prefer to sleep in my own bed—the bed I carved with my own hands before we were married. It's a thought I clung to while I lay shipwrecked on strange beaches and while monsters ate my companions from round about me and while I lay in my tent below the walls of Troy, and while I was washed on a plank of wood across the world-encircled sea.'

Penelope slowly nodded her head. 'Then I shall have the bed carried into the great west chamber. You will be comfortable there. I myself will sleep in the eastern-facing chamber. I would prefer it. Is that satisfactory, my lord?'

Telemachus could not believe his ears. 'Mother! What is all this? Why are you so cold with him? This is Odysseus! While he was gone your eyes were never dry of tears: not a day passed without you telling us how much you loved Odysseus!'

But Odysseus held up his hand. 'Quiet, boy. It must be as your mother chooses. But may I be permitted to ask you one question, lady?'

'By all means, sir,' said Penelope coldly.

'Then how exactly do you intend to move that bed? I carved it myself out of the crown of an ancient olive tree, and that olive tree grows in the centre of Pelicata Palace with its roots still sunk in the earth and its branches holding up the roof. Forgive my insolence, lady, but if you can move that bed of mine, I shall cheerfully sleep in the great west chamber or in the pig run or in the yard itself for ever and a day.'

Then Penelope leapt out of her chair—like a little dapple-coated deer she leapt over the hearth and into Odysseus's arms, covering his face and hands with kisses.

'Forgive me, my lord! But I was so certain that you were some imposter sent by the gods to break my heart! In twenty years you have hardly changed! I expected a stranger, grey and cruel and covered in scars. I didn't dare to believe that your face could be as lovely as the day you set sail for Troy! Say you forgive me! Say you do!'

Odysseus replied, 'My dearest Penelope, if you had not thought up some trick to put me to the test, you would not be a fit wife for Odysseus. The gods made us both quick of hand but quicker still of wit. And *now* may I go to bed in the bed of my own making?' And he took Penelope his queen by the hand and led her upstairs to the chamber and to the huge bed of olive-wood carved in the crown of a tree.

Sap still flowed in the trunk of the ancient olive, and here and there, spring leaves were unfolding along the boughs.

After one day, after two days, the feasting and celebrations were over. The dining hall was empty; the house at night lay sunk in sleep; the suitors lay in their graves, more still and silent than sleepers.

Then, at midnight on the third day, out from under the table crawled the thin young singer of songs whose life Odysseus had spared. He crept out of the palace and down to the harbour. He climbed aboard the smallest of the boats, slipped anchor and sailed out to sea, ahead of a gentle breeze. Wind and current and rowing carried him, in time, past Cephalonia and little wooded Zanthe, across the open sea, close by a narrow, stony island the shape of a ship, and into the harbour of Scheria. Here his old blind father sang stories in the court of King Alcinous.

Father and son sat under sunlight and starlight and talked in soft voices, sharing their separate songs.

Their stories they interwove into a new song. And they

sang their song at the marriage of Princess Nausicaa. They sang of a king (an ordinary man, not a magician nor one of the Immortals) who had fought under the walls of Troy and whose journeys had taken him from shore to shore of the world-encircled sea. They told how he had escaped death at the hands of monsters, giants, and whirlpools; how he had heard the Sirens' song and been loved by nymphs as lovely as the dawn, with braided golden hair. They told how, finally, he had returned home, to rid his palace of a plague of vermin with the help of his full-grown son.

When they had finished, the bride Nausicaa leaned forward and said, 'So, Odysseus's travels are over. Now he can sit under his vines and grow old in the shady places of Pelicata Palace.'

'Oh, no, lady,' said the younger bard. 'Odysseus has left Ithaca again already, and Penelope sleeps alone in the great olive-wood bed.'

'Why?' cried King Alcinous. 'In the name of all the gods, where has he gone *this* time?'

'He's gone with Telemachus, carrying an oar from one of his brightly painted boats. He's set sail for the northern shores of the world-encircled sea, and when he beaches there, he means to travel across the dry land to a place so far from the sea that no sea-bird can reach it from any direction; a place where there's no grain of salt in the earth, and where no inhabitant has ever heard the name Poseidon. And there he'll plant his brightly painted oar in the saltless earth and make a sacrifice of the finest of his black sheep to the great Earth-Shaker, the Sea-Shifter, the Earthquake-Maker himself. Perhaps then god and man can be at peace again, and the island kingdom of Ithaca will be safe from the vengeance of Poseidon.'

The guests at Nausicaa's wedding looked at one another and shook their heads.

'Such a journey!'

'Does such a place exist?'

'How long will he be travelling?'

'Will he ever come back?'

The two bards, father and son, shrugged their shoulders and stroked their hands over their harps to strum small, thoughtful, and harmonious tunes.

Nausicaa got up and stood by the window, looking out at the never-shrinking sea. The waves below her father's palace broke gently against the beetling cliffs and caressed the sharp pinnacles of rock. As one wave arrived, another was always drawing back again, out to sea, out to the open sea that is always travelling, always travelling, always travelling.

Geraldine McCaughrean is one of the most highly-acclaimed living children's writers. She has won the Carnegie Medal, the Whitbread Children's Book Award (three times), the Guardian Children's Fiction Award, and the Blue Peter Book of the Year Award, and is known and admired for the variety and originality of her books, as well as her stunning storytelling skills.

Among her other books for OUP are *The Kite Rider*, *The White Darkness*, *Stop the Train*, and *Not the End of the World*. In 2005 she was chosen by the Trustees of Great Ormond Street Hospital for Children to write the official sequel to *Peter Pan*. The result was *Peter Pan in Scarlet* which was published worldwide to huge critical acclaim in October 2006 and looks set to become a classic.

Neverland is calling again...

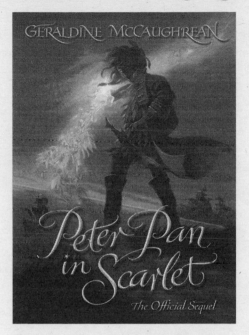

The first ever official sequel to J.M. Barrie's *Peter Pan*

Something is wrong in Neverland. Dreams are leaking out—
strangely real dreams, of pirates and mermaids, of warpaint and
crocodiles. For Wendy and the Lost Boys it is a clear signal—
Peter Pan needs their help, and so it is time to do the
unthinkable and fly to Neverland again.

But back in Neverland, everything has changed—and the
dangers they find there are far beyond their dreams . . .